The Butcher's Boy

Metzger's Dog

Big Fish

Island

Sleeping Dogs

Vanishing Act

Dance for the Dead

Shadow Woman

THE
FACE-
CHANGERS

THE
FACE-
CHANGERS

A NOVEL

THOMAS PERRY

RANDOM HOUSE

NEW YORK

All rights reserved under International and Pan-American Copyright Conventions.
Published in the United States by Random House, Inc., New York, and simultaneously
in Canada by Random House of Canada Limited, Toronto.

Library of Congress Cataloging-in-Publication Data

Perry, Thomas.
The face-changers : a novel / by Thomas Perry.
p.   cm.
ISBN 0-679-45303-2
I. Title.
PS3566.E718F33   1998
813'.54—dc21   97-34078

Random House website address: www.randomhouse.com

Printed in the United States of America on acid-free paper

2 4 6 8 9 7 5 3

First Edition

BOOK DESIGN BY LILLY LANGOTSKY

FOR JO, ALIX, AND ISABEL

If anyone dreamed he was a Falseface, it was only necessary to signify his dream to the proper person, and give a feast, to be at once initiated; and so any one dreaming that he had ceased to be a False face, had but to make known his dream and give a similar entertainment to effect his exodus. In no other way could a membership be acquired or surrendered. Upon all occasions on which the members appeared in character they wore False-faces . . . the masks being diversified in color, style and configuration, but all agreeing in their equally hideous appearance. The members were all males save one, who was a female and the Mistress of the Band. She was called Ga-go-sa Ho-nun-nas-tase-ta, or keeper of the Falsefaces; and not only had charge of the regalia of the band, but was the only organ of communication with the members, for their names continued unknown.

The prime motive in the establishment of this organization was to propitiate those demons called Falsefaces, and among other good results to arrest pestilence and disease.

Report on the Fabrics, Inventions, Implements and Utensils of the Iroquois, Made to the Regents of the University, January 22, 1851 by Lewis H. Morgan (reprinted in Elisabeth Tooker, *Lewis H. Morgan on Iroquois Material Culture,* 1994)

THE
FACE-
CHANGERS

1

J anet McAffee stepped out of the Baltimore Medical Center and winced as the icy air coming off the Inner Harbor lacerated her cheeks and forehead. Her eyes began to water as she lowered her head and searched for the taxi cab. At one time she would have called the sensation pain, but that was before she had learned what pain was. The chemical peel had only left her skin feeling tender and exposed, the way a sore tooth would feel if she drank iced tea.

The part of the makeover that had taken her by surprise was the liposuction. That had been the only part of the process that she had been secretly looking forward to, because it seemed like cheating away all the days she had convinced herself she was too busy to exercise and too hungry to turn down dessert. But the liposuction had cost her a week of hot, fiery misery before she had felt like moving again. Because they had sucked most of the fat from the places that a person rested on, stillness had not offered much relief. The doctors never told you that. Instead they drew lines on a photograph of your face to show you how clever the cut-and-stitch surgery was going to be. The mild discomfort from that was already half-forgotten and the scars were almost invisible.

She spotted the taxi cab parked beside the curb just outside the parking barrier, where the driver had stopped so he wouldn't have to pull a ticket from the machine to come into the lot. She resolved to be more specific next time she ordered a cab. She squared her shoulders and prepared to step away from the shelter of the big medical building into the wind. She felt a hand touch her elbow and shrank from it, tightening her muscles to clamp her arm to her side.

Janet whirled. A tall, thin woman with long black hair was standing beside her, looking into her eyes. The woman seemed to note her startled reaction, but it seemed neither to surprise nor particularly worry her. She said quietly, "Go back into the building and wait for me just inside the door."

"But that's my cab. I was just on my way—"

The woman interrupted. "Didn't they tell you I would come for you? It's time." Her eyes betrayed a small glint of amusement as she watched Janet's face.

Janet sensed a sudden weakness in her arms and legs. They felt heavy, but somehow empty, as though there were no bones. "All right," she said.

She stepped back in and watched through the glass door as the new woman walked up to the driver, said something to him, gave him some money, and stepped back to watch him wheel out and drive away. She turned and walked across the driveway and through the door, then kept going past Janet without looking at her. After five paces, she stopped, turned, and said, "This is it. If you're coming, come now."

Janet nodded and took a step. She could not help wondering if this single step was one of those enormous ones, like a step off the railing of a ship, but then she reminded herself that this wasn't like that at all. She had taken that step months ago, on the night when she had decided to make the telephone call. She had been busy preparing for this day for a long time—first quietly moving out of the condominium into the small apartment where everything was unlisted and nobody but the police knew she lived there, then enduring the makeover. This was only the next step, not the first.

She followed the tall, dark woman down the hallway and out the front door, then to a small green car that looked a lot like the one that Janet had owned until— No, she didn't want to follow her memory backward. This was a new beginning.

Janet got into the passenger seat and closed the door just as it began to move. The woman accelerated away from the curb and into traffic, then moved quickly into the next lane, then turned, turned again, and headed east. She was not exactly a reckless driver, but she was aggressive and sure, and those were qualities that made Janet uneasy.

Janet said, "I didn't think you would come for me here."

"That's why I did," said the dark woman. Then she seemed to change, as though she had thought about it and decided that there was no practical reason not to be friendly. "Everyone who has been wondering if you might try to disappear assumes that you'll do it in certain ways. What they're waiting for is to see you some night slinking out of your condo carrying a suitcase. Nobody disappears from a doctor's office." She glanced at Janet. "How did it go, by the way?"

Janet shrugged. "He says I'm doing great. I'm not supposed to see him again for six months."

"He did a wonderful job on you. Big improvement."

"Thank you," she said mechanically. It was a shock that this woman, who seemed so strange, would say something as normal and human as an empty compliment. "How do you know? We've never met before."

"I've seen a lot of pictures of you." She made another turn. "What have other people said? Has anyone who knew you before the surgery seen you since?"

Janet shook her head. "I'm a little low on the invitation list lately, and I didn't go out at all while my face still made people stare. The doctors and nurses are the only ones. And cab drivers."

The woman swung into a covered parking ramp, went up two levels, then stopped in an empty space and turned off the engine.

"Why are we stopping?"

"I need to give you some things." She reached into her purse and produced a ticket in an airline envelope. "Your flight leaves in two hours."

"Where am I going?" She pulled aside the corner of the envelope and read the ticket. "Chicago?"

"You'll be there for a while, but it's just a stop on the way. It will keep you out of sight until your plastic surgery is completely healed. You should show up at your final destination looking like a finished product—face, body, hair, wardrobe, credentials."

She handed Janet a small wallet that was stiff with cards. "Here's your ID."

Janet looked at the Mastercard on top. "Mary Anders. Is that going to be my name?"

"Just for this trip. You'll need to flash identification to get on the plane. If something goes wrong or you're stalled, you can't even get a room without a credit card. Use those."

Janet looked at the driver's license. The picture was the one she'd taken in a photo booth a week ago, but it had been touched up. It looked to her as though someone had scanned it into a computer and adjusted the color and texture to hide the surgery. She gazed at the picture. It was a young, pretty woman, but it was still her face. Maybe she would look like that after everything healed, and it made her hopeful again. She put the wallet in her purse with the ticket.

"Now let's have yours."

"Mine? What?"

"Your license, credit cards, and so on. Whatever you have with Janet McAffee written on it has to go."

"Oh, of course," she said. It had not occurred to her that she would have to lose things that took so little space. But of course she did. The dark woman watched impatiently while she took out her wallet, removed her driver's license, stared at it for a second as though she were saying good-bye to it, and set it down on the seat beside her.

"You'd better give me the whole thing. There's nothing in there that you're going to need."

"But what about later?"

The dark woman looked at her sympathetically and patted her arm. "I wish we had more time together right now, before you get on that plane, so I could help you through the hard parts. I really do. This has all been done before, and there's a right way. We don't know how long it's going to take for things in Baltimore to improve. It might be that those men will get caught trying to put a bomb in your condo tonight, or try to hire an outside killer who is really an undercover cop. Stranger things have happened. But you have to be prepared to wait a long time, and that means doing everything as though it were for keeps. It's not that much harder." She took the wallet and put it into her own purse. "Now for your traveling money. They told you to get a safe-deposit box nobody knows about, right?"

"It's not in there. I was afraid you'd come for me when the banks were closed. It's in a long-term storage place. The closest cross streets are Light and Fayette."

The woman looked at her with curiosity. "You mean by the courthouse, and all that?"

"That's right," Janet said apologetically. "I thought with all those policemen coming and going, it would be safer. It's so much cash . . ."

The dark woman didn't verify or contradict her theory. She seemed to be thinking hard. "Okay. Give me all your keys—condo, apartment, everything. I'll get rid of everything that might cause trouble later."

Janet handed over her keys, and the woman looked at them, then asked, "What about the safe-deposit box? Is the key in the apartment?"

"No, I have it with me."

"Then give it to me. I'll put your old ID in there with the rest of your papers."

"But I only have one key."

The woman smiled, but it was the kind of smile that told Janet she should have known better than to bring up something as foolish as that. "People lose them all the time. When this is over, you go to the bank. You tell them you lost it. They drill the lock." She held out her hand.

Janet handed over the key.

The dark woman seemed to hear something. Her eyes rose to settle on the rearview mirror. Then she turned in the seat and stared out the back window for a moment. Her smile was gone, and she looked intense, agitated. "We'd better get moving."

Janet tried to keep herself from looking in the direction the woman had been staring, but she couldn't help herself. "Did you see something?"

"I'm not sure, but I'm not in the business of hanging around to verify hunches. I just get people out." She started the car.

A black car had been prowling up the ramp on the far side of the garage. As soon as the noise of the green car's starter echoed in the concrete enclosure, the black car accelerated. It swung around the first aisle, where there were a dozen empty spaces, past several more aisles, and began to make the turn up this aisle.

The dark woman backed out of the parking space quickly, stopped with a jerk, threw the car into forward gear, and shot ahead. Janet tried to interpret what she had seen in a dozen sensible ways, but she could not. The black car could only have been trying to make it up the aisle before the green car backed out so it could stop behind it to block it in.

Janet turned in her seat to stare out the rear window. She could make out that the black car had silhouettes of two heads, but the upper part of the windshield was tinted, and she could not have seen the two faces in the dim light of the parking structure anyway. She had time to see it go past the parking space they had just vacated before the dark woman spun around the first turn of the ramp and descended so she couldn't see anything.

"I think they're coming," she said.

The dark woman didn't look surprised. "Are they the ones we have to worry about, or could they just be police?"

"I don't know. I've never seen them. They would just call me on the phone."

The woman's eyes kept flicking upward to the rearview mirror, then settling on the ramp ahead so she wouldn't hit anything. "I guess we'd better assume they are, since they don't seem to own a siren. I'll have to lose them while you go get your traveling money. It's Light and Fayette?"

"Yes."

"All right. We've got about an hour and forty minutes left, so this will be tight. Here's what we do. I can get us into the neighborhood in the next five minutes. I'll let you off somewhere nearby, and keep going. You go into the storage place and pick up your money, then meet me wherever I let you off."

"Okay."

"Then get ready."

Janet watched the rear window while the dark woman took several quick turns, sped down a narrow street lined with row houses, cut across a parking lot, then emerged on Light Street and drove past the intersection at Fayette. Finally, she turned in at the Harbour Court Hotel. There was a brick portal like the mouth of a cavern, then a circular patio with a fountain in the middle to keep cars moving around it in a circle to the lobby entrance.

The dark woman said, "Go through the hotel and out the other side. This is where I'll be. Don't look for the car, look for me. Now, move."

Janet slipped out of the car, the doorman dodged in front of her to open the door, and then she was in. She heard the sound of a car scraping its undercarriage, then turned her head to see that the black car had turned into the driveway too quickly just as the dark woman was accelerating to bring the green car around the fountain and out to the street. The two men inside seemed too intent on following the little green car to glance in the direction of the hotel entrance. They just leaned their bodies inward against the centrifugal force as they made the circuit, then bounced out again.

Janet hurried across the lobby, then out the other door, and nearly ran up the street toward Fayette. She stepped into the storage building's entry, rang the doorbell on the counter, and spent a few seconds catching her breath. It took three more rings to bring the clerk, who opened the cage and led her up to her storage cubicle. She was worried already. She had not exactly told the truth when she had allowed the dark woman to think the money was where it could be picked up quickly.

When she had locked the door behind her, she went to the big box where the winter coats were hanging in a row covered with dry cleaner's bags, and slipped her leather carry-on bag from between two of them. Then she began retrieving letter-size envelopes, each with ten thousand dollars sealed inside it, and placing them in her bag.

She took four from inside a pair of high leather boots she had not worn in years, two from coats that had inner pockets, three from the inside of Aunt Rosalie's giant casserole dish that had come to her because it didn't fit in any relative's cupboard, and had not fit in Janet's either. There was one envelope inside the little door in the back of the big wind-up clock that chimed every hour loudly enough to wake anyone trying to sleep in any dwelling smaller than an English manor house. Two were rolled inside the stemmed glasses and covered with tissue paper, and one slipped between the crystal decanters. She had once thought them pretty, but now anything associated with drinking made her depressed. It took a moment to push the bad painting of a sailing ship out of its thick frame and remove the false backing, then almost as long to collect the loose hundred-dollar bills she had packed there into their envelope.

There were two envelopes taped inside the carved Tibetan mask. She had been told that what the mask was vomiting through its fanged maw was supposed to be good luck, but she had never been able to feel comfortable about a culture so alien that it imagined good luck looked like that. She figured faith always worked that way—believing something frightening and unappetizing would be just the thing to make you happy. She supposed that attitude was why she had never married. Suddenly she wished she had a girlfriend with her so she could have said that aloud, but she was alone. At the moment, that woman waiting in the car was as close as she could come to a friend, and Janet somehow knew that the dark woman wouldn't have laughed.

She found one envelope behind her graduation picture, one in the battery compartment of a bulky old-fashioned portable radio that held four batteries, and three more tucked in with the receipts she kept with her old tax returns. That made twenty-one: two hundred and ten thousand. Oh, and five thousand in her purse. She had gotten into the habit of carrying that with her in case the very worst happened and she didn't even have time to come here.

Janet took a last look at the old things she had stored in the cubicle. She had judged all of them ineligible for space in her condo, but she had never been able to rid herself of any of them. She knew that as soon as the lease on the cubicle ran out, they would end up in a Dumpster. She felt a tearing sensation at the thought, paused for a moment, then re-taped one envelope on the back of her graduation picture, under the frame cover.

She went out to the counter, where the clerk was waiting. "Is there any way I can pay in advance for the next five years?"

"Five?"

She had said it without thinking it through, and tried to concoct a rea-son why he shouldn't think she was doing something crazy or illegal. "Yes. I figure with inflation, I'll save money over the long run."

He shrugged, and she could tell she had been wrong about him. If forced to think about it, he would probably have said that she was stupid, but he cared so little about her that he didn't bother. He reached under the counter and produced a blank rental agreement like the one she had signed four years ago. "Sign it, and I'll figure the charge."

He punched a calculator on the counter and did some elaborate math-ematical operation while Janet's brain silently screamed, "Just move the decimal point to the right! Four eighty a year. Forty-eight hundred, di-vided by two, is twenty-four hundred."

He said, "That will be . . . forty a month . . . times twelve months . . . times five." Janet waited while he gave her a chance to prepare for the shock. "Two thousand four hundred."

She had been counting out hundred-dollar bills while he'd completed his computations. "Here." She handed him the money and waited while he wrote up a receipt.

As she left the building, she felt a little better, a little smarter. Two hun-dred thousand was enough running-around money, and this way, when she came back to Baltimore, she would at least have something—a little cash, a few objects that belonged only to her. She had even avoided writ-ing a check, which would eventually be mailed to her condo and tell someone she had a rented storage space.

She glanced at her watch. It had taken her twenty-three minutes. She had used too much time. The dark woman had probably thought she would walk in, grab the bag, and run.

Janet hurried up the street toward the hotel, hating herself once again. She had worked hard for that money, invested it prudently each week for years, then carefully, over the past few months, had converted it to cash in five-thousand-dollar increments. She had hidden the cash in the way she had invested it: a little here, a little there. If the worst had happened, and someone had broken into her little storage area, she had hoped he might find one envelope and run away, assuming he had found everything. She had not considered that her chance of safety might be slipping away in the time it took her to gather it all.

The cold, steady breeze from the harbor punished her tender face as she hurried toward the hotel, but Janet felt that she deserved it. She had been too slow-witted to explain in advance to the woman who was helping her that the money would take time. That was unforgivable. Had she even made sure the woman knew that what those men had threatened to do to her wasn't just beating her up or something? Yes. She had told the person on the telephone all about it. The one on the telephone had been a woman too, or she might not have been able to say some of the words. The dark woman might even have been the one on the telephone.

Janet hurried through the hotel entrance, then walked as casually as she could across the marble floor of the lobby. She had been in the habit of wearing business clothes to the plastic surgeon's office. She had wanted to make the people there think she was a busy professional person, because being busy and prosperous seemed the same as being respectable. But now the disguise that had given her courage was making things worse. The high heels had always been just fine for getting out of a taxi cab and walking fifty feet to the waiting room, but now they were hurting her feet and making noises on the marble floor like a horse clopping down a cobblestone road. And the new sensitivity of the skin around her middle since the liposuction and tucks made her underclothes feel as though she were harnessed up to pull a carriage.

Janet kept her eyes ahead of her on the big glass doors across the lobby. A sliver of green made her hold her breath and stare, but when she saw it again, it was only the doorman in his green generalissimo's uniform lurking outside the door. There didn't seem to be a green car out there. Janet veered to the left a little so she could see the spot to the right of the door that was the logical place for the green car to be waiting, but she couldn't achieve enough of an angle.

She quickened her pace, goading herself with the foolishness of taking the time to pay advance rent on her storage space. Her sudden reluctance to part with a pile of gewgaws too old and tasteless to keep in her home was going to get the dark woman killed, and then Janet. They both could have been out of Baltimore by now if she had only kept walking past that counter.

She reached the door and looked out, but the green car wasn't in the courtyard. As she craned her neck to look toward the street beyond the portal, she felt the presence of someone behind her. She stepped aside to let them out the door.

The voice was almost in her ear. "Stay out of the doorway."

It was the woman. She took Janet's arm and led her toward the steps leading up to the restaurants on the second floor. "What happened?" Janet whispered.

"They were nastier about letting me lose them a second time." She changed her direction slightly, and they skirted the stairway, went out the door, and emerged on Light Street. "The car is down here." She brought Janet down Pratt Street, then turned into a parking area for the Convention Center. The car was parked between two big vans.

Janet came closer. The rear window had a small, round puncture, a milky circle of pulverized safety glass, and around it, a radiating spider-web of cracks. She knew instantly that it was a bullet hole, and she noticed that it was not on the left side, behind the driver's seat. It was on the right, where they must have thought she was crouching. The dark woman acknowledged her thought.

"Don't worry about that. Just get in. We're taking too much time."

Janet obeyed, wondering how anyone could not worry about that. She listened for some kind of assurance that what had caused the bullet hole was over, but none came. The car began to move away from the Inner Harbor, and she looked through the side and rear windows for the black car. What met her eyes were last glimpses of familiar sights—the National Aquarium, then the World Trade Center, and lots of other buildings that she had never been inside, but that she somehow felt she knew because she had driven past them so many times.

In minutes they were on the 295 expressway, then the 195, and every sign announced the approach of Baltimore/Washington Airport. But the dark woman pulled off the expressway and glided onto Dorsey Road, then stopped at a hotel near the southern edge of the airport.

"We'll have to take a few quick precautions," the dark woman said. "Come in."

She hurried into the nearest wing of the hotel with Janet struggling to keep up, and moved down the carpeted hallway, then into a room. She hurried to the closet. "They've seen you, and they'd be fools not to have figured out you might be heading for the airport."

"What can we do?"

"Get rid of everything they've seen, and show up a different way." She laid some jeans and a sweater on the bed, then tossed a pair of thick-soled running sneakers on the floor. "Put these on."

Janet put on the jeans and sweater, then sat on the bed to tie the sneakers, and the dark woman knelt on the bed behind her to braid her hair in a way she never wore it. "There's an airport shuttle that stops at all the hotels along here. Maybe we can catch it. They'll be expecting to see the car."

The woman took a small suitcase out of the closet and opened it. She put Janet's bag of money and her business suit and blouse into it. "Check the suitcase at the curb. You can't carry a bag of money on a plane and not have them run it through the X-ray machine, and maybe look inside. After you get to Chicago, throw the clothes away. Once they've seen an outfit, it's dangerous."

Janet tried to look in the mirror over the bureau, but the woman took her arm and pulled her to the door. "It'll have to do."

As they walked down the hallway toward the reception area, Janet thought about her appearance. She had not been allowed to see whether it was attractive, but it certainly was better. The clothes had a different look, but also a different feel. The running shoes made her a couple of inches shorter, and they made her walk differently, too. The woman seemed to know dozens of little tricks and shifts and be able to put them into play so quickly that the effect was not a collection of small details, but a transformation.

The dark woman left her and went to the front desk. She spoke to the clerk, then looked up over the clerk's head at the clock on the wall, and returned to Janet. "The shuttle bus is already due, so it should be here in the next minute or two."

Janet said, "Are you coming with me?"

"No. The way to get past them is to lose everything they've seen—the car, the clothes, the hair, and me. They'll be watching for two women, and once you're in the building, there's nothing I can do for you that the airport police can't."

"But the airport police don't know I'm in danger."

"Once you've checked your suitcase, go straight through the metal detectors. After that, whatever those men have in mind, at least it can't involve guns or knives. Then duck into a ladies' room and stay there until you hear the speaker announce that your flight is boarding. Walk directly to the gate and get on."

Janet stared out at the driveway, watching for the shuttle bus, but that made each moment tick by and upset her. "I know this is none of my business, so you don't have to answer."

"If I can't, I won't."

"What will you do next? If you're in a hotel, you don't live around here. Do you just get on a plane too?"

"The job's not over yet." The woman shrugged. "In a minute I'll get back in the car and drive toward Baltimore. If they're driving south toward the airport and see me coming in the northbound lane, there's no way they can get to me, but they'll think about it."

"What will they think?"

"Either we didn't go to the airport, and you're still with me, or you're already in the air. They'll realize that either way, I'm the one to follow, so they'll try, and fail."

Janet saw the shuttle van pull up and stop at the curb. As the driver jumped out, she could see three or four people already inside. He ran to the door and said, "Airport?"

"Yes," said the dark woman.

The driver snatched the suitcase and hurried to the van. Janet hugged the dark woman and whispered, "Thanks."

"Go," said the dark woman.

As Janet sat in the van beside a pair of elderly ladies, she could see the dark woman walking quickly toward the small green car to draw the killers away from her path.

As soon as the shuttle bus had safely made the turn onto the airport drive, the green car pulled away from the hotel. It moved along Dorsey Street for a half mile, then turned into the driveway of the Holiday Inn. The dark woman drove up to the front entrance, and two large men in their thirties got in.

The green car pulled away. As it passed under the Baltimore/Washington Parkway, the dark woman reached into her purse and produced a little Colt SF-VI revolver. She turned to the muscular man with blond hair sitting in the front seat beside her. "Get rid of this," she said.

He took the pistol and put it into his coat pocket. Then he glanced over his shoulder at the bullet hole in the rear window. "What was that for, anyway?"

"To give her nightmares." She looked in the rearview mirror and saw the top of the dark, curly head of the second man, who was bent forward as he ran his hand along the back of his companion's bucket seat. "Don't bother looking for a bullet in here," she said. "I packed the inside of the window with a couple of phone books before I did it."

She passed a sign that said "Patapsco Valley State Park," then pulled over at a wooded picnic area, and all three got out of the car. The woman opened the trunk, took out the tire iron, and leaned over the right side of the car. She swung the tire iron against the rear window three times, pounding the glass around the bullet hole into the back seat. She looked at the bigger hole, nodded to herself, and tossed the tire iron back into the trunk. "I saw a body shop down the road from your hotel the other day. Get the window replaced before you leave for home. And don't forget to tell them you're paying cash, so they don't waste a day writing up an inflated estimate for the insurance company."

The shorter man with curly hair said, "Are you going to fly back?"

"I'm going to keep her apartment occupied for a while," she said. "It'll take about a month to get a loan against her condo. Once the check clears, and I've cleaned her safe-deposit box and maxed out her credit cards, I'll turn up."

The blond man grinned, then sat on top of the nearest picnic table and lit a cigarette. "I've got to say, you kept us hopping. We actually lost track of you a couple of times."

She nodded. "Did you ever see Jane when she was getting somebody out?"

"See her? I thought somebody made her up. You mean there's a real Jane?"

The dark woman walked back toward the car. "Probably not," she muttered. "There used to be." She got into the driver's seat and started the engine. "Come on. If we trade cars now, you may be able to get this one fixed today and leave."

2

J ane McKinnon turned into the driveway, drove to the back of the big
old stone house, and strolled up the flagstone path toward the back
door. She would just have time to get dinner going and step into the
shower before Carey finished his rounds and started home. The feel of
the evening made her think of the ends of summer days when she was a
child in Deganawida, the air still and humid, the crickets just beginning
to compete with the faint calls of the red-winged blackbirds in the
marshy fields between her parents' house and the river.

She heard the muffled sound of the telephone ringing inside the house
and changed her walk to a trot. After two steps, the ringing stopped.
Maybe she could still catch the call while the person talked to the answering machine. She reached the back porch with her key ready, unlocked the back door, flung it open, rushed through the little cloak room,
across the kitchen, and snatched the telephone off the wall. She heard
the dial tone. She took a deep breath, then blew it out through her teeth
as she walked through the living room and into the den. She pressed the
button on the answering machine and heard her husband's voice.

"Jane? It's me. Can you meet me at the hospital as soon as you get
home? Thanks."

Jane reached for the telephone, then let her hand hover over it. He had
not said where he was, and his voice had sounded rushed. That usually
meant he was already on his way to the next patient's room. If she called
the main desk it would probably take them fifteen minutes to get him to

a telephone, and she could drive there in twenty. It would probably strike him as a refreshing change if she simply did as he had asked. The recording had sounded a bit like the voice of a man with car trouble.

She retraced her steps through the kitchen, swung her purse onto her shoulder, picked up her keys, locked the door, and backed the car out of the driveway. The drive to the hospital at this time of the evening was easy. The mild rush hour that Buffalo could manage was almost over, and the only heavy traffic that she could see was flowing out of the city toward her.

Jane pulled her car into the lot behind Carey's office building, around the corner from the hospital, and walked up the street, feeling the warm, humid air wrap around her. Winters in this part of the world were dark and fierce, but the summers were a sweet, guilty pleasure. Jane went around to the rear entrance of the hospital, so she could go up the elevator closest to Carey's wing.

As she turned the corner of the building, Jane saw the two police cars beside the emergency-room entrance, not exactly parked, just stopped and hastily vacated. One of them had its door open and the radio still crackling over a woman's voice chanting numbers and street names into the hot night air. Jane glanced across the parking lot at the row of doctors' reserved spaces to verify that Carey's black BMW was still there, and that no tow truck was hooked to it, then noticed the news vans beyond it. There were three of them, all with transmitter booms folded on their roofs. Beside one of them, a young man who looked like a carnival roustabout uncoiled a long double strand of electrical cord.

She kept walking without changing her pace, as though maybe she had always intended to take the long way around the building, or maybe she had noticed the police cars and simply decided that whatever the police were doing here, they probably would prefer not to have inquisitive civilians in their way.

It had been over a year since she had last been on the road, but she could not yet abandon any of the precautions: never stop walking in a place where there were policemen who had nothing to do but study faces; never stay in the vicinity of a camera crew long enough to risk having her face appear on a television screen.

The police had left their vehicles in a hurry without securing them, and the news vans meant that all three of the local channels had been monitoring their scanners and agreed that this was where the best story of the night could be had. She guessed that probably a policeman had been shot. She caught a glimpse of men in dark blue uniforms through the glass of the emergency-room reception area. The time when they had been able to act, to move quickly and accomplish something, seemed to be over. Now they were just waiting.

She walked more quickly as she approached the glass doors and watched them slide apart automatically. As she stepped inside the lobby she held her head steady and walked purposefully toward the elevators. She veered to stay behind the man holding the video camera on a young, blond woman with a microphone.

"Hospital spokesmen have confirmed that the suspect has been shot, and they characterized his condition as 'stable.' The police officers we spoke to were only able to tell us that the injured man is a fugitive and he is believed to have been armed."

Jane's fingers found the button to close the elevator door, then the button for the third floor, and she felt the sudden amplification of gravity as the elevator rose. She tried to fight the growing sense of dread. This had nothing to do with her. She was Jane McKinnon now, a respected surgeon's devoted wife who sometimes came to pick him up in the evening when he finished his rounds. Jane Whitefield was a memory.

She walked down the hallway, past the rooms where Carey's patients of the last day or two were recovering, learning to live without whatever he had cut out of them or sleeping off their anesthetic hangovers. As she came in sight of the nurses' station and began to crane her neck to look for Carey, she saw a door open near the end of the corridor. The first figure to appear made her take in a little breath. There were Carey's long legs and big feet, and his long arms below the short sleeves of the green surgical shirt. He still wasn't dressed to leave, but that was all right. He couldn't know that there was something downstairs that made her impatient to get away.

He saw her and hurried up the hallway toward her, but he didn't pause. His arm came around her waist and he spun her gently and pulled her along with him. He didn't let go, and she allowed his hand to guide her while she quickened her pace to match his.

"Got to talk to you," he whispered. His brows were knitted, and the sharp brown eyes seemed to be searching her face for something.

"Why are you looking at me like that?" she asked. "Is there a transplant patient who needs something I've got?"

"I love you," he said.

"You've already had everything that will get you," she murmured. "Anything else, you'll have to get me in the mood."

"Let's go in my office." As he led her into the tiny room, her eyes settled on familiar things: his briefcase, his coat. She watched him close the door and push in the button to lock it, then stop and lean against his desk. She felt the smile fading from her lips and became watchful.

He folded his arms across his chest, and she suspected she was seeing him as his patients saw him, just before he told them something that they wanted desperately not to hear.

Carey said, "I've got a patient and in fifteen minutes I've got to go in and repair a bullet wound in his shoulder. I want you to talk to him."

Jane stared into his eyes. She could see that Carey was making an enormous effort to keep his eyes on hers, unwavering, unblinking. She felt an unaccustomed chill, and when she identified it, she resisted the knowledge that came with it. He was building distance between them, trying to make her look at him the way a colleague or a patient would. That was why he was standing across the little room from her, not holding her or even reaching out to touch her hand. She recognized the stance with the arms folded in front of him. It was an unconscious gesture, using the arms to protect the midsection, where the guts and lungs and heart were. I don't expect to be attacked, it said, but I'm prepared for the possibility.

She felt a strong impulse to fold her arms too, to hug herself to ward off the hurt. This is my husband, who loves me. Why is this happening? "Why do you want me to talk to him?"

Carey sighed. It was coming. "He's in trouble."

She said, "What do you care?"

"I know him. He's a doctor. A surgeon. He was one of my teachers. There's some kind of crazy misunderstanding, and the police think he killed another doctor. I knew her too—when I was a resident in Chicago, she was a couple of years ahead of me. The whole thing is insane." Carey's eyes softened, and he held up his hands in a gesture of despair. "I know," he said. "You're going to tell me I can't possibly know he didn't do it. I can't make that judgment."

"No, you probably can," she said. "I'm just wondering how you can be sure nobody else can. Cops, judges, and district attorneys are better at telling who's guilty than people think they are. And when they just want to close the books on a case, the one they pick to hang it on isn't somebody like a surgeon. It's some loser with the right kind of criminal record and no money for lawyers." She gently put her hand on Carey's shoulder. "If you want to do something for him, let's start making some calls and get him some terrific legal help."

"What he's worried about isn't that he'll get convicted. It's that he won't get to court."

"Why not?"

"I don't know much. He's coherent, but we didn't have much time alone. He was agitated, in pain. He said something about being framed. He thinks there are people within some police department who are in on it, and whatever they put in their bulletin about him was designed to get him shot."

Jane tilted her head, as though she had heard an odd change of pitch. "The police here don't shoot unless somebody is in danger. Running away isn't enough."

"He's not lying about the bullet hole."

"I didn't say that. I mean something's missing, left out."

"Everything is missing. Everything is left out. I don't even have time to tell you what I know, let alone piece together what I don't know. I have to operate on him in a little while. All I ask is that you talk to him."

"No."

"No?"

"I mean, 'No, that isn't all you ask' and 'No, I don't want to talk to him.' " She said it without malice, preoccupied.

Carey's head nodded slightly, and he closed his eyes, as though he were waiting for a pain to pass. "You're right. I guess that isn't all I wanted. And it was a bad idea." He pushed off his desk and stood straight. "Well, I'd better go get ready to patch him up. If you'll wait, I think I'd like to drive home together tonight."

Jane was still motionless, her eyes staring at a little square of tile on the floor below him. Carey never did that, she thought. Even if they went out, they would come back to the hospital and pick up the second car before they went home. He was going to try to do something himself—slip this wounded man the keys to his car? She seemed to notice Carey only when his foot moved out of the square. "Wait."

"What?"

"You still haven't answered my question. What do you care?"

He winced. "A hundred reasons." He seemed to search his memory for one. "Remember I told you how I was almost washed out of surgical residency?"

"When they left you to sew somebody up and instead you went in again and redid the operation?"

"That's close enough. I saw signs that the patient was hemorrhaging internally, so I opened the sutures and stopped it. The surgeon I was assisting said I'd performed a procedure I wasn't trained for, endangered a patient, and so on."

"But this man saved you?"

"You know what he said? The charge that I wasn't trained was absurd, because I had just watched an outstanding surgeon perform the operation. It didn't work. Finally, he said if I went, he went."

"So you feel you have to do something because you owe him?"

"I'm sure that's partly true. I hope it is, anyway. But he didn't do that to save me. He believed that my career wasn't as important as somebody's life—no surprise—but that his career wasn't either." Carey was silent for a second, then said, "That's part of it, anyway. I know he's a good man, who certainly didn't do this."

"What's the rest of it?"

"I guess it's a feeling I have . . . a hunch." Carey's brows knitted. "In the last few years he's been doing research."

"You mean he's indispensable or something?"

"Nobody's indispensable." He paused. "This is going to be hard to put into words without sounding foolish. See all those?" He waved his arm at the collection of medical publications that lined the shelves over his desk. She recognized the familiar covers of the *New England Journal of Medicine* and the *Lancet.*

"Looks as though there's plenty of research going on."

"Right. The articles are short—just brief summaries of important things people discover in a month, doing medical research in a thousand places at once. It's impossible to keep up with all of it in even one specialty. But if one person could somehow hold a fair portion of it in his head at once and make the connections between discoveries that seem unrelated, and had the skills, and had the power to put it all into play, we just might make the next giant step."

"What giant step?"

He waved his arm in frustration. "That's just it. We don't know, exactly—can't know until it happens. It's like describing the wheel while you're waiting for somebody to invent the wheel." He glanced at Jane, then began again. "What if somebody invented a method that causes normal tissue cells to replicate quickly—the way some cancer cells do, only faster—so that surgical incisions would heal in hours rather than weeks or months?"

"You tell me."

"Surgeons like me could do things that we would never dare try now: virtually nothing would kill a patient if you could keep him alive for twelve hours. It might very well make procedures like kidney or heart transplants into historical oddities."

"The man down the hall is the one who's going to do that?"

"We don't know if anyone will. He's doing research in that area. It's rare for a person like him to turn to basic research, so there's been a lot of speculation, some tantalizing rumors. A few surprising early results have been published."

"So he might?"

"All I'm sure of is that he's something that seldom comes along. Twenty or thirty years ago, he was already one of the very best practicing surgeons in the country—the best hands, a temperament that was all concentration, an immediate understanding of the ways each technical advance could have been used to save the last patient, and how he would use it to save the next one. He's still doing it, year after year after year, getting better at it. And he never forgets anything, so all of that knowledge has been building. He's reaching a point now—a kind of peak—that hardly anyone ever reaches, because by the time you know that much, it's too late. Right now, he has as much scientific knowledge as anyone, the experience of bringing thousands of patients through the most difficult surgery, and he's so deeply respected that if he wants to try something, the money and the facilities will come to him. I don't know of anybody else like that. If he's lost—destroyed—maybe nobody will be in that position again for fifty years."

Jane studied Carey for a moment. "And if he isn't lost?"

"What do you mean?"

"I assume this process or formula or whatever would be patented, so we're talking about a lot of money? Nobel Prize, that kind of thing?"

Carey shook his head. "I know him. He's the one I picked to learn surgery from. I spent four years following him around from morning until night, listening to everything he said, watching everything he did.

He makes decisions to keep people alive, and when he does, nothing else matters to him: money, egos—his or anyone else's."

"What if somebody got in his way—this other doctor threatened to make the giant step impossible? What if all the thousands of people he might save would be lost unless he sacrificed the life of one single person? Would he do it?"

Carey shrugged. "It's an impossible situation. For one thing, that kind of act would require that he believed he was the only one in the world who could ever make the next step. To believe that, you'd have to ignore what's in all those medical journals—tiny contributions that add up. What I was telling you is that I have a feeling that he might provide a short-cut, and it would be a shame if we missed it."

Jane considered for a moment. "So we have a special man, who did you what's probably the biggest favor of your life, and who might be on the edge of inventing the cure for just about everything."

"I know," said Carey. "Why does a person like that need to disappear? An investigation will show he didn't do it, or a trial will, anyway. But he's convinced that whoever planted the evidence that he's a murderer has that figured out, and won't let it get that far."

Jane shrugged. "If there is such a person, that's probably what he would want. It's easy to get somebody killed in prison, and hard to keep a frame from falling apart. But if there is no such person, then he's as safe in police custody as he would be anywhere. Running is what you do if nothing else will keep you alive."

"I'm convinced that he can't be wrong about the existence of the framer. The police in Illinois didn't just pull him in for questioning. They arrested him and showed him a lot of manufactured evidence."

Jane stared at Carey for a long moment, then straightened. Her eyes had changed. They were quick and alert now. She began to pace. "We'd better get started. I've taken too much time with this. You know how rescue crews try to get a person to the hospital in the first few minutes— what do you call it—when you can still do something?"

"Golden time."

"Well, this is his."

"You've decided to take him out without talking to him?"

She looked at him in surprise. "This isn't between him and me. When you asked me, you made the decision. That doesn't mean I'll succeed, or that when it's over, you won't wish you hadn't asked." She walked past him to glance out the window. "Is there a policeman on guard with him right now?"

"Yes," said Carey. "They have him handcuffed to the bed in pre-op. He's been arrested."

"How bad is the wound?"

Carey shrugged. "Not life-threatening, but I don't have the pictures yet. He's lost some blood. The bullet passed through, but I'm guessing it left bone fragments. And he's not young."

"How 'not young'?"

"Sixty-seven."

"Healthy sixty-seven or weak sixty-seven?"

"Healthy."

"He'd better be. Describe him."

"I told you. His mind is—"

"Not that," she interrupted. "His looks."

"Maybe a bit over six feet. A hundred and sixty-five. Gray hair."

"Beard or mustache?"

"No. It makes your mask hot and itchy. He's a surgeon."

"Is the anesthetist someone you can manipulate a little?"

"Within limits. It's Shelton. He won't do anything illegal."

"He doesn't have to. You'll just have to give him good enough reasons to do what you want."

"Maybe I can get him to do that. He respects Dahlman, and if Dahlman tells him I'm right, he'll go along."

"Dahlman. Is that the patient?"

"Yes."

"Who's going to be in the operating room besides you and Shelton?"

"Darlene Brooks will be surgical nurse. Shelton will have one of his people. Sylvia Stern will assist me."

Jane stared at the wall to avoid being distracted. "How long will the operation take?"

"A half hour to four or five, depending on whether there are bone fragments, or if vessels need to be tied off or if I find nerve damage."

"All right," she said. "Here's what you do. Go in while they're prepping the patient, get rid of the cop and the handcuffs. Whatever you have to say, say it."

"No problem with the handcuffs, and the police don't go into the O.R. when we operate on a prisoner. But they do wait outside."

"Then Shelton. Have him order the full-dress general anesthetic, then change it to something else after you're in there."

"Something else?"

"This is your field, not mine. Say what doctors say—you're worried about his age, or something. Put him out for a half hour, do what you need to, then wake him up."

"I can't guarantee that I'll be able to do what needs to be done by then."

"And I can't guarantee anything will happen afterward either. Just make sure he'll live. If he'll be in terrible pain, shoot some local painkillers into him, but nothing that dulls his brain."

"I'll do my best. Then what?"

"Give the cops a little preparation. Tell them he's going to stay unconscious and the cops will contaminate his wound or hamper his recovery if they bother him before morning. Tell them where he's going to be afterward. Where would that be?"

"The recovery room."

"No good. We need to send him someplace else. Where would that be?"

"Intensive care—"

"Someplace where there won't be a million nurses watching him."

"His room, I suppose. I'm sure the police would like it if he were in an isolated place where he wouldn't attract attention."

"It will have to do. Work it out so that one of the staff talks to the orderlies and has him taken there. Then send her on an errand or something so somebody else talks to the cops. Don't do either thing yourself."

Carey held up his hand. "Wait. I'll work out the details and excuses. Just tell me what you want to happen."

She spoke patiently. "Get rid of the cuffs and get the cop to wait outside. Do your work in a half hour, and get him sent to his room. You keep everyone else assuming he's still in the recovery room until, say, two hours are up. The longer the better. Now, what's his room number?"

"It's 3205. But how are you going to wheel him out of the hospital?"

Jane shook her head as though she felt sorry for him. "There are cops and reporters in the lobby with nothing to look at but each other. If they see any patient being moved from this hospital tonight, they'll be all over him. He has to do what nobody thinks is possible. He has to walk out of here under his own power." She frowned. "Can you get me one of these surgery outfits with the mask and headgear?"

"Sure." He opened the door and went outside, then returned with a bundle of green cloth and plastic under his arm. "These should fit you." He put them into a plastic bag and handed them to her.

She stood on her tiptoes and kissed him, then threw her arms around his neck and kissed him again, harder. "I'll get word to you somehow. But don't expect to see me for a couple of weeks. I'm going to try to buy him enough time for the police to straighten it out and drop the charges. Now go tell him about me, so he has time to think it over."

"I don't have to."

She looked at him, puzzled. "What do you mean?"

Carey shrugged. "He remembers me. He knew that I was on the staff of a hospital in Buffalo, but not specifically this one. Anyway, he didn't come to Buffalo to get shot and admitted to a hospital. He was trying to make it to Deganawida. He was looking for Jane Whitefield."

3

Jane Whitefield McKinnon climbed the stairs and emerged on the fifth floor. She had chosen the fifth because that was where they put the cardiac patients, and it seemed to her that they would provide the greatest proportion of men over fifty. She walked with an air of certainty, as though she knew exactly where she was going, but as she passed each open door she flicked her eyes to the left to study the room. In the first two rooms the patients were impossible to see, because there were visitors standing around the beds. In the third, the curtain was closed because a nurse was doing something to the patient. She turned the corner, and was in the blind spot from the nurses' station.

The fourth door was closed. There was a sign on it that said, "Positively No Admittance." That was what they did when somebody died. Jane opened the door quietly and slipped inside. They had not moved the body yet: the bed nearest the door was empty, but the bed beside the window was covered with a sheet. There were intravenous bags and feeding tubes on a tall metal stand, oxygen equipment, and several kinds of electronic monitors on carts, but none of them was connected to anything. On the stand near the bed were a pair of glasses and an open magazine with a picture of a hooked bass jumping out of a stream the way bass never did.

Jane opened the closet, feeling a little hope. The clothes had not been packed yet. The man had probably been in the hospital for a long time, because the clothes looked a little warm for this weather. She took the tweed sport coat, charcoal gray pants, a tie, a blue oxford shirt, a pair of shoes. She put them into her plastic bag, then opened drawers until she found underwear and socks. In the next drawer there was a travel bag. She opened it and saw the usual clutter of toothbrushes and combs and shaving gear, but there was also a little kit for shining shoes. She slipped the polish and a comb into her bag.

Jane carefully collected the other belongings of the dead man and put them in a drawer, closed the curtain around his bed, then took a last look at the room. She opened the door a crack to be sure nobody was near, then slipped back out into the corridor. She took the sign off the door, threw it into a trash can in the hall, and hurried to the stairwell. She made her way to the hallway outside the outpatient recovery room on the second floor. She looked inside to verify that there was no outpatient surgery at night. The lights were off. She pushed the automatic opener so the double doors swung open, walked in, and watched them close behind her.

She hurried to one of the little half-cubicles along the wall, closed the curtain, and turned on the light. There wasn't much in the space: a straight-backed chair, a few cabinets. She changed into the lime-green pants and loose shirt Carey had given her, covered her shoes with the booties, stuffed her hair up under the plastic covering, and tied the face mask around her neck. When she hid her clothes and the bag in the cabinet, she found a box of tight latex gloves, so she put them on too. She went out into the central part of the big room, and looked around. There was a desk with telephones and incomprehensible monitors, and a few more cubicles. On the wall above one of them she noticed a television set like the ones in the patients' rooms.

She found the remote control hanging from the bed, and pressed the switch. On the screen she could see the same newswoman standing in the lobby of the hospital. This time the woman was almost whispering. "Lieutenant Ballard, the police press officer, is here, and he's about to issue a statement, so we'll listen in."

Jane heard a change in the sound, with microphones clanking together and some blips as switches somewhere were flipped, and then a man's voice. The wide torso of a plainclothes policeman filled the screen. "At approximately six-thirty this evening, police officers at the Main Street Greyhound bus station encountered a man who fit the description of a murder suspect from Illinois. They attempted to question the man, who became nervous and attempted to flee. When they gave chase, he appeared to them to be reaching for a weapon. One of the officers fired his sidearm, wounding the suspect in the shoulder. That's from the preliminary report, and it's about all we know at the moment. When we have more—"

"Lieutenant!" came a reporter's voice. "Can we talk to the officers?"

"Both officers have been relieved for the rest of the shift, and we're not releasing their names just yet."

"You said 'appeared to have a weapon.' Did he have one?"

"No weapon has been found yet."

"Who is he?"

Lieutenant Ballard looked down at a sheet of paper. "His name is Dr. Richard Dahlman, age sixty-seven. He is being sought by Illinois authorities in the murder of Dr. Sarah Hoffman, and was considered armed and dangerous. I have no further details about that case."

"Will he be sent back to Illinois?"

"No decision has been made about that."

"Will there be an extradition hearing?"

"I don't know."

"What's his condition?"

"He went into surgery about twenty minutes ago, at eight-fifteen. I'm told he's in stable condition and his chances of recovery are excellent."

Jane turned off the television set and glanced at her watch. It was eight thirty-two. She wheeled a gurney out to the elevator so she would look as though she had something to do, and put on her surgical mask as she ascended to the third floor. As soon as she was in the corridor, she could see room 3205. There was a uniformed police officer standing in the doorway, watching two orderlies wheeling a patient inside on a gurney. She stepped quickly toward the room.

"Hold it," she said, and the two young men stopped and looked at her, puzzled. She spoke loudly enough so the policeman would hear too. "His room's been changed. Let's get him up to the fifth floor so he'll be near the cardiac unit."

The two orderlies wheeled the gurney out of the room, then pushed it to the elevator. Jane was aware of the policeman standing beside her in the elevator, but didn't look into his eyes. He was young, at least a head taller than she was. His belt was so festooned with equipment—gun and ammunition, handcuffs, folding knife, and pepper spray, all in their own leather holsters—that she heard leather creaking every time he shifted his weight.

The door opened and the orderlies pushed the gurney out into the fifth floor hallway and followed Jane to room 5895. She opened the door and said to the policeman, "Excuse us for a moment." He lingered in the doorway for a second to glance into the room, then stepped aside.

Jane let the two orderlies lift the old man onto the bed, then said, "Thanks, guys."

One of them whispered, "Did he really kill somebody?"

Jane said, "That's what I hear." Her voice was an uninterested monotone that made the two men retreat out the door. Jane pulled the privacy curtain to screen the patient's bed from the door, then knelt down and released the brake on the wheels, and did the same for the bed with the dead man in it. Then she pushed the patient's bed aside, pushed the dead man's bed into its place, and pushed the living patient to where the dead man had been.

She looked around her until she found the oxygen mask, slipped it onto the dead man's face, slipped a surgical cap over the dead man's head, and looked at him. He was lying peacefully with his eyes closed. His hair and lower face were invisible. Jane began to search in the drawers around the room. At last she found what she had been looking for: two long, white Velcro strips. She tried to lift the dead man's arm, but it was stiff. She tugged him closer to the railing on the bed and tethered his arm to the rail at the wrist, then did the same to the other wrist.

She returned to the living patient by the window, then heard a knock on the door. She rushed to open it. The policeman was standing in the doorway, looking a bit sheepish. "I wondered—"

"Just a few more minutes," she said.

"I'm supposed to be sure he's restrained." He was fiddling with his handcuffs.

"Oh, you can't use those," she said. "He's been in surgery, and they're not sterile. He can't get out of the regular wrist restraints we use." She stepped aside to let the policeman look in and satisfy himself that the dead man in the bed was not going anywhere. He nodded. "I'll be right out here."

She closed the door and went to the bed by the window. She leaned down, and stared into the open eyes of Richard Dahlman. The pupils were dilated and the face had a drug-induced calm. She took the mask off her face and whispered, "You awake?"

"Yes," he said.

"Did Carey tell you about me?"

"Yes."

"Then sit up." She pulled his good arm and watched him strain to raise himself. She felt frightened. He seemed too weak to do anything, but she had to try. She spoke quietly and firmly. "This is going to be hard, so concentrate. We're going to try standing. If you fall, we're lost. If you feel faint, warn me."

She pulled his legs over the edge of the bed so they dangled a few inches from the floor. "Are you ready?"

He seemed to hesitate a long time, his eyes focused on the floor. "Yes."

She helped him down and held him for a moment. The hospital gown made him look old and frail. He was thin, but his bare back looked soft and boneless, and his buttocks were shrunken with age. She put her left arm around his waist and pulled his right over her shoulder, then began to move. Each movement of Dahlman's feet was fraught with risk and uncertainty. At first each shuffle gained them only two or three inches, but then something about the feel of the cold terrazzo floor on the soles of his bare feet brought back to him a sense of balance, and his shuffles became steps.

She talked to him in soft murmurs as she moved him into the bathroom. "You can do this," she said. "I can tell you can. If I sit you on the toilet, can you keep from falling?"

"Yes."

It occurred to her that his brain might be so far shut down that no matter what a human voice said, he would answer "yes," but that didn't change what she had to do. She eased him down on the toilet. "Just sit here for a few minutes, and I'll be back to get you out."

She closed the door of the bathroom and returned to the doorway. She opened the door to the hallway and beckoned to the policeman. He stepped inside.

"We've got a little problem," she said. "This room doesn't have a good oxygen connection. We'll have to move him back to the first room. Can you get me that gurney?" She pointed down the hall at the gurney she had left there.

The young policeman looked pleased. At last, he had something to do. He hurried down the hall and brought it back with him into the room. He prepared to reach for the body on the bed, but Jane stopped him. "Don't touch," she said. "You're not wearing scrubs. Go out and wait for me."

She pushed the gurney up beside the bed, removed the restraints from the dead man's arms, lowered the railing, and tugged the body onto the gurney. She re-adjusted the oxygen mask and the cap, restrained the stiff arms again, and took a couple of breaths.

Jane pushed the gurney along the hallway. She and the policeman moved the gurney into the elevator again, got out on the third floor, and pushed the gurney into room 3205.

Jane reversed the procedure she had followed the first time, hauling the body off the gurney onto the bed, pulling the covers over it, and then closing the curtain before she opened the door for the policeman. She said, "He's resting peacefully. Make sure that nobody disturbs him unless they have explicit permission from Dr. McKinnon."

"That's what I'm here for," said the policeman.

Jane wheeled the gurney down the hallway, into the elevator, and back to the room on the fifth floor. She opened the bathroom door and turned on the light with trepidation. She had been afraid that Dahlman would be lying on the floor unconscious, but he simply turned and blinked at her.

"All right," she said. "Climb aboard."

She helped him sit on the gurney, then swung his legs up and helped him lie down. She pushed the gurney back to the elevator, then punched the button for level B, below the ground floor, and pushed the gurney into the outpatient recovery room. She took three deep breaths, then turned on the light in the cubicle she had visited earlier.

"Time to get up," she said. She eased Dahlman's feet to the floor, then helped him to the chair. She retrieved her bag from the cabinet where she had hidden it. "Just rest and get your bearings, and let me do all the work." She knelt in front of him and slipped the shorts and pants over his feet and up to his knees, then put on the socks and shoes. She removed the hospital gown and gently slipped the shirt on over his useless left arm, then his right, and buttoned it.

His voice seemed to acquire some authority. "There will be nurses up on the fifth floor looking for me in a minute."

"No, there won't," she answered quietly. "They didn't know you were coming."

"Of course they did."

"Believe me, they didn't."

"But I'm a doctor. I know how—"

"Tonight you're not a doctor, you're a passenger. Do exactly as I say and you'll be outside in a minute," she said. "Do anything else, and you won't." She slipped the necktie over the back of his neck and quickly tied it.

"A tie?" He seemed wide awake now. His eyebrow raised.

"When somebody looks at you, if he thinks, 'patient,' then he might think, 'Which patient?' If he does, we're in trouble." She took his left wrist and removed the hospital's plastic ID bracelet, then slipped it into her bag. "Now we're going to stand up."

She raised him to his feet and knelt to pull his pants up. She buttoned and zipped them, then carefully slipped the sport coat over his left arm, then his right. She could tell that he was hurting, in spite of the painkillers, so she eased him back down before she opened her bag and took out the polishing kit she had stolen from the dead man.

"What's that?"

"Hair coloring," she lied.

"Do we have time for that?"

Jane moved around behind him and opened the can of brown shoe polish. "We'll make time. It combs in, like this." She began at the top of his head and worked downward, sticking the comb into the dark brown shoe polish and combing it into his hair. "When I asked Carey to describe you, the gray hair came up. He's not very observant—at least the way a cop is—because he's never been afraid, never looked at people suspiciously. And the hair is about all any of the others know about you, so put up with it."

Jane took off her plastic gloves, then stayed behind him while she took off the pale green hospital clothes and put on her skirt and blouse.

"What are you doing?"

"Disguising myself as a normal person." She stuffed the surgical clothes, the hospital gown, the shoe polish, and the gloves into the bag Carey had given her, and raised Dahlman to his feet again. "Do you think you can walk?"

He said, "I think so."

Jane held his good arm and steered him out into the hallway, then around a pair of sharp corners and into another wing. She kept whispering in his ear. "We're going out through oncology. They don't schedule chemotherapy or radiation at night here, and any cancer specialists would be upstairs, where the patients are. But we might meet someone. If we do, can you walk by yourself?"

"Yes," he said. "Not very well, but I can present like a chemo patient.

Notable pallor, physical weakness, nausea." He moved forward for a few seconds, then added, "Hair that looks like a toupee."

Jane found a trash can and discarded the shoe polish, then a wheeled laundry bin and left the hospital gown and surgical outfit in it. She glanced at her watch. It had been almost an hour since she had left Carey, and thirty-five minutes since Dahlman had gone into surgery. Dahlman's golden time was dwindling to nothing. She kept him moving as steadily as she dared down the long, empty hallways, past offices and labs that had closed doors and darkened windows, but each step was short and deliberate. Her mind kept bounding ahead, bursting forward to consider each foot of the corridor they still had to cross.

They passed an alcove with a big window and she turned her head to look out. There was nothing out there but the driveway and a cinder-block wall, and the blackness threw a bright, sharp-edged reflection back at her. She kept exerting the steady, gentle pressure on Dahlman's good arm. Her mind carried the sight of their reflection like a snapshot, and she studied it.

She could detect no errors so far. Whatever Carey's anesthesiologist had shot into Dahlman seemed to be wearing off. He bent over a little as he walked, but he didn't look as though he was protecting a bullet wound. The waxy brown polish had covered his gray hair, and it looked as though he had slicked it down with the kind of greasy stuff that some men his age actually used. The coat and tie helped. Dahlman looked like a man who had just come from visiting a patient, and Jane could easily be his daughter.

Jane led him around another corner and she could see the rectangle of the glass door ahead. Through it she could make out a few feet of dimly lighted sidewalk, and then inviting darkness. She wanted to push him, to get out of the light, away from the hospital before something happened. But suddenly there was movement in the darkness, and it startled her. In a second she could see that there were two men coming up the walk toward the door.

She let go of Dahlman's arm. "Walk by yourself. Do the best you can." She spoke evenly and forced her face into a smile as she glanced at the old man. From a distance, she knew, it would look as though they were having a pleasant chat.

"What is it?" Dahlman whispered. "What's wrong?"

She looked at him as though he had said something clever. "Two men coming up the walk. If they're cops, they won't be the ones who arrested you, because those two have been sent home for the shift. These haven't seen you before. Just act like we've visited Aunt Hilda, and we're going home. Don't rush, because we're not in a hurry."

"What if they've seen my picture?"

"If they say your name, laugh at the idea. Don't try to run, but keep moving unless you have to stop. If we're separated, turn right at the corner and go to 4997 Carroll Street. It's about a block. Wait for me behind the building."

As Jane moved toward the door she focused her eyes on the right objects: on the floor for two seconds, on her companion for two more, straight ahead for just a second and then at a spot on the floor ten feet ahead so she didn't appear to be looking at the men or not looking. She controlled her breathing to relax the tightness that was growing in her chest. She had been so close to the outside that she had almost begun to consider it accomplished when the sudden sight of the two men had startled her.

The fact that there were two of them bothered her. There were a thousand harmless reasons why two large men in their thirties might come up the walk together, but until one of them had been positively shown to apply this time, none of them brought any reassurance. Couples or solitary men might be doing anything, but men didn't usually travel in pairs unless they were working, or doing something that excluded women. These two weren't playing poker or bowling.

She touched Dahlman's arm again to move him along. The best place for them to see him was right outside the door, where the light would be behind him and his face in the shadow.

Through the glass she saw the blond one's eyes take note of the fact that Jane and Dahlman weren't going to turn at the end of the hall, but were coming out the door. Then he did something unexpected. He stopped, turned away, bent his head, and cupped his hands in front of his face to light a cigarette. His companion stopped and stood in front of him to shield him from the wind.

As Jane stepped out and held the door for Dahlman, she turned her face to feel the direction of the wind. She had to be sure. The wind sometimes whipped around in eddies beside big, tall buildings. She took five more steps, then watched the darker man point his finger toward the lighted lobby entrance and mutter something. The blond one agreed, and they set off across the lawn in that direction, walking slowly. Jane stared at their backs as she walked. As soon as she was five more steps away from the building she stuck her finger in her mouth and lifted it to feel the wind. "We might have a problem," she said quietly.

"Why? They ignored us," Dahlman protested.

"The blond one—the one that lit the cigarette—turned into the wind to do it."

"I'm not surprised. Smoking in this day and age requires a certain flair for ignoring the forces of nature."

"Don't you see?" she asked. "He was doing it just to turn his face away from us. He's thirty feet from a building where he'd have to put it out anyway."

Dahlman was silent for a moment. He looked over his shoulder, then winced and grunted from the pain. "Do you think they're policemen?"

"A policeman might recognize you, but he doesn't care if you see his face. Carey said you thought someone wasn't just trying to get you arrested. Is that true?"

"Yes. I think someone is trying to kill me."

Jane found that Dahlman was walking a little faster now, but it cost him great effort. They moved down the street toward the corner. Just as they turned up Carroll Street, Jane saw the two men coming away from the lighted lobby entrance of the hospital and walking toward the door where she had first seen them. She said, "We're in trouble. They didn't go into the lobby entrance. You're too weak to run, it's too late to hide, and I'm not carrying anything that would scare them"—the answer came to her as she heard herself say it—"off." She leaned close to him and said, "Can you keep walking?"

"I can, but—"

"Then do it. Walk straight up the street to the small brick building over there. It's Carey's office. No matter what anyone does, keep walking. Go around to the little parking lot in back. Sit down between the gray car and the brick wall. Don't move. If they follow you, try to watch them but don't let them see you. Got it?"

"I heard it," said Dahlman.

"Do it." Jane pivoted away from him, then stepped along the side of the hospital building. As soon as she was out of sight of the sidewalk she began to run. She knew that she must look insane running in a skirt, but in the narrow space beside the tall building nobody could see her. The weightless, flat shoes she had worn were better than she had expected.

She worked herself up into a sprint, dashing along the side of the building. Three stories above her, there were lighted windows where she knew that patients lay staring up at television sets that showed live shots of police officers milling around the hospital. Down here she was alone.

Just before she reached the lighted area at the far end of the building she slowed to a walk. She knew it would have to be the first try. She couldn't walk up and loiter, looking for an opportunity. It had to be there and she would have to read it instantly.

Jane took a deep breath as she stepped around the corner into the light. The three television trucks had their booms up and their dishes turned toward their stations' receivers. The ambulances were lined up in their spaces as before. No one was missing. There were five police cars now. Three had arrived after the emergency was over, so they had been parked in designated spaces with their doors closed.

She stepped along more quickly, her head held rigid, but her eyes scanning. She was closer now, and she could hear the same garbled radio noises she had heard when she had arrived. She passed to the right of the first police car, where she could see the ignition on the steering column, but the radio sound led her on past it.

The window of the second car was half open, and faint orange lights glowed on the dashboard. She angled away from the curb and passed the trunk. In a single, fluid movement, she reached for the door handle, swung open the driver's door, and was in. She turned the key, brought down the gear selector, and stepped on the gas pedal. She didn't let the car glide forward before she began the turn, because it would pass in front of the glass doors of the emergency room. Instead she wrenched the wheel to the left as far as it would go and swung around smoothly to drive the wrong way down the entrance lane.

Jane pulled out of the drive and accelerated up the straight, empty street away from the hospital. As she passed into the little splash of light under each street lamp she studied the interior of the police car: first the shotgun upright in the rack behind her right elbow, then the dashboard with its radio and mike and what looked like a computer screen, next some hard-sided notebooks that could be manuals or books of tickets or even the source of all of those forms that cops seemed to whip out when anything happened. It wasn't until she reached the bright intersection that she found the switches she had been searching for.

She made the turn, drove past the hospital, and began to look for Dahlman. She searched for the two pursuers, but she could not see them either. Could they have run hard and caught him already? She tried to imagine it. They would have needed to recognize him, see her part from him, decide she was going for help, dash to catch him, and either kill him silently and hide the body or push him into a car.

Jane was nearly at Carey's office. As she came to the parking lot, she spun the wheel sharply toward the entrance to make the car seem to have come from nowhere. As soon as her front wheels touched the driveway, she reached to the dashboard, switched on the red and blue lights, and stopped.

Just outside the beams of her headlights she discerned the two men walking toward the end of the building near a red car. If Dahlman had followed her instructions, then they must have seen him come as far as the building. If they were looking at the red car and not the gray, then they hadn't found him yet. Their heads turned in her direction, then away. Jane put her hand on the upright shotgun beside her and waited. The men didn't move.

Jane suspected they could see a head silhouetted in the windshield above the headlights, and she knew they could see the bright red and blue lights revolving on the roof. Maybe they could see Jane was alone, or even recognize her.

She closed her right hand on the grip of the shotgun, but didn't lift it. Of course it would be loaded. There would be no shell in the chamber, but there would be five rounds of number four buckshot in a line ahead of it in the magazine.

With her left hand she switched on the spotlight mounted on her door, and manipulated the handle to sweep the beam along the side of the building. She let the car begin to drift forward slowly in their general direction as she shone the light on the door of the building, then along the ground near it, inching her way along like a cop who had received a prowler call. Then she swept the beam ahead to the corner of the building. The two men were gone.

She hit the gas pedal and shot forward to stop behind her own gray car, then waited. Where was Dahlman? She craned her neck to look in every direction, but she saw nothing. Her breath came out in a hiss through clenched teeth. She had come too late. The men must have killed him, and she had let them walk away. She began to turn the police car around, then hit the brake. Of course: What had she been thinking?

Dahlman was a fugitive. If he saw a police car pull into the lot with its lights flashing, would he come out of hiding and climb in? She backed up quickly, opened the door of the police car, and ran to the row of cars parked behind the building. "Dr. Dahlman?" she called.

"Here," came the quiet voice behind her.

She whirled. "Where?"

Dahlman slowly stood up behind the low brick wall at the end of the lot. She stepped to the wall and helped him swing his legs over it.

"Did you see what they did when I got here?"

"They threw something over the wall. Over there someplace. I heard it but I couldn't see what it was."

Jane didn't need to see. She vaulted over the brick wall and walked the weedy patch between the two parking lots. She found first one gun, then the other only a few feet away, picked them up, and ran to the police car. She looked around anxiously. "Get in."

Jane helped him ease his body into the passenger's seat, then handed him the two guns. "Hold these."

She turned off the flashing lights and drove quickly out of the lot and up a dark side street, then turned and drove up another. She drove until she passed a house a mile away with its lights off and a FOR SALE sign stuck on the lawn. She stopped, backed up, and pulled into the driveway.

She opened the garage door, got back into the car, and drove inside. She opened Dahlman's door and helped him out. "Do you think you can walk a little farther by yourself?"

He said, "Yes."

"Then start walking up the street in that direction. I'll catch up."

"What are you doing?"

"Go," she said.

As soon as she could see that Dahlman was heading in the right direction, Jane closed the garage door, turned on the headlights, and found a rag hanging on a nail on the garage wall. She quickly wiped the steering wheel, the shotgun, the door handles, the shifter, then opened the trunk and found the foam fire extinguisher. She sprayed it liberally inside the car, then wiped the extinguisher off too, and tossed it onto the front seat. The foam would destroy any fingerprints she had missed. She turned off the headlights and stepped out the small door in the back of the garage. She walked along the house to the street and hurried after Dahlman.

When she caught up with him, she said, "I don't want you to faint or fall down. But can you walk a little faster?"

"Do I have a choice?"

"Sure. You could get caught."

He turned his head to focus his sharp gray eyes on her. "Suppose those men had seen your face—figured out that the police car was stolen? That you weren't a police officer?"

Jane shrugged. "They were still on foot in a parking lot. They could see I had a very big car, and suspect that there was a very big shotgun inside it."

"But suppose they had guessed that those were just part of the bluff?"

Jane looked at him with quiet sincerity in her eyes. "If they had guessed that, then one of them would have tire tracks on his chest, and the other would have a five-inch hole in his. This isn't a game."

4

J ake Reinert hung up the telephone, put on his jacket with slow
deliberation, lowered his weight carefully down each of the front
steps, and walked to his car. He had been Jane Whitefield's neighbor for
her first thirty-one years, and had lived beside her parents and grandparents for the forty years before that. Since she had married Carey
McKinnon he had found himself living beside an empty house. He had
watched the lights going on to illuminate unoccupied furniture in the
evening, then going off at bedtime, heard radios talking to themselves
during the day, and sometimes heard the telephone ring four times before the answering machine cut in. Burglars might not be fooled by all
that, but if they came in they certainly would not be lonely.

Jane's unexpected telephone call had disturbed Jake, but he was making an effort to hold his anxiety in abeyance. He started his car and drove
down the street toward Delaware Avenue.

The night air was chilly, and Jake began to feel better as the engine
warmed enough to permit him to engage the heater. If Henry Whitefield's daughter had called him at any hour of the day or night in any of
her thirty-three years and said, "Jake, I'm having trouble. Can you fly
down here to Peru and pick me up?" he would certainly have been on his
way to the airport. Tonight she was just asking for a ride home from a
movie.

Jake began to feel impatient to see her face and verify that this was all
she was asking. He glanced at his speedomoter and saw that his foot had

begun to get impatient too. Thirty-seven in a thirty-mile-an-hour zone wasn't exactly madness, but it wasn't especially smart, either. A man in his seventies could easily fail to discern some pedestrian in the dark, and then react too slowly to do anything but stop and back up over the body.

After about twenty minutes, Jake saw the bright lights of the marquee over the theater and began to search for an acceptable place to pull over. He failed to find one until he was abreast of the place, so he stopped in front.

There was a startling thump on the roof, and he looked over the back seat to see Jane standing there yanking the right rear door open. "Hi, Jake," she said. "Wow, it's hot. Is the heater on?"

"Evening," said Jake. He turned off the heater while she helped a man about his age slide into the back, then slammed the door and got into the front seat beside Jake.

"This is Dr. Dahlman," said Jane, "and this is my friend Jake."

The two men nodded, but Jake had already said "Good evening," and a second greeting seemed to him like taking a hat off twice. Besides, he was sure he had heard that name before, and might be able to think of something original to say if he could just drag out of his memory why the name was familiar. He pulled the car out into traffic.

The man was quicker. "I hope we're not getting you into trouble, Mr. Reinert," he said, and then Jake remembered. It was the name that they had kept interrupting the baseball game to repeat.

The confirmation of Jake's ability to sense trouble was not a sufficient recompense for the obliteration of his peace of mind. He turned to Jane and watched her face as he said, "Finding married life a little quiet, are we, Janie?"

"No," she said. "I like it." She looked strained, as though she were concentrating on biting something that she had between her teeth. After a moment she said, "I'm sorry to get you involved, Jake. I had no time to prepare anything sensible, so I had to improvise."

"It's flattering to be the first name that came to mind, I guess," Jake sighed. "What can I do?"

She turned her face to him. "Thanks, Jake."

"What can I do?" he repeated.

"Not much more than this. We've got to stop at my old house, so it's best if you just pull into your own garage. Dr. Dahlman, you may have heard, had a nine-millimeter bullet pass through him a couple of hours ago, so he's not at the top of his game, but we can bring him in my kitchen door. We'll only stay long enough to pick up some things I left there, and make arrangements for a car."

Jake nodded, then drove the rest of the way home. He pulled his car all the way into his garage, then got out to help Dahlman to the driveway of the Whitefield house and up the back steps. Jane closed the door behind them and then turned on more lights.

As he helped Dahlman into the living room to sit on the couch, Jake said, "Don't lean back just yet. There's blood showing through your coat."

He went into the bathroom, found a towel, folded it, and placed it between Dahlman and the throw pillow, then helped him lie down. He watched Dahlman's eyes rise upward toward the staircase, so he knew Jane was climbing the stairs behind him.

Dahlman whispered, "She said you were just a family friend. Why are you doing this?"

Jake shook his head. "Lie still. Gather your strength."

"Why are you helping me?" Dahlman insisted.

"They said on the news that you were a big doctor somewhere. Why did you kill somebody?"

"I didn't."

"Good," said Jake. "Then from now on, that can be the reason." He watched Dahlman close his eyes. In a few moments he seemed to be asleep. Jake heard the sound of a television set above his head, so he climbed the stairs. As he reached the top, he saw Jane moving up the hallway. "He seems to have dozed off."

"Good," she said. "He's going to need some strength." She walked into the master bedroom and Jake followed. As he watched her throwing things into the suitcase, it occurred to him that she had left an awful lot of Jane Whitefield in this house when she had become Mrs. McKinnon. She hesitated, took off her wedding ring, and quickly slipped it into a drawer.

Jane kept walking to closets, to dressers, to the suitcase on the bed, then turning to glance at the television set. She caught him watching her. "It's the only way I have to keep an eye on the opposition. Sometimes at the beginning, before the police know much, the newspeople will put it all on the air. There's a good chance this time, because they're all at the hospital trying to scoop each other."

Jake stared at the television set, but they had returned to their regular programming. Until the newspeople thought of something else to say, the Blue Jays were back to getting beaten in New York. He went to the window and pushed the curtain aside an inch.

"Not from there," said Jane. "If you want to watch the street for me, do it from the room at the end of the hall, where it's dark. What you're looking for will be a car with too many lights or too few. It will pass once, then come back. Don't move the curtain. You can see that much through it."

Jake walked off down the hall to the empty bedroom and did as he was told. He had been skeptical of Jane's instructions, but now he found he could see much better than he had expected. Through the curtain he could not only make out the sixty-watt lamp in Mrs. Oshinski's front window across the street, but even the dim patch of light it threw on her front lawn. He could still hear Jane hurrying around in her room, and he felt he could almost see her.

On the day when he had first realized what it was that she had really been doing for a living from the time she was in college until a good ten years later, he had experienced something that had never before happened to him—he had been struck speechless.

Nothing that had come to his lips had been worthy of a thinking man. "Cut it out" had seemed closest, but it was too paltry to meet the scale of the situation. Here was the quiet, pretty, and studious young woman he had known since birth, occupying the house where he had come just about every day until he and her father had both gone off to war, and— no, it was more than that. This was the only house that Jake had ever been welcome to enter without knocking. And when he did, he was expected to smile and sit at the table while the older Mrs. Whitefield, Jane's grandmother it was in those days, set something in front of him to eat. And here was this little girl, the product of all of those Whitefields, living under this roof while she engaged in the business of taking future murder victims—some of them with legal difficulties of their own—away from their troubles and making them disappear.

When Jane had finally agreed to marry Dr. Carey McKinnon, to Jake's immense relief, she had appeared to consider herself the last of her fugitives to be taken out of the world. She had not needed to spend time thinking of a new name, because her new husband had a perfectly good one that had been around western New York for a couple of hundred years. She had not needed to do much of anything except start being

Mrs. McKinnon instead of Jane Whitefield and let time do the rest. It had seemed to him that she had even begun to look different—the thick black hair hanging long and soft most of the time like a frame around her face, with just a subtle hint of an inward curl at the ends that hadn't been there before. Even the face itself had begun to seem different to him. Maybe it was just that she considered that a married woman could afford to devote more time to makeup, but he had attributed it to a change in what was behind the face. It had actually struck him that she had lost that sharp, watchful look that had disconcerted him a few times over the years.

But now, after only a year of that, here she was back in this house packing a bag while a wounded murderer rested up on the couch downstairs. He wasn't quite sure what to make of it. He knew for a fact that she had made a promise to Carey, and he could not imagine Jane breaking her word to her husband. That had been part of the new identity she had invented for herself—a woman who didn't do things like that.

But Jake had spent enough time in this part of the country and enough time in this very house to know that there were deeper issues involved. The Whitefields had always been very old-fashioned people.

And although the Whitefields and all of the Senecas Jake had ever met were scrupulously law-abiding, they made no secret that the impulse had not come from anything as recent as what a bunch of immigrants in Albany or Washington had voted. The laws simply happened to coincide pretty well with how the Senecas believed a person should behave anyway. The Whitefields were not shy in their judgments of human behavior, but they were traditionalists, and the founders of Seneca culture had not felt the need to include institutions like jails. The old-time Senecas had been in favor of revenge—famous for it. But they didn't feel that it was society's place to punish people: not that a person might not deserve it, but that, whoever you were, punishing somebody else simply wasn't in your job description.

Punishment was a matter that would be taken care of later—not by God, exactly, but close enough. The Senecas believed that the universe wasn't governed by one benevolent deity. There were twin brothers, grandsons of the first human being, a woman who had fallen from the sky. One twin was good, and when he was referred to in English he was called the Creator. The other was perverse, and one of his names was the Punisher. The European innovation of building jails and using manacles to restrain people seemed to them to be an unwise decision to redundantly build a small and rather amateurish Hell on earth.

As of tonight, Jake was beginning to suspect that he was seeing a new phase of things. He had always felt—no, hoped—that what Jane had done with the first part of her life was an instance of youthful optimism and high spirits taken to an extreme. But what if it was more than that? What if it was an expression not only of what she thought was right, but of who she was and had reason to believe her female ancestors had been, going back to Sky Woman? Jake was familiar with the idea that marriage reformed people—more in second-hand testimony than with his own eyes. But those stories were always that some guy stuck to his promise to stop doing something he knew damned well from the beginning was wrong. Jake couldn't think of an instance where a woman had saved her marriage by sticking to a promise to stop doing what she believed was right—not consistently and in a sustained way.

"What do you see?" Her voice startled him, and he turned to see her in the doorway.

"Nothing I couldn't have seen a week ago, if I had looked."

"Good."

"Why are you doing this?"

She stood absolutely still. He could see the silhouette of her thin, too small body, her long black hair combed back and tied in a tight ponytail, and it occurred to him that he had not seen her wear it that way since she had gotten married. She spoke quietly. "Carey asked me to."

Jake's mind seemed to him to choke for a second, then to start again, like an engine that needed to be taken out and run at high speed to burn off the deposits. "Why?" he said.

"Because if I hide him for a while, then we think the police will find that he's innocent. If we let him wait in jail, we think the police will find him dead in his cell."

She looked at him as though she were waiting in case something else needed to be said, but Jake couldn't imagine what it could be. She turned and disappeared in the direction of the staircase. Jake stared out at the empty street he had been staring at for seventy years. Carey was an educated man and a skilled surgeon, and that was why the whole world had agreed to put "Doctor" in front of his name. But he seemed to have taken a look at this situation and missed the important part.

Carey McKinnon had—by a series of circumstances that, when you analyzed them, came down to luck—been given a beautiful young woman who had the intellect, the courage, and the determination to do virtually anything, but who for reasons that were probably more biological than logical had decided to be his wife. What Dr. Carey McKinnon had seen fit to ask her for was that she go back on the promise he had extracted from her to stop putting herself in danger. Whoever this Dr. Dahlman was, Jake found himself silently praying that he was worth it—not to society, or some other word for a bunch of strangers, but to Carey McKinnon.

5

Carey McKinnon tried to think the way his wife would, and found it impossible. His brain wasn't as quick as Jane's was, and he had no experience at her kind of deception. He was reduced to trying to remember what she had told him to do. He had a difficult time bringing it all back.

Since she had left him he had been concentrating on the specific tasks that he had needed to perform to get Dahlman through the surgery. It had been one of the most nerve-racking procedures he had ever done: trying to be sure that he left no bits of metal or bone in the shoulder, that he sutured the torn muscular tissue and vessels properly without injuring tendons or nerves—so that one of the finest surgeons alive could heal and continue to perform surgery on other people. Every second, while his hands had been working, he had been aware that those eyes were open and staring into the overhead mirror: the eyes of his old teacher, evaluating, scrutinizing every move his fingers made.

Now he had to be certain that no policeman or reporter could ask him any questions. Certain parts of the job were obvious. He could not walk out the rear door of the hospital and stroll to his car in the parking lot. What he really needed was to disappear and reappear somewhere else.

Time was going by, and the longer he waited, the more likely it was that someone would begin to look for him. He put on his sport coat, walked to the fire stairwell, and descended to the first floor. He stepped into the unoccupied break room for the radiologists, walked past the coffee machine, opened the door to the little patio, and slipped onto the lawn.

Carey walked briskly along the side of the building to the street, then took the long way around the block until he came to his office building. He supposed it was smarter to go in the back door from the parking lot than the front door, so he kept going until he reached it. He could see that the usual collection of cheapskates had parked their cars in his lot so they didn't have to tip the valet-parking attendants at the restaurants down the street. That reminded him that he hadn't eaten dinner yet, and he was hungry. Hours and hours ago he had hatched some plan to take Jane to a restaurant. It might as well have been years ago.

Then he noticed that the third car from the end was Jane's. He stopped, paralyzed with alarm. He had assumed that she would be driving Dahlman out in her car. He looked at his watch. He had finished the operation nearly an hour ago, and Jane had been waiting for the first chance to slip him out. What if it had never come? He turned and started to walk back toward the hospital, then stopped. If he went back, he might be putting her in danger. If he found her, what could he do to help her?

He squeezed his eyes shut. What would she want? What had she said? Every minute that Carey stayed out of sight now would buy her another minute before anyone knew Dahlman was missing. That could last, at most, another hour or two if he didn't panic and rush back there.

Carey turned and walked slowly and reluctantly up the side street away from the hospital and away from the restaurants. The best he could do would be to go kill some time. There was a movie theater not far from here. The Rialto. He would watch a movie, eat dinner, and then come back. Later tonight there would be lots of questions, but he didn't have to face them yet.

Where was Jane? He tried to summon a picture of her driving off somewhere with Dahlman, but since he had just found her car parked behind his office, the picture wouldn't coalesce. He tried to imagine her on an airplane, but he was fairly certain Dahlman would not have been up to that—not the flying, but fighting the crowds and keeping himself from attracting attention during the long walks in an airport.

It occurred to Carey that he really had no idea what Jane would do in this situation. For the decade after he had met her in college they had simply been friends. They saw each other maybe once a month until the year before they were married. At that time he would not have guessed that she was doing anything secret and dangerous and illegal. He had not guessed until the night when she had told him. And she had initiated that conversation only to warn him that marrying her could put him in danger too. After that she had not talked about her old clients—told him the tricks she had used to make them invisible or throw off their pursuers. He had no clear, specific knowledge of how it was done. It was just something she used to do, and talking about it had made both of them uncomfortable.

Jane walked down the wooden steps to the cellar. The damp, musty air seemed to her like the house's breath. The house was a relic of the days when cellars were made of mortared stone and the beams under the floors were rounded logs with the bark stripped off. The coal furnace had been replaced by an oil furnace before she was born, and above the corner where the coal bin had sat there were still old ducts that led up to floor registers that had long ago been blocked off. She took the stepladder to one of them, pushed two sections apart, removed the small metal box hidden inside, and set it on the top step of the ladder. She took out a handful of cards and folded papers and shuffled through them.

In the past two years the only fake identification papers she had obtained were in matched sets, with her picture on one and Carey's on the other. There were some very good ones in the collection, as well as a few that wouldn't be ripe for some time. A good identity needed signs of a long history, with a real birth certificate and Social Security card, a couple of renewals on the licenses, visa stamps on the passports, and small but regular charges on each of the credit cards going back a couple of years.

Jane went past the recent identities, the ones she had made for a couple on the run. They were a part of her dowry that Carey didn't know about, and that she hoped he would never need to see. When she had retired from being a guide, she had known that people who were running would still come to her for a while, and there would still be people whose business it was to chase them. Some of the chasers might have heard of Jane or seen a little of her work, and would like the chance to get her into a small, quiet place somewhere and ask her questions until she died.

She found four identities for men who had birth dates in the 1930s, took four sets of cards she had made for herself, and then reached deeper into the heating duct to take out ten thousand dollars in cash. She put the box back into the heating duct, joined the two halves again, and carried the stepladder to the other end of the cellar to leave it with the tools and paintbrushes.

When she returned to her room she found Jake sitting on the bed watching television. He looked up when she entered. "There was just another news bulletin, but they didn't say anything about him being gone. They don't seem to know."

"Good," said Jane. "Do you think you have any clothes that you don't care if you ever see again?"

"Yes. All of them. I'll go put some in a suitcase."

"Nothing bright-colored, nothing new. You may not have noticed, but men over retirement age seem to have a lot of clothes of an earlier vintage."

"Yep," he said. "We're all timing it to wear them out at the moment of death so everything comes out even."

When Jake returned to the house with the suitcase, Jane had Dahlman sitting up on the living room couch and she was just finishing putting new gauze and adhesive tape on his shoulder and back.

Jake opened the suitcase so she could look into it. "Nothing to get him a lot of invitations, but nothing with blood on it, either."

Jane quickly fingered through the suitcase. "These are perfect. Thanks." She pulled out a plain tan shirt, slipped it onto Dahlman, and buttoned it quickly. She had taken the necktie off him by loosening the loop, so now she slipped it over his head again and tightened it, then helped him to his feet. "We'd better get going."

Jake followed her into the kitchen and watched her turning off lights and checking windows. "I'd like to go with you."

Jane shook her head. "Sorry. One geezer per trip."

"He's weak. You can't drag him around and watch your back at the same time."

"I said no," she said. "If you're so eager to take one more unnecessary risk, I'll accommodate you. Give me a spare key to your car. Call a cab tomorrow morning to take you to the airport. After he lets you off at the terminal and disappears, stroll over to the short-term lot, find your car, and drive it home."

"That's it?"

"No," she said. "Make sure this place is clean when we leave. Wipe off anything Dahlman could have touched. And when you think of it, tell Carey I love him."

6

J ane walked into the airline terminal and saw the clock on the wall. It was ten-fifteen already. The first flight out would have to do. But as soon as she was on the escalator and had ascended near enough to the top to see the second floor, she knew that it was too late.

It was likely that a stranger who seldom flew into Buffalo would not have noticed the change. The single sleepy security guard who spent most of his time talking to the airline man who weighed luggage and issued tickets was still downstairs at the door, but here on the departure level, where the people slowed down and formed a line to pass single file through the metal detectors, plainclothes policemen loitered, their eyes on the procession. The time was up. They had discovered that Dahlman was running.

She skirted the departure area and kept her eyes on the windows of the shops and restaurants. As long as she stayed away from the metal detectors, the cops would not consider her eligible for close scrutiny. There would be some kind of cut-off team up here too; if Dahlman got this far and saw the cops waiting, he might turn and head for the door.

Jane went into one of the shops and bought some items that wouldn't be wasted—toothbrushes, toothpaste, a hairbrush and comb, all in compact sizes for travelers. When she came out she joined the stream of tired passengers who had come off an airplane and were now headed toward the baggage area.

Jane was one of several in the group who stopped just before the escalators at the row of car-rental counters. She rented a big, roomy Oldsmobile Cutlass. In Buffalo the car-rental lots were all outside the door behind the terminal, so it took her only a few minutes to join the next crowd heading downstairs, get out the door and into the car she had rented.

She drove it to the short-term lot and helped Dahlman step out of Jake's car and into hers. She put the two suitcases into her trunk and drove out onto Genesee Street.

Dahlman looked alert and maybe even a little scared. "Where are we going?"

Jane shrugged. "There are police waiting in the airport, so right now we're only one very small jump ahead of them. What we've got is a big new car with a full gas tank, and that's about it. In a minute I'm going to turn left on Bailey Avenue. That's Route 62. By midnight we should be passing Warren, Pennsylvania. Then we switch roads and make a pretty straight run down to Pittsburgh."

"Why Pittsburgh?"

Jane said, "I know this is all very strange. You're in pain, you're weak, you're tired. In fifteen minutes we'll be out of the congested area and going through farmland, with a little town every ten or twenty miles. You can stretch out on the back seat and sleep." She turned south onto Bailey Avenue and accelerated slightly.

"I'm not ready to sleep," said Dahlman irritably. "I asked you a question, and I'd like an answer. What's in Pittsburgh?"

Jane glanced at him. The momentary glare of a set of oncoming headlights showed her the sharp little gray eyes glittering. At some point he was going to collapse, but until he did, his agitation had to be borne. "Okay, here's the situation. Staying in town is a bad idea. There's a term for people who thought they knew some city better than the local police. They're called 'convicts.' We don't seem to be able to fly out, so we're driving. We can't get on the Thruway, because there are toll booths, and in at least the first few around here, the State Police might be waiting for you. But once we cross the border into Pennsylvania, some of the searchers will be left behind. You're a fugitive from Illinois who escaped from custody in New York. Unless the Pennsylvania police have some reason to believe you're headed there, then you're just one of a thousand or so New York criminals they've been warned to keep an eye out for this year. You're very important to the Buffalo police because you embarrassed them by walking out of the hospital and you might be dangerous. To the Pittsburgh police you're just a name that's most likely to be somebody else's problem. They have at least a thousand murderers of their own to catch."

"I'm not a murderer."

"I'm glad."

"You don't believe me?" He was incensed.

Jane looked ahead and paid attention to her driving. If he had been young and healthy, she might have put him into the trunk and avoided the chance of his being seen at a lighted intersection. It was too bad he wasn't young or healthy. "It's not that I don't believe you. It just doesn't matter right now. I think that should be your first lesson," she said. "For tonight, it doesn't matter what you did or didn't do. If you could listen to the police radios right now—or even the television news—you would hear that you're an escaped murder suspect, armed and dangerous, probably desperate because you're wounded. They're warning each other and everybody else who's awake."

"I'm a well-known physician who has not only saved thousands of lives, but taught a fair share of the best surgeons in this country how to—"

"Then use your brain and think about it the way they do," said Jane. "If you've suddenly killed somebody who isn't related to you, it means you're crazy. The fact that you're a doctor who slipped out under their noses means you're devious and probably smarter than they are. The fact that you're famous only means they won't have to rely on one of those crude police drawings. They have lots of pictures of you—probably great ones."

He was silent for a moment, and she looked at him again. She decided she had better tell him the worst of it at the beginning. She spoke more gently. "If they can't take you under ideal circumstances, they'll kill you. It's not because they want to, but because they know that people like you seldom surrender."

"I'm trying to tell you that it's a mistake. All of it."

"And I'm trying to tell you that it doesn't matter. Don't imagine that your credentials and accomplishments will convince people you're innocent, or that you're harmless. Deep in the back of your mind you seem to have the notion that those things will make this come out all right—that the truth will save you. Maybe it will. But right now it won't, and right now is reality. The future is just a theory."

Dahlman sat in silence for a full minute. A few times he looked as though some retort was on his tongue, but each time he decided not to speak. Finally, he said with exaggerated patience, "It's just that you mentioned Pittsburgh. We could stop and see if we could get some help. I have friends there."

"No, you don't."

"I just told you—"

"Listen carefully, because this is important. You haven't told me who was chasing you hard enough to make you run to Buffalo. But I know who has been chasing you since then, and I think I know who will join in the hunt. You came through several states and committed crimes in two."

"What crimes?" His voice was irate.

"Fleeing to evade prosecution in Illinois and New York. That's if you didn't do anything else, and nothing happened on the way—like breaking into your own office in the university to get things before you left."

Dahlman was shocked. "That's absurd."

"That's a federal crime. School break-ins are investigated by the F.B.I. Crossing a state line while you were running is enough for them, though."

"I'm not some mad bomber. I'm a physician."

Jane sighed. There it was again. "They don't know what else you are, and waiting isn't a good way for them to find out. In one sense, it would be good for you if the F.B.I. does come in. They would take a very close look at whatever evidence there is that you killed someone, and at every piece of paper you owned. If there's anything that will clear you, they're more likely to find it than anyone else is, and they have no reason to conceal it. But in the short term, they're trouble, because they're better at finding people than any local cops can be. They make stopping in with out-of-town friends and relatives a very bad idea, both for you and for the friends and relatives. Your friends can be charged as accessories if they so much as fail to turn you in. It's hard to think of a friend you trust with your life but also don't mind putting in that kind of fix."

"I never intended to get anyone else in trouble. I was simply thinking of ways to make this easier."

"What we want isn't easier, it's less predictable. There are experts chasing you now. They're using this time to find out everything about you. You're hurt, so where will you go? Probably to a friend who is a doctor. I'll bet you know a dozen who would take care of you for a month without turning you in. Good for you. But twelve is a tiny number for the F.B.I. to check, and if they've already been called in they're busy tonight compiling the list of names and addresses. If you had them written down someplace when you left Chicago, the F.B.I. already has a list. They don't have to waste time flying around the country to find these people, they just have to phone the agents already in the cities where they live. I'm sure you had money—bank accounts and retirement accounts and stocks and bonds. Unless you kept it in cash a distance from home or in offshore banks under a false name, then forget it. The second you touch any of the accounts, bells and whistles will go off in the J. Edgar Hoover Building."

Dahlman glared at her angrily. "You're trying to get me to give up, aren't you? To go into some police station and turn myself in, because I'm going to be caught."

Jane looked into his eyes and held the gaze, unblinking, for a moment before she returned her eyes to the road. "No. I'm making sure you know at the outset what it costs when you decide to run. It isn't easy, and it isn't pleasant. And most of all, it isn't a sure thing. If you want to survive, you have to change who you are. You don't just get to run away from one bad incident in the past and keep the rest—the respect and gratitude you earned, the friends and family you love, the status you enjoyed. The past is what the police will use to find you. And I don't know much about those two men at the hospital, but I wouldn't want to make it too easy for them, either."

Jane had managed to plant a few bits of the truth in his brain, and over the next few hours his mind would be working out the rest, whether he wanted it to or not. She hoped she had said enough to keep him scared, quiet, and docile for the next few hours, while the trail was still hot and any mistake could be fatal.

Adult males had always been the most difficult kind of runner to guide. All of that self-reliance and aggression that they had painfully developed as survival characteristics got in the way and made their impulses foolish. It was true: women stopped and asked for directions, and men didn't. Even the way they looked was against them. Their hair was almost always too short to change much, the differences between the kinds of clothes they wore were minuscule. As she thought about Dahlman, what came to mind was a list of ways in which he was the worst ever. He was wounded and weak, and could easily get worse instead of better. If he did, she couldn't even take him to a doctor, because apparently in that closed, limited world, he was famous. And he was older, more brittle, and attached to his own habits of mind.

It struck her as odd that she had used the comparative: "older." Older than whom? Not just older than the usual male in trouble. Older than Carey. She admitted to herself that the worst mental habits that Dahlman had were familiar to her, because her husband had a milder, less irritating case of them. Dahlman never let a statement of fact go unquestioned and unexamined. Is it a fact? How do you know? Doesn't that contradict this other fact?

That was Carey, and so was the casual, unconscious assumption he had picked up in medical school that he was one of the good guys, so nobody would wish to do him harm. It was one of the qualities that she had always loved about Carey. It made him cheerful, pleasant, and self-assured enough to look goofy once in a while without getting defensive. He moved through the world smoothly, telling people what was good for them and quietly smiling through their irrational protests and retaliations like a parent waiting for a tantrum to end. She loved it now, when he was thirty-four. Would she love it in thirty years, when he had earned the kind of adulation and status that Dahlman had, when more confidence was heaped on top of the conviction and it started to sound a whole lot like arrogance?

As she drove along the dark highway all she could think about was Carey. The questions she had been holding in the back of her mind for hours tumbled into view. Carey had been adamant that Jane must never again drive along a dark highway with a fugitive in the seat beside her. The reasons had been carefully assembled and calmly presented. But all of the arguments had been made on the assumption that runners were certain kinds of people. Some had caused their own problems, and others were victims. The victims were usually women and children. There were people besides Jane Whitefield who would be willing to take the risks to save them. All Jane had to do was keep a list of those quasi-illegal organizations who hid abuse victims and make a call or two, and the person would be picked up. The ones who weren't exactly victims, just people who had acquired enemies but had not done anything bad enough to deserve to die just yet, could be handled differently. Carey had grudgingly conceded that if Jane felt it was justified, she could give a person like that a set of false papers left over from the old days, a handful of hundred-dollar bills, and a half hour of advice before she sent him on his way. Carey was very good at constructing fair, logical solutions to other people's problems.

She glanced at Dahlman. He was staring ahead, motionless. She looked at him longer and harder, waiting for him to blink. Was it possible he had just . . .

He said, "Don't worry. I'm not dead. I was just daydreaming."

Jane pulled the car onto the shoulder of the dark road. "Get in the back and stretch out. Maybe you'll be able to sleep a little."

He climbed out and lay down in the back seat. "Might as well. Not that it will be easy, now that you've convinced me I'm homeless, penniless, and friendless."

"Not friendless," said Jane. "You've got me." She didn't like the way that sounded. Maybe some reassurance would help him sleep. "The police and the F.B.I. will be working hard on building a case against you, and it would be a very unusual frame that could stand up to that kind of attention. All they have to do is detect some flaw that proves one piece of evidence against you is faked. If it's faked, the killer faked it, and that can't be you."

"Then all I'll have to worry about is a pair of men I've never seen before coming in the night to kill me."

"If the frame fails, killing you afterward won't put it back together," said Jane. "Those men will have other things to do—like making sure they're not caught." She forced a smile. "We just have to keep you out of sight a little while and let the police straighten it out."

As she drove along the dark road in silence, she wished that she were as sure as she had sounded.

7

Carey McKinnon walked along smartly, conscious of the sound of his shoes on the concrete sidewalk. Instead of worrying about his wife, he tried to review in his memory an article by an orthopedist decrying the effects of shoes that forced the foot to strike with high impact on the calcaneus at each step and the further skeletal deterioration caused by leather soles and hard rubber heels.

But there was little in the article that had surprised him, so he couldn't keep his mind on it for more than a few seconds. He turned the corner and saw the hospital building looming ahead, dominating the whole next block. He had never thought of the hospital as "looming" before. He raised his head, straightened his spine, and lengthened his strides. He had spent as much time away as he could possibly justify, and now he had to walk in, head for the third floor, and pretend to be the one who discovered that his patient was missing.

Everything he did during the next few hours would have to be deceptive and misleading. He had to delay the police, divert their attention, send them in the wrong direction, if possible. Jane was risking everything. From the second Carey had heard Dahlman say, "I came to find a woman named Jane Whitefield," he had wished he could throw himself in front of her. He wanted to hide her, deny she existed, and let the faceless, invisible threat take him instead.

Even as the words had formed in his mind, he had known that he could not do it. For most of his life he had been learning to believe passionately in human expertise. Nearly every day he detected the approach of someone's death and asked himself, "What is the best strategy to fight this? Who is the very best one to do it?" Sometimes he would clear his own schedule to prepare for the surgery, and sometimes he would instead make a telephone call to a superb practitioner of a particular procedure, an expert in a narrow specialty, and ask him to save the patient. When Carey had seen this patient—Dahlman—handcuffed to a gurney in the emergency room, he had known. Dahlman needed a specialist, not some clumsy amateur who would get him killed. Dahlman needed Jane.

He fretted as he walked toward the hospital. He worried that in the rush and the anxiety, he had not really explained to Jane who Dahlman was. Jane had a right to know everything, and Carey had the impression that what he had told her must have sounded incoherent. He found himself rehearsing what he should have told her.

Dahlman was truthful. Dahlman was no more knowledgeable than Carey about things that criminals did, but he had all of his faculties, and knew that he hadn't killed Sarah Hoffman. He was certainly capable of knowing that someone had planted evidence that he had killed Sarah Hoffman. No, Carey had told Jane that much.

What he had not told her was why a rational person—any rational person who happened to be nearby when this happened—should feel that saving Dahlman was worth enormous risks. That was more difficult. In a way, it was absurd that there had to be an excuse for saving a life. People, sometimes thousands of them in a single day, unhesitatingly threw themselves into battles to preserve the lives and privileges of degenerate kings and corrupt politicians. Dahlman was something that Carey could not have said aloud, even to Jane: he was a man who might be worth more to humanity than all the kings and presidents who had ever lived.

Carey could say the easy, verifiable part: Dahlman had already saved thousands of people in his operating room and had personally trained a few hundred of the best young surgeons now in practice. But the part that Carey was torn about was an assertion with no proof. He believed that Dahlman might be this generation's standard-bearer. Dahlman and Sarah Hoffman's quiet clinical research on post-operative regeneration of external epithelial tissue had produced results promising enough to attract the attention of a few nonspecialist journals. But what only

Carey and a few dozen others who had read the scientific articles had understood was that Dahlman wasn't just looking for a way to help surgeons produce evenly healed, aesthetically pleasing incisions.

The doctors who knew Dahlman, who knew the way he thought and were used to the understated, terse way he spoke, knew that the articles were hints. Working on the skin was almost inevitable because a researcher could see it and touch it. But the outer skin and the membranes of internal organs were both epithelial tissue. Dahlman was after game so big that even a whisper of it did not belong in a scientific article. It was nothing less than a way of making all surgery a minor procedure. Ultimately, maybe in another generation or two, it might provide a way of treating everything from heart disease to cancer. Huge sections of damaged tissue could be removed, and the body stimulated to replace them. And if Sarah Hoffman was already dead, then the seeds of that research—not what had been done, but what paths had been rejected, what would have been tried next, and why—existed only in the brain of Richard Dahlman.

Carey walked along trying to look unconcerned, but feeling his heart pounding. A very small, incidental part of this was up to him. He had to do what he could to help Jane carry this off. He had to become a disturbing, confusing element in the mixture, make a lot of noise, and appear to raise the hue and cry while really making a mess of it and adding to the delay. He had to buy Jane more time. If she was driving, a minute could put her a mile past a roadblock; if she was flying, it might get her off a plane and out the door of a terminal.

He realized that he had been describing an urge of his own. He would like to be with her, running away, not stepping toward the bright lights of the hospital. He wanted all of this never to have happened—wished he had never been alert enough to know that if he didn't ask the wife he loved to risk her life, then he deserved never to have been born.

He studied the building as he approached it. Was he imagining that there were more police cars than before? He probably was. When he had arrived at five there had been none, and then he had seen two out the back window. These had undoubtedly been parked in front all evening, and he had not been looking in that direction when he had slipped out through radiology.

He walked through the front door and stepped directly into a glaring light. "Dr. McKinnon?" said a female voice. "Can we talk to you?"

He had thought he had gotten past the newspeople. Their vans had been parked in the back, near his car. He looked down at the short, pretty woman beside him, and he recognized her as the one he had seen this morning when he had turned on the television to find out about the weather. She was wearing the same awful blue suit, and he felt sorry for her. Could she have been working all this time?

"I'm sorry," he said apologetically. "I have a patient to see right now, but I'll be around later."

The woman's face seemed to lose muscular control and go flat. The professional demeanor of concerned commentator had vanished, and for a second she looked confused. Then the eyes widened with excitement. Carey saw the change, and hurried toward the elevator.

"Dr. McKinnon!" she called, and he thought he heard her footsteps behind him. He went past the elevator toward the door to the stairwell, heard the elevator doors open, spun to step inside, and punched the CLOSE DOOR button.

He pushed the button for the third floor and tried to collect his thoughts. They already knew Dahlman was gone, and the newswoman had assumed he had known too, at first. But he hadn't wanted to let her be the one to tell him, and he knew he wasn't a good enough actor to let her record his reaction on camera.

He stepped out of the elevator and walked down the hall toward the room assigned to Dahlman. There were two men in sport coats, one gray tweed that matched the man's gray, bristly hair, and the other a brown that looked a little like one Carey had that Jane never let him wear. The men had plastic wallets stuck in their breast pockets so they hung over to display badges, one gold and the other silver. Carey pretended not to see them as he walked to the doorway.

The younger one in brown stepped into his path. "I'm sorry," said the man. "This is a crime scene." He studied Carey's face, as though trying to verify that Carey had seen his badge.

Carey turned his head to look in puzzlement at the older man, then back at the one in brown. "I understand. Dr. Dahlman is in custody, but I'm his doctor, and I'd like to see him."

The older man was holding a little spiral notebook in his hand and he consulted it. "You are Doctor . . ." He flipped a page. "McKinnon." It wasn't a question, but he said, "That right?"

"Yes," said Carey. He craned his neck to look in the doorway at the empty room, then looked at the policemen in surprise. "I operated on him earlier this evening, and he's supposed to be in there. Can you tell me where he's been moved?"

"I'm Captain Folger," said the man. "This is Detective Kohl. I wish I could tell you where he is. He's missing. If you'll come with me, you might be able to help us clear this up." He was reassuring and calm, but not quite friendly.

Carey knew it was time to start causing trouble. "What do you mean, 'missing'?" Carey simulated the amazement he might have felt. "That's crazy! He's seriously injured and tranquilized. You're trying to tell me he just got up out of bed? He was supposed to be restrained. And where were the policemen who were supposed to be watching him? We should be looking for him."

"We've already done that," said the policeman. "But he's not in the building anymore." As the policeman stepped off down the hall, Carey almost smiled. Jane was out. She had done it. The policeman said, "I think you understand we'd like to ask you some questions—about his condition and so on."

"Of course," said Carey. He followed the older policeman down the hallway, reminding himself that he couldn't let himself get lazy now. He had to think. The man had said "Captain" Folger—a very high rank, the sort of policeman who was in charge of a station, not the sort who wandered around looking for people.

Then Carey felt rather than heard something behind him: the younger one, Detective Kohl, was following a few paces behind them. Was he cutting off Carey's retreat, or was his position simply the result of starting to walk after his boss had? Carey decided that, for the moment, he had better not assume anything was meaningless.

Captain Folger opened the door to the conference room at the end of the hall, and to Carey's surprise, he went in and closed it behind him. Detective Kohl stepped to Carey's side. "Have you ever had a patient walk off before?" Carey decided he was trying to distract him.

"Usually if they chicken out, it's before I operate."

The detective seemed to think that was a very witty thing to say. He laughed, then said, "I guess he can't have gone far."

Carey shook his head. "I'm amazed he went anywhere. He's sixty-seven years old, he's lost blood, he's been bruised by the impact of the bullet, he's—"

"Oh, yeah," Detective Kohl interrupted. "I've seen it a few times, and I know what you mean. Whatever's going through his mind, he hurts."

He said it with a satisfaction that reminded Carey that this man was no friend of his.

The door opened, and Captain Folger beckoned and stepped aside. "Thanks, Doctor."

As Carey went past him into the familiar room, Folger began to recite names. Carey listened, aware that he should hold the names in his memory, but they were just words. "This is Officer Graley, Officer Wilchevsky, Mr. Marshall, and I'm Captain Folger, in case you didn't catch it before." Nobody stood to shake hands.

As Carey had expected, the captain did the talking. "Dr. McKinnon, I should say at this juncture that we appreciate any help you can give us. If you would be more comfortable consulting an attorney before you say anything, we understand: there's no way to predict whether you might open yourself up to some kind of malpractice litigation or other legal problems. It would cause delay that's probably unnecessary, but after all, we do need to respect your rights, too. Because this is an official police inquiry, it can't be off the record and could come out in court."

Carey admired the smooth, affable way the captain had spoken. It seemed to him that Folger had probably read him his rights and set a trap at the same time. If Carey was here to delay the police, Folger had offered him a simple way to do it. But that would confirm their suspicion that he was the enemy.

"I don't think that will be necessary," he answered. "Will it?"

"I can't give anybody legal advice," said Folger. "And I don't know anything about all these civil suits against hospitals and doctors. We just do the criminal stuff." He paused. "Want to go ahead?"

Carey nodded.

"Our logs say officers brought Richard Dahlman in here at seven-fifteen this evening. The hospital records say you operated on him at eight-fifteen. Is that right?"

So this was going to be about the subject of times. He didn't want to talk about times. That would help them isolate exactly when Jane had slipped Dahlman out, and if they knew when, they would know where it had happened. People might remember having seen Jane there. He answered with names. "Yes, I operated. Dr. Shelton was anesthesiologist and Dr. Stern assisted. The surgical nurse was Mrs. Brooks."

"What did you do to him?"

"I removed fragments of a bullet from his left shoulder—five, I think. Very small—particles, really. The main projectile had expanded as it passed through, and glanced off a bone. That seems to have been what caused the pieces to come off. It also caused a fracture with bone chips, torn musculature, and damage to a major vein. The main artery was not severed, and there appeared to be no significant nerve damage."

"How long did that take?"

"Not long. It couldn't have been more than forty-five or fifty minutes at the outside."

Folger looked at his notes. "The anesthetist keeps a timed record. Did you know that?"

"Of course," said Carey. "That's right. If you need exact times, you should get Shelton's notes."

"We have." He frowned, then handed the sheet of paper to Carey. "Is this his handwriting?"

"I guess so," said Carey. It said fifteen minutes and thirty-seven seconds. "He usually keeps his own notes." He handed the paper back.

"Fifteen minutes. That seems like world-record speed."

Carey shrugged. "Faster than it seemed to me, at any rate." He added, "No surgery is entirely without risk. We don't keep a patient open any longer than necessary. When I was sure I had removed the foreign objects that had shown on the X-ray, repaired the damage to the vein to stop the bleeding, and sutured the muscles, I closed."

"What kind of risk are you talking about?"

Carey cocked his head. "Infection, adverse reaction to anesthetics, shock and possible cardiac arrest, hemorrhage . . ."

As Carey spoke, he was aware of each of the people in the room. Did the young woman's squinted eyes and pursed lips mean she was trying to understand, or did she disbelieve something he was saying? How could she?

Folger was looking down at his notes. "Why were you the one to operate?"

Carey had not prepared for this question, and it astounded him that he had overlooked it. He constructed his response cautiously. "Dr. Leo Bortoni was the surgeon on duty at the time," he said. "When the patient was brought into the emergency room, I was on my usual rounds, visiting my surgical patients. I knew Leo was in surgery at the time. The procedure is to phone one of the surgeons on call, but of course I was on that list, and was already there, so I stepped in."

"And you met with the patient."

"I went to the emergency room to examine him."

"What was his condition?" Folger's eyes weren't on Carey's. He seemed to be glancing at the man in the dark suit across the table. What was his name again?

Carey sensed that some kind of trap was being prepared. "He had a bullet wound in his left shoulder. As I said before."

"Yes, but I was wondering if there was anything else. I mean, was he unconscious, delirious, anything like that?"

"He was weak, and in quite a lot of pain. The wound had bled profusely, but the E.R. doctors had it pretty well stopped by the time I arrived. He was conscious. He's a surgeon, so he was acutely aware of his condition and knew already that he would need to undergo a surgical procedure."

"What did you talk about?"

"That's about it."

"You were alone with him for a time, right? And you knew him personally. All of a sudden he shows up with a bullet wound. You didn't ask him how that came about?" So there it was. They already knew.

"Well, no," said Carey. "He told me that much. He said he had been wanted for murder and the police—one of the officers who brought him in—had shot him." Carey thought about it, and decided that if there was a record being made, then there was no reason he could not use it to preserve Dahlman's denial. "He said the whole thing was a terrible mistake. He had not killed anybody, and the person who had done it had framed him. I couldn't imagine Richard Dahlman as a murderer."

"Why?" This time Carey was sure. The captain was watching the man in the dark suit for a reaction, maybe for unspoken instructions of some kind.

"He's a distinguished surgeon and teacher of other surgeons who has never in the past committed a crime and, as far as I know, never lied about anything. I admit I haven't seen or heard any of the evidence against him. I assume it's pretty compelling, or we wouldn't all be here. But I think when you look into it, you'll find he didn't do it."

The captain was watching the man in the suit throughout Carey's answer. But who was he? Had Folger said "marshal"? Carey had a vague notion that marshals were the people who transported prisoners, or took them into formal custody in court or some such thing. But why would a police captain be deferring to somebody like that?

"Do you know this building well?"

Was he just giving Carey a chance to lie about something? "I ought to. I was born here," said Carey. "When I finished my residency I came back. I've been here nearly every day for a couple of years."

"Do you know how he got out of the building?"

Carey stared at the grain of the wood of the table. This was the question, he thought. It was best to ignore the implication, to pretend the word "know" had not been used. "If I were to guess, I would guess that he didn't get out: that he hid somewhere in the building and found himself too weak to go on, or fell asleep." It occurred to Carey that he might very well have made a terrible mistake. What if that had been Jane's plan? It would explain why her car was still parked behind Carey's office. It made perfect sense to put him in bed in another unoccupied room, slip a different bracelet on his wrist, and let him rest until the police had left the hospital. They had told him they'd searched, but why should they tell him the truth?

The captain shook his head. "No, that was what we thought too. But Mr. Pankowski's staff took officers into every room, every broom closet and storeroom in the building. We even searched every laundry bin and garbage can big enough to hold a man. He has definitely left the building. It's too bad you weren't here when it happened. They were beeping you, but—"

Carey was ready for this one. "They were?" He took out his pager and looked at it. He flipped the switch off and on a few times. "I wonder how . . ."

The man in the dark suit leaned forward and held out his hand. "I'm pretty good with those. Can I see it?"

Carey slid it toward him. The man picked it up, worked the switch, examined the display, opened the little hatch at the end, and took the battery out. He put the battery back. "You had the battery in backwards, with the poles reversed." He closed the hatch and flipped the switch with his thumb. The beeper went *bee-beep, bee-beep, bee-beep.* Carey watched him studying the display. He pressed the button twice more. Carey realized that he had been outsmarted again. The man was looking to see if other numbers besides the hospital's appeared. Then the man looked up at Carey, and his eyes carried an unexpected message. They said, "I know." But the eyes didn't look triumphant or reproachful; what the man seemed to feel was sadness, a mixture of sympathy and regret.

Carey's heart beat faster, and he tried to calm himself. The man had convicted Carey in his mind, but at least he was not writing a number down. That meant that Jane hadn't called. She was safe. Carey accepted his pager. "Thanks, Mr . . ." He frowned. "I'm sorry. Too many names at once."

"Marshall. You're welcome."

Carey knew he had to say something. "What a dumb thing to do," said Carey. "It must have been that way all day." Then his mind scurried to see if he had made a mistake. They could probably check the paging service to see when he had answered his last beep.

But the policemen seemed to miss it. The captain said, "Where were you this evening after the operation?"

"I had dinner and went to a movie."

"What restaurant?"

"I walked to Garibaldi's on Merman Street." He took out his wallet and read the credit card receipt. "It's 597 Merman Street."

"I know that place," said the captain. "What was the movie?"

Carey said, "*Finally Dead.* I guess the title should have warned me, right?" He smiled. "It wasn't very good. I didn't want to hang around the hospital getting badgered by newspeople, so I thought I'd waste some time. I got my wish."

"What would have happened if something went wrong with the patient?"

"What are you referring to?"

"You know. The things you mentioned. Dahlman starts hemorrhaging and needs to be operated on again. That kind of thing."

"After Leo Bortoni's shift, Arthur Hicks was on duty. He's a good surgeon, and there are always others on call. In my judgment, the best surgeon in an emergency would not be the one who's been working for fourteen or fifteen hours."

"But you wanted to be here. What for?"

"To check on him. It was my responsibility to ensure that my patient was responding well: to see for myself, in other words."

Folger glanced down at his notebook and looked surprised. "I don't think I have any more questions right now." He looked directly at the man in the dark suit. "Do any of you?"

The man in the dark suit was silent and motionless.

Folger said, "Thanks very much, Doctor. I assume you'll be going home from here?"

"I suppose so," Carey said. "Unless my patient turns up."

"We'll let you know if he does."

"Thanks." Carey stood up. The others remained seated, waiting for him to leave. He opened the door and stepped out, then turned around to close it. The last thing he saw confirmed his impression. The captain, the female detective, and the uniformed officer were all looking attentively at the man in the dark suit. The man in the dark suit was staring straight into Carey's eyes until the door closed.

Agent Marshall said quietly, "That's what I was afraid of."

Captain Folger shook his head. "It's hard to believe that a man like that would put himself in this kind of trouble."

Marshall sighed. "Have you ever read any medical books?"

"Can't say that I have."

"There's not much in them. You don't learn to be a surgeon by studying. After medical school you do four years of surgical residency at some hospital, helping out and doing the easy ones. Then you go find yourself the best surgeon you can, and you spend the next three or four years finding out how he does it and trying to learn to do it too. Dahlman was the one McKinnon picked out. McKinnon owes him what he has, what he does, who he is."

"It's a damned shame to see him paying off like this."

Marshall looked at the papers in the file in front of him and shook his head. "Fifteen minutes for a nine-millimeter round at twelve feet, and a sixty-seven-year-old is up and running. If I ever take a hit, McKinnon is the one I want to dig it out of me. He would have been, anyway." He tossed the file on the table and rubbed his eyes wearily, then squared his shoulders. "All right. Can you spare two officers around the clock for McKinnon?"

"I guess we'll have to." Folger turned to the policewoman.

"I'll put a team on it right away," she said.

"I'll have them take care of the wiretaps in Washington. The phone company will set it up so his phones can be monitored from there."

"Thanks. That will save us some man-hours."

"We'll do the lab work and print identification on whatever your people find here. Anything else you need, don't be shy. The worst I can say is no, and you know in advance I won't want to. I'd like to wrap this up in the next couple of days, but for now let's act as though it's going to get long and ugly."

8

As Jane drove along Route 62, she began to feel the old habits of mind coming back to her. Years of experience had taught her that the decisions she made during the first few hours would determine whether her runner was safe or merely a step ahead.

She was satisfied that she'd had no choice but to take Dahlman out of Buffalo tonight. The authorities would assume that a wounded man could not have gone far. They would look for him hardest in the immediate vicinity, and keep moving outward for a few days. They would knock on doors and interview everyone who could conceivably have seen or heard anything. For at least a month, it was going to be very difficult for a man in his sixties to show his face in Buffalo without getting a lot of inquisitive stares. If Dahlman so much as walked past a window, somebody might call the police. But if she could get Dahlman out of this part of the country, there was a good chance that wherever she took him, few people would have heard of him, and the local police would have their own fugitives to hunt.

The police were the immediate threat, but what they did made sense, so they were predictable. Her mind kept returning to the two men at the hospital. When she had pulled into the parking lot in a police car, they had hidden their guns in the weeds, so there was no possibility that they had anything to do with any police organization.

Who were they? She glanced over her shoulder at Dahlman. He was asleep on the back seat, so for the moment, she couldn't ask him any questions. The sudden arrival of people Dahlman didn't seem to have recognized, who were prepared to kill him in police custody, raised Dahlman's problem to a new level.

Jane had believed Carey when he had said that Dahlman had been framed for a murder. What that had meant to her was that some person who knew both Dahlman and Sarah Hoffman had killed her and hit on some unusually effective way of throwing suspicion in another direction. Jane had only temporarily suspended her disbelief enough to accept Carey's statement that Dahlman would not be safe from the framer if he went to jail. It was possible. If Dahlman had something to say that the killer was worried about, it wasn't that difficult to find a prisoner who could be paid to make sure he didn't live to say it.

But in Jane's experience, lone killers were shy about the process. The killer had to go to an intermediary, negotiate a deal for the second murder, and then wait to see whether the other side delivered or turned him in. Her skepticism had triggered her reflex to construct alternative plans. She had decided to listen to Dahlman's story as soon as possible, and then decide whether the threat was real. If she was sure that Dahlman was wrong, she would teach him to recite a plausible tale about why he had been scared enough to leave the hospital, then return to Buffalo and drop him off at the police station.

When she had picked up the guns the two men had hidden in the weeds, her skepticism had been obliterated. In its place was mystification. Dahlman's adversary wasn't some solitary amateur who had killed Sarah Hoffman and shifted the blame onto him. He was being hunted by professionals. That raised the possibility that Sarah Hoffman had been killed by professionals, and that the frame had been constructed by professionals.

What attraction would two doctors engaged in medical research have for people like that? Doctors had drugs. They tended to have money, houses and offices full of nice things, and cars that might interest thieves. Doctors engaged in research that had intriguing implications might excite a pharmaceutical manufacturer or a jealous rival. Sarah Hoffman might have had some secrets that Carey didn't know about—a gambling problem or a boyfriend who called himself a "developer" or "investor" or "consultant" but was actually a gangster. No answer she could think of was more likely than any other. Until she had asked Dahlman all of the questions and listened to all of the answers, she would know nothing. She didn't even know for sure whether Dahlman was innocent. Having armed men hunting him didn't exactly prove he had not murdered Sarah Hoffman.

Jane looked at Dahlman again. He was still asleep, so for the moment he was invisible to a casual glance from a distance, but if a policeman were to pull them over, he could hardly fail to notice that there was an old man lying there, and that he looked sick.

Jane was only as far as North Collins when she noticed the headlights behind her. She watched and waited, hoping they would turn off in Lawtons, then Gowanda, Conewango, Clear Creek, but they stayed there, just far enough back so she couldn't really see the car. When she slowed down, so did they. As she approached Jamestown she began to feel tense. Jamestown was big enough to have policemen who stayed alert at night, and the hour was just past eleven, when traffic was thin. If the ones behind were policemen, they could easily have called ahead and consulted with the local authorities. They would have asked them to pick a spot to set up a blind roadblock.

Pulling over a suspected murderer was a delicate matter. They would want a big complement of policemen waiting, and Jamestown was the last city of sufficient size to have one. They would want to do it in a place where he couldn't shoot bystanders, so it would be outside of town. No, she couldn't even count on that. Since it was long after business hours, they might choose to divert him into a cul-de-sac in an industrial area where he would be surrounded on three sides by high walls lined with sharpshooters.

Jane tried to decide whether her uneasiness was pronounced enough to make her turn off the highway onto another route. She studied the headlights in her rearview mirror for a few seconds. The car was still staying back a set distance—maybe a thousand feet on the long dark stretches and half that when she approached a town. It had done nothing suspicious, and that could be what was making her suspicious. Carey would have said she was driving like an old lady, but she had her reasons. What were theirs?

After eleven, on an open country road in good weather, people got careless, drove too fast, got impatient waiting for a safe place to pass. The driver of the car behind her never did those things.

Her tires made a new sound as she crossed a little bridge over Conewango Creek. She glanced over the rail at the quick flash of black water. If she remembered the route correctly, the road would cross the creek at least twice more. "Conewango" meant "in the rapids." The rapids were south of here, where there had once been a village. It was just before Warren, Pennsylvania, where the creek emptied into the Allegheny River. Tonight the stream seemed higher and faster than the last time she had been here. It had been a rainy summer.

She supposed it had always been a rainy summer. The Old People had a vast repertoire of procedures and medicines for success in war and love and curing disease and stopping whirlwinds, but she had never heard of one for making rain. They used to thank the Thunderers once a year for the plentiful supply. When European visitors of a literate sort visited Nundawaonoga in those days, they had all written descriptions of miles of fields growing tall with corn, bean vines twining up the stalks and squash beneath.

Jane stared at the empty blackness ahead, but a growing glare began to sear her eyes. The car behind her was coming up fast, and the driver had switched on his high-beam headlights. She tilted her mirror to keep the light out of her eyes and watched the car in the side mirrors. If he was trying to tell her he wanted to pass, she would be glad. But first she had to be sure.

She hugged the right side of the road and slowed down to let the car slip by safely. Then she watched. The car kept coming, moving a bit faster now.

Finally it swung into the left lane, and as it came abreast she turned her head over her left shoulder to look behind the glare of the headlights at the driver. She saw his head in silhouette, but all she could make out was that it didn't have the long hair of a woman, and it wasn't wearing a hat. The car glided forward and everything changed and came into focus at once.

A second head popped up from the passenger seat, the window started to come down, and she saw the face.

Jane stamped on the brake pedal, then turned the wheel to the left, toward the other car. She had predicted the other driver's reaction correctly. He was alarmed by the sudden swerve and the squeal of tires. His foot touched his brake pedal for an instant, but then he realized he had miscalculated: if she wanted to ram him, then he wanted distance. His foot jammed down on the accelerator, and he shot forward again.

Jane saw her hood slip behind the other car's trunk, missing it by inches, then keep turning. She concentrated on gauging the spin of her car. For two full seconds it was in its own motion and out of her control, the rear end swinging around with a shriek of friction. Her seat belt tightened around her hips and chest and she heard her purse slap against the inside of the passenger door and fall to the floor.

Finally, when it seemed as though the car could not do anything but keep spinning, the tires caught, the brakes held, and it came to a stop, rocking violently once, twice, but not tipping over.

Jane looked over the seat. Dahlman had his arms and legs spread, gripping the door handle with one hand and clawing the fabric of the back seat with the other, his face set in an open-mouthed breathless grimace. She found the white line on the pavement leading into her door, saw the bright taillights of the other car still diminishing at high speed, and regained her sense of direction. She straightened the car and began to accelerate northward, the way they had come.

"Who are they?" gasped Dahlman. "Police?"

"No such luck," said Jane. She watched the rearview mirror as she added speed. "It's the two men we saw outside the hospital." The other car was still going south, but then the taillights came on bright. They were stopping.

"How?"

"Maybe they were at the airport when I rented the car. Maybe anything. We're in trouble."

"What do we do?"

"Run."

She stared in the mirror just as she entered the first curve, and the mirror showed a flash of the white side of the other car turning around to come after them, and then she could see only the empty darkness of the trees beside the curve. She tried to remember in reverse order all of the sights that had floated past her window on the way south. Whatever she did, it had to be soon.

Her speedometer said fifty, sixty, seventy. At eighty-five, the big car was harder to keep on the right side of the white line, and each bump seemed to make it rise into the air and come down with a bone-jarring bounce. She knew she was putting some distance between them and the white car, but two men who had planned to walk into a hospital full of cops and shoot a patient who was already in custody probably had an optimistic view of the nature of risk. The fact that they were following her would add to their safety. All they had to do was get her taillights in view and keep them there. Any obstacle in the road might kill Jane and Dahlman, but the white car would have plenty of time to stop.

She said to Dahlman, "How are you feeling?"

"Rotten, but fortunately I was asleep when it happened, so I woke up on the floor and didn't see enough to give me a heart attack."

"I'm afraid we have to do something. If you're not up to this, tell me now and we won't try."

"I know what you're thinking, and the answer is no."

"What am I thinking?"

"You've disarmed them. You have their guns, and they have nothing. You want to arrange an ambush and shoot them. I won't permit that. I'll let you off somewhere with the guns, and drive on by myself."

Jane fought her way through competing thoughts, each in its own way important, but distracting. She had left the guns in Jake's car, because she had been trying to get on an airplane. Dahlman wasn't very observant, but he was unexpectedly brave. He wanted to take all of the risk on himself and let her escape—a completely impractical idea. He also had been lucky enough to live in the world all this time without learning anything about criminal behavior. The pistols those men had been carrying at the hospital were throwaways: ones they could use on him, then drop in a trash can before they walked out. If they had not left others in their car, they would never have come after him now.

Dahlman was naive and overconfident and insistent about matters he knew nothing about, but Jane supposed she should have felt glad. A man who would not use a gun to protect himself in a situation like this could be called many things, but he was certainly no murderer. Circumstances had presented her with the proof that she might have gotten around to wishing for later. Carey had been right about Dahlman, but it wouldn't matter unless she could keep him alive.

"You're wrong about nearly everything, but we have less than a minute for talk, so I'll do all of it. Those men aren't unarmed, so don't give them a target. Just do as I say."

"What's your plan?"

"To have you do as I say."

"I thought I had an option. What if I can't do this?"

"Then you'll die trying."

Jane turned the car quickly to the side and up a street in the little town. It ran along Conewango Creek a short distance, then reached a dead end. She parked the car between two others along the curb, got out, and hurried to the trunk. Dahlman stepped out stiffly and leaned on a taillight to watch her. She pushed the two small suitcases aside, then lifted the false floor of the trunk, pulled out the spare tire, tossed her purse into the trunk, and slammed it.

"Come on." She rolled the tire across the street and between two old brick buildings, then scrambled down a rocky bank onto a narrow muddy plateau. "Take my hand."

Dahlman let her help him down onto the mud and stared at her in confusion as she lifted the tire down beside them. She said, "I know you're not in any shape to swim, but that's what the tire is for. The rim is heavy, so it will float low, but it will hold you up. Cling to it. If you can't, I'll hold you."

Jane eased him into the cold, dark stream and placed his hands on the tire, then kept walking until the muddy bottom was no longer under her feet. She felt the current begin to pull them downstream. The momentum of the water tended to sweep them outward, away from the bank, but Jane resisted it, keeping her legs pumping steadily in a frog kick that didn't risk breaking the surface.

She saw the white car flash past over the bridge upstream, but she kept her eyes in that direction for several minutes because she knew it was too much to hope that the men would simply miss the turnoff and keep going. "How are you doing?" she whispered.

"Cold. I can take it for a while," said Dahlman.

"That's all you need to do." She changed her grip and began to push Dahlman downstream on the tire, using only her legs to propel them onward in hard surges.

It was probably a lie, she thought, but Dahlman seemed to find contradicting her either beneath his dignity or beyond his strength, because he said nothing.

The old, dim street lamps along the road above the stream and the faint glow of light behind the translucent curtains of the old two-story houses made the little town of Frewsburg look unreal, like a stop in an elaborate electric train set. It was after midnight now, and there were no cars moving along this road.

She kept looking back at the bridge, and she had almost begun to believe that the white car would not be back when it came into view again. She kept her eyes on it and felt a weight in her stomach. The car was slower now, prowling along the quiet street like a police cruiser. She could not see the men from this distance, so the car itself seemed to become the predator. It glided to the middle of the bridge and stopped.

Jane turned her face away and put her head under the surface, feeling the dark water pushing her along at its own slow pace. In the cold silence she thought and waited. She could not pull Dahlman under with her, but as long as his head was close to the tire, the shape would be hard to see and it wouldn't look like a man.

She held her breath for a long time, then surfaced on the downstream side of the tire and looked back. The car was moving again. It came off the bridge and turned up the street where she had parked. Jane rolled in the water and began to kick again, taking in deep breaths and blowing them out rhythmically, as she pulled the tire along with one arm.

She could tell that her memory had been right about the course of the little river. As it turned and meandered out of the hills toward Pennsylvania, there were lots of lazy curves. But these little old towns had all been built along rivers and streams that would run a mill, so there were probably narrows ahead where the water would get difficult. She needed just one big curve to do this right. The first one was too gradual, so she kept kicking. But as she did, the curve extended—not cutting back on itself but making a much bigger half circle to the east. She bent her arms to bring her close to Dahlman's ear.

"Are you okay?"

"Yes," said Dahlman.

"The worst part is over." Dahlman was lying, and so was she.

Jane raised her wrist close to her face and tried to read the dial of her watch, but the moon was hidden by clouds and she had not checked the time when she had entered the water, so the watch would tell her little anyway. She held the watch to her ear. It was still ticking. She was glad she had put the one Carey had bought for her in a drawer and strapped this cheap plastic one to her wrist. She had never worn anything that could be construed as jewelry while she was working unless it was part of a disguise meant to distract a viewer from her face, because jewelry was memorable. It was also precious, and that might make her hesitate to throw it away when she knew it was the sensible thing to do.

Jane floated in the stream as long as the curve lasted, then dragged the tire to the shore with Dahlman clinging to it. He stood up with difficulty, the water running out of his clothes, then sloshed along in the shallows, leaning on her, until she could bring him up onto dry, pebbly ground. She pushed the tire back out into the current until it caught and rotated downstream, the momentum slowly nudging it toward the middle.

Jane brought Dahlman up into a little park full of willow trees. She let him lean against the trunk of a short one with branches that drooped nearly to the ground while she wrung out his sport coat and emptied the water from his shoes. She twisted her long hair into a rope, then shook it out, and the shake turned into a shiver.

"I know you're cold," she said. "So am I, but I seem to remember it was a hot night a little while ago. Maybe we'll dry off a little on the walk."

"The walk?"

"I'm afraid so." She gripped his arm and began to ease him away from the tree to walk across a small open lawn.

He came with surprisingly little resistance, and it worried her a little, but he said, "Tell me what we're doing."

"I don't know if you were following the course of the steam," she said.

"I had my eyes closed most of the time."

"Well, it was a curve, like a horseshoe. We left the car at one end, and came out of the water at the other. The people who built this park probably picked the spot because of the curve. It's secluded, and there's water on three sides. We're going to walk straight north back to the other tip of the horseshoe, where we started—cut across the curve."

"But I saw them driving right along that street. By now they've found the car."

"I thought you had your eyes closed. But you're right. So what are they doing now?"

"I have no idea."

"First they looked inside it. They thought about breaking into it, but they saw that it has an alarm installed. I know they saw it, because otherwise we would have heard the alarm. They thought some more, and remembered that the car wasn't what they wanted anyway. They want us. The reason I rolled the tire along the street and onto the mud was so they would eventually figure out that we had gone into the water. First they'll look in all the alleys and Dumpsters and dark alcoves around the car, but at some point, they'll see the track, and ours beside it. Even they will know that a single fresh tire track leading into a creek wasn't made by a car. So they'll follow the creek looking for us."

"How can you be so sure?"

"I'm not. I told you what I think. And if they had done anything but park, we would have seen their headlights again." Jane was pleased. She had gotten him across the park, and now they were on a street leading away from the creek. They were heading straight for the car.

"What makes you think they're not searching the whole town on foot?"

"Just a guess." Her guess was that she had heard a story that they had not. When she had thought about the road crossing and recrossing the stream, she had remembered one of the stories about the Old People. Once, maybe two hundred years ago and maybe two thousand, there had been a small party of Senecas camped at a bend in a river. While they were sleeping, they had been stealthily surrounded by a much larger band of Cherokees. It must have happened on one of these winding waterways like the Conewango that ran south toward Pennsylvania and beyond, because that was the way the raiders had traveled in the endless wars. While his friends prepared for battle, a brave Cherokee had clung beneath a floating tree trunk and breathed through a hollow reed to reach the spot where the Senecas' canoes were tied, and cut them loose. When he had done it, there was no way left for the Senecas to escape.

But a few Senecas had caught the canoes beyond the river bend. Then they portaged across the narrow spit of land to come out upstream on the river again. They had kept paddling down and carrying the canoes across, until the Cherokees had concluded that a huge army of Senecas was gathering at the camp. The Cherokees had quietly retreated.

Jane did not walk quickly, just kept Dahlman moving at a constant pace. She could tell that the time and the sleep and the cold water and the fear had taken away the last traces of anesthetic that could have been in his bloodstream. Now his body was rigid with pain, but it made him seem stronger, faster. As though to warn her that his personality had not changed, he said, "You could easily be wrong."

"Yes," she admitted.

He persisted. "They could simply call the police anonymously and say they saw me getting out of that car and recognized me. We could arrive to find a hundred police officers waiting for us."

Jane said patiently, "I don't think that's what we need to worry about."

"Why not?"

"Because if having you in police custody was enough for them, they would have left you alone in Buffalo."

"What do you mean?"

"Those two men didn't show up because you had escaped from the hospital. We only saw them because they and I happened to know the last few minutes when the police would leave you alone, and which would be the safest hallway in the building. If you'll remember, we were on our way out, but they were on their way in." She added, "Carrying guns," to settle the matter.

"I sort of missed the implication," he admitted. "There's no way they could have known I wasn't still in the operating room, is there?"

"No."

"It's still not a very good plan."

"No, it's not," she agreed. "Let's hear yours."

Dahlman was silent. Jane looked behind her at the sidewalk. Their clothes were no longer leaving drips on the pavement. The moisture evaporating from her clothes into the night air seemed to be taking most of her body heat with it and leaving her shaking, but a casual observer would not glance at her or Dahlman in the light of a street lamp and know that they had been in the water. At this hour she had little to fear from casual observers anyway. They were getting close to the creek again, because she could detect the familiar scent of it.

She kept scanning the street ahead for the shapes of men on foot. At each intersection she lingered in the shadows of the big old trees and looked up and down to detect any movement, then hurried Dahlman across and into the darkness again.

When they reached the street where she had left the car, she ushered Dahlman into the shadow beside the corner of a house and whispered, "Wait here for me."

She slipped across the street and down the frontage road, staying close to the buildings. She came first upon the white car that had been following. It was parked three spaces back from hers. She saw no heads in the windows, but she approached it cautiously from behind the right side until her angle gave her a clear view of the interior. It was empty.

She hurried ahead to her rental car, clutching the keys. She went to her knees, examined the tires, then sighted along the top of the hood to be sure there were no spots where fingers had displaced the dust of the road. She lay on her back and stared up at the undercarriage. There seemed to be no booby traps.

Jane stood up, hurried back to the white car, took out her pocket knife, knelt in front of the hood, and reached under the grille. She felt around until she found the bottom radiator hose, then sliced it. She found the fan belt and cut that too. She stabbed the wall of the left front tire, then the right.

She ran to her rental car, started it, and swung it around to go back up the street. When she got there, Dahlman was already emerging from the shadows with a stiff, tottering gait. She got out and helped him into the back seat.

"Thank you," he said.

Far off, in approximately the direction they had come from, there came sounds: *Pop! Pop-pop-pop-pop! Pop!*

Dahlman was alarmed. "What was that?"

"Sounds like they've found the tire floating down the creek. They just killed it."

9

The sky was still dark when Jane crossed the line from Pennsylvania into Ohio, but by the time she was on the outskirts of Youngstown, whole blocks of street lamps were turning themselves off. Jane pulled into a gas station, filled the tank, and walked to the little building to pay for the gas. When she returned, Dahlman was still asleep.

She found a motel, checked in, then came back to the car and shook Dahlman. "Wake up, open your eyes, but don't sit up just yet."

Dahlman blinked up at the ceiling of the car. "Where are we?"

"Youngstown, Ohio. A motel. I'm going to take you inside in a second, when I'm sure there's nobody watching." She took a long look in each direction, then said, "Now."

She quickly walked him into the building and down the hall to their room. She hung the DO NOT DISTURB sign on the knob outside and closed the door. "Make yourself comfortable. Don't answer the door, don't answer the phone, don't open the curtains. I'll be back."

Jane drove out of the lot, along Bridge Street to Coitsville Center Road, north to King Graves Road, and west to the airport. She turned in the car she had rented in Buffalo and went to a second agency to get a new one under the name Kathy Sirini. On the way back to the motel she stopped at a big discount chain store and took a shopping cart.

She bought pairs of sunglasses for men and women, two kinds of hair dye, makeup, baseball caps, a big roll of gauze, a bag of sterile cotton balls, a roll of adhesive tape. She bought a bottle of peroxide, some Mercurochrome, Neosporin ointment, a bottle of alcohol. Before she returned to the motel she stopped on Route 224 at a take-out restaurant and bought four breakfast specials that came in foot-wide Styrofoam boxes.

She entered the room and looked around. Dahlman was invisible. "Anybody home?"

"I'm in here."

She walked into the bathroom to find Dahlman lying in the bathtub naked. "Oh. Sorry," she mumbled, and stepped out.

"Oh, for Christ's sake," said Dahlman. "Come in here."

Jane entered again. Dahlman glared at her. "You are a grown woman. You have definitely seen enough by now so that the sight of an aged person of the opposite sex can bring no surprises."

"I was being considerate," said Jane.

"Thank you," said Dahlman. "Now look at this wound, and you can be more considerate." He pointed to the hole in his left shoulder. "This is the entrance wound. Very neat and clean. A high-velocity bullet passed through intact. It was sutured expertly by a fine young surgeon. Come around to the back." He leaned forward. "What do you see?"

It was big and angry looking, and the white of his skin had a redness around the sutures. "Not so neat," she said. "The stitches haven't completely come apart, but they look . . . like they're unraveling. It doesn't seem to be bleeding."

"That's the lesion I'm most concerned about. When a bullet enters the body, it's still only nine millimeters wide with a rounded tip. After it's hit bone and burrowed through muscle tissue, it mushrooms and splays out, and the exit wound is worse. This one was closed as it should be. But last night's violent fall off the car seat undid that, and the swim in polluted water will have introduced contamination. What color is the tissue around it?"

"Red. I'm sorry."

He brushed her words away with his hand. "That was your job, and this is my job. If I get a raging infection, your job will have been a waste of time."

"What do we do?"

"Well, I think we should start by washing the wound with antiseptic. Any drugstore should have what we need."

"I bought peroxide, alcohol, Mercurochrome, and Neosporin."

He stared at her a moment, but she couldn't tell whether he was considering praise or a reprimand. "Yes. Well, help me dry off and we can get started."

Jane took his arm over her shoulder and let him lean his weight on her while he stepped out of the tub. Jane worked to dry his bony legs and feet while he dried the places he could reach. She finished with his back.

"Now let's lay out what you've got," he said. She brought in the shopping bag and he arranged the bottles and wound dressings. He looked at her again and conceded, "Very thoughtful of you."

"I had noticed that you had a hole in you," she said.

"Oh, yes. Well. You can wash up and we'll get started."

Jane scrubbed her hands until he said, "Let's start by washing the surface area around the wound with alcohol."

Jane took some cotton balls, soaked them with alcohol, and gently dabbed around the front of his shoulder. He watched her and frowned. "Here." He took a few cotton balls, soaked them, and roughly sloshed alcohol on the wound at the back of his shoulder.

Jane waited. It was only a couple of seconds before the pain clawed him. Every muscle in his body tensed, then quivered. His eyes squeezed tight, and beads of sweat appeared on his forehead. His breaths were shaky hisses moving in and out through clenched teeth.

He leaned forward, gripping the counter for a moment, as though he were about to faint. When the wave had passed, his voice was rough and croaky. "Now, let's use the peroxide the same way."

"I'd like it if we could do this someplace where if you faint you won't crack your skull."

"You're right," he said. "I was being foolish."

He walked into the bedroom and sat on the bed. "The alcohol is dry. Now the peroxide."

Jane slopped the peroxide on the entrance wound and watched him suffer. "That's better," he gasped. "It hurts like hell, but it ends. An infection would feel like that until I died. Just remember that. You're not causing someone pain. It's not you."

"What next?"

"Neosporin, then tape a sterile gauze pad over it."

Jane did as he directed. He looked down at her work, nodded, then lay on the bed on his stomach. "Now comes the hard part," he said. "This wound, the exit wound, is open. I can tell by the feel that infection has begun. It needs a bit more attention. Are you a good seamstress?"

"No," said Jane. She shook her head slowly as he looked up at her.

"Do you mean, 'No, I'm not a good seamstress,' or 'No, I won't do any sewing'?"

"A little bit of each," she said.

"Will you do it, or not?" He glared at her from the pillow.

"If you think it's necessary, I'll do it. But I don't have anything to sew with. I'll have to get something."

"There's a kit in the bathroom for sewing buttons on. Compliments of the inn. These are battlefield conditions, so you use what you've got."

Jane sighed. "All right. Tell me what to do."

Dahlman waited while Jane went into the bathroom and returned with the little paper packet. He didn't watch her, just began to talk. "We'll use white thread, because it's been bleached rather than dyed, and the dye is probably more poisonous. Soak the needle and thread in alcohol for a few minutes while we repeat the procedure we used on the entry wound to disinfect. When you're finished, take as many stitches as you can fit with the thread we have. Work outside the sutures that are there, by at least a quarter inch on each side, in a pattern that looks like shoelaces."

"How do I tie it off?"

"Take it in and out of the earlier laces a few times and then tie it in a square knot."

Jane went about preparing the needle and thread. When she poured the alcohol on his wound, he gripped the mattress so hard that she heard a sound like the sheet ripping, then went limp. But in a few seconds she heard him say, "Next the peroxide, please."

She used the peroxide, then waited until he said, "Now begin."

Jane forced her mind to stop thinking of his back as living flesh. She told herself it was the soft, buttery leather they used for couches and car seats. She sewed it as she would have repaired a piece of furniture, except that it bled. She had to catch the blood with cotton. When she had finished, she tied off the thread as he had told her to.

"Next, douse the whole area with peroxide again," said Dahlman. His voice was hoarse, all air and no vibration. "Then Neosporin and a full dressing of gauze and adhesive tape."

When Jane had finished she stepped back and waited. Dahlman lay still. Finally she detected from the sound of his breathing that he was asleep, so she covered him with the blanket and went to the table by the window. She opened a Styrofoam container, looked at the food she had bought, then closed it and sat down in the chair with her hands over her eyes.

Dahlman awoke an hour later, sat up, threw off the blanket, and walked to the bathroom, still as unaware of his nakedness as ever. He used the shaving mirror in front of him to look over his shoulder into the big mirror. He lifted the gauze and studied the wound. "I don't like the look of that. It's inflamed."

"What do we do?"

"An antibiotic. I'm afraid I can't just write a prescription, can I?"

Jane shook her head. "We'll have to do it another way."

"I've heard there's a black market for medicines," he said. "Is it true?"

"Of course it's true. There's a black market for everything. But they're not people we want to deal with right now. They're just like any other drug dealers. Antibiotics aren't their usual merchandise, so they'd have to make a special trip. That makes them curious. We'll just cut out the middle man and get it ourselves."

"How?"

"The way they do. What's the antibiotic?"

"I'd prefer Cipro. It's effective against the widest spectrum of bacteria, and I have no idea what was in that water."

"Spell it."

"C-I-P-R-O. But if that isn't available, any of the penicillins or cephalosporins would be worth having."

She picked up her purse and walked toward the door. "Get some rest, and try to eat something. I won't be back for a few hours."

Jane selected a gynecologist by talking to a woman at the hotel desk, who had a list of doctors for sick guests. She called and made an appointment for that afternoon. When she reached the office she told the nurse that she was on vacation and had forgotten her birth-control pills. The doctor took her right away, checked her blood pressure and heart rate, and wrote her a prescription for Orthocept pills. As she left the office, she slipped his pen into her purse.

Jane drove up the street until she saw a mailbox-rental store that advertised "Self-Serve Copies, 10¢," went inside, made a copy of nothing, then used the blank sheet to cover the doctor's handwriting and make a blank prescription form. Next she used the doctor's pen to trace his signature and the genuine prescription, substituting the word "Cipro" for "Orthocept."

It took Jane a little longer to find the right pharmacy. She looked for one on the other side of the city so the druggist would not be too familiar with her doctor's handwriting. She wanted one that was not part of a larger building, so all sides would be visible, and one that wasn't part of a chain, because there was no way to know what might come up on the computer of a chain store. After she handed in her prescription, she sat in a coffee shop in the strip mall across the street and waited. No police cars arrived, no stranger showed up to hang around the building. After an hour she went in, picked up her prescription, and paid for it in cash.

When Jane handed Dahlman the bottle of pills he looked at her with his eyebrows raised.

"Something wrong with it?"

"It's exactly what I asked for."

"That's why I asked you to spell it."

He took a dose immediately, then went back to the bed. "I've been thinking about you," he said.

Jane said nothing. She opened her suitcase and brushed her hair.

"Don't you want to hear what I was thinking?"

Jane stared at him over the lid of the suitcase. "Not if it's about me."

"Interesting," said Dahlman. "What I was thinking about was why a man like Dr. McKinnon would know the telephone number of a woman like you."

"A woman like me?"

Dahlman went on. "He had it in his head, you know—didn't have to look it up. I was thinking it was something like this. He did you a favor— maybe operated on you or a friend of yours. You told him that if he ever needed anything in return, he should call. The number just stuck in his mind. He's a brilliant man, with the sort of mind that things just stick to. And last night I came looking for you. The police shot me before I could make it to your house. I told Carey your name, and out came your number."

"You think he once took a thorn out of my paw?" Her face wore a mirthless little smile.

"Well?" He looked at her triumphantly. "Am I right?"

Jane picked up a new set of clothes and walked toward the bathroom. "I'm going to shower and change. Then I'm going to sleep for a few hours. You can watch TV quietly, or read if the light's not in my eyes.

When I wake up it will be dark. And then we're going to check out and drive on."

"You won't tell me how he knows you?"

"He knew my number because I'm his wife." She closed the door, and in a moment Dahlman heard the shower running.

Dahlman eased himself onto the bed. He had done it again. He had met a person he liked, and had studied her for a time, and found her so intriguing that he had allowed his curiosity to explode into life and hungrily turn her into a specimen for study. His life seemed to him a long and distressing series of incidents like this—a sequence of offenses that made him want to hide his face. He found himself wishing he could be back in the clinic in Chicago with the door closed and human beings kept far away, where he wouldn't be tempted to do something that would make him ashamed. He felt a sudden twinge in his shoulder and shifted his weight to his right side. "That's another reason," he thought. "If I were back there, I could make this thing go away."

10

It was time for the morning flurry of activity around the airport, and Marshall waited for the deep roar of the latest airplane to fade before he spoke into the telephone again. Now and then he looked down at what he had written in the little leather notebook that he carried. "Here's what I would like. The Buffalo police will be sending prints from the hospital, along with prints on file of the members of the staff who were supposed to be in the area. Anything out of the ordinary goes to me, and to them. Okay?"

On the other end of the line, Albert Grapelli spoke in a preoccupied way, as though he were writing. "Okay."

Marshall looked down at his list again. "When Dahlman walked out of there, he didn't take his medicine with him. He's supposed to have painkillers and an antibiotic. The painkillers we can't do much about because there are so many kinds on the market, and we can't even be sure he'll take one. But the antibiotic seems promising. The guy who operated on him was one of his old students, so let's assume they both believe in the same antibiotic. Now that he's on his own, he'll prescribe the same stuff for himself. It's called Cipro. If any pharmacist fills a prescription for it anywhere in the next few days, I'd like to have him interviewed."

Grapelli was silent for a moment. Marshall waited, then heard Grapelli take in a breath, so he knew what was coming. "John," said Grapelli. "Isn't that a little . . ." He corrected himself. "No, scratch that. Let's hear what else you want before I tell you what you can't have."

Marshall said, "Problem?"

"You know what I'd like? I'd like to know what you think is going on."

Marshall glanced around the little office that the airport people had lent him. The door was still closed, and under it he could see no shadow that would indicate someone was politely waiting for him to finish his call before they knocked. He said, "I think there's serious strangeness here."

"What kind of strangeness?"

"A sedated sixty-seven-year-old man doesn't hop out of bed with a gunshot wound and stroll past cops and newspeople wearing nothing but a hospital gown and a smile. I think even if all of the laws of the universe were temporarily suspended and he did, then you'd still have a wounded senior citizen walking barefoot and bare-assed down a well-lighted and well-traveled public street."

"I thought he stole a police car and drove it someplace?"

"I don't," said Marshall. "It's possible that it's just one of those jokers who see a unit sitting there during an emergency, take it for a joyride, and dump it. Unfortunately, the search for it took up maybe half the men and equipment the local police had for a couple of hours. They found it in the garage of an unoccupied house. That meant they had to surround the house and assault it as though he were barricaded in there."

"Should I send a team to tactfully explain that a man is short and round, and a house is big and pointy?"

"Not necessary," said Marshall. "They'll look stupid in the morning papers, but they're not. They had a wounded murder suspect and a patrol unit disappear at the same time. When they last saw the car it had a shotgun in the rack. When it turned up a mile away in a dark garage attached to an empty house, what were they going to do? No, they're good. Whoever took Dahlman out is better."

"What?" Grapelli elongated it into a drawl.

"Just a theory, of course," said Marshall.

"Who is it?"

"I don't know. Dahlman's surgeon knew him, so there's a connection that might make him want to help Dahlman. But the surgeon was accounted for during some of the time when the hard part had to happen—wheeling Dahlman out, bringing a getaway car, maybe stealing the police cruiser to create a diversion. The whole thing had to be cooked up in less than an hour, and executed in fifteen minutes. You can see the problem."

"Yeah, I can see it, all right. Multiple perpetrators of unknown number."

"If I say it out loud, then it's crazy time: maybe a conspiracy involving half a dozen people who work in the hospital."

"You mean doctors?"

Marshall said, "Whoever did it was smart. Doctors are smart. They also get to order everybody around in a hospital, have them wheel patients here and there with no questions asked. And maybe there was a cop who got talked into helping a prisoner escape, or maybe even one who got worried about the fact that he was unarmed when they shot him and took him out to finish him off. I'd say that for the moment, at least, we've got to let the Buffalo police take all the embarrassment while we quietly do everything we can to straighten this out."

Grapelli was silent.

Marshall waited, then asked, "New problem?"

Grapelli sighed. "I was just wondering what you would consider 'straightening this out.' "

Marshall said, "Getting Dahlman would be a start. I'd like to throw everything we can into his path and snap him up so he doesn't hurt anybody else. Then there's the surgeon. The Buffalo police are keeping an eye on him, but I'd like a wiretap on his phone."

"All right," said Grapelli. "We might as well solve the problem we know how to solve. Let's get Dahlman, and hope the conspiracy turns out to be a product of your imagination. What else do you need?"

"Printed circulars, news coverage, publicity. There should be lots of photographs of Dahlman in print. It's hard to be invisible with a hole in you."

"Done. What else?"

"I'd like to have a special agent assigned to take a close look at what happened in Illinois before he left: the evidence, the timetable, whatever else they have."

"Sure. I'll have somebody there tonight—" He corrected himself. "Today."

"I guess that's it. I'll let you know if anything else occurs to me."

"I'm sure you will," Grapelli said. "Where are you—at the Buffalo field office?"

"At the airport. I asked them to give me a little office near the security checkpoint for a few hours to watch for Dahlman."

"What do they need you there for?"

"I said that was what I told them. If he was going to fly out he would already have done it, but it puts me about fifty steps from the ticket counter if he turns up somewhere."

"You're going to do this yourself?"

"If I'm lucky," said Marshall. "Take care."

Grapelli stared at the dead telephone for a moment, put it back in the cradle, and then dialed Amery's number. He knew he was dragging Amery out of bed, but after he told Amery that he was the best one to go to Illinois, Amery's voice acquired that serious, professional manner that he cultivated, and Grapelli could hear the rustling of cloth while he got out of his pajamas or made his bed or something.

Grapelli was not exactly lying; if Marshall was doing something else, then Amery was the best special agent to go and make sense of a lot of evidence and interview the cops to find out where it came from. He hung up and sat at his desk for a moment, thinking about Marshall. On the day when the memo had been posted announcing that Grapelli had been selected to take over this job, Dan Phipps, who was retiring from it, had taken him out for a drink. Phipps had given him a brief summary of the hidden parts of this job—the problems his subordinates didn't know about because he had seen no reason for them to be distracted by problems they weren't paid to solve. He had said, "Listen to Marshall. He'll keep you honest."

"I like to think I can keep myself honest." Grapelli often remembered those words with regret. He had not given himself time to consider them, just said them automatically without first asking himself whether they were the best words to induce Phipps to tell him things he didn't know.

For a second, Phipps had let his face go blank and had stared at Grapelli. "We'll see," he'd said, and had returned to his drink.

Grapelli was sure it had taken him years to learn on his own what Phipps might have told him in the next thirty seconds. That was probably what Phipps had been leading up to when he had mentioned Marshall. It wasn't about Marshall; he was simply the most obvious example. Another supervisor had once said that if he had five like Marshall he could rule the world. The truth was the opposite. Marshall didn't think it was part of his job to help anybody rule anything. The complicated, intoxicating competition for budgets and the rising or falling in the chain of command that were played for keeps inside all government bureaucracies were not of any interest to him. Salvation was not in power, but in competence.

That was what Grapelli now believed Phipps meant that night when he said Marshall would keep him honest—not scheming and plotting, but spending the day ensuring public safety and then going home. As it was, Grapelli had been left to sort out for himself what was printed in the job description: "acting as liaison" to the following groups, "reporting to" this set of remote superiors, "in consultation with" these competing supervisors meant more than it seemed. And even the part that seemed clear—being a supervisor—was not what it seemed. How in hell anybody could consider himself to be "supervising" a disparate set of men and women who were usually hundreds of miles apart in situations where they had to make decisions instantly was not something that he had yet deciphered.

Grapelli felt an acidic burning in the pit of his stomach, because his train of thought had led him to his second lesson. The next morning, on his first official day as section chief, he had found an unlabeled audiocassette on his desk. Nobody seemed to know where it had come from. He played it, and heard his entire conversation with Phipps.

The microphone might have been planted under the table in the bar, but that would have required them to know what table Phipps would choose, and Phipps didn't usually go to bars. It could also have been a remote directional microphone, but there had been brick walls on two sides and a crowd of talking people between their table and the windows. When Grapelli listened more carefully to the tape, he was sure it wasn't made in either way. There was no sound of idle talk over it. His own voice was much louder, closer than Phipps's. The bug had been hidden on Grapelli's own body.

It had taken Grapelli an hour to go through all of the suspects and find that he could not eliminate a single one. They all had the technical expertise, the experience, and the nerve to plant a bug to eavesdrop on their boss and then shove the recording in his face. At this hour of the morning he wasn't in the mood to piece together the train of thought he had used, but he had reached a conclusion.

The one who had planted the bug was somebody who wanted to remind him that the ones who would judge him weren't the directors and assistant directors up the line, or the endless parade of ignorant and venal politicians who passed by somewhere above the directors. The people he had to satisfy were much closer to him, the ones whose lives would depend on decisions Grapelli made. The one who had planted it was the one who knew what thought processes the tape would set off—that he would spend some hard hours thinking about each of the agents in his section and not be able to find one who couldn't have done it, then appreciate the effectiveness of the tool that had been placed in his hands. It had to be Phipps.

It had taken him almost two years longer before he had learned enough to understand the rest of it. The suspect who was probably the most formidable, and the most capable of pulling a trick like that, was the one who would never have done it. That was what Phipps had been trying to tell him: that Marshall would keep him honest.

11

Jane drove west on Route 224 into the dark, flat Ohio countryside. For ten minutes she watched the pattern of glowing headlights behind her. Then, at the beginning of a long, straight stretch where she was sure she could see a mile or two ahead, she turned off the road and stopped until the line of cars had passed. She waited to be sure that none of the cars stopped farther down the road, watched her rearview mirror until there were no headlights, then accelerated onto the highway again. She was satisfied that she had not been followed.

"Are you up to talking?" she asked.

"I should be," said Dahlman. "I don't think I've slept this much since I was a child."

"I need to know exactly how you got into this mess."

"Why?"

Jane raised an eyebrow. This man had apparently spent a lifetime collecting and refining ways of being irritating. But she said patiently, "I think it will help. It might tell me all of the people who are searching for you, and that's useful, because they all search in different ways, look in different places, ask different people. If I don't know these things, I could take you right into someone's path."

"I didn't kill anyone," he said. "That isn't how this happened."

"I know."

He didn't seem to be willing to accept even that. "How do you know? Presumably most people who kill someone say they didn't either."

"They would also be willing to use a gun to defend themselves from someone who is chasing them. In fact, most people would. But not you."

"Oh. I suppose so." He seemed to respond to logic, and that made Jane feel more hopeful. "It's a very long story."

"I expect it will be a very long night."

Jane turned to look at him, and saw that his eyes were focused on a point in the distance. He seemed to be collecting his thoughts, and that was something Jane did not want him to do. She didn't want an account full of neat, clean summaries and judicious, erroneous conclusions. "Who do the police think you killed?"

"Her name was Sarah Hoffman. She was a friend and partner of mine for about ten years. She assisted me in surgery frequently. She was a fine plastic surgeon with her own practice, but at the time we started working together I was better known, and was being brought some cases that other people weren't."

"What sorts of cases?"

"Reconstructive surgery, mostly—usually people who had been terribly burned or injured. I was developing experimental methods for transplantation of tissue, and some post-op procedures that had brought promising results. It had struck me some time ago that these were the areas where the new developments could be made. We have thousands of surgeons who are now probably about as good at cutting as a human being will ever be. We have methods of magnification and nonintrusive monitoring and micro-instruments and lasers that make use of that dexterity in very sophisticated ways. But maybe seventy percent of the battle with restorative and plastic surgery involves allowing the body's tissue to grow and letting it make up for what we can't do with a blade— as well as repairing what the blade has done. Surgeons are the star quarterbacks of medicine: everything has been done to protect our part of the process and maximize its effectiveness. But at a certain level you do one after another. It feels like being a quarterback who throws a pass and is taken out of the game and put into another one before he even sees whether it's been caught."

"This isn't what you taught at the university, is it?" she asked.

"I was a general surgeon," said Dahlman. "For most of my working life, I probably performed more thoracic operations than anything else. The instruction I gave was almost entirely practical—in an operating room, teaching people who already were surgeons. I spent less time on post-operative work than most surgeons in private practice."

"What happened?"

Dahlman seemed mystified by his memories, like a man leafing through photographs who kept finding ones he had forgotten and lingering over them. As his eyes stared ahead of the two funnel-shaped beams of the headlights, his face moved, taking on a look of happiness, then sadness, then puzzlement. "I had good hands. By the age of forty I was one of the eight or ten most accomplished traditional surgeons in the country. I had been practicing at the University Medical Center since residency, and was already the Goldsden-Meara Distinguished Professor of Medicine. I was so busy performing surgeries and teaching young doctors like Carey McKinnon that I paid little attention to anything else. At sixty I was forced to do some thinking."

"Forced by what?"

"My wife died suddenly. An embolism. She was fine in the morning, and when I came home in the evening she was dead."

"Did you have children?"

"Two," he said. "My boy, David, was born the year we graduated from college. He was thirty-eight when his mother died, and living in California. My daughter, Terry, was thirty-six, married, and living in Paris. They both came home for the funeral, said the correct things to each other and to me, and went back to what they had been doing. When they were gone, I sat and thought, and looked around me. The kids were grown up and self-supporting in every sense of the word. They seemed to like me, but whatever emotional needs they ever had must have occurred during an earlier period, and my wife handled them while I was too busy to notice. So I was left with a lifetime appointment to an endowed chair, a series of vested pensions, paid-up life-insurance policies, and various savings accounts and investments that my prudent wife had accumulated for a rainy day she never lived to see. I found myself absolutely alone, with no real responsibilities, but no real connections either, and certainly no needs. That was a surprise. There were others."

"What others?"

"I suddenly realized, as though I were waking up, that I was sixty. What it meant was that the best work I would do with my hands either had been done, or shortly would be. I had to decide what to do next—how to use the next ten or fifteen years. I could spend the time training young surgeons, or use my name and reputation for medical causes—gradually do less medicine and more lobbying and fund-raising—or I could try to do some clinical research to solve the problems I'd noticed during the years of nonstop surgery."

"I take it you chose research."

"I found I didn't need to choose. As it turned out, my name and a letter from me did more for medical causes than my presence. My personality seems to irritate people. So I let the institutions write the letters and signed them for a couple of hours each week. My best teaching was done in the operating room, so it took no exclusive time at all. I spent my afternoons taking on the work I was telling you about."

"Where did Sarah Hoffman fit into it?"

"I selected her as my teacher. She taught me to perform plastic and reconstructive surgery, like an apprentice. When I was ready, I began to move ahead, and she followed. I learned from her that the surgery itself is more art than science—like being a sculptor. I became good at it, and my broader background in surgery gave me a wider range of techniques, familiarity with more of the situations that can come up, and so on. My credentials gave the universities and big drug companies an interest in keeping me abreast of the enormous amount of research they had been doing on various kinds of induced healing, artificial tissue, and so on. We both made great progress, became extremely productive. We published a number of articles, helped lots of patients."

"Carey seems to think there's more to the research than you're saying."

Dahlman smiled. "Carey. . . . He would see what it was instantly, and want it to happen right then, even if the others couldn't imagine it. He was that kind of medical student—always asking why we can't do better, asking for a finer instrument. He was right, of course. We were trying to reach the point where we could reliably induce rapid cell replication—persuade the body to do what it does anyway, but much, much faster and more completely."

"Did you succeed?"

"We had some success, but nothing as dramatic yet as what we're hoping—what I'm hoping for, and what Carey envisions. We understand a bit about the hormone that makes a human baby grow quickly during its first year of life. We know a bit about rapid cell replication in malignancies. There's already work being done on giving the body more of what it needs—exposing it to hyperbaric oxygen to stimulate healing, and so on. But ultimately, what we're talking about is speeding up time within the human body: an increased flow of blood to the wound, increased supply of oxygen and nutrients in the blood, a tremendously increased metabolic rate."

"How close were you to doing it?"

"We were just beginning. We weren't simply doing theoretical research. We were physicians trying to help the human beings who came to us, and that meant that most of our time with each patient went to applying the proven methods we had. When something was both promising and safe, we would get a patient's permission to try it."

"So what went wrong?"

"We took on a case of a sort that we seldom did—purely cosmetic. It was a man who simply wanted to improve his appearance. He came through Sarah's office, and she did all of the interviewing and so on at the beginning. The paperwork was handled by her nurse, Carol. Sarah used to take her own photographs, so that was done there too. Normally, whatever we had done together was paid for by the patient's insurance. Since this was purely elective surgery, it would be paid for by the patient. Normal procedure is to alert the insurance company anyway, in case there are complications. Records were created. That's an important fact. Then Sarah brought him to me."

"Why?"

"Why what?"

"Why did she bring him to you instead of doing it herself?"

"We usually worked together on particularly difficult cases. This one wasn't difficult, medically. But it was a patient who had certain requests, and one of them was my involvement."

"You just said you were concentrating on using your last years as a working surgeon efficiently. Surely there must have been somebody—some kid with a birth defect or something—that fit better. Or was using a healthy patient better for the research?"

Dahlman waved the question away. "I don't know that it makes any difference. Our motives aren't really the issue."

He was hiding something. "So tell me anyway."

"It was a combination of things. One was that Sarah had already made up her mind when she brought him to me. She was my partner. I owed her a lot. What was called for was a safe, familiar sequence of procedures. The difference between performing them on a patient who had no physical limitations and a patient who had suffered disfigurement was really only a question of the quality of results. And it would demonstrate the applicability of the methods we had learned in our reconstructive work to another whole category of—"

"He offered you a lot of money."

Dahlman slumped in his seat. "Yes."

"How much?"

"Two hundred thousand dollars."

"I thought you were set for life, and didn't need money."

Dahlman squinted, as though he were still trying to fathom what had been in his own mind, and having little success. Jane could tell that this part of the story was an irritant. "I didn't need money. Sarah was younger—I believe thirty-eight or thirty-nine. I could work for free; she couldn't. We had always assumed that she would naturally, gradually take over more of our joint work until I retired. The clinic and our research would revert to her. But at this stage the research was enormously expensive, and even the surgeries we did increased the deficit—sometimes because we took on the very sort of patient you mentioned. We had to give some thought to how Sarah would manage to continue the work without me. Two hundred thousand wasn't much, but it would help."

"You didn't like the decision, did you?"

"No. I didn't. But I couldn't deny the problem. We discussed it in very specific, practical terms that day. The question was, would we interrupt our real work to do forty tummy tucks and nose bobs, or do one complete, ambitious makeover for a rich patient who would serve as a demonstration for others?"

Jane said, "Tell me about the patient."

Dahlman said, "I never knew much about him. Sarah told me he wanted not only to have the best medical services available but to be of help. The fee was his idea, and we were to consider the excess a contribution. He had signed a standard agreement to let us publish whatever we learned in the course of his treatment."

Jane tested a suspicion. "Including pictures?"

"Including pictures. Of course."

Jane had guessed wrong, but she sensed that she shouldn't let Dahlman gloss over the patient. "Where did the money come from? What made him rich?"

"Sarah mentioned that he was the heir to the Hardiston fortune."

"Was his name Hardiston?"

"Yes. James Hardiston."

Jane still couldn't be positive: there probably were some living Hardistons. There was no way for her to verify her suspicion while she was driving along a deserted road in the middle of the night, but this was the first part of the story that seemed to sink when she put weight on it. Hardiston was a word that everybody knew: Bulova, Piaget, Timex, Cartier, Rolex, Omega, Hardiston. One of them was printed on your watch, and ten times a day, when you looked to see what time it was, you couldn't help reading it. Hardiston was undoubtedly the best of the bunch, because nobody could be named Timex, and half the school classrooms in the country had those big Hardiston clocks over the blackboard. Kids sat at their desks watching it out of the corners of their eyes. At three o'clock the red second hand reached the twelve, the minute hand clicked backward a half-step, then forward to the next minute, and the dismissal bell went off.

It was a con game as old as the Industrial Revolution. You just took some brand name that had started out as a surname and told the mark you were the great-grandson. If you could convince somebody your name was Pillsbury or Hilton or Doubleday or Kellogg or Hardiston, they thought they'd already done all the checking they needed to, and they started to get light-headed from the smell of money. "And you—or Sarah—thought the two hundred thousand might be only the beginning."

"Well, it had occurred to us."

"How did he know about you?"

"That was one of the things that impressed me. His forms said he had been referred to us by a doctor in Maryland. The doctor was real, and highly respected."

"Did you call him?"

"There was no reason to. He had simply told Mr. Hardiston that we would be the best specialists in the country for his needs. What was there to ask him—whether he meant it? Afterward I learned that he had given Hardiston copies of some of our articles from medical journals."

Jane's jaw muscles worked, keeping her mouth closed so she wouldn't succumb to the temptation to point out that this, too, was a confidence maneuver: the con man arrives with a fistful of recommendations and credentials, but they're all about the mark, not about him. "So you took him on."

"Yes. We performed five procedures over a period of about eight months."

"What exactly was wrong with him?"

"Nothing, really. He was healthy and had regular features. But the net effect of his face was not what he wanted, and I couldn't blame him: he had clearly never been considered attractive when he was young, and now his expression seemed forbidding, unlikable. And he was about fifty and looked older: lots of damage."

"What kind of damage—scars?"

"Nothing like that. His nose had been broken at some point—a souvenir of some adolescent football game—but the damage I meant was wear and tear. Some I would attribute to the sun, some to tobacco and alcohol and possibly other drugs, and the rest to age. He had some unflattering wrinkles that went with the sun damage—scowling and squinting."

"None of that sounds like anything he couldn't have had fixed on a slow afternoon the next time he was in Beverly Hills. What did you do?"

"We decreased the prominence of the brow and cheekbones and smoothed the skin with endoscopic surgery, performed rhinoplasty to make the nose thinner and slightly shorter, made the chin thinner and tapered it. In the process we did some traditional cut-and-tuck work here and there to remove wrinkles and sags, made the lips slightly fuller, and performed blepharoplasty on the eyes. We used a carbon dioxide laser to remove small wrinkles and uneven pigmentation. It wasn't the surgical procedures that interested him, it was the work we had done on induced healing and tissue regeneration. And it worked. When he left he looked like a different person—but that different person is a man about thirty years old."

"Did you do anything to his body?"

"Liposuction to relieve him of a middle-aged slackening around the middle."

"It sounds pretty good. I hope you're still around when I need a little help."

Dahlman's head turned toward her abruptly, and the stare was almost hatred. "He destroyed us."

"Did he?" Jane said evenly. "Tell me how." His pause gave her time to amend it. "Tell me how you found out, step by step."

Dahlman's anger seemed to slowly change to something like amazement. "It was strange, like being eaten alive, bit by bit. There were five of us involved in his treatment: Sarah Hoffman; her nurse, Carol Flanders;

me, of course; the anesthesiologist, Dr. Koh Wung; and his assistant, Celia Rodriguez. The first thing that happened was that Carol Flanders quit."

"Why?"

"She got an offer from a hospital in her hometown in Colorado. She had elderly parents there, and the job was, by any objective assessment, better than the one she had. We all advised her to take it. Working in a small clinical research facility like ours was rewarding, but it was also exhausting. We couldn't pay her the way a major hospital could, and there was no better job we could promote her to. So we wished her well, and had a little party for her on her last day."

"What then?"

"Nothing, for about a month. Then Dr. Wung left for a university hospital post in Boston and took his assistant with him. The final thing was that Sarah Hoffman was murdered."

He was skipping over parts of the story that Jane suspected must be huge. She would have to bring him back to them, but for now she needed to keep him talking. "How was she murdered?"

"At first it looked like a burglary. She was in her office, apparently late at night. Nobody knows why. She seldom did that. It's possible that she was trying to catch up on some paperwork because she hadn't yet replaced Carol Flanders. Or maybe someone called her and asked to meet her there. She was shot several times, but nobody heard it. The office was torn up terribly—not as though someone was looking for something valuable to steal, but as though they wanted to destroy all of it—file drawers dumped in the middle of the floor and set on fire."

"Did the police call you in to look at it?"

"No. The police came to me about a day later, because they wanted some idea of who might have done it, and why. By then they had decided it wasn't a burglary. That night I called Carol Flanders in Colorado to break the news to her gently. I got no answer at the number she had given us. I tried to reach her through her parents. They told me she had been killed in a car accident a couple of weeks before. She had been driving to Colorado to start her new job, and had never made it."

"Did it occur to you to call Wung?"

"Of course. His new university gave me a runaround. He didn't have an office listing, because he was to start in the fall, and the fall directory hadn't been printed yet. The personnel office in Boston at least knew who he was, but not where. I finally went to our university and talked to four people before I could get them to see that this was an emergency and to give me the emergency numbers he had put on his old personnel forms. The numbers were for relatives in Korea. I called his brother, and got another terrible shock. Koh was dead. I asked how, and all he would tell me was that he had gone on a vacation and died. His English was only slightly better than my Korean, and I don't speak Korean. He did understand when I gave him my name and phone number, because an hour later his sister called. She was screaming at me. All I could sort out at first was that Koh had committed suicide. Somehow they got the impression that he had been fired from the University of Chicago, and the job in Boston was a step down. Since he had been working with me, I must have gotten him fired, and the shame made him kill himself. I couldn't get the details—how they knew it was suicide, how it had happened—and asking again just infuriated her. I gave up."

"What did you do then?"

"I realized that the most urgent thing was trying to warn Celia Rodriguez. I called the university in Boston again. It was the same story as Koh—she wasn't supposed to start work until the fall, so they had no idea where she was, or even if she had arrived in Boston yet. I called Boston information, I even called Koh's sister again to see if they had found her number in Koh's effects. Nobody there had ever heard of Celia Rodriguez."

Jane saw it immediately. If Carol's accident and Koh's suicide and Sarah's murder had taken place in Chicago, the police would have jumped on them and initiated a search for Celia Rodriguez. But in Boston, nobody knew the connection, or that anything else had happened. She knew nobody there, so there was nobody to report her missing. Some murders got reported nationally, but not the suicides or car accidents of people who weren't famous. "Were you afraid?"

"I was angry. I went to the police and told them what I knew—that within a period of about forty days, all four of my colleagues had met deaths that were, at the very least, suspicious. At first I thought they weren't taking me seriously. Then, a couple of days later, two policemen came to my house."

"To arrest you?" There was no question that he had been arrested at some point, but she knew she should verify each bit of the story that she could hold on to as a fact, and the order of events made a difference.

"No. They were from a special squad that protects people. They told me they believed I was in danger. We talked for some time."

"Did you talk about who the criminal might be?"

"Yes. After some discussion, they agreed with me that Mr. Hardiston probably wasn't Mr. Hardiston. He was someone who wanted to change his looks to escape prosecution for some crime. They were desperate for the photographs—any copies I had of the ones Sarah took. But I never had any, and now I'm sure they were all destroyed, along with the medical records, in the fire in Sarah's office. The policemen tried to get me to describe the man. I've described him for you, as he looked before the surgeries and after. Could you find him?"

"I could find about a hundred of each in the next town."

"Exactly. They called the station and explained the situation to some superior, then came back to say that they had a plan."

"I'll bet."

"What?"

"What was their plan?"

"Since there was no way to identify the man, the safest way was to take me to a quiet place and hide me. I was to tell no one where I was going. I would have to live incognito for a time, and when the man surfaced I would have to reappear to identify him and testify in court. It would take lots of arranging, but if they didn't do it this way, they would risk losing me too. I was the only living person who could point out the man."

"You agreed to this?"

"I felt it made no sense not to cooperate. They took me to a farmhouse that night, over three hundred miles from Chicago. I was allowed to pack only those items that nobody would know were missing—some clothes, a few items of little value. Then we left."

"Where was it—the farm?"

"About ten miles outside a little town near Carbondale, called Hurst. I was there for three days."

"Then what?"

"It was strange—like a dream. They were very considerate. They even had a newspaper delivered each morning. One morning I got up and walked down the long dirt road from the house to the mailbox on the highway to pick up my paper. On the bottom corner of the front page was a story that said the police wanted me for questioning."

"How did you feel?"

"A bit disappointed, for one thing. The police had given me to understand that they were going to make my house look lived in, and if the killer made an attempt to break in, they would scoop him up. For some reason the deception hadn't worked, and they had given up hope of that. Otherwise, the police would never have revealed to reporters that I was gone. I also had some trivial concern about how the story in the paper would look to other people. It sounded almost as though I were a suspect."

"I take it the policemen had a key to your house?"

"Well, yes. As I said, they wanted to make it look as though I were still living there."

"When did your small worry turn into a big worry?"

"Three more days passed. The policemen were to deliver more groceries once a week. I wondered when they would come. The next day I stayed indoors all day waiting. Finally, I left a note on the table and went for a walk. When I returned, there were police cars parked in front of the farmhouse—not plain ones like the ones they had used before, but real ones, black and white, with lights on the roofs. I was excited. I knew that they would never show themselves like that unless the waiting was over, and they had found the killer. They had: it was me."

"Tell me about the arrest."

"I ran up, they threw me on the ground on my face, handcuffed my hands behind my back, pushed me into the back seat of one of the cars, and set off for Chicago. I told the policemen everything. I asked them to call the Special Protection Squad and verify my story. They just listened, but they called nobody."

Jane frowned. "What made them come after you?"

Dahlman threw up his hands. "I just told you that—"

"No," she said. "Forget the hiding part. I haven't heard anything yet that sounds like grounds for charging you with murder."

"They said they had wanted to ask more questions, couldn't find me at work, couldn't reach me by phone, and became concerned. They got a warrant and broke into my house. They showed me pictures they took. I recognized the place, but it had been altered. My wife's walk-in closet had been transformed into a kind of madman's shrine. There were pictures of Sarah pasted to the walls—dozens of them, with steak knives stuck in some, and holes or burn marks in others. And strange scrawls about killing her. One said her time was coming, and others had captions like 'Thief' or 'Betrayer' on them."

"When they showed you this stuff, did you have a lawyer present?"

"I had a lawyer. He had settled my wife's estate, and made out our wills before that. He called a criminal lawyer for me who was supposed to be terrific. I'm sure the man was competent, but . . ." Dahlman's voice trailed off.

"But he didn't believe you."

"He asked me questions like 'Do you know what day it is?' 'What year?' and then he said, 'I'm here to help you, but the best help I can give you is to advise you not to hide anything.' "

"Did he listen to your whole story?"

"He'd already heard it when I met him. The police had apparently been recording it when I told them the first time."

"No wonder he didn't believe you."

"I know. The idea that the police department had conspired to frame me for a murder seemed to be too much of a leap for his plodding intellect."

Jane sighed wearily. She had been dreading this moment. "There's a lot to be said for a plodding intellect."

Dahlman was offended. "What, exactly, do you mean?"

"Well," said Jane. "For starters, those two men who came to talk to you and then hid you weren't policemen."

"How could you possibly know?" He was furious.

Jane ignored his anger. "There are a lot of little things. One is that no city police department has anything called a 'Special Protection Squad.' Los Angeles and Chicago have both asked for money to begin protecting witnesses in gang-related trials, but so far, neither has gotten it. If the police want a witness protected, they don't hide him on some farm alone. They protect him—put a cop with him, or keep him in custody. A criminal lawyer knows these things. And if policemen think you're being watched and stalked by experts, they don't use your phone to call their office and discuss their whole plan. These weren't policemen."

"Oh," said Dahlman. Then he added, unnecessarily, "They were very convincing."

"The real ones were the ones you saw when you went to the police station. How did you get away from them?"

Dahlman shook his head. "That was the one service my attorney provided for me."

Jane frowned. "After all that creepy stuff in the house and the sudden disappearance to the farm, he got you out on bail?"

"No. The lawyer had them put me in a psychiatric lockup ward in the hospital for observation. I had worked in that hospital, and suddenly there I was—just like any other mental patient. The transformation was quite a feeling: a loss of identity, really. I was just another anonymous patient in institutional pajamas. Who I had been a week before meant nothing to them. I was there for observation, but I was given large doses of a powerful tranquilizer that would have made observing me a waste of time."

"Would have?"

"I pretended to take the pills, but hoarded them for four days. I didn't really have a plan yet, but I knew that if I took those pills, I never would have one. Then one day, an orderly turned up whom I'd known for some time. He used to work the surgical floors, but had transferred to the psychiatric wing because it paid better. We talked. He knew I wasn't crazy, and that I certainly hadn't killed my partner. He agreed to help me if I could keep him from looking guilty. So, we put the tranquilizer into his bottle of Snapple. I took his identification, keys, and clothes, then put him in a place they called the Quiet Room to sleep it off. I used his keys to get out of the ward, and used the money in his wallet to get on the bus to Buffalo to find you."

"This is something I've been waiting to hear. How did you know about me?"

He shook his head slowly. "It was an odd circumstance. It was less than a year ago. I was at a conference in Road Town on the island of Tortola in the British Virgin Islands. It was the week between Christmas and New Year's." He stared at her. "That's something you must know all about. If you have a conference of surgeons, it has to be in some holiday period when very little surgery gets done. If it's in the winter, it will draw better attendance if it's held in a warm place. In fact, Carey might have been there."

"Last year?" Jane shook her head. "Nope." Since they had been married, Carey had gone to very few of these doctors' conventions, and she was glad. She would have missed him, and she didn't like to go with him. She had spent too much of her life in airports and hotels already, and whenever she was in another, she felt a quiet uneasiness that one of the people who had a reason to look for her would turn up.

"I seldom go either. I went because I was reading a paper on a few of the post-operative techniques we had developed. That part seemed to go well. Then it was New Year's Eve, and I was scheduled to leave for home the next morning. I had developed a friendly relationship with a waitress."

Jane considered saying nothing. She had almost asked whether Sarah had gone to the Virgin Islands with him, but had decided to wait. At some point she was going to have to ask exactly what their relationship had been, but not yet. She decided to prod him a little. She raised an eyebrow. "A waitress?"

"Don't be ridiculous," he snapped. "The week in that hotel was frustrating. Most guests dealt with the manager and got nothing they asked for. I now believe he was the evil wayward son of some aristocratic family. Or they spoke with the concierge, who seemed to be there because she looked good behind the desk, but was utterly brainless. But this waitress would listen and get what was wanted. So I overtipped her and treated her with courtesy. That is all."

"She told you about me?"

"No. She knocked on my door at three A.M. and said there was a medical emergency. The hotel was full of surgeons, but in her eyes they had all disqualified themselves. Some had been drinking. I didn't drink. Some had come with wives and children, and I had come alone. Some had simply never noticed her, or had not struck her as approachable. So I was the one. She took me to a house. It was enormous, a villa of the sort you might expect to see on the Mediterranean, but wouldn't. The owner was ill, and apparently there was some problem about finding a surgeon who would admit him to the local hospital on New Year's Eve. Maybe it was true, and maybe it was just an excuse for drafting me. But I could tell the man had a hot appendix. We moved him to the hospital, I operated, and he was fine. It's a simple procedure. Medical students do it all the time. But he was grateful. He wanted to reward me. I refused. It's one thing to perform emergency surgery in a foreign country, but another to take pay for it. But he didn't mean money.

"He was positive that I had come to Tortola with a suitcase full of cash to hide in a bank down there. I said it was a medical conference, and he said that the reason they held conferences during the holidays was because the customs force was thinner and lazier then, and that's when American doctors and lawyers and politicians came to make deposits. I couldn't convince him. He just kept looking at me with a patronizing, knowing smile. The man was clearly a criminal, and the idea that some-one else could be honest seemed never to have occurred to him. Finally he wrote down your name and address and handed it to me. He said that since I was evading taxes, I might one day find myself in trouble. I said I wasn't. He said there were a million reasons why one day a person—any person—might need to disappear. I was to memorize your address and destroy the paper, and when my time came I should go there and ask for you. I destroyed the paper, of course, but the words he had written never seem to have left my mind. It was such an odd evening, and I'd never met anyone like him before."

"When the Buffalo police spotted you, you were on your way to my house?"

"Yes. I got as far as the bus station in downtown Buffalo. I was going out to find a cab, but I guess I looked suspicious, so two policemen ap-proached me and asked to see identification. I ran a few steps, they called for me to stop, and that brought me to my senses. When I reached into my coat to produce my stolen wallet, they thought I had a gun. That was something George Hawkes hadn't told me about."

If he was still calling himself George Hawkes, Jane thought, then his luck was holding. When she had met him he had made his living as a travel agent for money, taking it on trips from a jewelry wholesale oper-ation in California through Panama to banks in the Netherlands An-tilles to front corporations in Europe, and then back. One afternoon seven or eight years ago, he had been raided in Los Angeles by policemen who thought he was a drug dealer. But he had managed to see the signs just in time: the van that had been parked down the street, which occa-sionally wobbled a little, as though a person were moving around inside, and then the large, plain cars arriving from different directions all at once.

He had slipped out through the crowded produce market next door, carrying a great deal of money with him. Walking out ahead of the raid instead of getting caught in it did not, however, have the desired effect. His clients, who were innocent of drug dealing but deeply involved in the business of making unauthorized copies of feature films and selling them in foreign markets, had interpreted the facts in their own way. They felt he had absconded with their money. He had come to Jane.

After Jane had hidden him, she had gotten in touch with his former clients. She had then dictated a treaty. The former Harvey Fisk would

take his usual commission and return their money via the usual channels, which would then close forever. He would not engage in any illegal
activity again. They need not worry that at some time in the future he
would get caught and be tempted to trade information about them for a
light sentence. In return, they would never search for him, bother him,
or speak of him to a third party. Any infraction of the treaty by either
party would result in Jane, the referee, giving sufficient information to
the authorities to put the infringing party away.

Jane gave in to her curiosity. "How is he?"

"Oh, fine," said Dahlman. "Excellent health for fifty-six. Good physical
conditioning, muscle tone apparently from tennis and swimming. The
appendix doesn't really mean a thing." He noticed her expression. "You
didn't mean that, did you?"

"No."

"He lives like a king. And you know what? It didn't seem like anything
then, but now it seems like everything. He isn't afraid."

12

Jane drove through the dark country with tireless discipline. She kept her speed constant, changing lanes only when she needed to, never letting lines of cars build up behind her where a follower could hide.

The parts of Dahlman's story that were most incomprehensible to him were clear to her. The two men who had pretended to be cops had done it so they could interview him at great length. The questions they had asked were the ones that killers needed to know: Were there any pictures of Hardiston, or any medical records that had survived the fire in Sarah Hoffman's office? When Dahlman told his story, did it sound reasonable and rational, or disconnected and mad and unbelievable? If he had any witnesses they didn't know about, any evidence that would lend credence to any part of his story, that evening was the time when he would have produced it. Since he could produce nothing, he was perfect.

They had put him in suspended animation on the farm, convinced that he should go nowhere and talk to no one. Then they had pocketed the keys he had willingly given them, and returned to his house. They took a whole week to search every inch of his house and destroy any evidence he had missed that might corroborate his story, then plant all the evidence they could invent that he had gone insane and spent months working himself up to killing his partner.

Their plan had been very well considered. There had been five doctors and nurses on the Hardiston case. If all five had suddenly died in

Chicago, the police would have been in a frenzy. These killers had known that, so they had begun by culling the herd, luring the first three away and picking them off quietly. Even the order of the murders had been precise: the first was Dr. Hoffman's nurse, who had a car accident on the way to Colorado. She was the safest because when it happened she had already been separated from the others. The second was Dr. Wung, in Korea. His death and that of the nurse could not be connected, even in the unlikely event that anyone heard about both—she had never worked for Dr. Wung. The third was almost certainly Dr. Wung's assistant, Celia Rodriguez. As soon as her boss was dead, they had probably just grabbed her in Boston and buried her somewhere. Nobody would notice unless her body was found. She was a stranger in Boston. She had only moved because she was going to keep working for Dr. Wung, who wasn't expected to arrive for at least a month. Even then, when the vacation and relocation period was up, the one they would have missed was Dr. Wung, not the assistant he had said he was bringing with him.

It was very neat. They had killed three people—one between Chicago and Colorado, one in Korea, and one in Boston—in three different ways, without having either the police or the two doctors who had stayed in Chicago know that anything had happened.

That left only the two doctors in Chicago, Richard Dahlman and Sarah Hoffman. If either were murdered, there would be an immediate investigation. There was no way to avoid it. When that happened, the authorities were likely to try to ask questions of the people who had once worked with the victim, and they were going to find that a statistically unlikely number of them had recently died. So what the killers had chosen to do was to trigger the investigation themselves, so that the questions weren't asked until they were ready to hand the police a killer. They had made sure that before any question could be asked, the police had an answer.

If the investigation led the police to change the suicide or the accident or the disappearance into murders, they would not start looking for new suspects. They would already have in custody a proven killer who was clearly out of his mind, and who'd had as little reason to murder his partner as any of the others. The real killers must have planned the deaths in a hundred different ways, a hundred different orders to see which of the five should be killed when, and which would be left to serve as perpetrator.

The more Jane thought about it, the more sophisticated the plan they had chosen seemed. The one who would simply disappear had to be one of the three women, because that happened to young women fairly regularly in big cities, and hardly ever to middle-aged men. The one killed in the car accident had to be someone who could be fooled into traveling a long distance by car. That way there would be lots of chances to arrange it and the investigators who were stuck with it would have very little information. The supposed murderer would have to be one of the men, because men who went mad were more likely to do it that way than women were. Jane wasn't sure about suicides, but she suspected men did more of that too, and an anesthesiologist was the best candidate because he carried the means with him in his bag.

"What's our next stop?"

Jane remembered Dahlman. He had to be talked to. Human beings were terribly fragile. A person had to be kept informed, kept thinking and participating or he would begin to lose his connection with the herd, and that was the same as losing his connection with the world. "I'm not sure," she said. "I've been trying to think over everything you've told me so we'll know what we should do." She smiled apologetically. "It's not very comforting stuff."

His answer wasn't a snap, the way it had been earlier. It was quiet and regretful. "You said you wanted to figure out who was chasing us. Did you figure it out?"

"The police in Chicago are interested, of course. Most of the time, getting out of Illinois would do a lot to solve that problem. When there's a murder, the local police keep looking hard, but everywhere else you'd just be a name among thousands of others. The people who set you up took care of that. They've made it look as though you're unpredictable and dangerous, so for the moment you're probably near the top of the list everywhere. Since there are plenty of grounds for the federal authorities to come in, we have to assume that just about everyone in the country who hunts people for a living is looking for you."

"You think I should turn myself in and take my chances at trial, don't you?"

Jane shrugged, and slowly blew out a breath. "It's a hard question. Most of the time, if someone is wrongly accused of a crime, I would say yes. If there's evidence of your innocence that I haven't heard, I would still say yes. Is there?"

"Not evidence in the sense you mean. A lifetime of decent behavior doesn't seem to qualify." He was silent for a moment. "How do you think I would do at a trial? Be honest."

She squinted ahead at the road. "You've already been arrested. They got you a lawyer, everyone listened to your story two or three times, and they sent you to have your head examined. This is not a verdict, of course, but I think it's pretty consistent with what you could expect next time. Since you're clearly able to understand what's said to you, I would also guess that it was done as a necessary formality. You would be declared sufficiently sane to participate in your defense, and would stand about a seventy- to eighty-percent chance of being convicted."

"How can you put a percentage on it?"

"That's about how the average defendant does in a murder trial in this country. Your chances are actually a bit worse, but it's unrealistic to guess how much worse."

"Why would mine be worse?"

"A lot of reasons. One is that you've been made to look very clever and sneaky. You can't deny you escaped from a mental lockup by drugging someone, or that you slipped out of the hospital in Buffalo. Juries don't like that kind of defendant, because they assume he's a liar. Judges don't like them either, so the close calls would go to the prosecution. The people who framed you have already had weeks to clean up any loose ends, and the police have had more weeks to examine the faked evidence, so I can't hold out much hope that the frame will fall apart of its own weight."

"I can't live with this kind of injustice," said Dahlman. "I can't let them get away with what they've done."

Jane sighed. "Then maybe the best thing to do isn't to disappear, and I'm not the person you need right now."

"What do you mean by that?"

"I'm not in the business of ensuring that justice is done. I'm just one small person, not smart enough to assume I always know what justice is, let alone imagine that I can make things happen that are neat and symmetrical enough to qualify as fair. What I do is take people who are about to be killed and move them to places where nobody wants to kill them. If you want to disappear, you come to me. If you want something else—revenge, keeping your enemies from hurting someone else, peace of mind, justice, I'm not interested."

Dahlman was silent for a long time. Finally, he said, "I'm convinced that justice is a positive, verifiable, obtainable goal. I need you to keep me out of jail, but I'm not going to give up. I won't lie to you about that."

"Fine. Just don't imagine that you and I are going after these people ourselves."

"If that's necessary, I'll do it."

"Really?" said Jane. "Then I guess you'd better do as much weighing and measuring in advance as you can."

"What do you mean?"

"The authorities aren't looking for the people who framed you. That leaves only you to do something about it. But if you see any of them again, they'll be armed and trying to kill you. Will you let them?"

"Well, no," he said. "The last time it happened I was under the mistaken impression that you wanted me to help ambush and shoot them. Naturally, I refused. But letting them kill me doesn't serve justice. I would try not to let them do it."

"Would you try with a gun?"

"I would certainly be reluctant, but if there were no other way to preserve my life—and what I know—then maybe I would."

Jane shook her head. "The 'no other way' argument doesn't work in real life. When it happens, you don't have ten hours to work through each alternative to predict whether it will necessarily result in your death. You don't have ten heartbeats. You see them and shoot, or they see you and shoot. It's not about good and evil; it's about who gets to feel the eleventh heartbeat."

He nodded. "I suppose it could happen that way. There could be circumstances—"

"Yes," she interrupted. "There could. And while you're preparing for them, you'd better start working on the most likely of the circumstances."

"What's that?"

"There are—how many?—maybe five evil men searching for you. They're not using magic. They're probably watching TV to find out where you turn up next so they can go there too. The TV reporters get their information from the police. What that means is that the next person to aim a gun at you probably isn't going to be some slimy, conniving criminal who helped murder four of your friends. It's going to be some kind of cop. A good guy: in fact, the best of the good guys, because he not only hasn't done anything evil, he's taking a risk to protect people. And he believes in justice as much as you do. What are you going to do about him?"

She waited a few seconds while Dahlman tried to sort it out. Then she said, "I've been hoping all we had to do was keep you out of sight for a while, and let the police clear you. Now I don't know if that's going to work. All I can promise is that I'll try to keep you alive. I can't make things come out even."

It was two in the morning when Jane pulled off the highway into a gas station and stopped beside the row of pumps. The attendant in the little lighted building stood and stared out from behind his counter, and Jane studied him. He was probably nineteen or twenty years old, with a three-day growth of beard that had taken him much longer to grow, and a tattoo on the back of his left hand that he was going to live to regret someday. The only feature of it that she could see clearly was a spiderweb.

Jane said to Dahlman, "Sit tight while I pump the gas. Look away from him while I open the car door, because the light will come on."

She started to open the door when Dahlman said, "Wait."

She closed it again. "What?"

"I'd like to go to the men's room, since we've stopped. How do I get the key?"

"I'll get it for you." She kept her eyes on the gas station attendant. He seemed to be unconcerned now; he had gone back to watching the television set behind the counter, having reassured himself that he wasn't about to be robbed. "Anything else you want—a soft drink, candy? Tell me now, before the light goes on again."

"No," said Dahlman. "No, thank you."

Jane walked to the little building and pulled the door open. She could hear the television above the hum of the big refrigerator beside the door: "Los Angeles pulled a game ahead of the Padres in the West with a one-hit shutout at Dodger Stadium . . ."

She placed a twenty-dollar bill on the counter and said, "I'm at pump number five. And do you have a key to your men's room?"

The boy pointed to a key attached to a board on the wall above her head. She took it and turned to leave. She kept her eyes on the glass door of the refrigerator and watched his reflection. His head and chest were visible above the counter, and his eyes now fixed on her and remained on her as she walked away. She reminded herself that this was not a customs official in a foreign airport. It was a normal teenaged boy whose interests were limited to cars, music, and what he was staring at right now.

When Jane reached the car, Dahlman got out; she handed him the key and turned her attention to filling the gas tank while she watched the boy over the roof of the car.

The boy seemed lost in some kind of cogitation. He had stopped staring at the television. She hoped he was just waiting out a commercial, but then she saw that wasn't it. He came around the counter with a mop in his hand. Jane's mind worked on him. He was not the sort of person who had a mania about cleaning: there were packages of gum and cigarettes in the rack on the counter that would stay there forever because they had a film of dust on them. If his boss had told him to mop the floors, he would do it at the end of the shift, and that was not likely to be between two and three in the morning. It would be at six or seven.

She watched him closely. The boy left the cubicle and walked toward the men's room with his mop. He had no bucket. Jane turned off the pump, capped the tank, and moved quickly toward the lighted building.

Inside the cashier's station she worked frantically. She pulled the telephone cord out of its socket and stomped on the plastic connector, then jammed the wire back in. Then she stepped through the inner door into the mechanic's shop and gazed around her hungrily for anything she could use. There was a set of tire chains hanging on the wall. She took it, then hurried outside.

Dahlman was just coming out the men's room door. The boy edged past him with the mop. As soon as he was inside, Jane slipped the tire chain over the doorknob and clasped the other end of it around the upright pole that supported the overhanging roof.

Dahlman stopped, shocked. "Are you insane?" he hissed.

Jane seemed not to hear him as he followed her back into the shop. "How can he fail to suspect something if you lock him in the men's room?" Jane picked up the hammer on the workbench. There were wrenches of various sizes hanging from nails on the wall. She used one of them to pry out the nail it had been hanging from, then the two beside it.

"Give me the men's-room key," she said, and snatched it out of his hand. "Is there a window in there?"

He shook his head. Jane rushed past him, knelt beside the door of the men's room, and began to pound a nail through the door and into the frame. As she raised the hammer for another swing, she heard a loud bang, and there was a hole in the door a few inches above her head. She sidestepped away from the door. She had thought of the possibility of a gun when she had seen that there was no weapon hidden under the cashier's counter, but she had rejected it. Now the kid was scared and trying to save his life.

She hurried toward the car, but Dahlman wasn't in it. She ran back and found him inside the cashier's station, staring at the television. The image on the screen was his own face looking back at him. "I'm on television," he said. "They're saying incredible things about me . . ." He looked at her in disbelief. "I'm a serial killer."

"I wasn't able to tell you by the time I realized what he must have seen," she said. "When I came in, I could hear something about baseball scores. After I was outside I realized that it couldn't be a game at this hour. It had to be the news."

Jane looked inside the shop again. The vehicle parked in there was a tow truck. She hurried to it and saw the toolbox in the back under the winch. She opened it, and found the precious object she had been hoping for. It was home-made, just a foot-long strip of sheet metal that had been notched about a half inch from the tip. She took it, the hammer, and a screwdriver, and closed the box.

She grasped Dahlman's arm in her free hand and gently tugged him out to the car, then started it and drove back onto the highway.

"What are we going to do?" Seeing himself on television seemed to have destroyed the last of Dahlman's confidence.

Jane looked at her watch. "It's now two thirty-five. He could be in there an hour or so before somebody stops for gas and goes looking for him. But somebody could come along in five minutes. Either way, we've got to get as far as we can while we can. I don't think there's much chance a kid who works in a gas station won't give the police a good description of the car, do you?"

Dahlman held up his hands in a gesture of helplessness and shook his head. "I don't have any idea."

"It's obviously been a while since you were nineteen. Nineteen-year-old boys care about cars."

"I suppose so."

Jane frowned. "Don't go all limp and worthless on me now. Please. What we do next has got to work, or we're caught."

"What are we going to do next?"

"Take the map and look for the nearest airport." Jane knew approximately where the next airport was, because Akron was only about ten miles away. She had driven Route 224 before. It ran in nearly a straight line to the west across Ohio. Policemen looking for people had to watch the big interstate highways that ran in the same direction—80 in the north and 70 in the south—because people who ran were strangers, and strangers took the interstates.

"Right here." Dahlman pointed at the road map. "It looks like eight or ten miles, straight ahead. It's the Akron airport."

Ten minutes later Jane took a ticket from the machine at the entrance to the long-term parking lot, drove in, and began to search for the right car. When she found it, it was a nine-year-old Chevrolet Impala that had good tires and would not have been as shiny if the engine didn't run. She could see it had no mechanical locking device across the steering wheel, and there were no glowing lights inside that could be an alarm. She parked beside it and studied it. It wasn't in mint condition, so it wasn't somebody's old friend. More likely someone who traveled a lot had bought an old car he didn't mind leaving in airport parking lots so he could keep his fancy car locked in the garage at home.

"Get out with me," she said. "Open your suitcase, and keep your head down, as though you were checking to be sure you haven't forgotten anything. Warn me if anybody drives into the lot."

Dahlman opened the trunk and leaned into it to fiddle with his suitcase while Jane moved to the other car. He watched her while she slipped the long, flat strip of sheet metal into the space between the Chevrolet's window and door, and wiggled it a bit.

"What's that?"

"It's a slim-jim," she said. "Tow-truck drivers sometimes carry them because people lock their keys in their cars." She tugged upward and the lock button on the door popped up. "Keep looking for cars."

She sat in the driver's seat, used the hammer to drive the screwdriver into the space between the ignition switch and the steering column. She pried the ignition switch out of its receptacle with the screwdriver, yanked the wires out of it, and stripped back the insulation a bit. "Bring the roll of adhesive tape from the suitcase."

Dahlman carried it to her and watched. She taped the ignition wires together. Then she pumped the gas pedal once, and held the two starter wires together. The engine turned over. When it caught, she pulled the starter wires apart and listened. "Fairly smooth for a cold engine. It'll do."

She put their suitcases in the back seat, then walked down the aisle of cars until she saw the one she wanted. She popped up the lock button, took the parking ticket from the floor under the driver's seat, then locked the car again and went to find another one with a ticket in it.

When she returned to Dahlman she said, "You'll drive the Chevy. Follow me. I'm going into the lot at the terminal." She handed him one of the two stolen tickets.

Dahlman was agitated. "But we have a ticket."

"It says we came in the lot five minutes ago."

He was even more frustrated. "Why are we doing any of this?"

She looked around her impatiently, but no sign of headlights could be seen. "We can't drive the rented one any farther because the kid at the gas station saw it. If we leave it in this lot, the Youngstown office where we got it reports it missing. If we return it to their rental agency here, nobody reports anything."

Dahlman got into the car and did as he was told. When Jane had gotten them both out of the long-term parking lot, returned the rental car to the agency lot, and dropped the key in the lockbox, she climbed into the stolen Chevrolet with Dahlman and drove back onto the highway.

"How long can we go before the owner of this car reports it missing?" asked Dahlman.

"Maybe a day, maybe a month," said Jane. "It doesn't matter."

"You mean we're not going to keep it even a day?"

"No," said Jane. "It's time to get some help."

13

Jane guided the car up the quiet street above the little lake and stopped. The moment that the breeze through the open windows died, she could feel the weight of the humidity settle on her and make her arms heavy. She turned around to face Dahlman on the back seat. "Time to get up." She leaned closer to the steering column, pulled the two wires apart, and the engine was silent.

Dahlman slowly unbent himself, sat up, and looked around him. "Where are we?"

"Minneapolis. You slept most of the day. The sun will be down in a few minutes. How do you feel?"

"I'm a little stiff, but I don't feel as though the wound is inflamed, and that could be a wonderful sign."

He had not used a word like "wonderful" before, thought Jane. Maybe all it meant was that he really was getting better, but maybe it meant that last night's discussion about justice had made him decide to stop telling her the truth. "We've got to go for a walk now."

Dahlman ran his hands through his hair, made an attempt to straighten his clothes, then got out of the car. Jane locked the doors, then set off along the crest of the grassy slope above the lake. There were mallards bobbing on the darkening water, then lifting their heads to the sky to clap their bills in a shivering, jittery little movement to sift bits of food.

A car glided past on the road around the lake, and Dahlman moved a little lower down the slope, but Jane didn't join him. She stopped walking. "Don't hide yourself," said Jane. "The way is along the ridge."

"But it's the same direction."

"No. Come back up." She waited while he joined her. "I'll explain this as well as I can. There's a house a little higher up the hill at the end of the lake. There's a man in that house I want to see. In order to get into that house, you have to go a certain way. It shows another man that we're okay. This one is a very unpredictable, suspicious man—the sort of person who hits back first—and he's studying us through a spotting scope."

"A spotting scope?"

"You'll probably see it. It's a sixty-power telescope on a tripod at an upper window. In the day it is, anyway. When the sun goes down, they switch to a nightscope with infrared to pick up your body heat. You have to walk along the crest so they have time to get a good look at who you are and what you're carrying, and who else is nearby who might be following you."

"What happens if you're the wrong person?"

Jane shrugged. "It depends. If you're just enjoying the scenery, nothing. When I was here before they always had cars waiting with the keys in them, and beside the spotting scope there was another tripod with a Heckler & Koch G7 rifle on it. They have lots of options."

"Exactly who is this man we're going to see?"

"Just a man who knows how to get things accomplished."

"What's his name?"

"I don't know, exactly. It doesn't matter."

Dahlman let his frustration show. "That's not a possible statement of fact. You can't not know exactly. Either you know or you don't. You can't know a name approximately."

Jane frowned, and there was an edge in her voice. "I need to say a few things, so listen carefully. As long as I could, I've kept you in the part of the world that you're familiar with. People aren't entirely rational in that world, but they behave as though they were, and they make sure that their actions have to do with attaining reasonable goals—that is, things that they're allowed to want. Their way of getting them is by a logical series of causes and effects: you work, you get paid. You're patient, you get rewarded. You're pleasant, people like you. I kept you in that world for several reasons. You're a success in that world, so you know how it works and can move around in it without raising eyebrows. Something as simple as speaking grammatical English and holding a fork correctly makes you almost invisible. You also feel comfortable there, and that makes you look innocent. But the main reason I kept you in that world is that it's safer."

"Safer than what?" Dahlman's voice was skeptical.

"Safer than where we're going now."

"And where is that? What do you mean by other parts of the world? Are we leaving the country?"

Jane looked at him, and there was a touch of regret in her eyes. "I'm trying to prepare you for a shock. I hope it's not a big one, but it might be. The people we're going to see are not like you, not like Carey. I'd like to say they're not like me, either, but this isn't the first time I've been here." As soon as Jane said it she realized she had identified the hurt that had been constricting her chest. She was back in this life. It was as though she had happily fallen asleep in the old house beside Carey, and awakened with a start along this path by the lake. The place where she walked now wasn't a point in space; it was a point in time, in the past. Falling back into this place was not like being abducted. It was like being unmasked.

"You mean they're not honest."

"Categories like honest and dishonest don't apply to them any more than they do to your cat. These people have certain principles and habits and inclinations, but you don't have time to learn them all. Be alert. Be observant, and listen to every word that's said in your presence, but believe nothing unless I say it. Don't ask questions or express an opinion. You're a passenger."

Dahlman gave a little chuckle. "You're treating me as though I were a child. Speak when spoken to, and don't be afraid."

"Oh, no," said Jane. "That isn't what I meant at all. Be afraid. Just don't show it."

Dahlman walked along in silence for a time, then said, "Is that why you won't tell me his name? Are you afraid to?"

"No. One of the things he sells is forged identification. It's the reason I know him. But he's like a tattoo artist."

"A tattoo artist?"

"Every tattoo artist gets tired of waiting for the right customer to come in the door and ask for the right picture, so they all end up working on themselves. Some of the old pros are covered, from their toes to their collarbones. The man we're going to see doesn't concede that he should be permanently limited to one name, and he doesn't have to be, so he isn't. He uses an identity until he's tired of it, and then picks a new one. I know what he was calling himself last time. He was Paul Carbin. But it's been three or four years. He's probably been several people since then."

"Why did you bring me here?"

Jane walked a few more paces. "Until now, the police have probably been operating on the theory that you were still in Buffalo, or near it. The night we left, I had enough of everything on hand—money, forged IDs, clothes—to keep us out of trouble for a while if we got out and kept going. We were spotted last night at a gas station on an interstate in the Midwest, and that means we change our strategy. We've got to dig in somewhere, get an identity that's tailor-made for you, and then prepare to wait."

Jane led Dahlman to the end of the lake, then up the hill on the sidewalk to a Victorian three-story house with a stone-and-masonry facing that had originally been the foundation and at some point had been raised to the height of a man. She climbed the steps to the wide wooden porch and stopped to beckon to Dahlman. Dahlman hesitated, then climbed the steps, stood beside her, and looked around him.

There was a security screen door with steel mesh and bars set in so that it was much stronger than it looked from a distance. Behind that was a steel fire door with wooden panels glued on to fit the decor. For the first time, Dahlman noticed that the shutters on the lower windows were closed.

The fire door swung open and a thin young man whose pale skin didn't look entirely clean to Dahlman stared out with a bored, sullen expression. After a moment he muttered, "He said you could come in if you want to."

"We want to," said Jane.

The young man slipped the bolt on the screen and Jane stepped inside, then held it for Dahlman. "Come in," she said. "If I let it close, it'll lock."

Dahlman stepped in behind her. The room had once been a spacious foyer. There was a straight staircase leading upward to a second-floor landing, but the railing up there seemed wrong. It was out of proportion, the spokes too short and the base too high. Then Dahlman saw a pair of eyes peering down at him between the spokes. A girl about the same age as the boy at the door sat up, and brought with her a small, square-looking piece of black metal that Dahlman didn't recognize as an automatic weapon until she turned it away from him and he could see the short barrel in profile. She stood and sauntered off to dissolve into the shadows of the upstairs hallway.

"Well, what do you think of her?" The voice came from somewhere to the left of them, a loud baritone.

Dahlman turned his head to see that Jane was already staring in that direction, into a room beside her that looked almost as it should have. It was the library of the old house, and it was still lined with ornate oak shelves that held rows of leather-bound volumes. There was a tall, bearded, broad-shouldered man with a fat belly that showed a little between his T-shirt and his jeans sitting in a wing chair in the dimly lighted room.

Jane shrugged and walked to the entrance. "She's way too young to be sincere. She'll take your money and cut your throat."

The big man laughed and shook his head. "I was referring to the backup for the door. That's an innovation since you were here. See, they get past the door—"

"How?" she interrupted. "It would take a half hour with a battering ram."

"But if they did—say by guile and artifice—then Cindy opens up from the balcony with the Ingram. She's behind a layer of steel and bricks, and they're standing down here blinking." Dahlman saw the man's eyes settle on him thoughtfully. He didn't look pleased.

"What's your name these days?" Jane seemed to be trying to break his train of thought.

"Sid Freeman."

"Pleased to meet you, as usual," said Jane.

Sid Freeman's face was set and expressionless. "Who's he?"

"I was just getting to that," Jane said cheerfully. "He's my runner. His name is Richard Dahlman."

Sid Freeman stared at Dahlman for seven or eight seconds, then turned to glower at Jane. She avoided his gaze and looked around her as she said, "I don't see any of the old faces."

Sid Freeman snorted. "Death, plague, and conflagration on many fronts. Quinn got into the habit of wearing a Rolex and driving to unsavory parts of Chicago in a major piece of automotive extravagance. He made a stop one night while he was on the way to deliver a very big payoff, and the combination was too much for some people to resist."

"Sorry." Jane used the moment to inwardly celebrate the absence of Quinn. Sid was unbalanced, but Quinn had been frightening. She had once stood beside him at the window when he had the rifle pressed to his shoulder, watching an unidentified man strolling along the path by the lake. He had been gripped by a tense, aching longing to squeeze the trigger just to see the man's body jerk and the blood flow. Jane had stared into the spotting scope and said the man's earphone was a hearing aid, and his glasses were too thick to let him qualify as a cop. Quinn had kept the rifle to his cheek and his finger tapping eagerly on the trigger guard until Sid had taken a turn at the telescope and told Quinn not to fire.

Sid shrugged. "It's probably better that he's gone. He would have fallen eventually to a dirty needle or unpremeditated sex; he never considered an evening complete without both." He looked sadder as he said, "The lovely and talented Christie got caught in a sudden reverse of the natural order. She was killed by a New York cab driver. Actually, he wasn't a real cab driver—just stole it and spent the evening cruising hotels looking for a rich mark, when Christie was there making a delivery for me. But it makes a better story that way: CABBIES FIGHT BACK!" He laughed at the thought.

His laugh induced a sensation in Jane that wasn't exactly revulsion. It was the absence of pleasant surprise—what she might have felt if she had looked into an empty barrel and verified that it was still empty. Christie had been Sid's—what was the term? "Girlfriend" sounded like something playful and innocent, and their closeness had always seemed to be a fetid amalgam of eroticism and conspiracy. Christie had always been putting her lips close to his ear and whispering secrets that had to do with money. But Jane had been sure that whatever minuscule level of affection Sid was capable of, it had been reserved for Christie.

Jane said, "I assume we don't have to worry about anybody who's in the house right now?"

Sid Freeman shook his head so that his shaggy hair whipped against his forehead. He pushed it back. "Worry about the kids?" He gave an amused snort. "They're my greatest possession. They've eased the way out of my midlife tragedy and into my reclining years. I picked the first pair up to help me do some hunting—you know, to put Christie and Quinn to rest. They turned out to be ferocious—no hesitation, unencumbered by thoughts, either first or second. And they're sleek and beautiful to watch, like tigers. So I kept them and got some more. Four so far. I'm hoping they'll breed. But you don't want to climb in the cage with them, if you know what I mean: Sid Freeman doesn't indulge in the marital arts except with blue-haired ladies of his own generation. For you, of course, I'm willing to accept false ID."

Jane gave a little smile and shook her head slowly from side to side. "Not if you were driving the last bus out of hell and I was made of ice cream."

Sid Freeman shrugged. "Which, incidentally, is not an inaccurate description of your present predicament."

"That's how I know," said Jane. "I asked myself what I'd do for you if you got me out of this, and the answer already came back: 'Not a thing.' "

"You're not a spontaneous person," he chuckled. "But you wouldn't be here if something weren't making your little heart go pitty-pat. What is it?"

"Top of the list is that I had to hot-wire a car in an airport lot in Akron, Ohio. It's on the street with two suitcases on the back seat."

"J.C. saw it when you got out of it. Old Chevy?"

"That's the one," said Jane.

Sid Freeman stood up and walked across the foyer into the kitchen. Dahlman could hear him muttering, and then two or three pairs of feet walking across the floor and a door closing. When he returned, he said, "They'll dissolve it for you and bring in the bags." He stared at Jane in a leisurely way. "Is that it?"

Jane nodded at Dahlman. "I take it you know about him."

"Sure," he said. "They said he took a hot one from a constable somewhere." He suddenly poked his finger toward Dahlman. Although Dahlman was five feet away, the surprise made him involuntarily tighten his pectoral muscles and cringe to protect the wound, then wince at the pain it caused. "Right there."

Jane said, "He's been sewn up, he's got antibiotics, but he's going to need to stay in one place for a while and rest. While he's healing, I go out and prepare a place for him to be somebody else, do the necessary shopping, and come back."

"Big shopping?"

"I'll be gone one week, two at the outside. We both stay two more weeks after that. During that time you help me cook up a first-rate identity: family pictures, school records, work history, credit record, driver's license, the works. And I want a second identity that's almost as good, in case he's spotted using the first one. I could do it alone, but each step takes time and I don't want to use time that way right now. When we leave, it's in a good car with a clean title."

Dahlman watched as Sid Freeman's face took on a new expression. Dahlman could tell it was only an approximation of a face Freeman had once seen that had carried concern and regret, which he had found intriguing. "Ah, Janie," he moaned. "Where have you been? You're such a prize."

"I quit doing this about a year ago, on the stupid assumption I could have a life," said Jane. "Anything on that list you can't handle?"

"Let's see," said Freeman. He squinted down at his fingers as though he were counting them, then waved the whole hand. "All of it."

"Why not?"

"Janie, Janie, Janie," he said softly. "You disappear without a footprint—which, after all, is what anybody with a brain always thought you would do—but then you come scratch at my door, wet-puppy style, and talk as though you're still a fixture of the landscape. You nodded off, times changed, annelids turned."

"Annelids look pretty much the same on both sides," she said, unperturbed. "Now, human beings—"

"Sid's not human," Sid interrupted. "He's humanoid: two arms, two legs, wears corrective lenses, takes money."

"Oh, money," said Jane. "If we're just haggling about price, let's hear numbers."

"Sid doesn't haggle," he said. "Janie, I love you more than I hope for tomorrow's dessert. But I can't do business with you this time. I just let you in because you remind me of my mom."

"So your kids aren't chopping the Chevy for me?"

"They like the activity, so I threw that in as part of my lapse into sentiment. On the house. Besides, I can't leave a thing like that on my doorstep and expect to do business. But Sid can't fill your shopping list of goods and services."

"Why can't he? Did Sid get too rich in the last couple of years?"

He scowled. "Let's explore your problem."

"That's better. How much will it take?"

"You have this baggage with you, this multiple-homicide suspect, escaped from custody in two states. You know more about the rest of this game than anybody alive. You tell me who's hunting, what they'll use, and where the game ends."

Jane glanced at Dahlman, then answered. "If he were on his own, it would be over already, but he's not."

Sid Freeman shook his head. "I mean starting from now. Anybody making odds will say it ends by some TV zombie recognizing him and calling the police. The boys in blue don't need to go it alone, because the F.B.I. has already invited them to call in. So they do, and pretty soon there's a battalion. Are they then going to say, 'Come out with your hands up' loud enough for him to hear and reload? No. They're going to batter down walls and make everybody for miles around gulp tear gas. You and Foxy Grandpa will have many more holes than you started with."

"Will you miss me?"

"Will I have time? The next day, the F.B.I. demonstrates its zero tolerance of the brand-new Fleeing Felon Problem it just discovered by tracking down whoever gave you the papers, the car, the clothes, and whatever else they found near your bodies. They won't get me, of course, but they'll need somebody. They could scare clients, choke off a couple of my sources and suppliers. Very inconvenient. And for what?"

"What has it ever been for, Sid? Money."

He stared at her body from the feet up to the neck. "If you were carrying that kind of money among your various curves I'd see it, and you wouldn't leave it in a hot car, so it's on a pay-later basis, right?"

"I could get more during my shopping spree."

"I don't want to be depressing, but this time wanting to come back does not mean I'll hear your footsteps on my front porch. When your suitcases get here, I'll drop you someplace. Final word."

"You know who framed him," Jane said.

Sid's face froze in its mask of annoyance. It stayed that way for a few seconds. His mouth opened once to say something, then closed again. Finally the mask vanished and was replaced by another, softer one. "You drop off the radar screen for a couple of years. Do you think you invented the disappearing business, so you can take it with you when you go?"

She stared at him intently. She tried to remind herself that her instinctive feeling of dread didn't matter for the moment. He knew something. "Who is it?"

But Sid shrugged. "There are some people, and they're doing pretty much what you always did, only they're not going about it in this eccentric and self-indulgent way."

"What does that mean?"

"They're in a business, and they act like it. They charge what they can get, and they don't turn somebody away because he offends their nostrils. They give him what he can pay for. This, as you know, is a theory of business I subscribe to. On occasion they've sent to me for specific items of merchandise."

"Sent to you?"

"Yeah. They send the runner to pick up things, but don't come with him. There will be this typed list of stuff, practically pinned to his shirt, and he'll have the money in cash. I'm talking about runners who know zero. If I let them out the wrong door, they wouldn't be able to find their way back to the car."

"Like who?"

Sid threw up his hands. "Do I suddenly know names? Some up-and-comers from business school who looked at me like I wanted a handout for wiping their windshield."

"Any women? Kids?"

"No kids so far. A couple were women, but the kind that when they say 'the market' they don't mean a place you buy groceries. They're just men with suits that cost more and don't come with pants."

"And not one of them ever made a mistake and said who sent them?"

"Never."

"Did you ask?"

"Be assured," said Sid Freeman. "They always say it was a friend of theirs. But these are not people who would know enough not to say. Someone told them."

"What did they buy?"

"Not much overlap. What some of them wanted might get them a job as night watchman in a junkyard. One of the women got the full glamour makeover—birth, Social Security, credit, diplomas, transcripts, job references, old tax returns, doctored photographs of her standing in front of the Denver capitol building hugging one of my guys who was cleaned up to look like a boyfriend, passport, shot record."

"You came up with all that, and she said nothing? It must have taken a month."

"You have to understand that this is a very unpleasant young woman who came to Sid's door with a suitcase full of money. No incentive to establish a social relationship, and Sid doesn't haggle."

"Didn't the proportions strike you as wrong?"

"They did seem a bit off," said Sid. "But I kept an eye on the television and checked a lot of newspapers and magazines. There was nobody who looked like her, no disappearances of famous people, or of anybody about the same time who rated a line of print."

Jane's eyes rested on Dahlman, but he sensed that she was listening to something. "Your boys are back."

Sid looked away from her. "See how reliable? The future is in good hands."

Jane was still staring at Dahlman. "What about him?"

Sid looked at Dahlman too. "What about him?"

"How did you know he wasn't some madman who really had killed his friends and run off? If you got the story from television, what was there that told you?"

Sid stared at her uncomfortably. "I think it was his cunning plan to go live in a farmhouse. Was he going to stay there forever? Who would buy that as a plan? I mean, not counting the police."

Jane shook her head. "The world is a wondrous place, Sid. Naive credulity is rampant. What did they buy from you? The photographs they left in his house?"

"Just the gun. That's how I remembered the name. It was a tricky business, because it had to come from a legitimate dealer that never saw the buyer, but be registered in the name Dr. Richard Dahlman."

"Registered?" said Jane. "Then it was a suicide gun?"

"That's what I think now, after all the dust that got kicked up. I think the idea was to shoot them both and put the gun in his hand. Maybe they figured it was safer to just kill her: no matter how hard the police look at a murder it's still a murder, but a murder-suicide doesn't always include a real suicide. If the suicide doesn't hold up, they start looking for some-body else." He frowned at Dahlman. "They obviously put too much con-fidence in police marksmanship."

Jane said, "Are you going to help us, or not?"

"I still like money," he said. "But something in my mind keeps telling me, 'Janie and these faceless guys are about to bump into each other. Who's coming home to dinner?' Your suitcases are waiting."

Jane walked to the door, picked up Dahlman's suitcase and reached for hers, then saw the keys beside the handle. She could see that the papers beneath them were a car registration and a pink slip with no names on them. She straightened and turned toward Sid Freeman.

"Just fresh horses, that's all," he said. "It's the quickest way to get him out of my place of business."

14

Jane drove the new car down the hill and along the parkway beside the lake. Dahlman stared ahead for a few minutes. Then he said, "It's astounding. I've been rejected by even the worst criminals."

"Oh, Sid's okay," said Jane.

" 'Okay'?" Dahlman said. "He has no mercy, no morality, no—"

"Don't get launched, or I'll be listening to what he doesn't have all night. He got us out of a very hot car and into one we could keep forever if we were careful. That's more than any number of nice law-abiding citizens could do. He also told me some things we might have died finding out."

"He probably told you lies . . . nonsense," said Dahlman. "He's probably on the telephone right now, telling the people who are after us exactly where we are."

Jane shook her head. "Once you're in a car, he doesn't know exactly where you are."

"I don't know that he's not following us."

"I do." She sighed. "Sid doesn't have a set of rules. He has to make his decisions as they come up. All things being equal, he would rather I lived than that my enemies did. He knows that he can't affect the outcome, so it's unwise to try too hard. But he gave us what we needed."

"He said several times his only interest is money."

"Nobody is only interested in money. Sid wants to be important, and he lives on impulse, so he needs money. But the way he gets money means he has to live in isolation in a house with bulletproof walls and armed guards. He won't sell us out."

"Why wouldn't he?"

"To those 'faceless guys,' as he calls them?" said Jane. "They have not endeared themselves to Sid. They've been so careful to be sure he doesn't know who they are that he can't get word to them to negotiate a price for us. He resents that, and he resents them. They don't come in person to talk to him. I do."

As Jane drove through the night, she thought a bit about Sid's dead companion, Christie. She had always been the one in the background, floating around like the bad fairy. Jane could picture her now, with her anorexic body, close-cropped red hair, and nocturnal pallor, watching with a smug look on her face as though Sid's visitors were there for some sadistic amusement of hers. It had come as a surprise to Jane that Christie's sudden absence had made so little difference—not to Sid, but to anyone. Jane had always suspected that Christie had done most of the thinking—concocting the plans and then cajoling and manipulating Sid into executing them. But the atmosphere of the strange household, an uneasy tension between agonizingly slow, patient scheming and temporarily suspended violence, had not changed since Christie had died. Nothing had changed. The teenaged girl Jane had seen watching from the staircase had even looked a little like Christie.

Memories of Quinn were not so easy for Jane to exorcise. During the long minutes while she had been walking Dahlman to Sid's house, Quinn had been the one she had been thinking about. Christie had made her uncomfortable, but Quinn had frightened her. Quinn had been a changeling—not a fugitive, but a person who had experienced some voluntary midlife transformation. He had been something else once—she had heard lawyer, she had heard insurance investigator, she had heard detective.

Sid had told Jane that one day Quinn had simply stumbled on a truth that Sid considered obvious: that if he never again let anything interfere with his inclinations, he would, inevitably, have everything he wanted. The discovery had been exhilarating, and it had liberated his imagination. He had thought of a great many things that he wanted. But now he had undergone a second transformation. Quinn's change from alive to dead had been an immense step up.

It was two A.M. when Jane reached the outskirts of Waterloo, Iowa. She turned off the main highway and spent twenty minutes driving up and down the streets, studying the little city. When she was satisfied, she found a motel and checked in. Then she woke Dahlman and hurried him into the room before anyone else was awake.

As she opened the suitcases, she asked, "Are you up to having the bandages changed?"

"Yes."

Jane undid the bandages on his back and chest, then said, "I can't tell how you're doing as well as you can. Take a look in the mirror."

Dahlman squinted at the bathroom mirror, turned on all the lights, poked the wounds, turned this way and that. "I'd say considering the age of the patient, he's doing pretty well."

"That's what I thought," she said. "Let me wrap you up again, and then we can get some sleep."

It was evening when Dahlman awoke to find Jane sitting on the other bed watching him. He saw that she had repacked the suitcases, and that clean clothes were laid out on the bed for him.

"Are we leaving?" he asked.

"We're not going far," she answered. "I've rented an apartment."

She drove Dahlman to a one-story building across the town, and pulled the car into a space under a carport that had eight other cars in it. She helped him into the back entrance of the building, hurried him down the hall and into a door marked 3, then went back to the car to unload.

Dahlman looked around him. The apartment was furnished with cheap furniture that seemed clean and sturdy. There was a small kitchen that was separated from the living room by a low counter, and on the opposite side, a bedroom that seemed to be situated so that little light or noise was likely to reach it in the daytime. He heard Jane come back and heard her unlatching a suitcase.

Dahlman opened a cupboard and saw a sparse collection of china and glasses. He peered into the refrigerator and was surprised to see that it was already packed with food. "It looks like an awful lot of food," he said.

"I wanted you to have enough," said Jane.

He turned to look into her eyes. "You're leaving?" He had assumed she was unpacking her suitcase, but she had been unpacking his. Hers must still be in the car.

"I wasn't lying to Sid when I told him I had to leave you for a little while."

"How long?"

"I may be back tomorrow, and it may not be for two weeks. How long depends on what's out there."

"But what's your plan?" He seemed frightened.

Jane stepped away from the doorway into the kitchen. "It's not much of a plan. You said before that you're healing okay, and there are no complications, right?"

"Right."

"So now we use up some time. If you're not traveling or making noise or even going outdoors, nobody sees you and you'll heal. And the longer we keep you safe, the more likely it is that something big will happen."

"I'm supposed to sit here waiting for something big to happen to me?"

Jane smiled and sat down at the kitchen table. "Not to you. We've got problems because your story is peculiar, and that makes it newsworthy. There are a lot of murders in this country—maybe a hundred a day. But for two days, the face on television and in newspapers has been yours. It's very much in our interest to have the newspeople stop putting it in front of everybody's eyes. And they will, as soon as there's something bigger, or odder, or more compelling to replace it. If the stock market crashes or an airplane blows up or the chief justice is caught soliciting an undercover cop, your picture will disappear and people will forget about you."

"I wonder how long that will take."

"We can't know that. Of course, there are people who know it's in their interest to prolong your notoriety as long as they can. The F.B.I. will probably try to release intriguing tidbits each day. Even if they know a lot, they'll feed it to the reporters a pinch at a time. One day it'll be places where somebody may have seen you, and the next day, inside details of your previous life. They'll get people you operated on to say you did a great job but were not very friendly—"

"How do you know what people will say?"

"I don't," she said. "I'm guessing."

"I'm extremely friendly," he protested.

Jane shrugged. "I suppose I'm not seeing you at your best. It doesn't matter. News articles aren't statements of fact. They're some writer's attempt to flesh out very small bits of information into a full, coherent story. Lots of things about you will be twisted to fit a pattern of behavior, like a profile. If we're lucky, they'll concentrate on the things that aren't true; those won't help anybody recognize you."

"But what about the trial? Any potential jury will have heard all this nonsense."

Jane frowned at him. "No matter what we do, a jury would hear it from the prosecution. Let's see what we can do to keep from having a trial."

Dahlman stared at her. "I remember you said that it wouldn't be wise to go to the authorities before I have a way of defending myself. But at some point, after they've studied the evidence and found it isn't as neat and perfect as it sounded, why shouldn't I?"

Jane could feel a headache developing behind her forehead. She closed her eyes for a second, then opened them and said, "I want this to end the same way you do. I thought at the beginning that we could slip you away for a short time, let the police catch the killer, and bring you home. But it hasn't happened yet. I think we have to start thinking about the possibility that it isn't going to happen soon."

"I don't think the situation has changed. What's different?"

"What has changed is what we know. The killer isn't some amateur, and it isn't some psychopath. It isn't even one person. There are some people making a good living doing what I used to do. They helped somebody disappear—this 'Hardiston' guy—and now he's just about home-free. He has a new name, he's in a new place. But there's still one living person who saw the way he used to look and saw the way he looks now. Just one."

Dahlman stared at her.

Jane waited. Then she asked, "Enough said?"

"Yes." He began walking around the apartment again, looking closely at each piece of furniture, then at the four walls.

"I'll only be gone for a week or two."

He gave a reassuring little smile that vanished after he was sure she had seen it. "I'm not uncomfortable alone. I've lived alone for a long time. I was just thinking how much this reminds me of the place where the two policemen put me—only they weren't policemen. I don't mean it's the same physically. There's just something about spaces that have been closed up for a while . . ."

"It's probably got the same feel because this is the way the game is played, and those men seem to know it. The best place to hide is where nothing in your daily life forces you to put your face where lots of people see it. Sometimes a farm is good. So is a small town, as long as it's not small enough so people ask about you, and not a rich small town, where police check out newcomers."

"When are you leaving?"

"Soon. Tonight."

He came back into the kitchen. "Then in case I don't see you again, I would like to thank you. I can see I haven't been an easy companion, and it seems no advantage can come to you from helping me."

Jane saw that he was telling her that he was ready. She slipped her purse strap onto her shoulder and stood up. "You'll see me again."

"You've taken me away from the police and away from the people who wanted to kill me. Now I'm in a place that seems to be safe. It wouldn't be unreasonable to expect that this is the end of your services."

Jane walked to the door and put her hand on the knob. "Don't open the blinds, don't answer the door. Don't go outside unless you're sure the building's on fire, and even then, leave by the bedroom window. And don't forget to take the rest of the antibiotics. When I come back for you, what I want to find in here is a man, not a body."

Jane waited until Dahlman gave her a single nod. Then she slipped out the door. When she closed it behind her, Dahlman listened for a few seconds, but he heard no other sound.

15

I t was nine o'clock in the evening when Carey McKinnon finished his rounds. The six patients he had operated on in the past three days were all doing extremely well. He wondered whether he had been somehow overcompensating for his anxiety, and therefore doing a better job. Maybe he had been concentrating on the clear, logical work of surgery as an escape from the unpleasant and unmanageable realities that were waiting for him outside the O.R. But maybe he had been unconsciously scheduling the easy ones for this week, and pushing the risky, demoralizing surgeries off for later. Both of these possibilities were, in different ways, disturbing, but at least he could test the last one. Mr. Caputi certainly was not an easy one. His pre-op physical exam had shown elevated blood pressure, he suffered from emphysema, and he had a history of complications in earlier surgery. Mrs. Trelewski had been rushed into surgery from the emergency room, so scheduling had nothing to do with it.

It was entirely possible that he had been focusing his mind more intensely on the practiced movements of his hands. Certainly he was doing something like that now, as he walked along the street in the dark. If things had been as usual, he would have been thinking about Jane. Maybe he would be on his way home to have a late supper in the kitchen with her, and he would be forming a picture of her in his mind. The picture was almost formed, but he pushed it away. Thinking about his work was safer, and it kept his features set and impenetrable—no worry lines, no frowns.

They would be looking for signs that he was weakening. Every moment when he was not in the operating room there seemed to be someone observing him. When he was out and on the move like this, sometimes he would see them. Tonight it would be the team of two big, benevolent-looking policemen who always worked in the evening. Usually one of them would be in a car parked near the back entrance of the hospital in sight of Carey's reserved parking space. The other would be in one of the waiting areas or the gift shop off the main lobby.

He knew that behaving as though nothing had happened was the right thing to do. It was also completely insane. He was not trying to avoid creating suspicion: the police already suspected him. And the policemen weren't pretending not to be policemen. Both sides were engaged in a long, silent face-off that had become like a dialogue . . . or an interrogation. It was as if he had said, "I know you think I had something to do with Richard Dahlman's escape." They would answer, "What makes you think that?" He would say, "Because you're watching me." And they would answer, "What makes you think we're watching you?"

He was aware that, sooner or later, their patient immovability was going to end and someone was going to say, "Where is your wife?" They must have noticed by now. If they could devote policemen to sitting in cars and watching him, then they must have done a background investigation on him, or simply asked his colleagues at the hospital about him. They must know he had a wife.

The thought re-activated another bit of anxiety. Several of his colleagues had been questioned by the police, even a couple who had not been on duty the night Dahlman disappeared. A few of his close friends had said things like "Carey, what's going on? Why are they asking so many questions about you?" The ones who made him anxious were the ones who had said nothing to him. He suspected that a few of them must be trying to build distance between him and them to preserve their careers. Others might even have told the police things that were incriminating.

Carey made his way along the sidewalk in front of his office building toward the parking lot in back, where he had left his car. He had been walking this same route every day at least twice for a couple of years. When he was scheduled for surgery in the morning he would park in the hospital lot, then walk to the office around one to see patients, then back for his rounds. Since Jane had been gone, he had made a point of parking at the office and walking to the hospital, so it had become four trips. As he came around the corner into the shadow of the building, the blackness seemed to congeal in front of him into a darker black. It was the shape of a person, but some template in his brain had already measured it as small, thin—a woman. He was too late to keep his body from giving a jerk to defend itself, but then he held himself stiffly and finished his step to pretend it hadn't.

The shape took a step backward out of the shadow, and became Jane. Carey drew in a breath, but she was holding her finger over her lips, so he blew it out. She took his arm and silently pulled him through the office door, guided him down the dark hallway, and hurried him out the front door to the curb, where there was a car he had never seen before. She pushed him into the driver's seat and went around the car to sit beside him. As he stared at her in incomprehension, she kissed his cheek and whispered, "Drive. I want to see who follows."

Carey drove up the street, then turned up the second side street, then turned again at the next corner, zigzagging through the quiet streets while Jane stared out the back window. Finally she rested both shoulders on the seat and seemed to relax.

She looked at him. "You can talk, you know. That's why I rented this car. Nobody could have put a bug in it. So let's hear some sweet nothings."

"I love you," he said. "How bad is it on your end?"

"Pretty bad."

"Here too. I was hoping that by now Dahlman would be safe in Illinois again, and we could forget about him and go back to living a normal life."

"Me too." She watched him as she said, "I'm afraid that's not exactly imminent." He looked as though his lungs were deflating. Then he straightened, and began compulsively glancing in the rearview mirror. When he had seen her, his hopes must have ambushed him, she thought. "But I'm curious," she said. "What could a fellow like you mean by a normal life, and what makes you so sure you want one?"

He looked at her, and his lips slowly came up into a smile that turned into a small, rueful laugh. He was Carey again. "There are many ways of assessing these matters," he said. "But I find that what the term really means is frequent sex."

"Why, you terrible man!" She leaned close and kissed his cheek again. "No wonder I couldn't stay away."

"What else can you tell me that will make me happy?"

"Nothing happy. Dahlman's recovering from your hasty ministrations. I had to go over your shoddy tailoring with a needle and thread in a motel room."

"I'll bet that wasn't your idea. Did he teach you the coroner's stitch?"

"Sort of like laces?"

"That's the one."

"I'm surprised he didn't call it that. You're such a morbid bunch. I left him in an apartment so I could come back here and play house for a bit."

"You mean he's already doing that well?"

"No, but I figured you'd be doing that badly."

He winced. "I think I am. The police knew within a couple of hours that I worked with Dahlman years ago. They know I had something to do with his escape."

Jane frowned. "Are you positive?"

"Yes. They don't know what, exactly, or I'd probably be in jail."

She stroked the back of his neck softly. "I'm afraid that's not necessarily true."

"It's not?"

"No," she answered. "If you're right, then they're probably watching you to see if someone comes to visit you or calls—either Dahlman or a co-conspirator. Your phones will be tapped. As your co-conspirator, I can tell you that having them listening really dampens the urge to put that quarter in the pay phone. If I had, they'd have me. And they'd have you."

"We're in trouble, huh?"

Jane shrugged. "Let's say we're in a delicate position. It doesn't sound as though we have much hope of convincing the police we're innocent bystanders. The only thing we can do now is to convince them that what we're guilty of is relatively minor and that they'll never have enough evidence to be sure we'd be convicted."

"What are you talking about? Helping a murderer escape from the police—how can that be minor?"

Her voice became quieter and more worried. "It's not. It's major. Minor is something like neglecting to notice that an innocent man walked out of a hospital. We have to do everything exactly right, and that means understanding the game. The police know it inside out, so they start way ahead. Dahlman isn't a murderer unless he goes to trial and gets convicted, right?"

"I guess, so . . . yes."

"Until they catch him, he's just a murder suspect."

"The distinction isn't exactly enormous."

"It means nothing to most people, but it's important to us now. The police think they're going to catch him. They think that when they do, he'll either tell them who helped, or they'll find a witness, or pick up some evidence with him that proves it—not to them, but to a jury. They also think it's possible—even probable—that by watching you they'll hear or see something that will help them catch him. That's their priority. They think he's a killer and they want him yesterday. If they charge you or put you in jail, it will be in the papers and on television. So you won't be good bait anymore. Even Dahlman wouldn't be dumb enough to call you."

"Even Dahlman? He isn't a stupid man."

Jane sighed. "No, but he doesn't seem to be able to get over the idea that the world will spontaneously come to its senses—that his résumé will convince people he's innocent. I think I've scared him enough to make him stay put until I get back."

"What do we do?"

"What you do is play yourself as convincingly as you can. You're not worried, you're not scared. You're a doctor who operated on a patient, and that's all you know. If they ask you for theories, you don't have one."

"They already did."

"What did you say?"

"That he was probably still in the hospital. I said I didn't know anything about the murder. I didn't think he would kill anybody. Since I hadn't seen any evidence, I couldn't prove it. In other words, I played dumb."

"See?" she said with a smile. "All those years of practice paid off. Make sure your schedule stays as busy as ever, and keep at it. Do nothing that surprises them."

"I think I just did," he said. "Didn't I?"

"Yes, but it's not serious. Just because they lost you for a while doesn't mean you planned it. I had to talk to you alone, and this could be the last chance. Have they asked you about me yet?"

"No."

She frowned and considered. "I guess that's good, because it doesn't put anything on the record. Here's the story. I was out of town when Dahlman arrived. I'm home now, but this is powwow season, and I'm involved in Native American political issues, so I'm making the circuit—coming and going for much of the summer."

"But why tell them something like that?"

"It's not really telling them anything but my race. They'll already know that much about me. Trust me on that. It's been going on all my life: 'This is Jane. She's an Indian.' So we'll use it. The F.B.I. will run a trace and turn me up on some list or other: maybe one of the groups I belonged to in college, or just the Seneca enrollment list. It will give them an independent verification from their own sources, and that usually makes them overconfident. I'm going to give you a schedule of powwows and festivals and things. When they ask where I am, you look at the schedule. If they want to see it, let them."

"Won't they find you?"

"No. The doings are simultaneous and overlapping, all over the country. It'll look like an itinerary, but at any given time I could be anyplace or on the way. If I get the chance, I'll call once in a while at the right time from the right place. If I do, we'll talk about nothing. No code words, no clever tip-offs you make up on the spot."

"But what if—"

"What if nothing. The people they'll have monitoring our phones decipher telephone codes for a living. We're no match for them." As they passed an intersection, Jane looked away from Carey. "Oh, that's too bad," she said. "They're looking for us."

"How do you know?"

"I just saw two police cars on parallel streets, like a grid search. I was hoping the two we left at the office would be dumb enough to sit tight for a few more minutes." She paused for a moment, then said, "We don't have much time, so I'd better say this now."

"That sounds ominous."

"Afraid so," she said. "It's unlikely that this whole thing is going to end well. The only hope Dahlman has—or we have, either—is if we can keep him from going to trial until the evidence isn't all against him. All we have going for us is—"

"You," he interrupted. "We have you. Or I do, anyway."

"Very sweet," she said. "I love stupidity in a man. The time could come when the situation gets to be impossible—you lose track of me, or Dahlman ends up dead, or the police show signs that they're ready to put you away. At that point what I want you to do is this: go to Jake's house without letting anyone follow you. I'll leave a packet with him. It will have identification for both of us, passports, a lot of cash, and things like that. There will be an address in the packet. Go there and wait for me."

"What if you don't show up? You know how flighty and unreliable women are. How long should I wait?"

"If I'm alive, I'll be there. If I'm dead, what will I care? You have my permission to fly to the Middle East and start recruiting a harem."

"Hmmm," he said. "Something to consider."

"Of course, you'd be wise to make sure I'm really dead."

"I'll wait at least an hour before I get started. By the way, how in the world am I going to get anywhere if the police are about to arrest me?"

"I'm not sure if I should tell you. But I will as soon as I've gotten a better look at who's doing the watching."

"Jane?"

"No, I won't give you advice on how to find the women. Find your own women."

"I'm being serious."

"All right."

"I'm sorry. I'm sure you know that, but I have to say it anyway. If I had known what was going to happen—that this was going to destroy our lives—I would never have gotten you into it." He looked at her sadly. "I'm sure you know that, too."

She shrugged. "There's always more than one way to look at it. If we hadn't done this, you would have found Dahlman murdered in his hospital bed. That's not speculation—I saw the two men on their way to do it. Then we would have had to try to live with the knowledge that a man you admired and owed a big debt came to us for help, but you refused because you wanted to keep your nice, safe life. Could you do it? Could I? It wouldn't have killed us, but that wasn't the person I wanted to marry. I wanted to give myself to a big, strapping, manly blockhead who could be counted on to sacrifice himself to my every whim. But if you wouldn't for Dahlman, you wouldn't for me either. This sort of behavior is what I wanted, I guess. So I deserve it."

"Thanks," said Carey. "I knew I could find comfort in there somewhere."

"Where?"

" 'Manly.' It has a positive, endearing connotation, and definite sexual overtones."

"It does not."

"Oh?" said Carey. "It certainly does. Try the reversal test. What if I were describing you and used the word 'womanly'?"

She thought for a moment, then shrugged. "Okay, you got me. I must have been thinking about you in shameful, lustful ways. Pull over there at the curb."

"You can't be serious."

"You're a prude all of a sudden?" She laughed. "No, but I'd like to drive. This is probably the last time when there can't possibly be anybody spying on us or eavesdropping. If they happened to spot us on the way to the hotel I picked out, I would be a very disappointed girl."

16

Marshall sat behind the cashier's counter of the little gas station on a chair that must have been purchased in the sixties. The burlap-colored upholstery had a texture like military webbing, and six cigarette burns that were becoming familiar to him. The chrome on the frame had worn thin and begun to show rust specks. He said, "So you were sitting right where I am now?"

Dale Honecker said, "Yes sir," and nodded his head emphatically. "I heard a car, so I stood up to look."

"What could you see from here?"

"The old guy, and a woman driving. She gets out—"

"Wait," said Marshall. "She gets out. Which side?"

"This side. He's on the other side." Marshall thought about it. The gas cap on a Toyota Camry was on the left side, so she should have been on the other side of the pumps, where she wouldn't have to drag the hose across the car to fill it.

"Are you sure?"

"Uh . . . yes." So she was trying to keep the passenger away from the gas station, where the boy couldn't see him, thought Marshall.

"Then what?"

"Then she gets out, walks in, hands me a twenty, and says she's going to fill it."

"Describe her," said Marshall.

"Long, dark hair . . ."

"How old?"

"I don't know. Maybe twenty-five. Thin, pretty."

"Eye color?"

"I don't remember."

"What were you thinking?"

"I . . . I don't understand."

"It's very late at night. A car pulls up. You probably haven't seen many cars since around midnight. You look out the window. Why?"

"Because you get kind of jumpy sitting here alone in this lighted room all night. When somebody pulls in, I take a look to see if they look like they might rob me."

"Good. So what did you think when you saw this car?"

"I guess I felt kind of relieved. An old guy and this woman probably aren't about to stick me up."

"It's kind of an odd combination, though, isn't it? You didn't recognize Dahlman right away, did you?"

"No."

"So you had to think they were something else, right?"

"I guess so." Then he amended it. "I didn't really think."

"You're a night cashier in a self-service station," said Marshall. "When I used to work dull night shifts, and somebody came in, I used to play a little game, and sort of make up stories about them. You've got an old guy who pulls in with a woman maybe a third of his age, it's kind of interesting."

The young man looked alarmed. "I didn't make none of this up."

"I don't mean that," said Marshall. "I meant you might have thought, 'This is a father and daughter. He's sick, and she's taking him to the emergency room, but suddenly she sees she's out of gas. So she's in a hurry, maybe looking scared.' Or, 'This is some rich old guy who's making a fool of himself with a woman who's probably a hooker.' Or, 'This is an undercover policewoman who's taking the editor of the local paper on a ride-along to show him a crime scene.' " Marshall paused and waited. The young man's blue eyes were opaque, like marbles.

"I guess the last one."

Marshall wondered if he had heard correctly. "You mean you thought the woman was a police officer?"

"No," said Dale. "I didn't think anything. But if it was one of them, that would probably be the one. She wasn't scared or nervous, and she seemed kind of . . . tough. Not like prostitutes."

"Have you seen prostitutes?"

"Yes . . . not exactly. I mean I think I've seen them, but seeing them on a street isn't proof that's what they are. What I mean is she didn't look like the ones looked that I thought might be."

"Was she carrying a purse?"

"I don't know. I don't think so." He blinked and seemed to achieve clarity. "No. She pulled the money out of her jacket pocket."

"Wearing jewelry?"

"No."

"Not even a ring or a watch?"

"Maybe."

Marshall felt sorry for the boy. He said, "Okay. We'll get back to her. You took her money, turned on the pump, and sat down again to watch TV."

"No. She asked for the men's-room key. I gave it to her, then sat down. The news was on. I saw the picture of Dr. Dahlman, and he looked familiar. It was because I'd just seen this old guy in the car. But I wasn't sure. So I took the mop like I was going to swab the men's room. When he came out I got a good look. It was him."

"You're forgetting something."

"I am?"

"The gun. It's usually hidden by the cash register, over here?"

The boy nodded.

"What made you decide to take it with you?"

"I thought it was the smart thing to do. I mean, the guy was supposed to be a killer, right?"

"That's what I hear." Marshall felt tired, but he decided that it was part of his job. The kid was nineteen, and he had a long way to go. "Let's talk about that for a minute. You're alone. You see a man who's a killer, so you pick up a gun. What were you planning, a citizen's arrest?"

"Me? No. I just wanted to see if it was him."

"If it was, what would you do—shoot him?"

"Call the police."

"If that's what you wanted to accomplish, I have a suggestion. You see him. You duck down behind this counter, pick up the phone, and call the police right then. By the time he finishes filling up and using the men's room and paying, it's possible the cops could be here. At that time of night they're usually not too busy, and out here they can drive a hundred miles an hour without fear of killing anybody. They might very well have ended it right then. Or, you could have waited until the car left, watched which way it went, and then called the police."

The boy was confused. "But I wasn't sure."

"I understand the way you felt. But I've known a lot of cops over the years. They like getting called out for nothing a lot better than they like working around bodies."

The boy's unlined face seemed to elongate. "It was for self-defense."

Marshall's eyebrows knitted and his dark eyes looked apologetic. "I sympathize with you. There are so many decisions in a situation like this. One of the problems is that armed killers don't react the way you want them to. If you pull out a gun and say, 'Freeze,' they hardly ever do. They try to shoot you. They don't hesitate, but you do. Or they turn and run, and you have to decide. Maybe this is just some guy, running because a gas station attendant suddenly pulled a gun on him, and he has no idea he resembles some wanted killer. But maybe he's a killer running to get behind something and open up on you. If he's guilty, you can't let him reach cover. He knows you recognized him, and he knows you're alone late at night, and that the next thing you're going to do is call the police. If you make it to the phone, his chances will go from so-so to zero." Marshall rapped on the wallboard beside him and listened. "This wall won't stop a bullet." He seemed to remember something. "And in this case, you've got this woman to figure out."

"To figure out?"

"Well, who could she be?"

"I don't know."

"That puts you in a hard place. You saw on TV that the man is suspected of being a killer, but there wasn't anything on the news about her. It could be she's a hostage."

"He let her come in to pay. She couldn't be."

"Maybe he's got her month-old baby lying on the back seat. Maybe she's a hitchhiker he picked up, who knows nothing about any of this." Marshall gave him a moment to assess the possibilities and dream up a few of his own. "On the other hand, it could be she's an armed killer too. Before guns come out you've got to make a decision about her. Either protect her, or kill her—it's hard to do anything in between, because all a gun can do is put holes in people. Will you put one in her?"

The boy was lost, floundering. His blue eyes squinted, blinked, but this time it didn't seem to clear his mind.

Marshall pressed him. "Suppose you were in that position right now. What would you do about her?"

"I don't know."

"Make your best choice. Now."

"I don't know!" He was sweating, frustrated, angry. "What? What's the right answer?"

"You fired a round. Did you know what you were shooting at?"

"I fired through the door. I heard bangs, and I thought they were shooting at me."

"Who was?"

"Whoever was shooting."

"And what they really were doing was nailing the door shut. Right?"

"I guess so . . . well, yeah."

Marshall nodded and thought for a moment. "You've worked in a gas station for a while. You must know that firing blind through a door in the direction of the pumps is a little risky. You must have thought you were saving your life. In that half second you had a brief, clear vision of what you were shooting at. Was it him, or was it her?"

"Mmmmm." The boy was straining, trying to see it and feel it again.

"Who?"

"Him."

"Are you sure?"

"Him. I was afraid of being killed, and he was the killer. I saw him right there a few seconds before, coming out. I wasn't thinking about where she was. When I heard the bangs, I fired at him."

"But not her."

"Not her." He was full of indignation and shame. "Who is she?"

Marshall shrugged. "You're the only one who's seen her. When you thought your life depended on it, what you guessed was that she wasn't the problem. So for the moment, she's a woman he picked up who doesn't watch much TV."

"But I'm not sure of any of it."

Marshall said, "No, but one thing we know is, if they're both hardened killers, neither of them is any great shakes at it."

"Why?"

"All they had to do was look at the hole in the men's-room door, and fire eight or ten rounds at it. Then you and I wouldn't be having this conversation."

Marshall stood in the lot at the Reliable rental agency in Akron and watched the forensics team going over the car again. The preliminary notes were in his hand, and he knew that what the two women and two men were doing now was wasting time. In his twenty-two years as an agent he had watched this ritual hundreds of times. The F.B.I.'s big edge was in lab work. If there was something in the car that they had missed the first time—really, the first four times, because there was only room in the car for one person to search—then it was probably a sample that wasn't big enough for the lab to analyze.

The car had a few hairs left by unidentified people, none of whom happened to be a female with long dark hair or a gray-haired male over fifty. There were fingerprints of the sales agent who had moved the car to the cleaning area, the man who had vacuumed it, hosed it off, and wiped the chrome and windows, then filled the gas tank and parked it in the ready space. It had a few prints on the hood latch, the air filter cover, and the gas door from the man's colleagues in Youngstown.

The part about Youngstown had brought its own complex of worrisome facts. The car had been rented in Youngstown by a woman named Kathy Sirini, whose credit card bills went to a P.O. box in New York City. Someone had turned the car in at Akron, fifty miles west of Youngstown and a day later. Marshall's experience told him that things didn't look good for Kathy Sirini. Someone—presumably Kathy Sirini—had been seen at a gas station, heading west in this car with a man suspected of killing another woman. The car was left in the rental lot at the airport, but Kathy Sirini hadn't bought a ticket. She hadn't rented another car. She hadn't made any new charges with her credit card, although it had been three days since then and she was far from home.

The New York office was trying to find her apartment now, but the P.O. box made it difficult. A lot of young single women in New York lived with roommates or boyfriends who had signed the lease—or in rent-controlled apartments in the names of people who had moved on decades ago. It was possible that whoever cared about Kathy Sirini wasn't going to report her missing until she was a week late at the end of her vacation, or she missed the family reunion in Nebraska. Kathy Sirini was almost certainly dead.

The case had begun with the kind of disorder that most undermined Marshall's sense of well-being. The death of a young woman doctor was disturbing: it seemed to have exacerbated the sense of waste that he always felt when he came close to a killing. The probability that she had been murdered by a man like Richard Dahlman made Marshall feel jumpy and unsettled. The case seemed to want to force its own conclusion on the investigator, and the conclusion was that sanity was only a fragile and temporary balance in the human organism, like perfect tuning. At any second, any human being might subtly, invisibly change and start coldly, methodically butchering his friends and neighbors. It was not inconceivable that such a thing could happen, and a good many people close to the case seemed to have accepted it already. But from the beginning, Marshall had been turning up facts that didn't fit, and didn't go away.

Richard Dahlman was the wrong kind of man for the sudden, self-destructive kind of murder. The ones who did this were younger—fifty at the oldest. They were rarely successful in life, and seldom well-educated. They were modern society's casualties: men who kept getting dead-end jobs and then losing them, getting connected with some woman and then losing her too, because the failure or the bitterness or the accumulating evidence that the future was never going to be any different drove her off. Each time one of them loaded all of the clips for his assault rifle and barricaded himself in his apartment, the newsmen would say it was totally unexpected, and it was. But after the investigation had been completed, Marshall always found a list of incidents—threats that got more and more specific, outbursts that were more and more violent—that retroactively charted a kind of downward trajectory.

Dr. Dahlman seemed to have no trajectory. He had succeeded at everything. He had maintained what appeared to be a loving marriage for over thirty years, until his wife's death, and nobody had yet found any evidence that her death had been suspicious. He had raised a set of normal, or at least high-functioning, children, and had managed to gain the respect of a couple of generations of other doctors.

The evidence the police had found seemed to show that Dahlman had quietly developed some festering mental delusion that had led him to kill his partner. The strange little shrine to his secret hatred of his victim was standard, recognizable evidence of madness. There were the usual photographs, the little possessions like pens and notes that he could have taken without her missing them. That was what searches turned up when a killer heard supernatural voices and saw the act as sacrifice or fulfillment of some metaphysical destiny. But the killing itself didn't fit the pattern. It should have been ritualized in some way, not faked as an interrupted burglary. That was what killers did when they wanted to collect on an insurance policy.

The premeditation, the ability to lie with conviction, the habit of looking at any new configuration of human beings as an opportunity, suggested something far more ominous than a simple mental breakdown. And Dahlman's behavior since the killing was carefully calculated and self-preserving. He was not acting like someone who had lost control, but like someone who was exerting control of a very special sort. It was just possible that when Dr. Dahlman had constructed his little shrine he had not been gearing up for the killing: he had been coldly, rationally thinking about the risk that something might go wrong, and building himself a defense. It was the sort of thing a sociopath would do, and they usually had histories. They didn't wait until they were sixty-seven. This train of thought led Marshall back to Kathy Sirini, the girl with the long dark hair who had rented this car.

He sighed. He could see that every part of the car that was covered with black fingerprint powder also had tape marks where the print had already been lifted. The forensic people were beginning to give one another inquiring glances.

"What do you say?" he asked. "Think you've found everything?"

The senior specialist, who would have been a fair match for Dale Honecker's description of the woman in the gas station, said, "We've got about all we're going to get. I guess we can release it now."

"Better have the local police store it for the moment," he said. "Somebody may want to look it over again later."

"Later?" She cocked her head.

"If her body turns up."

She nodded with no trace of surprise and turned away to take charge of the preparations. He could tell she had thought of the possibility that she wasn't just verifying a sighting of a fugitive and looking for fibers from what he was wearing. If the next big rain washed Kathy Sirini's body out of some hillside between here and Youngstown, the car would be evidence in a second murder trial. It was just possible that by the time this was over and enough of Dahlman's history was known to make it coherent, there would be indications that there had been other bodies in other places.

17

The big stone house under the maple trees, where Carey McKinnon and his father and grandfather and all of the McKinnons since the 1790s had lived, built on land that before the McKinnons had arrived had belonged to her own relatives, the house where she had come to stay with him and be his wife, was now a prison.

Outside the front window one of the guards jogged past in a dark blue sweatsuit. The woman's hair was gathered in a ponytail and in her ear was what looked like the earphone for a transistor radio, but there was no reason for a person to talk back to an AM station.

If Jane stood to the side of the front window she could just see the corner of the Water Department van parked two doors down the street. The day after she had come home the van had appeared; two men in coveralls had set up highway cones and reflectors and gone back inside. Each morning they had taken out their equipment—toolboxes, surveyor's transits, even a compressor, and then done nothing.

Jane had spent the following two days cleaning. The microphone in the dining room attached to the underside of the antique sideboard was so amateurish that she was sure it was there to get her to take it out and assume there wasn't another somewhere else. The ones in the living room were relatively good: nobody but Jane was likely to manipulate a hand mirror and a flashlight to see a microphone stuck to the inner wall of a chimney, and the funnel shape of the fireplace probably acted to amplify sounds. The one in the table lamp had not just been stuck there. The base had been taken off and the wire split, spliced, and reconnected so the house current powered the microphone.

That was ominous, because it meant the technicians had been warned of the possibility that the surveillance might continue beyond the life of a battery. The kitchen had been bugged the same way, under the ventilation hood, with a little rewiring.

Jane had not bothered to try to find the bugs in the master bedroom. She had instead devoted her energy to the least likely guest bedroom, at the end of the hall, and taken it apart. The lamps were clean, the bed was clean, the bathroom was clean. She had taken all of the drawers out of the dresser because the backs and undersides of drawers were a favorite location. She had unscrewed the heat registers and the hollow rails of the towel racks. Since the F.B.I. was probably involved, she had unplugged the telephone. Devices existed for picking up and amplifying the faint signals that still came down the wire when the receiver was in its cradle.

That night she and Carey had slept in the master bedroom as usual, with a tape recorder running. The next night she and Carey had undressed in the master bedroom and turned off the lights. Then Jane had turned on the tape recorder and led Carey down the hall.

On her seventh day at home, Jane wrote Carey a note. It said, "I need Cipro, tape, dressings, etc. Can you get them?" Carey scrawled "Yes," and reached to crumple the paper, but Jane held his hand and shook her head. The noise would be recognizable. Later she lit it at a stove burner, dropped it in the sink, and ran the ashes through the garbage disposal.

On the eighth day, before Carey came home from the hospital, she prepared him a written list marked "August":

Cherry Creek Powwow, Eagle Butte, South Dakota
Crow Creek Powwow, Fort Thompson, South Dakota
Rosebud Fair and Rodeo, Rosebud, South Dakota
Looking Glass Powwow, Lapwai, Idaho
Makah Festival, Neah Bay, Washington
Shoshone-Bannock Indian Festival and Rodeo, Fort Hall, Idaho
Chief Seattle Days, Suquamish, Washington
Omak Stampede Days, Nespelem, Washington
Grand Portage Rendezvous, Grand Portage, Minnesota

Ni-mi-win Celebration, Duluth, Minnesota
Land of the Menominee Powwow, Keshena, Wisconsin
Passamaquoddy Ceremonial, Perry, Maine
Ponca Indian Fair and Powwow, Ponca City, Oklahoma
Wichita Tribal Powwow, Anadarko, Oklahoma
Intertribal Indian Ceremonial, Church Rock, New Mexico

She randomly assigned dates to the August gatherings without regard to the real calendar. Then, to complicate everything, she added, "Remember, August is the month of the Green Corn celebration for all of us Hodenosaunee. I might make it to Cattaraugus, Tonawanda, Six Nations, Oneida, Onondaga, Akwesasne, Allegany, or Tuscarora near the end (30th or 31st). I'll try to call." She smiled. Just that list would give the F.B.I. plenty to sort out, and if they decided to keep an eye on her, they would have plenty of women with long black hair to look at. She stopped for a moment, and repeated the thought to herself: plenty of black-haired women.

She spent most of her time studying the police. Each morning the policewoman would put on her running suit and jog past the house at the same hour. The shift changed right after that, so no doubt she went home for her shower. The new shift included two men who followed Carey to work at 6:30, and two men to putter around the Water Department truck and monitor the bugs. Jane began to experiment with these two to see what happened when she left the house.

The answer was not unexpected. If Carey was already at work, then one man followed and the other stayed in the van to monitor the bugs. If she drove to the market, or drove to the river and jogged five miles, or went out, drove around the block, and came back, as though she had forgotten something, one man followed and the other stayed in the van.

She had been half-expecting that when she left, the man in the truck would head for the house to read their mail, but if they worked for the F.B.I., she supposed they would have read it before it was delivered. And the men obviously felt that hearing a live call from Dahlman instead of listening to it on tape ten minutes later was critical, but searching the house periodically to get evidence on Carey was not. That was a good sign.

Jane began to introduce variations on the routine in order to get them bored and overconfident. Sometimes she was in a big hurry, heading straight for the Thruway just above the speed limit. Once she drove to the airport, but that didn't seem to make the follower nervous. Once she left late at night, and still the chase car kept its distance. The only way she could get them to add a second car was to pick up Carey and drag his follower along with hers.

On the ninth day she opened the newspaper and read the headlines: LAWMAKERS CAUGHT IN F.B.I. STING. There had been yet another patient, quiet effort to offer bribes to a group of congressmen, but judging from the article, the F.B.I. had become more sophisticated in the past few years, and played the game the way it was normally played. They had not dressed up like visiting Middle Eastern potentates. They had not had sleazy bagmen hand over briefcases full of cash in motel rooms. Instead they had gotten the cooperation of four genuine lobbyists, who had gone to congressional offices during business hours and offered checks made out to congressmen's campaign funds in exchange for their explicit promises to sell their votes. The F.B.I. had then waited until a bogus law had been introduced and the congressmen's votes recorded. It was good, but it wasn't good for Jane. The old stings had been more vivid, and drawn more attention.

She looked down the page. There was a train crash near Boise, Idaho, the murders of three policemen in New Jersey. On the second page there were a few hot local issues, including a chemical company caught dumping waste in Lake Erie at night. Pages three and four ran the international stories that were probably important but didn't sell newspapers. The second section of the paper had human-interest stories and what amounted to free publicity for various events arranged by public-spirited groups. She kept turning the pages and searching, but there was not a word about Richard Dahlman.

That afternoon she went to the public library on Main Street in Deganawida. A few minutes after she had gone to the corner to search the newspapers of other cities, Amy the librarian appeared at her shoulder. "Jane . . ."

Jane looked up and smiled. "Hi, Amy."

Amy took off the silver spectacles that she wore only when she was working. "I know this is going to sound crazy . . ."

"Really?" asked Jane. "Then I'd love to hear it."

Amy's eyebrows tilted apologetically. "There's this man who pulled up across the street just after you came in."

Jane said, "Tall, kind of cute, like a young prizefighter with dark, curly hair?"

Amy put on her glasses again and looked over them at Jane. "I thought he was a little creepy."

Jane shrugged and looked back down at her *San Francisco Chronicle*. "He's waiting for me, all right. He's not a creep, though. He's a policeman. He doesn't wear a wedding ring, and with the hours he keeps I don't think he's married."

"But you are, you bad thing."

"I was offering him to you. It's not social. He's got me under surveillance."

Amy was shocked. "Why?"

"It's nothing, really. Carey operated on that man a couple of weeks ago. You know, the one who was supposed to be a murderer?"

"Well, of course I knew that. But why are the police . . ." Then her eyes widened. "It was a woman he killed. Did he threaten you or something?"

"No. I never met him," said Jane. "But Carey used to know him. I guess they think he's dangerous."

"You didn't even ask them?"

Jane shook her head. "The one out there isn't bothering me, and if there's any chance we really are in danger, it would be nice to have our own family cop." She stared into Amy's eyes. "Of course, you wouldn't mention this to a soul, right?"

Amy said, "Of course not." After a few seconds she drifted off toward her desk to pretend she wasn't studying the police officer in the parked car. Jane was satisfied. Unlike most people, Amy actually wouldn't volunteer anything about it, but if anyone happened to notice it, she would feel she had to explain. Jane was glad that the explanation made a better rumor than anything so familiar as a woman cheating on her husband.

Jane went through ten newspapers from major cities. Most of them had headlines about the congressional scandal. A few had pressing local issues that bumped the Washington story to the bottom of the page. Not one ran anything about Richard Dahlman in the front section, and only four mentioned him at all. He was old news. She had no illusion that the F.B.I. would let him be entirely forgotten. If they had to, they would probably release a negative progress report just to get a few lines of print.

For the next few days, their spokesmen would be kept busy with the congressional sting. It was clearly an instance when they had fearlessly done what they were supposed to do, and done it superbly, so they would have to devote the week to weathering the publicity. They had enough experience to know that the network news shows would run with the scandal, and that they would never devote two segments to interviews with the same F.B.I. men on the same night. It wasn't good TV.

Jane smiled at Amy as she left the library. Amy glanced again at the police officer's car, and returned Jane's smile conspiratorially. Jane felt a little guilty. Amy wouldn't have smiled if she had known that the cop had no purpose parking this close unless his car was equipped with a directional microphone that would pick up the vibrations of speech on the big front windows of the library.

Jane's time under surveillance with Carey was like a play in which nothing ever happened. At breakfast each morning they spoke about the probable temperature and the likelihood of rain while they held hands and caressed each other gently and soundlessly. In the late morning when Carey was out of surgery, he would call her on the telephone and say it was because he had forgotten to tell her what time he would be home for dinner, or ask her if she had paid the electric bill, or say that he had run into someone at the hospital who had sent her regards. He never said it was because he wanted to hear her voice, and knew that very soon she would be gone and he might never hear it again.

In the evening, she would sometimes drive to the hospital to take Carey out to dinner and then wait for him in his office down the street while he made his rounds of his patients' rooms. During the long nights they would be entwined in each other's arms with their eyes open, not daring to speak for fear their jailers would hear and know they were in the wrong room.

During the day, Jane made her movements erratic, her routes unpredictable, and her destinations dull and quotidian. If she wanted to shop, she drove to a shopping center on the Youngmann Expressway or the New York State Thruway, got off at the wrong exit and then drove back, parked in the lot for one store and walked to another. If she wanted to go to a restaurant, she would go in the front door and leave through the back. When she drove out to the reservation to visit her old friends Violet and Billy Peterson, she parked on Sandy Road and walked through the chestnut grove to come out across from their house under the big hemlock.

Three times, Jane left the house just as a shift of watchers was about to be relieved by a fresh team. Nothing she did seemed to disconcert them. They operated on a series of situational models that they all knew, so no unexpected movement caused them to hesitate or confer. The person nearest to a car, from whatever shift, went after her. That officer followed her until she stopped, and then that person was replaced. The one time she made her move when there happened to be two people from different shifts in the same car, they both went after her.

On the tenth evening, Jane posted her bogus schedule on the bulletin board beside the telephone and called to make a plane reservation for a morning flight to South Dakota in the name Violet Peterson. She pulled her car out to the street, parked, put a suitcase in the trunk, and went back into the house.

Before long, the surveillance team saw Dr. and Mrs. McKinnon leaving the house. This time Mrs. McKinnon wore a light blue summer dress and carried a large canvas shoulder bag. A single car with two team members followed the black BMW to a small Italian restaurant on Main, then remained outside to watch them through the front window.

The directional microphone picked up little that seemed reportable. The subjects of the surveillance said they loved each other. This was not news. The male said that he wished he were accompanying the female on her trip. The female said she wished it were possible too, but that his job was to keep cutting open unsuspecting patients and removing things until he had paid for her trip. The ironic tone she used was familiar to the listeners, and the topic only confirmed for the team what they had already learned from the wire tap and the stationary observation vehicle: the female subject had made a flight reservation under the pseudonym Violet Peterson, packed a bag, and left it in her car on the street.

The team then followed the McKinnons to a large shopping plaza where they had followed Mrs. McKinnon before, and watched them enter a large movie theater complex called Cinema 12. It was observed that, after studying the marquee where the times and titles were posted, the female subject picked Theater 5, where a British-made film that was reputed to be romantic was about to begin. The male purchased two tickets, and the couple entered the big lobby and walked to the set of doors with a number 5 above it in blue neon.

One of the watchers, Officer David Foalts, bought a ticket for Theater 5, went in during the opening credits, and sat alone in the back row. The second, Sergeant Roger Horowitz, stayed in the chase car to watch the door and the BMW and monitor the radio.

After the film began, Mrs. McKinnon stood and walked up the aisle. Officer Foalts's training told him that he had options. He could remain where he was and assume that Mrs. McKinnon would go to the ladies' room or the snack counter and return. Ordinarily he might have gone out to the lobby and verified the obvious while keeping his eye on the only nonemergency door to Theater 5, then followed her back in. But the standing order was to watch Dr. McKinnon at all times, while Mrs. McKinnon's situation was not quite as clear.

It was just possible that leaving the theater at the beginning of the film was her way of luring Foalts away from her husband. Officer Foalts decided not to risk letting Mrs. McKinnon see him make a move. Mrs. McKinnon's call to the airline had been the first thing either of them had done since the beginning of the surveillance that showed promise of revealing anything. His superiors in the Buffalo police department and his colleagues in the F.B.I. would be very upset if she were spooked into canceling her trip.

Foalts stayed in the back and watched Dr. McKinnon. After what seemed to him to be a long time, he heard the door to the theater behind him open and close. The complex was new and well designed. A person had to enter a little anteroom and walk two paces before opening the inner door, and in that time, the outer door would automatically close to prevent a splash of light from disrupting the movie. Officer Foalts saw the shape he had been waiting for float down the aisle past him—a tall, thin woman, the long, straight black hair hanging at the back of the pale blue dress, the canvas shoulder bag. The shape found McKinnon in the dim light from the screen and sat down beside him.

Foalts stayed in the back until the film was about to end. He slipped out the door through the tiny anteroom and waited in the rear of the lobby near the back entrance that opened into the enclosed shopping mall. When the film in Theater 5 ended and the crowd streamed out, he faded into it and followed the couple outside. He rejoined Sergeant Horowitz in the chase car, and when the male and female subjects got into the BMW and drove away, the two policemen followed.

The BMW returned to the McKinnon house, and the team observed lights going on in the upstairs rooms, then going off. Officer Kemmel in the monitoring van heard the usual footsteps, the usual swishing noises of clothes being taken off, water running, toilets flushing, the clicks of light switches, the creaks of bedsprings. There was even less conversation than usual. The male subject said, "You'd better get some sleep. You have an early start," and the female said, "Uh-hunh."

At five A.M. the next shift observed a tall, slim woman with dark hair leaving the house and driving off in the car that had been parked in front. A team was waiting for her at the airport. As expected, the woman checked the bag that had been in the car trunk, then went to the downstairs desk and showed identification that said she was Violet Peterson. F.B.I. agent William Grey surreptitiously photographed her while she was waiting for her plane and moved off to transmit the photographs electronically. Agents Leah Caldicott and Ralph Mandessi boarded the flight to Chicago after her.

A second set of agents, using Grey's photographs, waited for her at Chicago, where they followed her onto the flight to Rapid City, South Dakota. They reported that in her entire journey, she appeared to meet no one, and to speak to no one who didn't work for the airline.

In Rapid City, she went to a car-rental agency and picked out a red Ford Escort. She drove the car from Rapid City east on Route 90 to Wall, near Badlands National Park, then took 14 north, switched to 63 outside Hayes, drove north across Cherry Creek onto the Cheyenne River Indian Reservation. She checked into a motel in Eagle Butte, and the F.B.I. agents settled in to wait. It was ten hours since she had driven to the Greater Buffalo International Airport, and seventeen since she had left the Cinema 12 complex. Then the subject of the surveillance showered and went to sleep.

At approximately that moment, Jane Whitefield was driving into the parking lot behind the apartment complex in Waterloo, Iowa, still trying to decide what her present to Violet Peterson would be. She supposed it would have to depend on what sort of inconvenience the F.B.I. caused for Vi and Billy. If they held Vi overnight in some women's jail and frightened her, then a bouquet of flowers would seem like a pretty empty gesture. If she just got to spend a week or two at a few major Indian get-togethers at Jane's expense, then anything more than the flowers would offend her.

Jane had no doubt that Vi had done the job properly. When Jane had arrived in the ladies' room at Cinema 12, Vi had already been waiting. She had quickly changed from her jeans and sweatshirt into Jane's pale blue dress, then helped Jane braid her hair, pin it into a bun, and fit the baseball cap over it.

Jane had said, "Are you sure you can handle this?"

"What's to handle? I'll have a plane ticket in my own name to take me to a legitimate party. Billy is envious."

"I'm sorry I can't tell you what this is all about."

Violet had shrugged. "It's about a small favor for a clan sister." Then she had given Jane a little push.

When Jane had turned back and kissed her cheek, she had caught a glimpse of the two heads and torsos in the bathroom mirror. There was a blur of shining black hair, Violet's skin a half shade darker than Jane's and her eyes black, but their shapes were almost identical. Even the little turn as Violet raised her shoulder to shrug off the peck on the cheek was familiar: Jane had done it herself.

Jane had left the ladies' room, slipped into the gaggle of people leaving Theater 8, hurried across the lobby to the rear entrance that opened onto the shiny floor of the mall, and kept walking. She had not looked back until she'd reached the far end of the mall and made her last check to see if the policemen had followed. Then she'd gone out, found the car that Violet Peterson had left for her in the lot, and driven it into the night to the south and west toward Iowa.

18

M arshall watched Dale Honecker pick up the color photograph of the dark-haired woman that had been taken at the Buffalo airport. He pinched it with his fingers at the edges as though it were a glossy print, probably because somebody had once told him he would ruin a picture if he touched it. This one was printed by a computer. Honecker rested it on his lap. He squinted, then held it at arm's length. In a minute, he was going to say yes, that's the one, and Marshall would have to put him through a few tricks to be sure he wasn't just saying yes because it would please Marshall.

"No," said Dale Honecker.

Marshall's mind raced. Had he piled so much weight on the side of caution that he had paralyzed the boy? Could there possibly be two women? "Okay," said Marshall evenly. "How about these?"

He handed the boy four photographs that he had printed out from the Wanted List. All of them were pictures taken at bookings, so the women had little black placards under their chins with white NCIC numbers and lines behind them that gauged their height. The boy leafed through them carefully. He handed Marshall one of them. "This looks a little bit like her, but it isn't her."

Marshall looked at the picture. It was Smithson, Wanda Dee, wanted in Alabama for manufacturing and sale of methamphetamines. She had a triangular Anglo-Saxon face with a thin, pointed nose and deep, clear blue eyes. Her hair was long and straight, parted in the middle, and it was bright, luminescent blond. Marshall said, "Something in particular about her?"

"The eyes, I think," said Honecker. "And I guess the hair too."

Marshall studied the boy. "I thought the woman you saw had black hair. And the eyes . . . you didn't know what color they were."

"Yeah, I guess so," said the boy. He frowned uncomfortably at the floor. "You know those police artists? Maybe if you could get one of them . . ."

Marshall nodded unenthusiastically. "You might be right. The problem is, I haven't had very good luck with them in the past. It's possible my bosses will send one to you at some point, but as a rule, they haven't worked too well for me. I heard somebody say once, 'If they were any good as artists, why would they want to be cops?' But I think it's more complicated than that. There's something about the way faces get recorded in the memory that isn't like a photograph. You remember something distinctive—the style of the hair, or the shape of the eyes, but your mind doesn't hold on to the rest. Maybe you can describe what you saw in words, and maybe not. So the artist has to fill in the blanks with something he thinks you must have seen. Then everybody in the country looks at this line drawing. We get calls turning in all the young women who have long, straight hair and pretty eyes. Now, that's quite a few. In fact, I'd say that they're one of our greatest natural resources."

"It was just an idea," muttered Honecker. "Trying to help."

"I know," said Marshall. "We appreciate it, too. But see, I don't know if she did anything, and if she did, sketches can come back to haunt us in court. Usually if you hold the picture up next to the defendant, you have to stretch your imagination pretty far to convince yourself they're the same person. This makes juries extremely nervous." He smiled. "If I bring you the right picture, you'll recognize it?"

"I guess so," said Honecker.

Marshall stood up and walked to the front door of the Honecker house. There were four flies buzzing and making crazy circles to batter themselves against the screen. They could smell the dinner Honecker's mother was making in the kitchen. Marshall said, "We'll find the right one. And don't get impatient. It may take time."

He slipped outside the screen door without letting the flies in, then crossed the wooden porch and went down the steps. He was convinced now that Dale Honecker's memory was not going to be the answer. Honecker had seen the woman, but within seconds he had also seen a dangerous killer. His instinct for self-preservation had forced his attention away from her.

As Marshall drove onto the highway he conceded that there was no basis for adding anything to what he had already published about the woman. She had long, dark hair, and she was young. He had allowed himself to imagine that she was Jane McKinnon, going around the country on some misguided amateur attempt to save her husband's old teacher. But the boy had just looked at a clear, fresh photograph of Jane McKinnon taken at the Buffalo airport, and said it wasn't.

Marshall had no choice but to lean toward the hypothesis he liked least: the dark-haired woman was likely to have been Kathy Sirini, the young traveler from New York who had rented the car in Youngstown. Dahlman had gotten her to give him a ride, and somehow either won her over or kept her ignorant while she drove him to his next stop. Then he had killed her and buried the body somewhere out here in the Iowa countryside, not to be discovered until a month from now, when some farmer went out to check the alfalfa in the north forty and smelled something awful.

19

Dahlman seemed affable, almost manic tonight, talking as though he had done nothing but wait for her to come back so he could have someone listen. And Jane listened politely while she prepared dinner, making a sound only when he paused. As Jane and Dahlman finished their dinner in the little apartment's kitchen, he said, "It's been an interesting exercise, living here for twelve days. It's been nearly half a century since I've lived in a big apartment building with people at close quarters like this, but things never change at all. The games the children play are the same. Has anyone ever found out how they all learn that awful chant—nyah-nyah nyah-nyah-nyah? They seem to be born knowing it."

Jane said quietly, "You've had a hard time, haven't you?"

He made a face. "I can't complain. I've been safe, and I'm healing nicely. And I've done a lot of thinking."

Jane said, "What about?"

Dahlman said, "Have you ever been in prison?"

"Yes," said Jane. "A couple of times, but not much longer than you were."

Dahlman nodded. "It's not entirely different from this. You can't talk to anyone, really, or open the door." He said, "I would like to apologize for getting you involved. When I heard of you, I wasn't sure you even existed, but there seemed to be no reason not to look. There was no other direction that led to any destination at all."

Jane sensed that something big was coming. "It doesn't really make much difference how this happened."

"It does," he said. "You see, I was sure you weren't going to come back, and I'd be rid of you. But here you are. I think it's time for you to go back to your husband. I'll go in the opposite direction for some distance before I'm caught, so there won't be any obvious connection with you."

"Sorry," said Jane. "It's a lousy idea."

He waggled his head in frustration. "I'm sixty-seven years old. I've had a satisfying life, and a useful one. But it's mostly over. If I'm caught, the people I care about—my children, a few colleagues, my patients—will never believe I'm a murderer. All of that matters. But the rest of this doesn't. If I go to jail, my productive life is over. If I stay in hiding, my productive life is over. Even if I'm cleared, it could take five years of jails and lawyers. I won't be able to return to operating on patients at the age of seventy-two."

"I don't know what will happen, and neither do you," said Jane. "It could be that you'll think of something that cures cancer."

"And it could be that you'll go home and save the world from hunger, or bear the child who rids the world of ignorance."

She laughed and shook her head. "This isn't the heart-transplant business. You don't look down at two people on stretchers and say, 'This one is young and that one is old, so I have to save the young one because she has more potential for the future.' The truth is, there isn't much chance for either of us. There's none at all if you give up."

"Why not?" he asked.

"They're already convinced that Carey helped you, and by now they've got their suspicions about me," she said. "If you get caught and convicted, it won't exonerate us. It will just change our crime from obstructing justice to accessory to murder. And if you get killed it's worse, because if there's a trial our side at least gets to say something."

Jane moved into the living room. Dahlman looked at her in disappointment. "I see."

Jane stopped at the door of the bedroom. "I'm tired. I've been driving for a night and a day. Wake me if you smell tear gas."

Jane lay on the bed and closed her eyes, consciously letting the muscles at each of her joints relax—first the toes and fingers, then the ankles and wrists, knees and elbows, shoulders and hips, then slowly, each vertebra along her back to her neck. For a time her mind struggled with bright impressions of headlights and the reflective signs along the superhighways, and white dashes between lanes shooting toward her out of the darkness like tracer rounds. Then darkness came, and Jane began to dream.

In her dream she was lying in the darkened apartment. She heard a sound, like something scratching against the door. She tried to ignore it for a time, but then she realized that she would have to get up and see what it was. She walked to the window beside the front door, stood on the chair, and looked out over the top of the blinds. On the little concrete slab outside sat a big black dog. With its keen senses it was aware of her instantly, and it turned its broad head upward to look in the window at her.

Jane stepped to the door and opened it. "Go home, boy," she whispered. "Home."

The dog turned and began to walk down the sidewalk into the dark, and Jane had an overwhelming feeling that she had to follow. She stepped onto the little slab and quietly closed the door behind her, then walked off after it. The dog reached the small circle of light from the street lamp at the intersection, then stopped and looked back at her. Jane stopped too. The dog came to her, then started across the street, and Jane went with it.

She followed it until she came to a small city park with big trees and a tiny old-fashioned bandstand with a roof on it. As she approached the bandstand, she saw that one of the pillars was out of symmetrical alignment. Then the pillar moved. It was a man. Jane called up to the man, "Is this your dog?" She turned to look down at it, but the dog was gone. Part of Jane's mind knew that she was dreaming: when she'd stopped looking at the dog, it had ceased to exist.

The man's soft, gentle voice made Jane's eyes water and her throat tighten. "What the hell am I going to do with a dog?" It was Harry's voice, and Harry was dead.

Harry the gambler stepped forward into the moonlight. He was as she remembered him, a bit on the short side and balding, with clothes that had once cost more than they should have but had been worn too long. She even remembered the expression that appeared on his face now—apologetic and regretful. "I'm sorry to make you come out here, honey. But I find it hard to go into a little furnished apartment like that. You understand."

It was true. The first step into the apartment had triggered Jane's memory of the place where Harry had died—the color of the carpet, the arrangement of the windows—but while she was awake she had forced the thought out of her mind. Harry shrugged his shoulders and the suit coat rode up on his arms, so he tugged the cuffs, then lifted his chin to straighten his tie. Even in the moonlight she could see the big, crude stitches the undertaker had used to close the place where John Felker had cut his throat. They were like the ones she had taken in Dahlman's back.

Jane climbed the steps and put her arms around him. His body was cold and thin. Jane said, "I'm sorry, Harry. I'm so sorry. You got killed in an apartment like that. And it was my fault that he found you."

Harry stepped back and lowered his head, but his sad eyes were still on her. He snapped his fingers. "Must have slipped my mind."

"I've wanted to tell you something for a long time, but I couldn't," she said. "It wasn't that I didn't think you were important enough, and didn't try to protect you. It was a mistake."

He looked away for a second, then tried to smile. "Will you please stop nagging me about that? I'm just dead, not immortal and all-forgiving." He reached out and tried to pat her shoulder, but his hand was cold and stiff. "I'm sorry I had to come now."

"Why did you?"

"I'm an expert on long shots."

"You're not an expert," she said softly. "An expert is somebody who wins."

Harry nodded. "I won a lot and lost a lot. By the time I came to you I didn't look like much, but I felt the same. I felt young, like I had plenty of life left." He sighed. "You gave me a few extra years. Nobody else would do anything."

"And?"

"You're about to lose your ass."

"How?"

"That old man is six feet two, thin and craggy, and sixty-seven. You disguise him, he ain't getting any shorter, younger, or less craggy. How long is this man going to stay invisible?"

"I don't know," Jane admitted. "Who's going to find him?"

Harry shook his head sympathetically. "All the horses cross the finish line eventually. Who cares which one is first?"

"I do. I finally have a life of my own, Harry. I love my husband. I wanted a future—kids, an old age maybe."

Harry threw up his hands in despair. "That's why I'm scared for you, honey. A perfect example."

"Of what?"

"You don't even know what game you're playing. Your personal life is not on the table tonight." He sighed mightily, then gave a little shiver to shake off the topic. "Somebody's in a business you happen to know a lot about. They got a client's face changed. They killed all the people who saw both the old face and the new face except one. They got the murders blamed on the one that's left."

"How do I stop them?"

"You don't stop them. Their guy is vanished, resettled somewhere. Yours is a murder suspect. The hand's over. Hear that clicking noise? It's the sound of them raking all the chips over to their side of the table."

"If it's over, why are you coming into my dream?"

"Me?" said Harry. "I'll be with you forever. I'm your mistake."

"And now Dahlman too."

"Don't count him until it's over."

"But you said it was over."

"I said that hand was over," Harry corrected her. "It's not you and Dahlman against them and their client. Dahlman and the client are just stakes. The game is between players, not chips."

Harry walked toward the other side of the bandstand, and as he approached the steps, she reached out toward him.

"Wait, Harry," she said. "Don't go."

Harry stopped and turned to her. "I never really was much use to anybody. I should have left your sleep alone."

"What do I do?"

"You win, and Hawenneyu, the Right-Handed Twin, gets a point. Or you lose, and Hanegoategeh, the Left-Handed Twin, gets a point, and the brothers grow another player to take your place."

"How do I keep Dahlman alive?"

Harry's brow furrowed, as though he were trying to formulate a way to divulge a secret he wasn't supposed to. "Why can't just any yokel fan the deck face-down and pick out the king of spades?"

Jane awoke, trying to answer, but Harry was gone. She sat up. "They're all the same." She got out of bed and began to pack Dahlman's suitcase.

It was nine-thirty in the morning three days later when Jane walked Richard Dahlman into the front entrance of the complex in Carlsbad, California, for their appointment. The architecture of the place was an artifact of a Spanish California that had sprung spontaneously from the imagination of an architect sometime during the 1920s and had taken hold. Certain parts of the state looked as though the Spanish colonists had left behind not just a few missions, but an array of shopping malls, restaurants, and office buildings.

The stylized script embedded in the far wall of the lobby said "Senior Rancho," and Jane remembered that what Los Angeles County called its big prison in the sparse hills above the city was Honor Rancho. She whispered to Dahlman, "How does it look so far?"

"It looks comfortable, like a campus . . . if a bit impersonal."

She used the time as they walked. "Remember. You're Alan Weems. You're not a doctor. You know nothing. I'll tell all the necessary lies. I'm your daughter Julia Kieler. And don't keep looking at your hair in the reflections of the windows. White hair makes you look distinguished."

The receptionist directed Julia Kieler and Alan Weems into the office for the appointment with the "intake counselor," who introduced herself as Mrs. Paxton but called Dahlman "Alan" from the instant she saw him. After a few seconds she had the receptionist usher Alan through the lobby into a large garden. Mrs. Paxton told him, "We want to be sure this is a place where you'll feel at home. Why don't you make contact with the other guests while Mrs. Kieler and I talk some girl talk?"

Jane sat at a table in a small office while Mrs. Paxton went out and returned with some forms. It was the sort of office where customers answered questions and the counselor interpreted and compressed their answers to fit on lines.

"Tell me about your father," said Mrs. Paxton. "What sort of medical care does he need?"

"None that we know of," said Jane. "He's pretty healthy."

"I could see he's ambulatory; no obvious problems. Is he forgetful?"

"No more than I am. Here's our situation. He retired three years ago. Since my mother died about ten years ago he's lived alone in the old house. He's cooked and cleaned for himself, shopped, and so on. But he knows that might not always be possible, and right now he doesn't especially want to. He's still physically active—likes to walk and swim. But he had a bad experience a few months ago, and he doesn't want to live alone anymore."

"What sort of bad experience?"

"I guess you could call it a carjacking. The man wanted his car, and when my father resisted, he shot him. He's okay now, but it's been hard for him."

Mrs. Paxton's eyes were wide with exactly the right mixture of shock and sympathy, as though she had a recipe. "I should say so. The poor man."

Jane shrugged philosophically. "He wants to sell the house, and go live somewhere where he can spend time with people his own age." She added, "He won't live with me. To tell you the truth, I think my friends and I bore him."

Mrs. Paxton nodded. "He's definitely a fit for our Level One," she said. "We have many people in similar circumstances. Each person lives in what amounts to a condominium right here on our grounds. There's a swimming pool, golf course, square dances and social dancing, exercise groups, all supervised by our professional staff." She looked conspiratorial as she said, "Many of our guests feel agitated and depressed if they spend too much time watching the news and reading unpleasant stories in the papers: they want to forget those things. So we try to keep them busy."

"What's Level Two?"

"Two?"

"Yes, you said he was Level One. What's Level Two?"

"Those are people who need some nursing care or who need a helper because they're not capable of living on their own. Level Three would be people who need a greater degree of attention. Some are no longer ambulatory, and some need constant supervision."

"Where are they?"

"The fourth building over." Mrs. Paxton spun in her chair and pointed out the window with her pen. "The one that looks like a hospital."

Jane picked out the building. It looked modern and well-designed, and she could see a few white-coated attendants pushing white-haired people in wheelchairs onto a lawn. The whole operation looked clean, efficient, and humane, but seeing it gave her chills. She told herself it was the air-conditioning.

"We'll tour the whole facility in a few minutes, but I want to wait for your father." Mrs. Paxton gave her conspiratorial smile. "Old people detest being rushed. Do you have any questions about the fee schedule?"

Jane said, "Let me see if I have it right. The fee is a fixed monthly charge."

"Yes. For your father that would be this figure." She held up a glossy brochure and pointed to a number with her pen. "It will remain the same as long as he's at Level One. If he were to move to Level Two, he would incur an additional charge." She pointed to a second figure. "That pays for a companion. At Level Three, the charge is the same. It won't increase during his stay."

"Really?"

"Yes. You see, our typical guest is on a fixed income. He wants to know that the Rancho isn't going to pull the rug out from under him."

"If you don't mind my asking, how can you do that?"

"I'm just talking about our fees. You have to remember that a patient who reaches Level Three probably would have high medical bills also. Some is paid by Medicare, and the rest by the patient himself or his private insurance carrier. But our costs don't go up much, so the fees don't either. You also should know that for the first few years, your father will be overcharged. As he ages and needs more care, the surplus he paid will have gone into the trust and been invested."

"That works?"

Mrs. Paxton grinned. "So far. We've been here since 1948."

Jane tried to communicate a low-level worry. "If my father decided to stay, would he be free to leave?"

"Of course."

"I mean, suppose one day he decides he wants to hop on a plane and visit me, or go to Europe. What would he have to do?"

"Call a travel agent, I suppose. Our regular shuttle bus would take him to the terminal and pick him up."

"There's no way he could be prevented?"

"No. If you wanted to do that you would have to go to court and have yourself granted a conservatorship of his person. But you haven't said anything that would indicate—"

"I didn't mean to," said Jane. "I just want to be sure he can do as he likes." She said, "What about crime?"

"Crime?" Mrs. Paxton seemed confused.

"I saw private security guards, gates, and fences."

"Oh," said Mrs. Paxton, suddenly sympathetic. "This is a small, quiet seaside community. He wouldn't have to worry about that sort of thing. Of course, there's no place in California that's very far from a freeway, so we can't let strangers come onto the complex. If you came to see him, you would give your name at the gate, and they would find it on a list, so you'd be admitted immediately."

Jane kept at Mrs. Paxton, asking the questions she thought a daughter would ask, and Mrs. Paxton seemed to have prepared for all of them.

When Dahlman returned from his walk, Mrs. Paxton went off to get an electric golf cart for their ride around the grounds.

"Well?" said Jane.

"Not bad. It's not the way I had hoped to spend my old age, but the people I met seem happy. It must be incredibly expensive."

"I've seen the price tag," said Jane. "It's outrageous, but it would be a bargain at ten times that much. You can move around freely and do as you please, and if you want to leave, they'll drive you in a shuttle with five or six other people your age. Outsiders can't come in except to deliver groceries and cut the lawn. With any luck we won't have to pay for long."

"What about the other campers?"

"Guests. She says a lot of them come here to forget things like newspapers and television, and the staff tries to keep everybody too busy for them. That should help. The hair should help. The more you behave like Alan Weems and the less like . . . anyone else, the better."

He considered for a moment. "I suppose it's not on the list of places I'd go to look for a fugitive."

"Why can't just anybody spread a deck of cards face-down on a table and pick out the king of spades?"

Dahlman looked at her impatiently. "Why?"

"It's not a trick question."

"Well, to begin with, they're all the same. The king of spades doesn't look any different from . . ." He paused, then nodded.

Five days later, Alan Weems was installed in a condominium at the Carlsbad Senior Rancho. His belongings were said to be "in storage" in Michigan. He arrived with only a few suitcases full of clothing that was as new as the suitcases, a large box of recently purchased books, and a valise that contained "personal papers." He said good-bye to his daughter privately, and she was recorded as leaving the gate at midnight.

20

At 3:35 A.M. Violet Peterson awoke to the sound of many feet walking through the high grass outside her motel room. She silently eased herself off the bed, stepped into her jeans, pulled a clean sweatshirt over her head, and then sat down on the bed to tie her sneakers.

By the time the door burst open, she was sitting at the small table by the window, her purse across the table from her where they would see it immediately, and her hands palm-down on the tabletop.

Before the door swung far enough for the knob to bang the wall, the first man in had barreled across the room to her left like a football player, knelt behind the bed, and rested his elbow on it so his rifle would stay trained on her chest. But the second was already in place by that time, since all he did was sidestep through the doorway to his left. The third crouched in the doorway and swept the room with his eyes, his rifle turning wherever he looked. The fourth stepped past him and turned on the glaring light.

Violet watched the proceedings with intense interest. It was good that Jane had explained how to receive such visitors. She spent the next few moments thinking about her daughter and her son, and marveling at how having them had changed her. At one time she had been very impressed by her own physical beauty—even awed by it, since it was unearned and had come unasked for—and she would, at a time like this, have been terribly afraid that something would happen to shatter it. But having her children—not just bearing them, which had distorted that body temporarily and proved for the rest of time that it was not delicate or fragile, but watching the children grow and devoting her life to them—had moved her beyond little fears.

The moment when the first one, Victoria, had begun to walk and talk, Violet and even Billy had in some subtle way become the old generation, superseded by the next. She was very afraid of these men because they might make some mistake and obliterate her children's mama. She knew that reason dictated that she be afraid for herself, and she told herself that she would be; she had only put it off until she had time to think.

The fourth man through the door advanced close to her cautiously, taking little side steps. She could tell that much of his caution was devoted to staying out of the gun sights of his friends. He snatched her purse off the table and then said, not in the brutal shout she had been expecting, but in a quiet, normal voice, "Listen carefully. I want you to keep both hands in sight at all times, and away from your body. Now slowly stand up and turn to the wall."

Violet stood up with her hands out like a tightrope walker and stepped to the wall. Before she expected it, big, strong hands pushed her forward so her hands had to lean against the wall, then quickly moved up and down her body, but the touch was not personal. It was like a strong wind riffling her clothes. Then other hands grasped her wrists and brought them around behind her. She felt the handcuffs click shut and she began to feel better.

Jane had told her that this was the time she should eagerly await, because it meant the real danger was over. Once the handcuffs were on, the men would begin to relax and there would be little chance that they would make some mistake and hurt her.

The men kept her standing there for a long time, her face a few inches from the wall. She could hear men going through her purse, shuffling through the money Jane had given her, like a bank teller counting it. She could hear the little slap as each piece of plastic was placed on the table—her driver's license, her credit cards. She heard the click and snap as they opened her suitcase, and the quiet rustle as they examined the clothes. Somewhere beyond the bed, men were systematically opening drawers and moving furniture.

It was the man who had taken her purse who grasped her shoulders and turned her around. "Sit down, please."

Violet obeyed. A new man was standing outside the doorway talking quietly with one of the raiders, their backs turned away. This one wore a dark gray suit, and he seemed to be in charge, because he couldn't dress like that and do all these acrobatics, breaking down doors and diving onto floors with a rifle.

The new man was a person to whom other people brought things. One man showed him the contents of her purse, then brought them back and returned them to the table. Others, one at a time, would go to him and whisper the way the first one had.

Finally, the man turned and looked in at her. He was big, not athletic-looking exactly, but the way that soldiers looked. He nodded at something one of his men whispered to him, but he didn't take his eyes off her. They were brown, but light brown, not the brown that most of the people she trusted had. They looked thoughtful and tired. He walked in the door past two men in dark blue golf shirts and khaki pants that Violet hadn't noticed before, who were sprinkling black fingerprint dust on the furniture.

He sat down at the table across from her and stared into her eyes for a moment. "I'm Special Agent Marshall," he said.

"Hi," she answered in a small voice.

"You know that you've got a serious problem?"

"No," said Vi. "I don't."

He pushed a few of the cards closer to her on the table. "You boarded an airplane under a false identity. You used these cards to rent a car, a hotel room, meals. That's fraud. Forgery. Now, I know that you planned to pay the bills. Otherwise you would have no hope of fading back into being a law-abiding citizen when this was over. That was one of the reasons why my boss got tired of having people follow you around the country, and decided that I should have this talk with you." He waited.

Violet watched with curiosity. He seemed to be waiting for her to say something important. If he knew she was going to deny it, then what was all of this about? No, he must be expecting her to admit it and say she was sorry.

She detected a subtle change in his eyes. She had been waiting for a change, but this wasn't the one she had been expecting. She had assumed he would turn cold and cruel and contemptuous. Instead, he was like a man listening to a small, faraway sound. He knew something was wrong, the way Billy knew when he listened to the hum of their car's engine. He must be very intelligent. For the first time, Violet was a little afraid of him.

He said, "What's your name?"

She answered, "Violet Peterson."

His eyes had a new intensity. "What's your husband's name?"

"William Tanaghrisson Peterson. He's a professor of psychology at the University of Buffalo."

"Jane McKinnon bought your plane ticket. Is she a relative? Are you related to Jane McKinnon?"

Violet nodded. "Not in the way you keep track of these things, but the way we do."

"I see," said Marshall. He stared at the table, where he had arranged her ID cards and licenses and tickets. He seemed to turn his mind inward, as though he had received a blow and he was testing how much it hurt. "I wish you hadn't done this."

"Done what?"

"She was under police surveillance. The F.B.I. thought it was following her around the country for over a week. You've been obstructing a murder investigation."

"I flew out of Buffalo on a ticket with my own name on it. I'm here for a legitimate purpose. I don't know anything about a murder investigation."

"What legitimate purpose?"

"This week I was here for the Cherry Creek Powwow. Next I had planned to go to Wisconsin for another one."

"You're from New York. You must be some kind of Iroquois, right?"

"Seneca."

"The people here are Cheyennes. In Wisconsin they're what— Ojibway?"

"I was going to a Menominee celebration. You don't have to be a Menominee. You could go, too. I've always wanted to make the powwow circuit, but there was always a reason why I couldn't. This time I could."

"Was that Jane's idea?"

"Not really. Senecas made a point of traveling around to visit other nations a thousand years ago."

"Has she done it?"

"Quite a few times, I believe. She used to be very political."

Marshall's face was sad. "You're not afraid of what's going to happen to you now, are you?"

Violet surprised herself. "I know you can make things very hard and unpleasant for me right now. But I know that if I wait, there's a limit, an end. You have to let me out because I haven't done anything wrong. At that point, my side gets to take its turn."

"Your side?"

"My lawyers. I don't know you, and I don't know anything about this murder, and I don't know how watching Jane would constitute an investigation. Maybe it does, but maybe it doesn't. I don't know what this really is, but I know what it will look like. It wouldn't be the first time that police have used public safety as an excuse to harass members of a troublesome and politically active minority group who were going to a peaceful assembly."

"Don't worry," said Marshall. "I've been around long enough to know better than to arrest people who want to be arrested." He stared at her hard. "But that's not the real penalty for obstructing a murder investigation."

"What is?"

"Thousands of people get murdered in this country every year. We don't catch all of the killers. Even if we find the man we're looking for, get him convicted and put away, we'll probably never know what else he did while we were looking for him. A body is being found somewhere tonight. Right now. We may not ever find out who that person used to be, let alone who killed her. Will you ever be absolutely sure that the man we're looking for didn't do it during the extra week you bought him?"

21

Jane flew to San Francisco as Julia Kieler, then boarded a flight in San Francisco for Rochester, Minnesota, using a driver's license and credit card in the name Diane Fierstein. The old habits had come back almost too easily: never start in the direction of your real destination, never miss a chance to put a pursuer you haven't yet seen at a disadvantage. She spent the flight lying back in her seat with her eyes closed.

What was Carey doing right now? He was probably asleep, even then holding the attention of the police at home. These days he had little possibility of getting himself into more trouble, but no possibility of freeing himself of suspicion. Jane's practical purpose in going back there had been to present the police with a dull domestic scene that would make them lose interest in him. She supposed she should have known he would already be under surveillance, and that showing up would not change that. But the surveillance had a positive side: as long as the police were watching him, he was safe.

Was Violet Peterson safe? Jane had needed Vi as a decoy to break herself out, but that left Vi and Billy in the same state as Carey—frozen in place, watched and suspected, but not exactly in trouble because nothing they had done could easily be restated as a criminal charge.

She was more confident about placing Dahlman in the retirement home. As long as the money held out and he didn't need the services of a doctor, he would almost certainly be safe. But the price of keeping him away from the police and his enemies was keeping him away from her too. Whatever else he knew would be of no use to her, because he was placed in storage like the others.

As she stepped off the plane into Rochester Municipal Airport, she wondered whether she had prudently provided for the safety of her family and friends, or simply locked in place everyone who might have helped her. She rented a car, drove it in a circular path to be sure she had attracted no attention at the airport, then committed herself to Route 52 and headed north.

She thought about her enemy, trying to feel for a solid, recognizable shape in the dark. She had asked Sid Freeman if he had ever seen any women or children among the clients sent to him. There had been few women and no children. Jane searched her memory again for a census of her own runners. After a few moments, she was sure: the people who were in jeopardy, but who had no relatives or friends or co-conspirators at hand ready to help them, were more often women or children than men. The people whose only option in times of danger was to run were the weak and the young. Most men would turn and fight unless the odds were absurd. They only came to her after they had tried on their own and failed. She didn't have to spend any time wondering about the discrepancy. The one thing that few women and no children had was money, and Sid had said the face-changers were in it for money.

But who were they? There had been two men who had gone to Dahlman in Chicago after the death of Sarah Hoffman and posed as policemen. There had been two different men who had shown up at the hospital in Buffalo to kill him. They worked in pairs. That might be useful, too. At the very least, if she saw two men behaving suspiciously, she would know enough to get out of their way.

Runners had come to Jane because someone had told them that her kind of help existed, if they could only make it as far as her door. It had always been one person telling another—sometimes a social worker who had gotten tired of telling clients that the system had no way to protect them, or maybe the prisoner in the next cell, who had been whispering her name to himself like a mantra for years. Even if the face-changers had turned disappearing into a practical business, their operation could only work by quiet confidences and tips, too.

But the people who came to them needed to have money, and that made certain differences. If the word had simply gotten around among people who had troubles, then the face-changers would have to spend much of their time turning unacceptable runners away. That could go on for only a short time before one of the rejects got caught by the police and traded the face-changers for a lesser charge. No, someone must be doing an initial screening of the clients, maybe even recruiting them.

The screener had to be somebody who came into contact with potential clients. There had to be some place where this secret operation touched the surface, some person who met prospective clients and heard their stories, and then said, "If it's that bad, and you have no defense and no way of getting past it, there may still be a way . . . if you're willing to spend the money."

Maybe it was a banker. There were certainly bankers who catered to people who had reason to expect that some day they might need to disappear: drug dealers, money launderers, gun runners, embezzlers. Or it could be a stockbroker, the one who invested and hid illicit money in the maze of electronic transactions that flashed from computer to computer each day.

It could even be a receptive, sympathetic bartender who worked in the right spot. People who stole a lot of money seldom did it so they could stay home in the evening and watch television by themselves. No, Jane realized, a bartender was wrong. There were bartenders who made extra money by trafficking in information and introductions; some would tell you where to place a bet or buy drugs, or would give a whore your room number. A few would even set up a meeting with a man who would kill your rival for you. But those were rare and unreliable sources of income—for the dishonest bartender, certainly, but even more so for the dealers and prostitutes and bookies, and the market for disappearances was much sparser than the market for drugs, sex, or gambling. The bartender would have to chat with thousands of people, each of them when the bar was empty or nearly so, before one of them asked him the right question. It might take a hundred years to meet three clients.

The screener had to be somebody who spoke privately with a lot of people whom he might expect to be in serious trouble at some point. They had to come to him and volunteer to tell him their stories, because if the trouble was public enough for a stranger to hear of it and approach them, then it would be too late to disappear. They had to tell him what the problem was, and that would require that they believe they could reveal it without getting in worse trouble. That sounded a lot like a lawyer.

The lawyer would be a specialist in criminal law. Judging from the sums that had been spent on Hardiston's plastic surgery, it would probably be the sort of practice that didn't take many small-time cases. Armed robbers got a lot of police notice and press attention and public concern. The only thing they didn't get a lot of was money. They were, as a rule, not good candidates for disappearing. They were temperamentally unsuited for taking instructions, which was why their job prospects had narrowed down to showing up in places where cash changed hands in plain sight so they could grab it.

The people Sid Freeman had described sounded like white-collar criminals who had gotten away with serious money. In Jane's experience, that kind of runner was easy to hide. In order to get that far, they must have taught themselves to lie and pretend to be something they weren't for an extended period of time. They had to be smart enough to have worked themselves into positions of trust, where they could skim profits or take kickbacks or accept bribes or offer them. Before you could get into trouble for insider trading, you had to be an insider. And before you could be charged with tax evasion, you had to make enough to owe taxes.

The lawyer would have to be highly regarded—not just in the underground, but above the surface. People who were in the position to pay a couple hundred thousand to get the right plastic surgeon probably had millions. When a person like that got into trouble, his first impulse was to get himself the biggest, fanciest lawyer he could find.

Jane sensed that she was taking this too far. There was no evidence that it was a lawyer at all. She decided to put the screener out of her mind. The ones she had to face now were the pairs of men who weren't sitting in offices somewhere. They had been out getting false identity papers made and transporting clients from place to place. They had also, when the job required it, had the stomach to kill people who had seen their client's face, and had the cunning to frame one of the survivors for their murders.

They had not come from the world the clients inhabited. Just knowing that Sid Freeman existed put them in the category of people who had connections rather than credentials, and who bought their coats a little loose so the gun wouldn't show. At least two pairs of them, and maybe more, had managed to operate in a coordinated, effective way in different parts of the country at once. Two of them were good enough to have convinced Dahlman they were policemen, and the other two had managed to anticipate the route Jane would take to get Dahlman out of Buffalo, which was better than the real police had done.

For the past few minutes a quiet, insistent alarm had been sounding in the back of Jane's mind, and now she allowed herself to acknowledge it: these men had certain disturbing qualities. They had a comfortable working knowledge of where to obtain illegal commodities: good fake IDs, guns without histories. They had been up to carrying out a regular massacre on the medical staff at Dahlman's clinic. They had been knowledgeable enough not to simply make Dr. Sarah Hoffman's murder look like a botched burglary, but to make it look like the way an intelligent but inexperienced killer would go about making it look like a botched burglary.

They all worked undeviatingly to fulfill a fairly complex and delicate plan of action, which would indicate that they had received very specific orders from somewhere. They were as brutal and violent as anyone, but also unusually patient and organized. The foot soldiers acted with the sort of discipline that came only when failure carried a more convincing probability of reprisal than the legal system offered. And they worked with a benign and respectable above-the-surface screener, the friendly face who could make that crucial phone call and get you a favor. There was a lot about this that smelled as though Dahlman had fallen into the path of some small, fledgling enterprise of the Mafia.

As she thought more about it, she sensed that the framing of Dr. Dahlman didn't feel like Mafia work. They were imaginative enough to concoct it, and professional enough to carry it off if they wanted to, but would they want to? They had thrived for five generations by keeping things simple. If they had wanted five people silenced, they would have swept through the clinic that day and killed all of them at once. Ornate, rickety constructions designed to throw suspicion in all directions—this wasn't Mafia style at all. They never wanted to cast suspicion in other directions. The protection of all of their existing operations demanded that everyone know who had done it.

She considered the possibility that these men might have something to do with law enforcement. But no, that wasn't right either. There were certain standard signs. When people like that needed arms that couldn't be traced, they took them from the piles of confiscated weapons that had supposedly been destroyed. They didn't need to go to anyone like Sid

Freeman. And they didn't need any false IDs from him, either. They had access to the equipment for making real ones in false names.

As Jane drove along the dark highway, following the Mississippi toward the north, she picked out the constellation the Old People had called the Loon, and began to navigate by it. The world had changed so much since then, and none of the changes had been anything that mattered. The foot trails had been straddled by wagon ruts, then covered over with asphalt. This stretch of land had always looked like this: flat prairies covered in the summer by long grasses.

The Grandfathers had come here regularly on foot in groups of three or four warriors. Just to get as far from Nundawaonoga as she was now, they needed to pass through the countries of enemies: the Eries, the Shawnees, the Miami, Kickapoo, Potawatomi, Sauk, Fox, Mascouten, and Iowa. They had done it by moving in silence and covering their tracks carefully. They had followed a course parallel with the main trails but had stayed off them, just as she was doing now. When the Europeans came they called these little bands "skulking parties."

What they really represented was the customary way of making war. When a Nundawaono died, the women of his clan—his mother, sisters, and aunts—would ask the men of other clans, who were their husbands, to make up for his loss. This they did by traveling to the land of an enemy people and bringing back a prisoner. It was what men did for women, what one clan did for another, what the clear-minded did for the bereaved.

If the grief of the women was inconsolable, the prisoner would be tormented to demonstrate his bravery, killed, and eaten so his power would still belong to the people. But usually, the prisoner would be adopted to take the name, home, family, and responsibilities of the lost Seneca.

When a life was lost it weakened the side of good and order and happiness by one, and robbed the people of the services of a human being. It made the side of chaos and cruelty and disorder and darkness a little stronger. Whether or not a person had ever heard of the Twin Brothers, that much was undeniable.

It seemed odd to her that tonight the only force in motion was a skulking party of one small, weak Nundawaono woman. But she had seen enough fighting to know that it had probably always seemed that bad to the ones who had to slip quietly through the forest into the country of enemies, and she had been to this part of the battleground before.

22

The electric alarm clock gave an insistent high-pitched chirping sound, and the woman rolled over to reach for it, her long black hair streaming behind her on the pillow. She turned it off and listened to the sounds of cars and trucks moving on the street below the window: New York. She squinted at the display on the clock. It was three A.M. She slipped out of bed quietly, then padded across the carpet to the bathroom, closed the door, and stepped into the shower. The warm water came out in a hundred hard jets and made her skin feel alive again. She could not possibly have had more than two hours of sleep, but she was already alert.

She emerged from the bathroom with one of the hotel's big soft towels wrapped around her, and saw that the man was just sitting up in the bed. His voice was hoarse when he said, "It's still dark. What time is it?"

She moved closer and smiled down at him apologetically. "It's three-fifteen. I'm sorry, but this is part of the game, too. When you have to travel, you try to do it in the dark when nobody else is likely to see you."

He reached out and grasped her hand, then gave a gentle tug that made her sit on the bed. She let him kiss her neck. "That's all," she announced, and stood up. Her eyes softened. "It was wonderful. But if you make me forget I have to get you out of here on time, then it won't happen again. The flight to Morocco leaves at six, so you'd better get in the shower."

He swung his legs to the floor, rubbed his eyes, then ran his hand through his hair, stood up, walked to the bathroom, and closed the door.

She waited until she heard the shower running, then opened her suitcase. She pulled out a blue skirt and jacket and put them on, then reached to the bottom of the other section and took out the clothes that she had selected for him.

As she spread them on the bed, she studied them critically. The gray suit looked surprisingly good. It had been bought at a thrift shop in Chicago. The shoes had been picked up in a big discount chain store in North Carolina, and the shirt had been left behind by another runner months ago. It was just the right sort of outfit. Tracing it would lead a person in all directions at once. She heard the shower stop, waited a minute, then went to knock on the door.

"David?"

He swung the door open, took the toothbrush out of his mouth, and said, "Change your mind?"

She rolled her eyes. "Afraid not. It's nearly three-thirty. We have to be outside in about fifteen minutes."

David dried himself briskly as he walked out of the bathroom. He looked at the unfamiliar clothes she had laid out for him, then picked up the suit. "Where in the world did you pick these up?" He tossed the coat back on the bed and stepped into the pants.

She put her arm around his shoulder and looked up at him with amusement. "You've got to go through customs. Your passport belongs to a teacher in North Carolina. You have to look like a teacher. If you dress like a successful lawyer, they're going to take a second look."

He looked closely at the necktie she had picked out for him. "This isn't so bad."

She grinned. "I must have slipped up."

He stopped in the middle of tying it, not sure whether she was serious, so she tightened the knot herself. "You're a teacher, not some hayseed. You can't afford a Savile Row suit, but you can buy a nice tie to dress up the suit you can afford."

She walked around the room wiping off surfaces with his damp towel, then went into the bathroom, wiped the handles and faucets, and dropped the towel on the floor. As she came out she studied him judiciously.

He noticed, turned around once, and looked at her inquiringly.

"You'll do." She glanced at her watch. "Time to go. I'll slip out and look for our ride. You take the suitcase, go down and check out."

His face went slack, and he didn't move. She could see that he was embarrassed. "I . . ."

She snapped her fingers. "Sorry. I forgot you don't have any money left. I'm not used to getting up this early, I guess." She went to the window and looked down at East Forty-ninth Street. "They're here already. Let's go."

She opened the door handle with a handkerchief, then closed it quietly and followed David Cunningham down the deserted hallway to the elevator. After the door had closed them in, she said, "You take the suitcase out and put it in the trunk. As soon as I'm finished at the desk I'll join you."

David walked purposefully across the lobby and out the front door. A blue car with two men inside pulled up at the loading zone. The big blond man in the passenger seat got out, took the suitcase out of David's hand, and said quietly, "Get in the back seat."

David sat in the car and the door closed. The man behind the wheel was the smaller, curly-haired one he had met months ago, just after his troubles had started. The man turned his body in the seat to smile at David. "You're in the home stretch now. How does it feel?"

"Better than I expected," said David. Much better than he was allowed to say, he thought. The woman had said she didn't want any of the others to know that she had spent the night with him. He could hardly blame her. She was unattached and so was he . . . now, anyway. She had a right to do what she wanted, but she was in a business surrounded by men: criminals, when you came down to it. She was probably smart not to give them the impression that she was accessible.

He heard the trunk slam, then both doors opened and he saw the dark woman slide into the front seat. The big blond man got in beside David, and the car pulled away from the hotel. David felt a bit cheated. After last night, he would have expected her to sit in the back beside him—that she would have wanted to be near him for the ride to the airport. She had told him she wouldn't be able to fly over to North Africa for a visit until late fall, maybe even December.

Women were always trying to give the impression that they were more romantic than men. But the minute it was over, what did you hear? "Yeah, yeah. The earth moved, you changed my life, you're the best, now let's get downstairs so you can buy me dinner." This one had a way of dropping the temperature from cool to cold. He had said, "You know my real name. Don't you think it's time I knew yours?"

She had answered, "I have lots of names, and they're all real." He supposed that in her business, she had to be that way. The people who had something to run from got to change their names and looks, then disappear. She had to stay around while they went off to places like Morocco.

He had accidentally reminded himself, and it made him frightened. He had made it this far, but the only real hurdle was still ahead of him. Staying free all this time was no big accomplishment, because he had not been face-to-face with a federal official since the last time he had walked out of the courthouse.

He still couldn't believe that he had let this happen to him. When that Mullins character had come to him and presented the scheme, it had seemed simple. All he had to do was take the cash a bit at a time, and place 80 percent of it in an escrow account against the purchase of an imaginary piece of real estate, as though the man were building up a down payment. Then he would make out a check to a different name, hand it to the same man, and keep his 20 percent in cash. Deal closed. Of course, it was money laundering. He didn't like that part of it, but he had liked getting an under-the-table payment in cash. Everything had seemed fine, even after the man had stopped showing up. After he had missed four consecutive weeks, David had begun to see the three hundred thousand in the escrow account as found money.

That was when the man's boss had come to the office. His name was Maggio. He had explained to David that Mullins had been a professional bagman, merely delivering Maggio's money. If David would simply hand over the check for seven hundred and fifty thousand, he would be on his way. It was then that David had seen it all, as though it were carved in his forehead. Mullins had fooled them both, but Maggio was never going to believe it.

David had considered calling the police. He would be disbarred and convicted of money laundering, tax evasion, and some currency-reporting violations. He had considered asking Maggio for time to pay the money back. But he could tell that this man was not the sort for that. Had he actually said that he had killed Mullins? No. David had inferred it from the way he had spoken about Mullins in the past tense from the beginning, always with a weary, philosophical distaste. Finally, David had written out the check for seven fifty, and begun to pack his bags so he could be gone before the check bounced.

Her voice jarred David. "He doesn't have any money with him. Did you take care of that?" She was talking about him.

The blond man beside David said, "There's five hundred in cash and two thousand in traveler's checks in his flight bag."

"Good," she said. She turned in her seat so she could see David's face. "David, remember. When you get to Morocco, take a cab from the airport to your hotel. Spend a few days resting up and getting used to the climate. Don't go right to the bank and start withdrawing lots of money. They could put you under surveillance for a day or two just because you're a foreigner."

"Don't worry," said David. "Once I'm on that plane, I'm a different person. I'm never going to hurry again." The car coasted to a stop on a quiet street lined by brownstones. "Why are we stopping?"

"We're going to change cars here," said the curly-haired driver. "Just sit tight while we shift your luggage to the other car."

David sat alone in the back seat while the others got out. He watched them through the rear window until the trunk lid went up and he couldn't see them anymore. After a few seconds, the blond man opened the door and said, "Come on." When David was out, the man took his arm and ushered him around the back of the car.

David didn't see the gun come out, and the silencer never touched the back of his head, so he never felt anything. He saw the dark woman looking into his eyes with an expression of intense curiosity. The bullet passed through the back of David Cunningham's skull and emerged high on his forehead, and the blond man gave him a hard push from behind. His body toppled forward against the rear bumper and bent at the hips over the rim of the open trunk, so his head and torso were inside. The two men grasped David Cunningham's legs and heaved them upward to push him the rest of the way in, and the woman closed the lid over him.

In a moment the woman had taken David's place in the back seat, the two men were in the front, and the car was making its way toward the Queensboro Bridge.

The curly-haired man looked over his shoulder at the woman. "Morocco?" The blond man beside him chuckled.

The dark woman said, "One of the things he thought he was running from was the federal government. Was I supposed to tell him Biloxi?"

"It just has a ring to it, that's all: 'Your money is in a bank in Morocco.' "

"Just make sure you bury him deep," said the woman. "And I keep thinking about the clothes. Maybe you should strip him first, and burn the clothes someplace far away."

"All right," said the curly-haired man. "You going straight to the airport this time?"

"Yes. Drop me at the United terminal." She tapped the blond man on the shoulder. "So bring me up to date."

The blond man said, "The girl we have on hold in Chicago is getting restless."

"Is everything ready for her at the other end?"

The blond man shrugged. "Pretty close."

"When it is, move her." She stared out the window at the buildings as they drifted past. She muttered, "I know you haven't killed Jane yet. If you had, you would have been falling all over yourselves to tell me."

23

Jane arrived in Minneapolis and registered at the Copley Hotel because it was too big and ornate and comfortable for a woman who didn't want to be noticed, then bought the best street map the gift shop had and went out to find an apartment and do some shopping. She had very specific requirements for the apartment, so she wasted very little time.

Sid Freeman had always been proud of his little stronghold, even in the days when he was calling himself Harlan J. Hall or Mrs. Dilys Mankewitz and he had not yet reinforced it with steel and stone. But even in those days, Jane had been alert to its vulnerability. Sid required that every visitor approach the house from the same direction and move along the rise above the lake shore so that his lookout—usually Quinn, when he was around—could study the visitor through a rifle scope. Sid and his sniper had an elevated, unobstructed view of the path all the way from the other end of the lake to his door. What Sid had not provided was a way of keeping a third party from seeing the path too.

Jane visited an apartment in a big house two blocks west of Sid's. It was slightly higher on the hill than Sid's house, and obscured by the leaves of two long rows of tall oak trees along the old, quiet streets.

The apartment was on two levels, with a kitchen and small living room on the second floor and a staircase that led to a bedroom at the peak of the house. It had once been the attic, so it had a low sloping ceiling and was hot, but the landlord had installed an air-conditioning unit in the front window. It had a separate entrance down an enclosed staircase to the driveway. Jane walked back to the front window and studied the view of the lake over the air conditioner, then took out a pen to sign the lease.

Jane left her apartment and went out to buy all of her furnishings at once. At a sporting goods store in a mall she found a sixty-power spotting scope on a tripod. At another sporting goods store she bought a nightscope with infrared enhancement. She had known Sid for years, and if those were what he used, they were what was necessary. The electronics were slightly more chancy, because she wasn't yet sure how much of what she bought would work at this distance. She knew that the only way to solve it was to buy everything that might work: two video cameras, a directional microphone, a tape recorder, a scanner that the salesman slyly assured her would pick up conversations on cell phones. Then she went to a giant appliance discount store and bought an air-conditioning unit exactly like the one in the front window of her apartment.

Jane set up her gear in the late afternoon. She knew that night was the time for watching the path, because Sid dealt with people who tried to stay indoors in the daytime. She took the motor and refrigeration coils out of her new air conditioner so it was nothing but a metal box with louvers, and used it to replace the original one. She put the video cameras inside it, plugged them in to run on AC power, and aimed them between louvers at a spot on the path through the park that was open and close enough so that with the zoom lens set properly she could get a clear picture of anyone visiting Sid Freeman's house. Then she placed the spotting scope and the night-vision scope in the air conditioner beside the cameras.

The directional microphone took a bit more thought. It had a dish-shaped receiver that was too big to escape notice in a window, and putting it behind a pane of glass or a set of blinds would muffle sounds. It occurred to her that the proper way to use it was to make it look like a TV satellite dish and place it on the roof.

Jane spent fifteen minutes trying to decide whether the roof was merely her best hope or her only hope, because best hope was not good enough for Jane Whitefield. Her parents had brought her up without concealing that the world was a place composed of materials that were much harder and more enduring than human flesh and bone. Nothing she had seen since then had caused her to forget it.

Her father had been an ironworker, one of hundreds of Iroquois men who had traveled the country in little crews, working on big construction projects for much of each year. There was a myth in the society at large that the Iroquois men were simply lucky that they had inherited some odd blank on their chromosomes in the spot where other people carried the gene for their fear of heights. They walked the high girders that formed the skeletons of skyscrapers, and clung to the cables that spanned bridges, and made good money. But one of those men had been Henry Whitefield, and he had told his daughter the truth.

There was no such thing as a genetic immunity to fear. Three hundred feet looked the same through his brown eyes as it did through the blue eyes Jane had inherited from her mother. Things of the mind were controlled by the will, not by chemical codes. A man who needed to feed his family simply taught himself to weigh the risk against the benefit without adding in the fear. It was probably two years later that the cable holding the steel I-beam that suspended Henry Whitefield so high above the river snapped.

Jane had been eleven that summer, and she had been three thousand miles away from that river in Washington, but she had seen him falling, over and over in her dreams. Sometimes she would be up there with him, not standing on anything as he was, but disembodied, watching him in his red flannel shirt and blue jeans, looking so small up there surrounded by sky. And then the cable snapped and he was lost, his arms flailing and his legs kicking for second after second, all the way down. But sometimes she would be inside him when it happened, and that was worse. She would be looking down all the way at the dark water and the big rocks along the edge, watching for a long time as they rushed up toward the eyes she was looking through.

Jane hated heights. The roof of this house was steep. It was a three-story house at the street, but on the lower side of the hill where the directional microphone needed to be placed, the ground sloped away, so it was four stories high. The risk was not inviting. All she could do to mitigate it was to prepare herself. The next morning she went out to a sporting goods store and bought a baseball and a pair of leather gloves. Then she stopped at a military surplus store and picked out a hundred-yard spool of olive-drab seven-strand para cord. She wasn't sure whether that meant it was used in parachutes, but the label guaranteed that the minimum tensile strength was five hundred and fifty pounds.

That afternoon she unrolled some of the cord from the spool and set to work on it. Every two feet she tied a strong knot that held a loop a foot in diameter. After thirty feet, she decided she had tied enough loops. She unrolled another hundred feet of cord, then cut it. Next she sliced open the laces of the baseball in two spots, worked the end of the cord through one hole and out the other, and tied it securely. She opened the side window of her bedroom. Below her she could see the top branches of a big sycamore, and she half-formed the notion that if she fell she could clutch at it to slow her fall, but then dismissed the idea. She wasn't going to fall.

That evening, when she heard her landlords' car start, she hurried to the window. She watched the wife get into the passenger seat, then saw the headlights go on. The car backed out of the driveway, then drove off down the hill toward the main thoroughfares, where the restaurants and movie theaters were. It was time.

Jane opened the window at the side of the house. She leaned out, held onto the frame with her left hand, lowered the baseball about ten feet, and began to swing it back and forth in an arc. It gained momentum, swinging faster and faster, higher and higher. Finally, as it reached the bottom of its arc and began to climb, she changed its direction slightly so it came up, high over her head above the overhanging eaves of the house. She let go, heard the hard ball hit the roof, bounce once, and then roll down the other side of the peak.

She paid out more para cord until the line went slack, then quickly went down the stairs and outside to the driveway. The ball was lying on the pavement with the cord hanging down to it from the roof. Jane pulled the cord slowly and patiently, dragging more and more of it out her upstairs window and over the roof. When it stopped, she climbed upstairs and found that one of the knots she had tied to make loops had snagged on the rain gutter. She searched the back yard until she found a rusty rake, went up to her room and used it to push the loop up over the gutter onto the roof, then pushed the next few up after it. Next she returned to the driveway and pulled the para cord tight again. She wound the para cord three times around the trunk of the tree beside the driveway, tied it securely, and hurried back to her room.

When she had the directional microphone and its electrical cord strapped to her back with a belt, she pulled on her gloves, gingerly put one leg out the window, and looked down to place her foot in the nearest loop of cord. She felt her lungs huff, as though a pair of hands had clapped together against her ribs to squeeze her breath away. She raised her eyes a little, grasped the cord, and swung out above the ground.

She climbed slowly, using each loop as a foothold, then reaching to grasp the next one to pull herself up until she was just below the gutter. Then she reached over it and felt for the next loop. When she found it, she pulled herself over the gutter onto the roof. She held on to the rope as she crawled up the steep incline to the chimney. She freed herself of the directional microphone, set it where the chimney would hide it from the street and the slope would hide it from Sid Freeman's house, then aimed it at the spot where she had parked her car on the night when she had brought Dahlman here.

Jane began the slow descent from the peak of the house, paying out the electrical wire as she went. When she reached the place where the para cord bent and went over the gutter, she felt the worst of the fear. She clung to the para cord and let her legs go out while she lowered herself with her hands, then bent at the hip and felt with her toes for the next loop.

When she found it, she felt a relief so strong that her breath came from her throat in raspy whispers. It took a short time to climb down to the level of her window. When she reached it and pulled herself across the sill she lay on the floor, trembling for a moment. The arches of her feet hurt from unconsciously trying to bend them to cling to the loops of the cord like hands.

When she stood up, she felt energized. She had not fallen. Now she had to clean up. She ran downstairs to cut the cord free of the tree and pick up the baseball. She returned to the room and pulled the cord back over the house into her window. Then she went back to watching the path along the lake.

It was early the next morning before she adjusted all of her equipment for the last time. The microphone and one video camera were trained on the most likely spot for a car to park along the lake. That was the only place where the face-changers would say anything to their rabbits. After that, until the rabbit returned, he was on his own. The second video camera was aimed at the approach to Sid's house. At this range the built-in microphone might even pick up a bit of what the lens saw. Then Jane lay on the bed and closed her eyes.

By watching all night and working all morning, she had reset her internal clock to become nocturnal. When she closed her eyes she had to endure three very clear and convincing versions of herself losing her footing on the high, steep roof, then sliding down the rough shingles, scrabbling with her fingers so the nails broke, then being launched over the edge, where she made one desperate grab for the gutter. Each time, that only got her turned around, so that she plummeted toward the ground headfirst like a diver, the wind blowing her hair and the ground coming toward her so fast it seemed to swell to fill her field of vision like an image in a zoom lens. Then her heart would stop for an instant, and she would be awake again. While she waited to see it for the fourth time, she fell into a deep sleep.

She awoke at sunset and went to check her equipment. She played each of the tapes on fast forward, but none of them had picked up anything but a woman walking a dog by the lake, at least a hundred cars passing on the road above it, and four little boys who had come to give bread to the ducks.

She had dinner and rewound all of her tapes. When it was dark she put the earphones on and listened to the microphone and watched the lake with her night-vision scope. Late in the morning she turned on her recorders and video cameras and went to sleep.

Jane watched the path this way, night after night. She ate simple meals that didn't require her to be away from the window. She performed extended versions of the Tai Chi movements to keep her muscles loose and her joints flexible. She left the house only during daylight, when visitors were least likely to come along the path, and when she returned she checked the tapes her recorders had made. She resisted the growing temptation to turn her attention toward Sid Freeman's house, because she knew there was no more to be learned there. All she could do was make Sid's protégés think his house was her target and kill her.

She kept her suitcase open, and the only clothes that were out of it were the ones she was wearing at the moment. She had a second, larger suitcase that she would use to carry the cameras and recorders and earphones. The directional microphone could stay on the roof if it didn't come down the first time she tugged the power cord. One thing she knew for certain was that she was not going up on that roof after it.

Each evening after dinner she cleaned the apartment completely before she sat down to watch the path. If she had to leave quickly, there would be two or three door knobs to wipe off, and the place would yield no prints. She even composed a note and typed it on a typewriter on display at an office equipment store. It said, "Dear Mr. and Mrs. Stewart, I'm afraid I've been called away urgently. My mother back in Florida has had a stroke, and I need to be there to care for her immediately. Thank you so much for your kindness. I'm enclosing next month's rent to cover the inconvenience while you find a new tenant. Regretfully, Tamara Davis." She had put the paper into the typewriter and taken it out with a tissue in her hand, then slid it into an envelope the same way so it would carry no prints.

With that, she decided she was ready. In the Old Time, a lone Seneca might have come to this very place to watch the lake. In the wars of the forests, all attacks were surprise attacks, and the best strategy was to become indistinguishable from the forest, to wait and listen and watch. Enemies needed to be studied until their strengths and vulnerabilities were known and the time was perfect. Relations with distant tribes of the west were fluid and shifting, so they were studied for signs of impending trouble.

Each night she sat at her window gazing at the familiar picture she could see through her night-vision scope. By now the bright green image had become flat like a painting—an unchanging arrangement of shapes that her mind simply verified each time she leaned to the eyepiece.

But the green painting had small living elements. Owls nested high in the canopy of leaves at the top of the stand of old maples across the lake to her left, where there were no houses. Every few nights she would see one glide out of the high place, suddenly swoop into the brush, and rise clutching a small shape that must have been a mouse, then flap its wings to return to the confusion of dark leaves. The ducks that swam on the surface of the lake in daylight were gone by the time she took her post each night, but she had studied the tapes to see them return to their nesting places in the reeds to the right of the owl trees. To the far right, near the road that ringed the lake, she had found squirrels. To amuse herself she had switched on the infrared scope to pick up their body heat as they slept in their ramshackle piles of dead leaves in the high overarching limbs of the sycamores.

The only human shapes that moved across the green painting regularly were two people she called Woman with Dog and the Sad Man. Woman with Dog seemed to work late five nights a week. Jane saw her car appear on the hill at around midnight and pull into the driveway of a big house up one of the side streets across the lake. The light would go on only in an upper window, so Jane was sure the woman lived in a converted upstairs apartment like hers. Then the woman would reappear in a sweat suit with a retriever on a leash, and go for a long walk in the park. The Sad Man usually appeared some time later. He seemed to come from a distance. He walked steadily, but not quickly. He slouched forward and looked down at the ground, as though he were wondering whether this was the night to burrow into it.

The other visitors were ephemeral. One night, after Jane had watched a middle-aged man selling crystal methamphetamine to a college-age boy, a man and a woman pulled to the curb near the spot where Jane's directional microphone was trained. Jane's spine straightened, she turned on her cameras, and recorded the sounds her microphone picked up. The scene began as she expected. The man was alert and watchful, looking around him for other people, then moved the car with its lights out so that it was precisely in the ideal parking spot, shielded by bushes, barely visible from any side but Jane's.

Jane put on the earphones, and the man said, "This isn't a good idea. I don't want to do this. Please." That didn't sound right. The woman's voice said, "What are you afraid of?" Then she suggested, "The police?" and the man said, "Well, that's not unreasonable, is it?" Jane increased the magnification of the zoom lens of the video camera aimed at the car, turned up the volume of the microphone, and began to prepare. She had her suitcase closed, her keys and purse on the bed, and was on her way to the window with the big empty suitcase to begin collecting her electronic equipment, when the sounds began to change. She stopped and listened. They were having sex.

Jane had started to turn off her electronic equipment, then stopped. It wasn't out of the question for one of them to be a face-changer and have that kind of relationship with a runner. This wasn't the time for it, but since it wasn't beyond the realm of human behavior, she couldn't dismiss these two people just yet. She waited, keys in hand.

Finally, the man said, "Next Friday?" and the woman answered, "I'm sorry, but it's my anniversary, and it's very important to me. How about Saturday?"

Jane thought about that a few times afterward, but never was confident that she understood. Each of the false alarms during those few weeks made her faster and more efficient, but each one made her more impatient. She seemed to have done to herself what she had done to

Carey. She had left him in a kind of paralysis, where he could do nothing but stay where he was and allow every tiny movement he made to be watched. Now she was trapped too, sitting in a room watching a static landscape, waiting to detect some minuscule change.

One night another man and woman arrived and stopped in the same parking place. They behaved so much like the other couple that she was almost sure it was just more sex. The woman said, "Are you sure no one will see?" and the man was the one who said, "Don't worry." But then he said, "Just walk straight ahead along that ridge. Then go up to the big brown house, stand on the porch, and knock. By the time you get there they'll be waiting."

24

Jane watched the woman walk along the dark path toward Sid Free-man's house. She was about twenty-five years old with a good figure and a face that might be pretty under white light. But in the dim green glow through the eyepiece of the nightscope, the skin looked ghostly and the hollows of the eyes were deep gashes of darkness. Her hair seemed to be dark, cut above the shoulder, then curled and puffed to stand out a little. She wore a dark sweater and a pair of jeans, but Jane did not consider drawing any conclusion about her from the way she dressed tonight.

She carried a big shoulder bag, and Jane watched the way she handled it. At first it hung on her left shoulder with her hand resting on it. Jane watched her head moving in little jerks from side to side, looking for human shapes and listening for footsteps, and wondered if the woman was carrying a gun in the purse. Then the woman stopped, frozen for a moment, and listened. After a few seconds, she recognized that the sound she had heard was a car going by on the street, and she went on, looking anxious. She slipped the strap over her head and across her chest and clutched the bag with her left hand, but never touched the metal latch. She didn't have a gun in there. She had money for Sid Free-man, and she was protecting it as though all she had to worry about were purse snatchers.

Jane turned the nightscope away from her and watched the man. She wrote down the license number of his car, then reached to turn up the volume on her directional microphone, but found she already had it all the way up.

He was in the shadow created by the roof of the car, and there were no streetlights nearby, so he was a shadow in a shadow. Jane picked up a small ticking sound, then recognized it as the sound car engines sometimes made when they were hot. The man's hand came up to his mouth, then went down again. The other hand came up and there was a bright flash, then a blinding glare. Jane blinked, then instantly understood he was lighting a cigarette, but the nightscope made it look as though a flare had exploded in his face. She turned to the eyepiece of the video camera in time to see the next two seconds. The automatic light meter on the video camera let in more light than a human eye would, so she saw his face clearly until the cigarette caught and he closed the lighter. He was the man she had seen outside the hospital in Buffalo—the blond one who had turned into the wind to light a cigarette.

Jane listened to the recorder as she hurriedly prepared. She wiped off the door knobs, tore the sheets off the bed and threw them into the suitcase with her clothes, then began to dismantle her equipment. The cameras, recorder, and scopes went into the second suitcase. She turned off the light in the room before she took her empty air conditioner out of the window and re-installed the original. She carried her first suitcase and the empty air conditioner down to the car, then returned. Finally, with a little trepidation, she yanked the wire at the side window and coiled it as the directional microphone slid down the roof. It stopped at the gutter and she tugged it over, then barely kept it from swinging against the side of the house as it fell. She pulled it in the window, put it in the big suitcase with the rest of her equipment, and took a last look around before she locked the door. On her way to the car she left her good-bye letter in the landlords' mailbox.

Jane drove out onto the side street, away from the road by the lake, then made her way along the streets on the hillside, keeping herself far above the waiting man. Whenever her route took her out of sight of the car for more than a block, she began to feel anxious. Each time she came to a turn or a stop sign, she would crane her neck to be sure the car had not moved. But when she had nearly completed a half circle to come out beyond it on the road, she saw that it was gone. The woman must have just come to pick up something Sid already had prepared for her.

Jane's breath caught in her throat. She turned right and let the car gain speed as it coasted down the long straight street toward the lake.

She had considered it essential to get out of Minneapolis without again coming into the sight of Sid Freeman's juvenile delinquents, but now she had no choice. She had to hope they would just see her car passing and classify it with all the others that happened to move along the lake shore each night. She was aware that there were a few problems that weighed against her. It was now after two in the morning, so there were few cars on any of the streets of this residential area, and none on the lake drive except hers. Another was that Sid's kids had very good optical equipment and nothing to do but look. If Sid thought she was breaking the rules, he would regretfully tell them to kill her.

She speeded up. When the road veered away from the lake she felt as though a weight had lifted from her chest. Jane had come to the house from a dozen different directions over the years, so she was familiar with all of the ways a car could go, but tonight she had no choice but to pick the most likely. The man would follow the surface streets until he came to Interstate 94, take it down toward the central part of the city, then branch off onto one of its tributaries—394, 494, 694. There was no telling which one he would take, and they went in all directions. He would disappear.

She pushed the car harder, going as fast on the empty streets as she dared, and finally she saw the green car pass under a streetlight ahead of her. She lifted her foot off the accelerator and let her car coast down to the speed limit. She would have to be cautious now. The fact that there was so little traffic had allowed her to find the car, but it would also make her headlights stand out in its rearview mirror.

After two more blocks, the car swung up a ramp and onto the interstate. Jane gave them a few hundred yards, then followed. She let a big truck flash past her as she came into the right lane, then pulled up to hide behind it. Jane forced herself to be patient. All she needed to do was stay far enough back from the dark green car and keep other vehicles between them, and she would be invisible. After a few minutes she tagged along with a passing Mercedes, and stayed behind it until the green car took the airport exit.

Jane followed long enough to see it turn into the airport drive and stop at the curb in front of the terminal, let the woman off, and pull away. Jane took a few seconds to study the woman in the bright lights as she walked from the curb to the terminal; then Jane continued on to the long-term lot, parked, and ran for the shuttle bus back to the terminal.

She stalked the departure level, scanning each waiting area until she found the woman sitting a few yards from a United Airlines gate. Jane looked at the television monitor above her on the concourse and learned that a flight to Los Angeles was leaving in twenty-five minutes.

Jane walked up and sat beside the woman, but didn't look at her. She said quietly, "I'm sorry, but we've had to change your itinerary. We think you might have been followed to the airport."

The woman looked at her, and Jane watched her work her way through a sequence of emotions, trying to find the one that fit. First she was startled that a stranger was talking to her, and felt afraid. Then there was a second when the words she had heard acquired meaning and she felt relieved: this woman beside her wasn't trouble. She was here to get her out of trouble. But that brought a new, undirected fear. Now the trouble had no face—it was everywhere. When Jane judged the woman had reached the right level of receptivity, she said, "Here's what we do. You're going to get up and go into the shop over there. The first one. When you come out, just go in the other direction, down toward the baggage area. Go outside and get on the shuttle bus for long-term parking."

"All right." The woman prepared to stand.

"Wait," said Jane. "First give me your ticket."

The woman looked puzzled, and behind the inquiring look was suspicion. "Why?"

Jane nodded toward another woman sitting across the waiting area. "We're going to send a decoy in your place."

The woman was filled with admiration: Jane was clever and devious, but best of all, Jane wasn't alone. There was a whole team here to keep them both safe. She handed Jane the ticket and Jane put it in her purse. The woman stood up and walked toward the store.

Jane moved across the concourse and waited a few minutes to see whether anyone separated from the crowds that passed by and approached the woman in the gift shop. No one did. Apparently the face-changers had not placed anyone here to be sure she actually made her flight. Jane walked down to the ground level, stood at the telephone booths along the wall, and waited. She looked at the woman's ticket to Los Angeles. The face-changers had not made the mistake of paying for it out of some general account. The ticket was in the name Melinda Kelly, and it had been charged to a credit card in that name.

Jane had taken the ticket from the woman partly to see what it revealed, but also to keep the woman from having options. As long as the woman had the ticket in her hand, her decision would not have been final. She could still get suspicious, change her mind, and step onto the plane. But now that Jane had the ticket, the woman was committed. Her mind would be busy thinking up reasons why giving it to Jane had been a great idea. Jane went out the door and walked down the sidewalk to the next terminal. She watched the woman come out of the United Airlines terminal and step onto the next shuttle bus. When it moved farther up the drive to Jane's terminal, she stepped on too. The ride was quick, and Jane spent part of it watching for the green car that had dropped the woman off at the airport, and the rest watching for any other car that might be following.

When the bus stopped two rows away from Jane's car, she got off. After a second's hesitation, the woman did too. Jane walked to her car, opened the passenger door for the woman, got in, and drove out of the lot.

"Where are we going now?" the woman asked.

"We'll still head for L.A.," said Jane. "We'll just use a less direct route." She was silent for a few seconds, so the woman would remember she had not told Jane where she was going. "It's more painful, but it's worth it."

The woman said, "What's your name?"

"I don't have a name."

"Then what do I call you?"

Jane said, "That reminds me: you can't be Melinda Kelly now that you've made a flight reservation in that name. You'll be Darlene Hunt and I'll be your sister, Ann, for the moment." She glanced at the sad, scared face beside her. "Your older sister. After the first time we use those names, we'll be somebody else. If you have to make a move, don't be the same person in two places in a row."

"I know," said the woman. "They told me that."

"Good," said Jane. "Just so I don't waste my breath, what else did they tell you?"

"To stay where they put me, live there quietly, and not make friends too quickly. Not to do anything that will get my picture in the newspapers or on TV, not to buy anything on credit, get married, get sued, call the police, apply for a passport." The litany came out as though she had been forced to repeat it a few times, then had recited it to herself until she had come to resent each word of it separately.

Jane accelerated, but stayed in the right lane because it was easier to see headlights overtaking her from the left, and while she was still in the

208 THOMAS PERRY

populated area where exits came every minute or two she could take one without much notice if she needed to. "It sounds as though they gave you the basics, anyway." She gave a reassuring half-smile. "Don't worry about this little detour. To tell you the truth, I think it's a false alarm."

The woman's eyes brightened. "Really? How can you tell?"

Jane shrugged. "You were about to get on your flight to L.A., right?"

"Right."

"If somebody had been following you—and I'm talking about anybody now, from a serial killer to the F.B.I.—the place to stop you would have been before you got into the waiting area. A person who wants to kill you has to make a move before he goes through the metal detectors or he'll have to do it in public with his hands. And cops aren't just interested in you. They want everyone around you, too. They would have moved in at the moment when you were getting out onto the curb—used a car to block the driveway in front of the terminal and arrested both of you before you made it to the door." The woman's earnest, unlined face was just attentive. It showed no more reaction to one kind of pursuer than another. Maybe she didn't know who was after her.

She said, "So why did you go along with it—take me away like this?"

Jane gave a rueful smile. "It's my job." Then she added, "I guess they didn't give you lesson number two. This is the price of disappearing."

"What is?"

"You're going to spend a lot of time looking over your shoulder. When you see something that might be trouble, you don't wait to see if it is. You go."

The woman didn't seem disturbed. She looked out the window at the fronts of stores and houses. "I like it better this way."

"Are you afraid of airplanes?"

"No. It means I have a little longer before I have to be alone. Probably forever."

Jane studied the rearview mirror for the next ten minutes, giving herself time to think. The face-changers had given her a few tips. Maybe they had told her a little bit about what being a runner was going to feel like, and maybe she was simply shrewd enough to have figured it out for herself. Jane decided she needed an advantage. She said, "Whatever happened back there, I don't see anybody following. Are you a good driver?"

"Yes," the woman answered. There was a peculiar edge to her voice that Jane couldn't quite identify. "I know that sounds odd coming from me, but I am."

Jane wondered why it would be "odd coming from me." It was the answer to a direct question, not a boast. Maybe it was just normal modesty magnified into something worse by the experience of prolonged dependence. She decided it was too risky to ask more questions now. "All right, then. I'm going to pull up here at the next exit and let you drive while I sleep."

Jane decided that before she risked going to sleep while this woman was awake, she had better test her. When the car had stopped, Jane waited for the woman to get out and come around to take her place before she relinquished the driver's seat. She was fairly certain that she had the woman fooled, but if she was wrong, the woman seemed alert enough to see that her best move would be to drive off while Jane was walking around to the passenger seat. But instead, the woman used the time to adjust the driver's seat to her shorter legs.

Jane got in and said, "The entrance ramp is right up ahead. Get on it, head west, and keep going. If I sleep more than four hours or you run out of gas, wake me up."

When they were on the highway heading in the right direction, Jane lay back on the seat, used her jacket for a pillow, and relaxed her muscles. She watched the woman drive for a few minutes and decided that whatever the woman had meant, she was not an incompetent driver. Jane closed her eyes. Over the past month she had gotten used to sleeping in the morning, but it was close enough to morning already.

Jane was operating on rough guesses now. She knew that she had to keep this woman off balance—to be smarter, quicker, more sure of herself. The simplest way to buy herself an edge was to sleep while the woman was awake, to rest while the woman wore herself out. And if the woman was craving company already, then she would be craving it more in a couple of hours. Jane let the vibration of the tires on the road and the unchanging rush of the wind against the surfaces of the car soothe her and lull her to sleep.

25

There was bright morning sunlight glinting off the chrome and mirrors of the cars ahead when Jane opened her eyes and sat up.

"You're awake," the woman announced.

"How's it going?" asked Jane.

"It's about fifty miles to Sioux Falls. If I don't see a ladies' room in a couple of minutes, I'm going to die."

Jane leaned closer to look at the fuel gauge. "Pull off at the next exit. We'll get some gas and use the rest room. We'll find a place to eat breakfast."

"There's nothing around here but these tiny little towns."

"Good," said Jane. "Everything we want will be close together."

They pulled onto a two-lane highway that had obviously been superseded by the interstate. A hundred yards farther on, they found a little business district dominated by a single blinking stoplight hanging across the intersection. Jane got out to fill the gas tank while the woman disappeared into the ladies' room. Then they parked across the street in front of a diner that called itself a "family restaurant."

As they ate in the little diner, Jane reflected on what she had just learned. The woman had never spent time in small towns. She didn't know how they worked, or even what was in them. People in small towns needed all of the services that people in big cities needed—a store or two, a gas station, some kind of restaurant.

Jane studied her as the local people talked in cheerful tones at the counter. Sometimes they included someone who came in the door, or others who were at tables. The woman ate with her eyes down in a kind of embarrassment at the discovery that people in the diner talked to each other from table to table. When a girl of about twenty got up and walked around, then picked up a newspaper that had been left at an empty table and scanned the headlines before she went off to work, it seemed to strike her as tragic—as though the girl had been scavenging scraps from a plate.

There was no question that she had lived her whole life in big cities. People who had not come in the door together must be strangers, and strangers should avoid and ignore each other. Making eye contact was not only a breach of propriety, it was dangerous. Raising your voice across a room to talk to a stranger was something city people did when they had gone crazy enough to stop keeping themselves clean. Jane decided to get her outside before she got too uncomfortable. She paid the bill in cash and left an unmemorable tip.

When they were in the car again, she told the woman, "If you want to sleep, it's your turn." Jane was reasonably confident that the sun would keep her from getting much rest.

"Not yet. I guess I shouldn't have had coffee."

Jane drove back out onto the highway. She said nothing as she drove, until she could feel that the silence was making the woman as uncomfortable as the talk in the diner had. That was another sign of a person who had always lived in cities. If you weren't a stranger, you had to fill up all the time with talk.

"Are we going to drive all the way to Los Angeles?" the woman asked.

"I think so," said Jane. She had known the woman had planned to fly to Los Angeles, but she had not known whether she had been intending to fly on to some other destination. L.A. must be where she was going to live. "The safest way to lose yourself is in a car. It's anonymous." She looked ahead at the road. "When they call me in, it means they think it's time to take precautions."

"Do you have a gun?"

Jane looked at her in surprise. "I have several."

"I mean now."

Jane said, "No."

"Why not?"

"Because I can't conceive of a way that having two pounds of metal strapped to me would help me accomplish what I'm trying to do now. It doesn't make me drive faster or keep your face from being recognized."

"It would be safer."

Jane sighed. "I'm sorry, but I was called into this at the last minute to pluck you out of an airport. I don't know anything about you except the name they gave you, and nothing about the kind of trouble you were in. Do people shoot at you?"

"Oh," said the woman. She looked disappointed. "That explains it."

"Explains what?"

"Why you let me drive. That's what got me here. I caused a terrible accident."

Jane nodded sagely, as though that made sense: hit and run? "How did that happen?"

"It was so stupid. I can remember the whole thing exactly, every detail—what I was feeling and thinking."

Jane shrugged. "So tell me. It's a long way to California."

"Well, I lived in Baltimore and worked in Washington. I had only been in my job for about four months."

"Wait," said Jane. "Back up. Why did you live so far away?"

"That was another mistake. It's as though every decision I ever made was leading up to this. My first job out of college was in Baltimore."

"Doing what?"

"I was an investment specialist for a mutual fund."

"And when you got another job you didn't want to move."

"Right," said the woman. "But there's more to it than that. I worked for this mutual fund in Baltimore. I did fine for four years. I worked hard, made solid investments. One day I put a big bet on Wonderfair Drugs. I had researched it. The price-earnings ratio was great, they were positioned in good areas, they had a big enough market share, they had spectacular young management."

Jane noted that the woman was one of the ones Sid Freeman had described. Jane could tell she was bright, ambitious, and probably very professional: Sid must have hated her.

"One thing that attracted me to Wonderfair was that the biggest shareholders were two British companies that I knew about—very conservative, very solid, very smart. One was a marine insurance company, the other an oil and chemical company. Together they controlled about forty percent. If they wanted a piece of Wonderfair, so did I."

"Sounds reasonable," said Jane. She knew she was about to hear why it wasn't.

"One night—it was day there—a tanker sank in the Indian Ocean. The oil company was on the hook for a billion dollars' worth of oil and a billion-dollar ship. The insurance company had to cover both. But there were other problems. The ship was grossly off course in clear weather, so it looked like a sure bet for lawsuits, enormous fines, and maybe having their other ships temporarily barred from some of the European ports where they delivered. They had big contracts with other companies and a couple of governments to deliver specific amounts on specific dates. That turned small trouble into big trouble. They knew instantly that they weren't going to be able to perform. They didn't have the reserves. It's still not clear to me how much of this loss was going to get covered by the insurance company, but it doesn't matter, because they acted together."

"Who acted together?"

"The second the market opened, both companies dumped Wonderfair. It was nearly ten o'clock before we knew where the shares had to be coming from. At about four the news about the ship came out, and I began to piece it together. They were converting to cash. The excuse was that they had to hedge against their losses. What they were really doing was jumping on the opportunity to increase equity."

"I'm afraid I don't get it."

"That's not a surprise," she said. "I didn't either. The oil company was a terrific business. The marine insurance company was a terrific business. But the minute the word got out, their stock was going to drop. The way these things work, the stock nosedives on the headline. Then, after a few days, people realize that the disaster is not going to be that big a deal, and it goes halfway up again. Three weeks after that, it's business as usual. They knew their own stock was going way down. So when it did, they bought back all they could get their hands on. The money they used was the money from their stock in Wonderfair Drugs."

"What happened to them?"

"Not only did they pick up a huge block of their own stock at a disaster sale, but all the buying was enough to start the move back upward in the price. They were rich, and they got richer."

"No," said Jane. "I meant Wonderfair Drugs."

"Their stock tanked. The company lost a quarter of its value in an hour, fifty percent in a day. For a while people thought that if the smart money was leaving, so should they. After a month or two, people realized nothing was wrong. Wonderfair became an ideal takeover target, so they got gobbled up by a competitor that was actually a weaker company. But that was later. I lost my job that day."

"Just like that? One catastrophe?"

"It's a tough business. The timing was bad for me, because they happened to be looking for somebody to fire."

Jane said, "What did you do then?"

"Looked for a job, of course. It took ten months. I got really good at telling that story. Every time I had an interview, the person would say, 'Why did you leave the Gray Fund?' so I would tell it. Then I would say, 'You know, I learned a lot from that series of transactions.' "

"Was it true?"

She laughed. "No." Then she said, "Or maybe it was. I learned that just about anything can happen. Which is good, because it has."

"I take it that the place where you found a job after ten months was Washington."

"Yes," she said. "I didn't dare move until I was sure it would last. It was a good job, doing essentially the kind of investment analysis I was trained for. But I had trouble getting to know people, trouble feeling secure, trouble getting myself to concentrate. Maybe it was my fault. I guess I was still trying to get over my last experience, maybe holding something back because I had committed myself completely the last time and gotten burned. But the people at the investment bank didn't exactly extend a warm welcome, and everything was sort of . . . tentative. At first, anyway."

"But things changed?"

"A few months later, when I was just about over my jitters, I made a big score. I picked a winner. It came just as completely out of nowhere as the one that got me fired. I saw a pair of companies in one business. They both made a component for compact ultrasound imaging systems. They sold to military suppliers, companies that made medical equipment—just about anything where you need to see through something solid. One company held the patent, and one licensed it. I was assuming I'd invest with the company that invented it and held the patent. But when I went to talk to their management, I sensed problems. The CEO was the inventor, and all his company did was make that one component. He was an egotist, and he seemed to be enjoying his wealth just a little too much: his clothes, his car, his office, his plane. The other company was dependent on the ultrasound business, but you could tell they wouldn't always be. They were hungry and serious, developing products of their own. So I gambled on them. A month later, the news comes out that the inventor has been bleeding his own company. It's insolvent. Presto. Suddenly there's one company making the component. The stock I bought tripled."

"So you were a hero."

"I was a hero," she repeated. "And I no more deserved it this time than I had deserved to be fired the last time." She smiled. "People at the bank suddenly noticed me. I think that they had been trying to keep from being friends because they knew they might have to fire me, and it would be painful. But now I was in the club. No, that's not right. I was being invited into it. The one who did the inviting was my boss."

"Who was she?"

"Not a she. A he. That was part of the problem. He was a single man about five years older than I was. He was nice-looking, and he was just about the only one who had ever talked to me before any of this."

"You had a crush on him."

She nodded. "A big one. He asked me to dinner at the Hay-Adams Hotel for a Friday-night celebration of my victory. That was Tuesday. I got all agitated thinking about it, bought a dress, took it back, bought another one. Some of the time I was nervous because I was so happy, and some of the time I was nervous because I was dreading some sexual-harassment thing: I mean, there are nice restaurants that aren't in hotels. I would think, 'Well, okay. Suppose he does try to talk me into something? If it's got nothing to do with my job, then he's just a single guy talking to a single girl.' Then I'd think, 'But how can it not have to do with my job? He's my boss.' You get the picture. By the time we left for the restaurant, I was thoroughly confused. I was listening to every word as though I were a prosecutor."

"Did he say anything you objected to?"

"No," she said with a sad little laugh. "I think that he actually had something in mind. But he sensed that I was bracing for it, so he didn't. If only he had, and I had said yes, I wouldn't be here. I'd still be me, only I'd actually have a life."

"I'm not sure I get it. That caused the accident?"

"We had dinner at this beautiful, romantic restaurant. I was so uncomfortable and crazy by then that I gulped down a martini before we got to the table and half a bottle of wine with dinner. That wasn't a problem for him, but I was tipsy. I was also beginning to feel desperate and weepy, because even though I'd had more to drink than I was used to, everything was clear. I liked him a lot, and I'd had a great chance alone with him, and blown it completely. I tried to prolong the dinner to start all over again and pull it out. All I could think of was after-dinner brandy. Things just got worse. I was dumb and tongue-tied, and by then he was tired of thinking of bright, cheerful things to say. He took me back to the office, where my car was parked, waited until I was inside with the doors locked and the engine running, and left."

Jane felt sorry for her, partly because she wasn't blaming it on somebody else, and partly because she had been foolish as the manipulators and opportunists never were. "What did you do?"

"I cried. Then I opened the windows wide and started to drive. I missed my turn for the 295 parkway. I made a U-turn and came back looking for the sign for the entrance, didn't see the light change, and crashed into another car." She was wide-eyed, then jumped when she said it, as though she were feeling the shock again in her body. "It was so loud. On TV there's a kind of crunch sound, but it's really a bang. After that there was glass breaking and tires squealing sideways on the pavement. It was awful. I was hurt and bleeding and drunk. I was outside of the car, but I didn't remember standing up and opening the door and all that. The windshield of the other car was gone and the man was lying on the street. He wasn't dead, but he looked horrible. I couldn't bring myself to touch him. I ran to a phone booth and dialed 911. When they answered I didn't know the name of the cross street. I had to run a block back down there and look. But when I got there, the police car was there already. Suddenly I'm blowing into a tube, then I'm in handcuffs, and then I'm in jail."

"What then?"

"He died. The man died." She looked at Jane anxiously for a reaction. "I was charged with manslaughter. I had been drunk. There was some suspicion that I could have saved him if I'd done the right things, or maybe the prosecutor was just implying that. At my trial my boss had to testify. He never looked at me, or said a word to me. I lost my job, of course."

"Was it manslaughter?"

"No. The jury said I was criminal, but not that criminal—the D.A. had overcharged me. So I served ninety days in jail for the drunk driving. When I got out I got sued."

"His family?"

"Among others. He had an ex-wife, and she had been getting alimony. He was thirty-six, and that meant that I owed her twenty-nine years at thirty thousand a year. He had a live-in girlfriend who sued his estate for half. Then the estate sued me to get it back. He had no insurance, so the doctors, the hospital, and the ambulance service sued me. The funeral home hadn't been paid because ex-wives and girlfriends aren't legally responsible, so they sued me too."

Jane was very careful to sound bright and sympathetic. "So you decided to disappear?"

The woman looked at her in surprise. "I wasn't innocent. If I made it sound that way, it's a mistake. I killed him. I did it. I wasn't going to hide from it."

"Then what are you hiding from?"

"They were going to kill me." She looked at her lap. "I actually considered letting them."

"Who was? Who was going to kill you?"

"His friends. They were calling all the time, following me, watching me for a chance. They said that money wasn't enough; that I was going to die, they were going to do horrible things to me. I told the police, and they came over and took notes. I don't know what happened to the notes. I could tell they didn't believe me. They seemed to think I was trying to make it look like the people who had sued me were criminals so I wouldn't have to pay them."

"Did you recognize the voices?"

"No."

"Did the ones following you look like anyone you had seen before—in court, for instance?"

"I never saw them. Afterward they would tell me on the phone where I'd been, what I was wearing."

"Did you pay the judgments against you?"

"Well, no. I was going to, and I still want to. But when I found out I had to run away, that was the first thing they told me. It was going to be expensive, and I would have to pay in cash."

"Who told you?"

"Your people. They said that when you run, cash is safer. They needed to be paid, of course, and there was a lot of overhead. They told me not to use the credit cards they gave me to run up bills because I couldn't pay right away without getting traced, and that would make it much harder to go back later."

Jane pondered the woman's story and felt another wave of pity for her. She was smart, but she seemed to use the little she knew to help people delude her. She wanted to go back, so she was willing to believe that avoiding fraudulent credit would keep her clean enough to surface later. She didn't seem to know that running was a crime, too.

Jane supposed that she couldn't expect this woman to have figured out that people who wanted to kill her probably wouldn't want to talk to her on the phone first. The ones who did call probably weren't friends of the deceased. They might very well be people who wanted to give her a convincing reason to disappear. She had not even questioned it.

Jane weighed the next question with care, then decided it was safe. "How did you happen to hear about us?" Even if everybody heard from the same screener, this woman wouldn't know it.

"From the police."

"What police?" Jane tried to keep the impatience out of her voice, but her mind was already making connections.

"Sergeant Gilbert, from the Witness Protection Squad. He asked me what was being done for me, and promised to look into it. A couple of days later he was back. He said the other police didn't believe me, but he did. By then I was crying and begging him to help me, but he couldn't. I wasn't a witness in an investigation, because nobody was investigating the threats. Finally, he told me where to go."

"What did he tell you?"

"To call a number and ask for Jane."

26

"Jane." That was what the woman had said. Jane's mouth was dry and her stomach felt as though at its bottom there was a layer of loose stones. She kept her expression empty, but her mind was rushing around picking up small bits of information she had stored and rearranging them in new patterns.

Jane felt a surge of annoyance at this poor, stupid woman. She had been sent to people she knew would give her false identification papers, but it had never occurred to her to wonder whether the person who sent her might not have a false ID of his own. She had never thought of calling the police department to find out whether there was such as thing as a Witness Protection Squad.

The face-changers had developed a routine, or at least a method they had used more than once. They had a man who was spectacularly good at impersonating a plainclothes police officer, but who was definitely not one: how could he be a cop in both Chicago and Washington? Both times all he had needed to do was appear at the right time, after the real police had come and gone. That made the victims forget that they hadn't exactly called him. He had probably read about this one in the newspaper.

Jane tried out the theory that the name Jane was a coincidence. It didn't sound convincing. She had spent thirteen years taking fugitives out of the world, and by now there must be a couple of hundred new people all over the country who had come into being because she had invented them. People—even vulnerable, scared people who knew better—sometimes said more than they should. And the person they told would be even less likely to keep the secret. Jane had been a guide for only about two years when the first total stranger had shown up at her door with a story of how he had heard of her that didn't include the name of anyone she had ever met.

Getting to be too well known was just one of a dozen occupational hazards that quietly, invisibly grew to increase the odds against her. During those years it had become more difficult to slip into an airport and fly out quickly and anonymously, more complicated to forge a driver's license or a vehicle registration, harder to invent a personal history for a runner that would stand up to the instant credit checks that had become routine. The forces of order—the businesses and agencies that were engaged in ensuring that each person keep the same labels from birth until death—had become more sophisticated. When Jane had guided her first runner out of the world it had still not been unusual to meet an adult who had never been fingerprinted; now it was hard to find a child over five who hadn't. Computer terminals installed in police cars carried information on everybody, and there were only two states left—Vermont and New Jersey—where licenses didn't carry the driver's picture.

Jane had always known that if she didn't get herself killed, the time would come when what she did would become impossible for her. It had never occurred to her that by then her name would be so widely circulated that someone else would assume it.

If these people were using the name Jane, and visiting suppliers and contractors that Jane had once used, then they were creating a universe of new problems. It was only a matter of time before one of her old runners, some person she had risked her life to help, tried to see her again and got killed by the face-changers. No, she thought: blackmailed. The runner would come to them, maybe because the place where she had put him had suddenly become dangerous. The face-changers would play him the way they had played Dahlman and the woman. And as soon as they knew enough about his problem—who he was and what was after him—they would own him.

Jane had an uncomfortable thought. That wasn't really very different from what Jane was doing to this poor, naive woman beside her. She knew exactly what they were doing and exactly how they would go about doing it, because the methods weren't theirs, or even hers: they were simply how the business was done. Jane had often carried identification that made her a policewoman, because on the rare occasions when she thought she might need to provide herself with a gun, that was the only explanation that would be universally acceptable.

She had also manipulated runners and sometimes even used a bit of coercion. She had said to them, "You are in a dangerous, unfamiliar world. If you now act according to your own experience and instincts, you are certain to be killed. If you do precisely as I say, you have a chance. If you do not, then I will step aside and whatever is after you will catch up." Even if Jane had not said the words, they were inherent in the situation. Jane had used guile and threats to keep her runners alive, but those methods didn't need to be used that way. She knew it and the face-changers knew it. They knew everything she knew.

The woman said, "You're so quiet. Is something wrong?"

Jane turned and forced her face into an utterly convincing beatific smile. "Not at all. I was thinking that things could hardly be going better."

"Really?" The woman's face was trusting, open. She was asking permission to feel relieved, and Jane gave it to her.

"Sure. Nobody is following us, the road is clear, and we should be in L.A. in about two more days."

"Do you think it's safe to go to the same address?"

"Well, for a while I was thinking of diverting you a bit. That's what we do when there's trouble. But I don't see any reason for it now, do you?" She watched the woman's face, wondering why the lie made her feel so little guilt.

It was early in the morning on the third day that Jane detected the sudden wave of fast traffic overtaking them and surrounding them on its way into the city. No matter how many times Jane came into Los Angeles, it was always new, always just changed, and about to change again. The city was always reaching outward to grasp more of the landscape into itself, so that now the places with names like Antelope Valley that had made sense once were just parts of the continuous network of freeways and subdivisions that was a hundred miles long and eighty wide and growing.

At eleven, when they reached a part of the city that Jane knew, she pulled into the parking lot of a big motel and registered. They had to wait until noon to take possession of the room, so they had lunch in the restaurant beside the lobby and then picked up the key. When they were in their room, Jane sat at the table by the window. She held out her hand. "Can you let me see the driver's license they gave you?"

"Sure."

Jane watched her fish it out of the wallet in her purse. Then she copied the words onto a receipt. "Janet McNamara, 19942 Troost Avenue, North Hollywood, CA 91607." She held the card under the light and turned it to examine the holograms on the front, the magnetic stripe on the back, and the photograph. "Very good," she said as she handed it back.

They were careful and meticulous, and in this woman's case they'd had plenty of time to get the details right, because she had never been in any real danger: they had made the death threats themselves. Jane stood up. "I'm going to look your new apartment over. One precaution while I'm gone: pretend the telephone doesn't exist. Don't call in to announce that you've arrived or something."

"Why not?"

"I could give you a list of reasons. But the big reason is that it's contrary to our established procedure."

"What does that mean?"

"It means we don't do it."

"You mean the home office sends you memos and directives and things? Do you have a manual?"

Jane chuckled. "No. Look, you have two kinds of vulnerability. One is that you'll make a mistake and get caught by the people looking for you."

"That's the only vulnerability I knew about."

"The other one is that somebody else will. Some other client gets spotted and watched, but doesn't know it. He calls in to the office. Now the police have the office number and address. They tap the phone. You call in, and they have your number and a recording of whatever you say. So there's a rule. The fewer calls the better. It protects you if somebody else is caught, and it protects everybody else if you are. Now I'd better go earn my pay. Do you have the apartment key?"

"I'm sorry, I forgot," said the woman. She reached into her purse, pulled out a set of keys, and removed one from the chain. "Here."

Jane took it. These people were good with details, she thought. They hadn't given the runner one key that stood out in her purse and looked important. They had hung it on a chain with a dozen others—door keys, car keys, luggage keys—so it might open anything or nothing; it was part of a fully developed, convincingly complex life. "Thanks. I'll be gone for a long time unless I find something wrong over there and want to get you out fast. Stay out of sight as much as you can. If you get hungry, eat at the place where we had lunch and come back."

Jane spent a few minutes watching the car from the hallway before she slipped into it and drove toward the freeway entrance. Now that she was in the city where the face-changers expected the woman to come, she felt the need to take every precaution. She knew the Los Angeles freeway system well, because she had used it other times with other runners. She put traffic jams between her and cars that might be following, and twice used ramps to slip off one freeway and onto another going in a different direction before she emerged near the address.

First she drove a circuit of the neighborhood, looking at other apartment buildings and single-family houses. There were no windows that had opaque shades with the rollers set too low so someone could look out above them, no flashes in the bright sunshine that could be lens reflections, no men loitering on balconies in the middle of a workday. She drove around again, studying the vehicles parked nearby, paying particular attention to vans and four-wheel-drive vehicles parked along the streets. There were none with men sitting behind the wheel, none that pulled out when they saw her approach for the second time.

Jane parked on the street near Janet McNamara's apartment building, took out her suitcase, and walked into the little lobby that passed through the building and looked out on a small, desolate swimming pool. She avoided the elevator and walked down the hallway and up the stairs, listening for the thuds of feet, the sounds of a television set, for anything that would tell her who lived here and where they were at the moment, but she heard nothing.

When she found apartment 208, she stopped and studied the floor to see if there was any indication of wires under the thin industrial carpet, then cautiously inserted the key in the lock and opened it. A tiny piece of red fluff, like lint from a sweater, was released by the door near the hinge and drifted to the floor in the hallway. Jane smiled. It was an ancient trick for determining whether anyone had been here without going inside to check. If the fluff was there, then there was nobody inside waiting for her.

Jane slipped inside, locked the door, and looked around her. The apartment was small and simple, but the face-changers had furnished it in advance to keep Janet McNamara from making mistakes while she did it herself. Jane went into the bedroom, looked in the kitchen drawers and cupboards, the refrigerator. They had even bought her enough food so she wouldn't have to go out until she had been here for a week.

Jane searched for the best hiding places. She moved a chair from the kitchen into the living room and stood on it to unscrew the grate from the heating duct high on the wall across from the entrance door. Then she took one of her video cameras out of the suitcase, set the lens to manual and focused on a space near the doorway, used a piece of tape to cover the red light that showed when it was on, pushed it two feet back into the heating duct, and replaced the grate.

On her way out she replaced the bit of red fluff, then went down the stairs to the street. The building next door had an apartment for rent, but when she had roused the manager and gotten him to open it for her, she found that the windows afforded her no view of Janet McNamara's apartment. She would have to do this the hard way. She watched the neighborhood for two more hours, then drove back to the motel.

When Jane walked in, Janet McNamara was on the bed watching television. She turned it off as though she were hiding something. Jane turned it back on. "No need to turn it off for me." There were two men in suits chatting about futures and options across an oddly shaped marble table. In a second or two the men were replaced by a table of figures.

Janet McNamara gave a comic wince. "They told me to start weaning myself away from the market stats, so I won't be tempted to invest."

Jane sighed. "They're right about investing. I know very little about you, but if I were looking for you, that's one of the ways I'd go about looking. I'd buy all the mailing lists of investors I could."

"I know," said Janet.

"On the other hand, somebody should have told you that you can't expect to last very long if you go against all your preferences."

"I don't remember hearing that."

"Watch the channel you like. Please yourself in quiet ways. While your enemies are standing around watching airline terminals and hotels at all hours, you want to be curled up in a cozy place feeling content. You'll last forever, and they'll give up."

"I like that," said Janet. "Of course, in my case it doesn't have to be forever."

Jane glanced at her without letting her see. She still didn't get it. The face-changers had convinced her that she just had to slip away for a while to outlast some imaginary death threats, and had gotten her to do things that would make it too hard to ever go back. "Maybe not," she murmured, and hated herself for it. She hated herself more for what she was about to say. "The apartment is fine. In the morning I'll check once more, and then move you into your new home."

27

Jane entered the building alone. She made her way to Janet McNa-mara's hallway and up to her door, then opened it and watched the piece of red fluff fall to the floor. This time she let it stay there. She used the kitchen chair to climb to the vent in the living room, then removed the grate, retrieved the video camera from behind it, and played the tape back on fast forward, staring into the eyepiece. The tape was a still, un-changing shot of the closed door. She slipped the camera into her bag and went out to get the woman who was not Janet McNamara.

Jane brought her inside and closed the door. While Janet walked around the little apartment looking dazed, Jane told her, "I'm positive nobody has been here since I came in yesterday, and nobody seems to be watching from a building or a car around here. That's the best I can do."

"It's . . . cozy, isn't it?"

"What?"

"It's kind of small and tacky. The apartment."

Jane brought herself back to the business of resettling. She had seen this before in runners of her own who were used to having money. It was probably made worse for Janet McNamara because she had spent her life in old eastern cities with big, heavily ornamented buildings. Los Angeles was alien to her. Jane stepped back into her role. "It's small and cheap be-cause it gives you a low profile. These apartment buildings are full of young women from somewhere else who work as receptionists or secre-taries or shop clerks. They don't make a lot of money, and they spend most of it on clothes and car payments and going out. What you want to do is make yourself look so much like them that a stranger would need a microscope to pick you out of the crowd."

"I guess that makes sense," said Janet. Her voice was not enthusiastic. "Am I on my own now?"

Jane had not yet decided how to bring up the next issue, and this seemed like an opportunity. "Not yet. There will be a person who comes to be sure you're settled. He probably won't know why you didn't take the plane. Don't tell him."

Janet's head spun to look at her. "Why not?"

Jane had hoped this woman would be exhausted and preoccupied enough to lose her curiosity, but she had not. Jane waved a hand in a vague gesture. "Another standard procedure that protects everybody. We try to compartmentalize everything. But there's always one of us who wants to know what everyone else is doing. It's pretty hard to pry information out of a person who keeps secrets for a living, so people ask the client."

Janet's expression seemed to move through suspicion into certainty. She raised an eyebrow. "That's what you've been doing to me, isn't it? You've been asking me all these questions, and the reason you didn't know the answers already was that you weren't supposed to."

Jane smiled sheepishly. "Caught me." She let her face reflect the uneasiness she was feeling. "But I wasn't doing it out of idle curiosity. There are a couple of guys in this scheme that I'm not sure about. They seem unprofessional."

"What do you mean, 'unprofessional'?"

Jane shrugged. "Arrogant, overconfident. Maybe a little too casual about the rules. That's the kind of person who gets caught. They may be fine. But if I'm right, I don't want them to know too much about how the rest of us do things. So if somebody asks, tell them you saw a man staring at you at the airport, so you slipped out and took a bus."

Janet looked a little worried. "I'll try."

"Succeed," said Jane. "It's important. If one of them finds himself in a jail cell some day, one of the things he'll think about is what he has to trade. If it's you, then you're in deep water. If it's all of us, then you're in deep water with no lifeline."

Jane took a last look out the window of the bedroom, then said, "Good luck."

Janet gave a brave little smile. "Thanks. I don't know if there was anything to worry about, but thanks for being on my side. It made me feel a little better about everything."

"Good," said Jane, and slipped out quickly so she wouldn't have to look into those trusting eyes. She made her way down the stairs, then out the door and around the building, reassuring herself that there was no sign that the face-changers had arrived early.

She knew it wouldn't be long. They had dropped a runner at an airport with a plane ticket four days ago, and she had never shown up at the end of the line. She knew they must have spent the first three days the way she would have: examining everything they had done to find a mistake, then trying to discover whether the runner had been picked up by the authorities for some mistake of her own.

Jane walked down the street to the spot where her car was parked, got in, parked again on the street behind the building, and began the long wait. For the first two hours she walked. The days on the road had made her muscles feel slack and her joints stiff. She was used to exercise and motion, and the walking helped her get over the feeling of confinement. When the face-changers came, they would case Janet's building as she had, and look for the same signs she had: heads in parked cars, windows in nearby buildings that looked as though they were being used for surveillance. A lone woman walking down the street looking as though she belonged here would be of no interest to them.

After she had walked enough, she spent some time driving. She bought gas, ate a quick dinner at a Chinese restaurant a few blocks away, then changed her clothes to avoid becoming familiar to the people who lived in the neighborhood.

Jane wondered whether she was making a mistake. She could have told Janet the truth, then taken her away and resettled her. She could have done it on the first night in Minneapolis. No, she reminded herself. At that moment it would not have worked. The woman believed the face-changers had saved her from people who were going to kill her. Jane was just some woman who had appeared from nowhere. But maybe now, after spending four days with Jane, the woman would believe what she said. No, Jane had gotten her to believe, and then spent the whole trip lying to her.

Jane knew it didn't matter whether she could have done something else. She hadn't. She had done this. She had put the woman right where the face-changers hoped she would be. Now Jane would wait for the contact person to show up, and follow him. Nobody would know that she had ever seen Janet McNamara. Jane would learn about the face-changers without sacrificing Janet. That was important. Having Dahlman tell the authorities his story was a pointless exercise. Having a second client of the face-changers describe the disappearing process and identify some of the people who had arranged it would be another matter. As long as Jane left the woman where the face-changers had put her, she would be safe, and Jane could come for her whenever she was ready.

At ten, the lights in Janet McNamara's apartment went off. At eleven, Jane drove by the building again, and the lights were on. As Jane moved her car to the end of the block, she studied the cars parked nearby. The face-changers always seemed to work in two-man teams, so she was looking for a car with one man in it who might be waiting for a partner who had gone inside. She walked past the building and glanced into the lobby, but there was no one loitering there. But when Janet had met the bogus policeman, he had been alone. The man who had taken her to the Minneapolis airport had been alone. Maybe they only used pairs to kill someone.

She studied the building. The lights were still on in Janet McNamara's apartment. There were other lights on in the building, but only in the stairways and halls. Eleven o'clock wasn't that late.

Jane cautiously stepped around the building to the driveway and peered at the back of the building. The building's parking lot was built to hold ten cars, but there was only one car in it. Eleven o'clock wasn't that late, but it wasn't that early, either. At eleven o'clock there should be cars. Her mind raced. She knew why there had been no sounds when she had come here during the day. She had assumed that everyone must be at work, but she had been wrong. There was no "everyone." It was just Janet McNamara, and she had a visitor.

As Jane moved to the back of the building, the logic of it seemed simple and inevitable. The face-changers were in the business of hiding people, and they were doing it on a large scale and planning to stay in business, maybe even expand. They would need places for lots of people. Why not buy an apartment building or two in big cities? A runner had to be in constant fear that he might do something that would arouse the curiosity of his neighbors. But a fugitive had little to fear from his neighbors if his neighbors were fugitives too.

Jane tried to fight off the decision that she was about to make. The most important thing for her to do was to stay out of sight until the visitor was in his car, and then follow him. But when Jane had conceived the idea, she had thought that this apartment building was full of people. The fact that it wasn't might not change anything. But it might mean that the man in Janet McNamara's apartment could kill her and there would be nobody to hear it. The risk had suddenly become unacceptable.

She hurried up the stairs, then slipped into the hallway and stole along the corridor until she came to the door beside Janet McNamara's. She tried the doorknob, but it was locked. She put her ear to Janet's door. She could hear nothing but a pair of muffled voices in conversation. She stepped back to the other door and took out her pocketknife. She carved out a little of the wood beside the knob until she could fit the blade beside the jamb. She inserted it to nudge the bolt to the side, then pushed the door open.

Jane closed the door and moved across the room, then quietly opened the window closest to Janet's apartment. She could hear the voices more clearly now. The tone still seemed even and monotonous, but she looked around her. If the tone changed, she would need something she could use as a weapon.

The apartment was furnished exactly like the one beside it. She looked in the kitchen for knives, but found there were none. That was more than an oversight. It could hardly be anything but a precaution to keep the runner who would live here from committing suicide. No, she decided. It was to protect themselves from a runner. If all a runner wanted was to kill himself, then anything would do—an open window, an electric socket.

Jane turned on her heel and stepped to the pole lamp by the couch, unplugged it, and began to dismantle it. She removed the shade, unscrewed the bulb and socket from the pole, and disconnected the insulated wires from the switch. She pulled the cord all the way out of the long wooden pole, unscrewed the heavy metal base of the lamp, and removed it. She looked around the apartment. There were no extension cords. She ran to the closet and found a vacuum cleaner. She pulled the cord out all the way, then cut it and brought it across the room. It was at least twenty feet long. She listened at the window for a moment. There was tension in the voices now, but she still couldn't make out any words.

She knelt on the floor and worked faster. She ran the vacuum cleaner cord all the way up the hollow wooden pole of the lamp. She reconnected the ten-inch loop frame that went around the bulb to hold the shade in place. She pulled the two sides apart so they were two prongs, then connected the two bare wires at the end of the cord to them.

As Jane worked, she was acutely aware of the sounds of the two voices in the next room. They were louder, more rapid. The woman's voice had a cry in it now. She was scared, maybe hurt. Jane ran into the hall, then plugged the cord into the wall outlet beside her. She put her ear to Janet McNamara's door and heard her say, much louder, "Don't. You don't need a gun."

Jane rapped on the door, ducked back, and waited. The footsteps were heavy: the man. She held the pole in both hands. The door handle turned, the door opened an inch, then stopped.

Jane said, "I was going by outside and heard someone yell. Is everything okay?"

Her tentative, apologetic female voice made the man sure it wasn't the police or armed men who had heard, so there was no tension in his voice. "Oh, sure. We're fine. Just a little family discuss—"

Jane hurled her shoulder against the door. She felt no resistance as the door swung freely six inches inward, then hit something solid. Then it swung inward again and she fell into the room. The man was staggering backward, his hands cupped together covering his nose and mouth.

As Jane regained her balance, the man's eyes opened and he reached under his coat, groping for what could only be a weapon. Jane shouted, "No guns!" and jabbed the prongs of her pole lamp against his elbow. A line of blue lightning flashed between the prongs.

The jolt stung the man into a reflex like a spasm. His left hand chopped down from his bleeding nose and lip, his right hand shot out of his coat, and both lunged for the pole. Jane yanked it backward, but he was too quick.

His hands missed the wooden pole, but the metal prongs wouldn't come away from him. His body jumped, froze, then gave a convulsive jerk, and the lights in the hall went out. The man collapsed to the floor.

Jane poked at him with the pole, and heard the woman scream, "Stop it!"

Jane kept her eyes on him as she said quietly, "The electricity's off. The circuit breaker popped." She opened his coat with the pole, quickly crouched to snatch the pistol out of the shoulder holster, then retreated two paces and aimed it at his chest. She waited a few seconds, then cautiously knelt and put her hand on his chest. She moved the hand up to his carotid artery, then took it away.

She stood and glanced across the room at Janet McNamara. She was leaning against the wall. Her hands were at the sides of her face like claws clutching at nothing, and her teeth were bared as though a scream had been caught in her throat. She was wearing a flannel night-shirt that had been unbuttoned in front from the neck to the thigh.

"Put on some clothes," said Jane. "This place doesn't seem to have worked out."

28

Jane drove out of the quiet neighborhood, down Colfax Avenue, east on Ventura Boulevard, and up the entrance to the Hollywood Freeway. Finally she looked at Janet McNamara. "Are you up to having a serious talk?"

"I don't think so." After a few seconds, she said, "But if I won't, I'm in worse trouble, aren't I? I'm lost, just as though I were floating on some dark ocean. Nothing in any direction—left, right, above, below."

Jane reached out and touched the woman's shoulder, but the woman cringed and shrank back. Jane said, "Sorry, I didn't mean to startle you."

"Is that man dead? Did you—did we—just kill him?"

"If he's dead, I killed him. I'm not interested in sharing the blame," said Jane. She looked at the woman. "Did he rape you?"

The woman glared at her, but said nothing.

Jane said, "No matter what he did, it's over. I'm not going back there to kill him again."

"So he is dead."

"I'm asking about you. I need to know if I'm looking for a doctor or an airport."

"He didn't. I'm sure you know exactly what happened. You set this up."

Jane held her breath for a few seconds, then let it out. It had to be now. "I don't actually work for the people who hid you. I didn't set this up. I took you there because I wanted to see them without having them see me. When I realized they had arranged to meet you in an empty building, I got worried."

"What are you saying? You don't work for them? You said you did. You said—"

"I lied."

The admission stopped the woman, made all of the evidence she was arranging in her mind irrelevant. Or maybe it didn't: maybe this was the lie. "Why should I believe you're telling the truth now?"

Jane looked into her eyes for a moment. "I'm not telling you the truth because I've suddenly become a sweet person." She turned to look at the highway ahead. "I'm doing it because I think it's to my advantage right now, and I don't think it will cost me anything in the future. Listen carefully, because the truth doesn't come trippingly to my tongue, and I use it only as a last resort. I've been trying to spy on those people to learn who they are and where they are so I'll be able to destroy them. I was waiting for them in Minneapolis, and saw one of them taking you to the airport. I had two or three seconds to decide whether to follow him or to divert you. I picked you."

"Why?"

"I thought you might tell me things. I knew the man driving you to the airport wouldn't."

"What are you—some kind of policewoman?"

"No. I'm Jane."

"You're . . . I don't understand."

"For thirteen years I was a guide. I took people who were in danger and moved them to places where they weren't in danger. I gave them forged papers, taught them how to stay hidden, and left. Sound familiar? It was quiet, it was private. It wasn't a business. But people heard about it. Now the ones you met seem to be using my name."

The woman's eyes flashed. "You used me to get revenge because they stole your trade name?"

"No," said Jane. "These people have become a danger—to people I hid over the years, to people I love who have nothing to do with the disappearing business, and to me. I did use you." Jane stared at her, unblinking. "But here you are."

"You mean you put me in a fire and pulled me out before I got burned?" She was angry and Jane could tell that her vision was narrowing—she was literally seeing red. "Well, it wasn't in time."

"You said nothing happened."

"Something happened. Not that, but something."

Jane kept the emotions she felt from slipping into her voice. "What happened?"

Janet McNamara's body began to shake. It was a slow movement of her head, the tears hidden as though she were refusing to give in to them. Then she sobbed, and gasped in a breath. The next sob was loud, as though she were angry at Jane for causing it and was defiant. But she didn't sob aloud again. Her shoulders shook harder for a minute or two, and then she lifted her head and spoke just above a whisper. "I found out that I'm not smart, and I'm not strong, and I'm not brave."

Jane's tone was gentle, reasonable. "He was a man who hurt people for a living. He had a loaded gun. You had nothing. Smart is being able to walk away at the end of it. You're smart. He's not."

The woman seemed to let Jane's words go past her, because she had something to tell. "I went to bed, and when I woke up he was standing there in the bedroom doorway. It was like one of those dreams where there's something big and awful that you can't quite see. I sat up so fast I was dizzy. He said he was there to check on me." She glared at Jane. "Just as you said he would."

Jane didn't answer. The woman needed to get something said, so she didn't try to interrupt her with some disclaimer that would have to be a lie.

The woman looked out the windshield. "I pulled myself together a little bit after that. I remember actually laughing—a nervous little laugh—because finally something was happening the way somebody had said it would, and that meant everything was on track again. But it wasn't. He said, 'Get up,' and switched on the light. He turned away, so I thought it was some clumsy attempt to be polite, because I was only wearing my nightgown. But when I got up I saw he was going through my stuff: my suitcase and my bag. I said, 'What are you doing?' and he said he was collecting the money I owed."

"Did you owe them money?" asked Jane.

"No," said the woman. "I paid all the expenses, and gave them fifty thousand dollars. That was supposed to be it. But he said I was mistaken." She looked down at her hands in her lap.

"Did he explain what he meant?"

"I didn't really listen carefully to the rest. There was something about extra expenses because I wasn't on the plane, and that meant they had to look for me. And fees for other things. Once I knew where this was all leading, it hardly mattered what he called it."

"Did you argue with him?"

"Sure. I wasn't trying to run away from things I'd done and live in luxury or something. He was taking the money I was going to need to stay hidden and get started again. I was desperate. I started to yell at him."

"And then what?"

"And then I stopped."

Jane looked at her closely. "You figured it out, didn't you?"

"Yes," said the woman. "I did. It was one of those surprises that come, and when they do, the biggest part is wondering how you could be so stupid that you didn't know before. All you had to do was step out of your own skull and look at yourself from anywhere but your own eyes. I saw him looking at me, and saw that the shouting didn't make him nervous. He raised his voice too, but he wasn't mad. He was just showing me he wasn't afraid of being heard. He could make all the noise he wanted."

"And you couldn't."

"No. I couldn't. I saw it in his eyes. They were . . . amused. I don't mean he thought I was funny. I mean that he was watching my face while it all occurred to me, and he was enjoying each step."

"Each step?"

"I'm thinking, 'Why am I yelling?' The reason you yell is to bring other people—neighbors, passersby, police. If that happens, I'm going to be caught and shipped back to Washington and put in jail. Or maybe it's more basic, less civilized. I'm angry, like an animal. My throat tightens and my mouth opens wider. But what does my animal anger mean to this other animal? He's much bigger and stronger and faster than I am, and he knows how to fight—has fought. So yelling is not only pointless, it's actually self-destructive. Yelling and fighting were out."

"You said he was watching you figure that out. Did he say anything?"

"He said, 'The maintenance fee will be five thousand a month.' "

"What's a maintenance fee?"

"I'm surprised you don't know. Or maybe you do, and you want me to say it. He said they'd continue to check on me to be sure I was okay, and if I needed things, they would get them for me."

"What sorts of things?"

"Renew my licenses and cards and things. Even that had never occurred to me. I had a wallet full of fake cards, but what happens in a year when they've expired? What if I needed a college transcript or a reference for a job?"

"Did you agree to it?"

She shrugged. "I told him I didn't have enough money. When I ran away I had two hundred and five thousand dollars. I paid them fifty to help me. I put up another twenty-five for expenses: that Sid Freeman guy, plane tickets, hotels, cars, hair, clothes, and I don't remember what else. He was taking another twenty-five right then. So if I never spent anything at all—never even bought any food—I could only pay for twenty-one months. Then I thought, 'Well, okay. Maybe I can find a job quickly, and that will buy me more time.' Isn't that amazing?"

"It sounds fairly sensible."

"No, it doesn't. What I'm telling you is that it took me maybe five seconds to hear it, and accept it, and get used to it, just like the yelling."

"You didn't have much choice, and you had already figured out that arguing with him tonight wasn't going to get you anywhere."

"I didn't have any choice at all. I was being robbed and I couldn't fight or yell for help. I was getting scared. I thought about running. I was in a strange city across the continent from anything or anybody I knew. I had no credit cards or licenses or identification except the ones they had given me, in a name they chose, and no hope of getting any others. How far would I get? But the big, big surprise was that it took me maybe five more seconds to see everything that had happened the way it really was."

Jane wondered if she did. "How was it, really?"

"They had promised to make me disappear. I had thought of it as hiding, but it wasn't. They made me cease to exist, and what was left was this woman that they had invented. Whatever they decided was all right with me, because it had to be. They owned me. I was already not really evaluating what he was telling me, because I knew it was settled. But I was listening, because I had to know what he wanted so I could do it."

Jane guided the car onto the circular interchange for the San Diego Freeway and accelerated up the long hill to the south toward the airport. "It's over now. Don't blame yourself. If anybody is to blame, I guess it's me."

The woman looked at her with glazed eyes. "I should hate you, but I don't seem to be able to bring back enough of myself to feel it. I think it, but it's just something I know is appropriate, not an emotion."

"It's a start," said Jane. "Being in a situation like that isn't something that changes you into a different person. He was holding a gun on you."

"No, he wasn't. If you want to know what really happened, I'll tell you. He said I would pay them five thousand a month. I said I couldn't for very long. He said a smart girl like me would think of a way."

"This isn't necessary," said Jane. "You don't have to talk about it."

"Yes I do," said the woman. "I said, 'What's that supposed to mean?' So he reached out and tugged my nightgown so the hem came up over my knees. He said my legs weren't bad, so there might be hope. I batted his hand away and pulled back from him. He just stood there and put his hand on his hip. That opened his coat so I could see the gun. He never touched it, just looked at me and waited." She squeezed her eyes closed, and Jane saw tears stream down her cheek. "I said, 'You don't need the gun.' And I started to take the nightgown off. He didn't even have to ask. I've never done anything like that in my life, never thought of it. I just knew that was what I was supposed to do, and I was thinking I would save myself some little bit of nastiness if I just did it."

Jane said, "This isn't what I want to know."

"But it is what I want to tell you. It took about fifteen minutes to reduce me to that. He had come to make sure I understood that I would have to do what they wanted, and this was the most painless way I had to tell him that I got the idea: he didn't have to hit me or cut me or something. And you know what? Before it happened, I was already used to it. It had already sunk in, and seemed perfectly natural in the new order of things. I had already learned that I could get by without my money, and now I told myself I could get along without whatever this was, too. But having to be hit in the face or have an arm broken, or even having to stand there and listen to him saying it, and then have to do exactly as he said, seemed worse than just getting it over with quietly. Then you came in."

Jane drove in silence, watching the lanes behind her. At the last second, she decided to drive past the Century Boulevard exit. The Los Angeles airport was too big, too obvious, too chancy. She kept going.

The woman said, "You've lost all respect for me, haven't you?"

Jane looked at her and shook her head. "No."

"Oh, that's right. You didn't have any respect for me in the first place. Why should you? I did a terrible thing and ran away. And now this."

Jane said, "I've been trying to tell you that you did the best you could under the circumstances. That's all anybody can do."

"Not you," she said with hatred. "You didn't volunteer to strip for that man. You came in and zapped him. No hesitation, no fear. But I'm not like that, and if I were, I wouldn't have the slightest idea of how to do it."

Jane shook her head sadly. "There was lots of hesitation, and that's why you got into trouble. I'm sorry. I misread the signs at first. The reason he wasn't afraid that anybody would come when you made noise was that there's nobody else living in the building yet. They undoubtedly own it, and you're the only tenant at the moment. His car was the only one in the lot at almost midnight, so I came in. And I do feel fear."

"No you don't," said the woman. "You don't know what it is."

"I've felt convinced that everything has fallen apart and I'm surrounded and outnumbered and unthinkable things are going to happen and I won't be able to do anything. Not anymore."

"You just decided to stop?"

"In a way. I've been at this a long time. The problems all have shapes now, and I try to guess what might be done to get rid of them. What I'm afraid of is that I'll miss something, that I won't move fast enough, or I'll guess wrong. Those are fears I can do something about, so I do. It doesn't leave as much space in my brain for just being frightened. It's a trick, and you're going to have to learn it."

"I can't." The tears came again, and the big, gulpy sobs shook her body. "I can't. I don't know what to do."

Jane said quietly, "I'm going to take you somewhere now. I'll give you new identification that will hold up until I can tailor something for you. I'll give you a quick course in how to get along."

"And then what?"

"After that, if you've paid attention, you'll get along."

"That's it?"

"That's it."

29

Jane let her choose her own name, but she didn't know how. Jane sighed and asked, "What's your real name?"

"Janet McAffee."

Jane shook her head in surprise. "I'll bet they don't do that very often."

"Do what?"

"Give a runner the same first name. The reason to do it is because you're used to being a Janet, so a new last name is no big mental strain. A hundred million women have done it without much fuss, and we're all prepared for the possibility from the age of ten. But it means they didn't think anyone would be looking for you very hard. Now they are, so you'll have to do better this time. With your hair and eyes you don't have to be Irish. Is there anything else you've ever wanted to be?"

"I don't know. How about French?" It was a moment or two before she admitted to herself that it was because of her college roommate, Denise Fourget. She had always envied the way Denise looked, the way she moved and talked. She spent a few seconds feeling foolish, and another few seconds asking herself whether it mattered where the name came from, then chose the name Christine Manon.

Chris Manon was not sanguine about Cleveland. It was no more run-down or dirty than Baltimore, but the old buildings didn't seem to have the eccentric grace of the ones she was used to. They weren't even as old. She suspected that when the summer ended, it would get cold in that ferocious, windy way that midwestern cities did, with snow that was frightening instead of pretty. But those were petty complaints, and she was ashamed to say them out loud.

The apartment Jane rented was not even as nice as the one in Los Angeles. It was drab, and had endured a lot of damage over the years that seemed to have been repaired by a landlord's handyman instead of a real carpenter. There were mismatched tiles here and there in the foyer and hallways, and the cheapest kind of faucets in the kitchen and bathroom.

Jane had been very pleased when she found it. "Second floor is best, so always try for it. If the building has three or more floors you can slip out when you need to and go up or down the elevator or the stairs, then out the front or back door. A visitor can't easily climb in your window, but you're low enough to go out with a rope. You can see the street better than they can see your apartment." Jane had put on the mailbox the name Joseph Manon, and assured her that any mail for Christine Manon would still get to her.

Christine Manon's main occupation was watching Jane. Each morning she watched her go through her Tai Chi exercises, stretching and contorting but never stopping, always in motion at the same slow, constant pace so she moved from one position to another and each pose was already changing into something else. Then Chris waited while Jane went outside to run. Sometimes an hour later she would catch a glimpse of Jane coming up the walk, taking long, fast strides with her head up and her neck straight, landing each step on the ball of her foot. Jane's movements seemed always to be the kind that should require her muscles to be tight and straining, but they weren't. The word that came to Christine's mind was "coiled." She was preparing herself for something.

It was three days before Christine worked up her nerve enough to say, "I want you to teach me how to fight."

Jane looked at her skeptically, then said, "You needn't expect to see them again."

"I can't be sure."

"You're going to be invisible, and they're not going to strain much to find somebody who can't come up with five thousand a month. They have richer clients, who are running from worse trouble. And if they were to come, you don't fight. You run."

"But what if they do come, and I can't run? Please. I know I'm not very promising, but I know that you can help me."

Reluctantly, Jane had walked to the kitchen, taken out a big pot and set it on the stove, then put a long-handled ladle beside it. "Make some sauce, make some stew, the kind that simmers for twelve hours. Keep something going whenever you're feeling that way."

"You mean if I eat something I'll feel better and stop imagining things?"

"No. It's boiling water, only thicker. If somebody comes in, he'll smell it, but he won't be afraid of it. The smell makes him think nothing's wrong. If you need to hurt him, you throw a ladleful in his face, dump the rest on him, and run. Don't stop to look back. He'll probably have third-degree burns, but he'll also be very angry."

Christine picked up a long butcher knife from the counter and looked at it.

Jane shook her head. "That's not your first choice. A knife is good only if he never sees it. The boning knife is a better size and shape. Using one takes a strong stomach, and you can't do it from a distance."

"Why a distance?"

Jane took the knife out of Chris's hand and led her to the kitchen table, then sat across from her. "This isn't going to sound good to you, but here it is. You are a woman. No matter what lessons you take, or how hard you work at it, you are not going to meet one of these men in an even hand-to-hand fight and not get killed."

"Then what about all those self-defense classes and things? Karate and all that."

Jane shook her head sympathetically. "There are people who make a good living by teaching scared women a few quick moves that might buy them ten seconds to get away. Good for them. But they also manage to imply to a lot of gullible ladies that lesson number six hundred and forty-seven will make them formidable enough to overpower a serious attacker. It doesn't work that way."

"Why not?"

Jane seemed to contemplate her for a minute. "What's the simplest way to put this? Athletic-equipment companies have been studying this stuff like crazy for years, trying to design gear especially for women. It's a gold mine, so they're working hard. One result I saw was a baseball glove they had developed just for women. It had to be smaller, but also compensate for the fact that the average American woman has fifty-five percent less strength in her hand than the average man."

"You're telling me I should give up? It's completely hopeless?"

Jane shook her head. "No. I'm telling you that pretending a woman is a man with long hair will get you killed."

"What won't get me killed?"

"Recognizing what you can do, and practicing."

"Practicing what?"

"A man has more upper body strength than you can ever have, so you never compete with it. Practice staying out of his reach. A woman is more flexible. We can bend and stretch more, kick higher. If you work hard at a few moves, you can become very fast. But above all, you fight dirty."

"I'm willing to do that, but what do I do?"

"Think about it clearly. If he hits you once, the fight is over. So you always hit first. Each movement of your body must be a surprise, and it must be capable of disabling him—if possible, permanently. You want to put out an eye, dislocate a kneecap, crush a trachea. Always use a weapon if you can. Never let him suspect that you intend to fight until after you've done the worst you can to him—not the worst you think is necessary: the very worst." Jane paused. "That's most of it."

"I don't want most of it. What's the rest?"

Jane shrugged. "That comes with time. It's mostly learning how a man fights with a woman. If you watch boxing on TV you'll see men dancing and circling, bobbing and weaving, keeping their guard up. That's what they do if they think the other person is their equal. They know you're not, so they're very sloppy. Usually they don't even try to hit you—just grab you and you'll give up. That gives you one enormous chance. Use it wisely, because there won't be another."

For three days Christine practiced in the middle of the living room. Jane told her, "Learn just one sequence of moves: six punches delivered just as fast as your arms can move—left-right-left-right-left-right to his nose, eyes, throat—then the side kick to the knee, pivot, and run. Always the same."

Christine was insulted. "Always the same? I mean, it seems too simple."

"If you were going to do it twice, it would be. But you're not. You only have to surprise him once. You practice it until your body simply does it without bringing your mind into it. He has to make decisions, you're already in motion."

Christine practiced in the living room while Jane watched. It reminded Christine of a dance rehearsal, with the choreographer studying everything she did. A few times Jane jumped up and corrected her. "Not just arms," she said. "Your arms aren't enough. Up on the balls of your feet, and explode off your back foot. Your whole body has to deliver it, and it has to be a poke, like a piston, not a swing." Jane did it all with such speed and force that Christine felt a little frightened of her. She tried to imitate the moves precisely. Jane watched with tentative approval, then said, "See his face in front of you. Faster. Harder. Body, not arms."

During these days in Cleveland Jane tried tracing the license number of the car that had brought Christine to Sid Freeman's. She claimed her car had been dented in a parking lot and a witness had left a note with that number on it. The Minnesota Department of Motor Vehicles gave her the name of the company that the car had been rented from. Jane decided not to call the company: knowing the false name the man had used to rent it would get her nowhere.

Jane called the Los Angeles county clerk's office to find the owner of the apartment complex at 19942 Troost Avenue in North Hollywood. In exchange for four calls and a fee, Jane learned that the owner was a corporate entity called 19942 Troost Management and its address was the bank that held its checking account.

On the fourth day, Christine walked quietly to the doorway of the bedroom and stopped. Jane was facing away from her, throwing clothes into a suitcase. After a second or two, when Christine was sure she had not shifted her weight or even breathed, Jane said, "I'll be back in two days."

"Where are you going?"

"To meet someone."

After Jane was gone, Christine sat in the middle of the living room and stared out the window at the upper branches of a tree slowly swaying against the cloudy sky beyond it. She thought about Jane on an airplane. Pretty soon the silver airplane would rise up to pierce those clouds like a little needle. Christine was already alone.

The silence of the apartment was suddenly palpable, and it forced her to think. She kept coming back to a nagging worry that was almost like guilt. She had let Jane save her life, then spent all of this time with her. Had she remembered to tell her everything? Probably it wasn't worth anything to Jane, she assured herself. And Jane wasn't the problem. Christine was the one who had to be afraid. She had only a few secrets left.

30

Something just below Violet Peterson's chest was clutched again by the throbbing of the drums, quickened and carried along with their rhythm. The wild, falsetto voices of the singers rose and fell and made her throat contract with theirs as she waited in the crowd. This was the part of the doings that she had found she loved the most. It brought back the amazement that she had felt as a small child, when the sound of the drums had held her in some space between physical and emotional, and the wailing male voices that were clearer and a pitch higher than the voices of normal life had seemed to come from somebody far older and more important than her uncles and cousins.

Violet glanced at her watch. It was seven o'clock, and the Entry was beginning. She saw the four men of the honor guard moving up into the big circle. The first of them carried an American flag; the next, a blue one with pictures on it she couldn't make out that she supposed must be the flag of Oklahoma. Then there were two men carrying feathered staffs. They all wore Cherokee gear—beaded buckskin shirts, tall horse-hair roaches on their heads with feathers jutting out at angles. She recognized some of the medals pinned to their shirts: two—no, three—purple hearts, a silver star. The one with the American flag had a few she had not seen before.

She had gotten used to the way powwows went. It seemed unsurprising that the honor guard was always made up of combat veterans, because that was the way people had done things in the Old Time. Next came the traditional male dancers, mostly older men who wore not replicas of costumes but the family heirlooms of twenty or thirty nations. Tonight, in this group, there were plains shirts made of deer that had probably died before Custer, embroidered with trade beads and porcupine quills, and bear-claw necklaces and eagle-feather war bonnets. Then came the grass dancers with long fringe, then the fancy dancers, wearing iridescent colors that didn't exist a hundred years ago and bells and turkey-feather bustles and hoops and war paint.

Next came the traditional women dancers, then women in jingle dresses with cones made of the shiny metal tops of chewing tobacco cans, clacking together as the women danced. Then there were the women fancy dancers, with dresses embroidered and beaded and even sequinned so they reminded Violet of hummingbirds. Nearly all of the fancy dancers wore a single feather in their hair, something that in the Old Time would have been about the same as wearing your husband's breechcloth. The shawls were breathtaking, worn over the shoulders and held out in the dance like the wings of birds.

Violet looked around her at the crowd. Before she had hit South Dakota she had never seen anyone wearing a cowboy hat except on television. There were lots of people here tonight with them, and she was starting to get used to them.

Even two of the F.B.I. stalkers had worn them tonight. The man with the little mustache and the blond woman posing as a couple were wearing black ones with fancy decorations on the crowns. She supposed that the black ones must be evening attire, because the sun during this afternoon's doings would have baked their brains. She took another look at the woman. She had a cute shape—probably from all the exercise they got running and jumping and aiming guns at decent people—but she had made a mistake with those blue jeans. They were way too tight. Violet almost felt sorry for her, because she just didn't know any better than that.

She turned away from them and checked on the man with the glasses. He seemed to be fascinated, watching the dancers come in. No, she remembered. He was watching her. No matter where his eyes were when she looked at him, that was what they were all here for, and they were distressingly good at it.

She moved back from the dancers and began to circulate in the crowds. She paused at a few of the booths. At some they sold turquoise and silver jewelry from Arizona, reddish gold from the Black Hills, some beaded moccasins that were sort of like the ones she had at home, some tall ones like boots that the Apaches made. There were Navajo blankets and rugs, a lot of baskets, Hopi pottery. She stopped and bought some fry bread with powdered sugar and a Coke. She could get used to this stuff, she decided, but it had to be loaded with calories.

Behind her she could hear the blaring amplified voice of the master of ceremonies making the opening speech, then some words that must be a prayer in his own language. Then the drums began again, and the grass dancers were out in the circle. They wore costumes with two-foot fringe swinging from their arms and backs and around their legs as they whirled and dipped and spun, doing the Kiowa dance that was supposed to stomp down the tall grass so the night's festivities could begin. The stomping down wasn't literal. She had seen an Ottawa on a tractor-sized lawn mower cutting the grass on the day she had arrived. It was a preparation in the Indian sense, the way Seneca negotiators used to tell the whites they would uproot brambles and cut down tall trees to clear a path to the spot where negotiations would take place. It just meant they would make things right.

The grass dancers were spinning and stomping wildly now, working up a sweat. People around Violet were nodding their heads in time with the drums and smiling to themselves. It was a nice feeling, being out here in this rolling country with strange bright-red dirt and fragrant grass, all being Indians together.

Violet was a bit of a conservative in her own ways, and had always favored the old Seneca songs and dances and customs. She understood the words and had the feeling that they were about her and her family and their relationship with the universe. But the powwow circuit was about just being Indian. It was probably something like the great councils had been, when dozens of nations who had little in common, speaking unrelated languages and wearing all of these different costumes, had traveled thousands of miles to come together in the same circle for a time.

If it hadn't been for the F.B.I. agents following her around like circling vultures, she might have enjoyed it even more. Maybe when it was all over and she had time by herself in the old house at Tonawanda, when new sights weren't being flashed in front of her eyes every few seconds, she would formulate the spectacle into some general impression that would fit into her head all at once.

She had been gazing around her at the groups of dancers and celebrants as she walked, but now she found herself in the middle of a dozen costumed dancers she had seen in the entry of the traditional women. A voice beside her ear said, "Vi."

Violet turned. In front of her stood a Seneca woman got up to look the way women had not looked since the 1790s. On her cheeks were painted two vermilion circles from the eyes to the chin, and four broad red lines made by a horizontal swipe of the fingers crossed her forehead. The part in her hair was bright yellow. Handsome Lake had dissuaded women from painting themselves in this fashion because it was calculated to attract the gazes of men they weren't entitled to entice. The woman wore the old-style beaded moccasins, leggings, skirt, and overdress, and around her shoulders was a dark blue shawl embroidered with daisies and apple blossoms. But still, she was Jane Whitefield.

She spoke in Seneca. "I see three people keeping watch over you. Are there others?"

Violet forced her eyes toward the circle as though she were watching the dancers and answered in Seneca. "The woman with yellow hair, her husband, and the one with glasses."

"Have they spoken to you yet?"

"Oh yes," said Violet. "They raided my hotel room in Eagle Butte."

"I'm sorry," said Jane. "Were you afraid?"

"Of course," she admitted. Then she quickly added, "But I'm fine."

"What did they do?"

Violet risked looking into Jane's eyes for a second. "Nothing. But they were prepared to shoot you when they came in. They were all ready, you know."

"I thought they might be," said Jane. Violet saw a flash of white teeth smiling in the red paint. "It's a good thing it was only you."

"It's not a good joke, Jane."

Jane shrugged. "It's the only joke we have. Tell me about Carey."

"He's exactly as you left him," said Violet. "He's so worried about you he looks like something hurts."

Jane said, "I came to tell you to go home, Vi. Tell Carey where we were when you saw me." Jane's body seemed to pick up the beat of the drums. She began to dance a little, moving slowly away into the crowd.

"Wait," said Violet. She reached into the pocket of her jeans and slipped a small piece of white paper into Jane's palm. "One of the agents gave me that. It's his name and the number you call to get connected directly to him. He said it was in case I change my mind. Keep it in case you change yours."

Jane closed her fingers around it without glancing at it. She said, "Please, Vi. Don't worry about me." Jane looked over her shoulder at the crowds of people of both sexes and all ages, wearing every kind of gear and ornament that had ever been seen on the continent, almost all of them with hair that gleamed black in the floodlights above the field. "They can't even see me."

Jane walked out past the man in the glasses, nearly brushing his shoulder as she went, then slipped between the man and the woman in cowboy hats. They looked at her, but they saw only a flash of bright paint and the clothes of a woman who might have lived long ago.

31

When Jane returned to Cleveland she seemed different to Christine. She spent the first day in the little apartment staring at the wall. On the second, she went out for the whole day. She came back with shopping bags full of new clothes, some hair dye, and a shoulder bag full of hundred-dollar bills. She sat Christine in the living room beside the telephone.

"What's going on?" Christine asked.

Jane said, "I had hoped to avoid doing anything as risky as this, but nothing that wasn't risky has worked. When that man pretending to be a policeman came to you, he gave you a phone number that you were supposed to call and ask for Jane. Dial it."

Christine frowned and looked at her, but she could see that she wasn't supposed to say anything. She dialed the number and handed the telephone to Jane.

Jane listened for a moment, then broke the connection. "Try again."

Christine dialed the number again; Jane listened, then hung up. "They must have found the body."

Christine picked up the receiver, dialed the same number, and listened to the voice. "The number you have reached is out of service. If you feel you have reached this number in error, please hang up and dial again." Christine set the receiver down.

Jane took a deep breath and blew it out again. "I was hoping they needed to keep that number open, because they had other runners out who might need to get in touch. But they're too smart. They must have used it for initial contact only. Maybe they used it just for you."

"What were you going to do?"

Jane sighed. "Tell them I had embezzled some money and needed to disappear."

Christine realized that her mouth was open. "You wanted to be their client? But they saw you."

"Two of them did. One is dead."

"Still . . ." said Christine.

"It doesn't matter," Jane said. "It isn't going to happen." She walked into the bedroom, tossed the bag of money on the bed, and looked at the shopping bags doubtfully. "Those might fit you."

"I can't believe you were going to do that." She realized that she sounded foolish. "What are you going to do now?"

Jane shrugged. "Go back to Minneapolis. If I can find more of their runners, it's possible I'll learn who they are, where they are . . ."

Christine looked at her for a moment. She couldn't keep it a secret, but she wasn't sure how to admit she hadn't told Jane everything. "Other runners? Like me?"

"Yes," said Jane.

"Then I guess I have something to tell you. It didn't seem like it was important, and I kind of forgot—"

"Tell me."

"I was in Baltimore when the policeman told me to call the number. The woman on the phone said to wait on a particular corner. A car drove up and a man took me to an apartment, and explained what I had to do: get plastic surgery, collect money, and get ready to go. Then they flew me to Chicago, put me in another apartment, and had me wait some more. I lived there for a long time—a couple of months—and they would come about once a week with groceries and things. They said they were getting ready to move me someplace where I could live permanently. I kept asking, 'Where am I going to live?' and they'd say, 'We're looking for the perfect place,' or, 'We're getting it ready.' Each time they had some agenda. Once they took my picture for IDs. Sometimes they told me things about how to stay hidden, brought me new clothes . . . things like that. There was a closet in the apartment that was locked. One day they opened it up, and it was filled with boxes."

"What kind of boxes?"

"About the size that copy paper comes in. About a foot wide and two feet long. They were all wrapped in brown paper and sealed with packing tape. One of the men put stickers on them and they carried them away."

"Stickers?"

"Mailing labels." She looked a little uncertain. "I wasn't supposed to go near the closet. One man would carry a couple of boxes down to the car, and when he came back, the other would carry a couple. After a while, they got careless, and they were both outside at once, so I looked: 80183 Padre Street, Santa Barbara, CA 93101."

"Why do you remember the address after all this time?"

Christine made a face. "I had this stupid idea that it was like the underground railroad or something. Somebody had been in this apartment first, then got moved to the next place. That meant that the address in California was where I would go next. So I thought about it a lot. One day one of the men asked if there was any reason I couldn't live in California, so that made me sure. I didn't find out that I was wrong until I saw the address on the driver's license Sid Freeman gave me that night. Ten minutes later you were there."

"And you forgot?"

"Not exactly," said Christine. "I figured it was the place where you would take me." She frowned. "I'm wrong a lot."

Jane was pacing, looking at the wall, then turning and walking toward the opposite wall. The intensity of her eyes frightened Christine. "Is there anything else that you saw or heard that I don't know?"

"No, I don't think so."

"What about the name? Was there a name on the labels?"

"Oh, I'm sorry," she said. "It was C. Langer. I wasn't going to snoop, but I glanced at the pile of boxes and that was what I saw first. It looked like the name was 'Clanger.' It seemed like a joke, at first."

Jane spoke quietly, as though to herself. "It is a joke."

Jane was quiet again for a full day. When Christine awoke the next morning, Jane was in the living room as usual, but she was not finishing her exercises. She had used the time to make a transformation.

She had braided her hair and rolled it into a bun behind her head. She was wearing a pair of photosensitive glasses with big lenses that made it difficult in the bright morning light to tell what color her eyes were. She had replaced her usual jeans and sneakers with a light gray skirt and jacket. It wasn't as though she was a different person, Christine decided. It was as though she was a different type of person.

Christine had gotten used to thinking of her as a sort of athlete—someone who wasn't exactly deprived, but who denied herself, subjected herself to some kind of harsh, unforgiving discipline. The physical changes were minor, when Christine analyzed them, but the attitude of the woman before her was different. The word that came to Christine's mind was "spoiled." Jane looked like the kind of woman who spent a week out of every month in some spa having massages and wraps and special diets. She looked like the pampered and ignored wife of some fancy doctor.

"I guess this means you're leaving again."

"Yes," said Jane. "I have a few things to tell you before I go, because this time I may not make it back."

Christine found herself backing away. She wished she had never told Jane about Santa Barbara. When she felt the chair against her calves, she realized what she had been doing, and sat down.

Jane said, "You know that you've been used by the people you paid to help you. What you don't seem to know is this: there never were any death threats. It's just a way of drumming up business—selecting the ideal runner. There was no risk for them, because nobody was after you."

"Why didn't you tell me?"

"Because I was using you to get to them. I told you that much. You deserve an apology, but you won't get it from me. If I had it to do over, I'd do it again. Now I want you to spend some time thinking about what you're going to do."

Christine heard the words, and it occurred to her that she had been trying to avoid saying them to herself. She said, "You mean if you don't come back?"

"If I don't call you or show up here within a month, then I'm not coming. If you think you can make a decent life beginning then and starting from here, without ever going back, then do it. If you think you can't, call the number that I left by the phone in the kitchen and ask for Mr. Marshall. Tell him everything that happened."

"Who is he?"

"An F.B.I. agent. He'll arrest you."

"Arrest me? I could go back to Baltimore and get arrested. Why should I call him?"

"He's working on the case of Richard Dahlman, the other runner I told you about. You can give him answers he can't get any other way. The details from his case will make what happened to you a lot easier to believe. If you help him, he might be able to help you find the least painful way back to where you started."

Christine's eyes welled up. Not tears, Christine thought. I don't want to cry now. "That's what you think I should do, isn't it?"

Jane looked at her, and Christine could see that she was feeling sorry for her. "I don't know. The decisions I've made for you haven't done you much good. This one's yours."

"Please," she said. "You know, but you're not telling me."

Jane touched her arm and spoke quietly. "This isn't your life. This is just a nasty detour, like a sickness." She picked up her suitcase and went to the door. "Give us both a month. No more." She opened the door and slipped out.

32

Jane found her seat in the airplane, sat down, and felt a cold, empty sensation in her chest. She was about to go west again, away from Carey instead of toward him. She had spent most of the summer trying to find people who had done terrible things and left Richard Dahlman to take the blame. But Richard Dahlman was in a pleasant retirement home in Carlsbad, and the one who was surrounded by policemen, watched, and suspected was Carey. It couldn't go on much longer. Something Jane tried had to work.

She slowly forced herself to stop thinking about Carey and tried to think instead about what she had to do to set him free. But every time she tried to plan what she would do when she arrived in Santa Barbara, she began to lose her resolve. It was impossible to think about Santa Barbara without bringing back a horrible memory.

Harry the gambler had been so hot that she had not wanted to know where his final hiding place would be. She had been afraid that she would be caught and that whatever they did to her would make her reveal it.

She had taken Harry to Lewis Feng's shop in Vancouver, where she could buy him a whole prefabricated identity, not just a few good papers like the ones she could have bought from Sid Freeman. Lewis Feng had not dealt in new names. Lewis's specialty had been creating unoccupied spaces in the universe, then holding them until the right customers arrived with the right sums of money. The driver's license, the credit cards, the Social Security card, the car registration, even the apartment had been obtained in advance and kept current, waiting for the right purchaser. Most of Lewis's customers had been rich ethnic Chinese from Hong Kong, Taiwan, Malaysia who foresaw that some day they might want the chance to slip into the United States. But Lewis had kept a number of surnames that weren't necessarily Chinese. So Harry had filled the space of Harry Shaw, and Jane had left him in Vancouver.

Harry had made no mistakes. He might have lasted forever if Jane had not met another runner who had convinced her that he, too, deserved the very best kind of identity, one with an impeccable provenance and enough age. Jane had taken John Felker across the country into Canada and left him at Lewis Feng's shop. The next time she had seen Lewis Feng she was staring at a picture of him in a newspaper above an article that called him "the victim." The next time she had seen Harry she had been looking down at him from the rim of an open grave. And the next time she had seen John Felker, he had been busy cycling the bolt of a rifle for his second shot at her.

Lewis Feng had placed Harry in a small apartment on a quiet street on the outskirts of a medium-sized community at the edge of the country. Harry had been killed in Santa Barbara. Jane reminded herself that it was a coincidence. Harry had been put there because it was a place where a lot of middle-aged people could be seen doing nothing. It was a place where Harry would not be able to play the horses in person. If he wanted to organize a game of cards, he couldn't be stopped, but in Santa Barbara he probably would not find himself sitting across the table from other pros, who would know who he was and what his location would be worth to them.

The face-changers must have picked Santa Barbara for similar rea sons. It was still a place where a stranger could appear to be minding his business without having a business that was evident. There were a couple of colleges, lots of tourists, lots of conventions, lots of retirees from someplace else. It was a place where you could give a runner a history and assume it wouldn't be deeply scrutinized.

Jane got off the plane in Sacramento, then took the whole day driving south down the long highway through central California, and arrived in late afternoon. Santa Barbara still looked pretty and peaceful to her, wedged in the pocket between tall mountains and the ocean.

When she parked on Anacapa Street and walked to State Street, she could see that the pedestrian traffic was thicker and faster and busier than the last time. Visitors were the city's main industry, and it looked to her as though business was expanding. The parts of lower State Street that used to cater to fishermen and divers and surfers had been replaced by a mall that might have been moved in one piece from Beverly Hills. Jane had stayed alive by reading changing configurations of people, and this change was one that added to her safety. It was not hard for a strange woman to stay invisible on a street crowded with strangers.

Jane waited until night to drive to Padre Street and find the address Christine had given her. It was a small white house with a low porch and a tiny patch of green grass between that and the sidewalk. The front windows were blocked by opaque white horizontal blinds, but she could see tiny slices of light behind them.

Jane drove past the house once each hour. The lights were still on at midnight, but were off when she came by at one. At two she made a list of the cars parked on the street nearby, because they probably belonged to people who lived on the block in houses that, like C. Langer's, had no garage. One of them was probably his.

At three she parked her car around the corner and walked to the house for a closer look. The night was warm, and the smell of jasmine was overpowering. She left the deserted street and walked quietly beside C. Langer's house. The windows were the sliding kind with wooden sashes and a latch between the upper pane and the lower. They were all closed and the latches locked, but there were no signs of an alarm system. Jane studied the lock on the kitchen door and the placement of shrubs between the windows and the street, then walked the fences along the sides and back. By the time she returned to her car she was confident that if she needed to, she could get in without making much noise or being visible from the street.

It wasn't a bad spot to place a runner. It was quiet and private without looking as though anyone had gone to any effort to make it so. It had three good ways out—two that would put C. Langer on another street in ten seconds. That was the way to keep a runner alive: keep her out of sight, and give her an escape route she could use if something went wrong.

Jane stopped herself. She had unconsciously slipped into the assumption that C. Langer was a woman, just because Chris was a woman, maybe because the house looked like a woman's. But Sid Freeman had told her that most of the clients he'd seen had been men. C. Langer was probably a man. It was also possible that this runner wouldn't be some stockbroker who had driven drunk, or a banker who had been unable to keep customers' accounts from merging with his own. There was no guarantee that the face-changers wouldn't take on a runner who was dangerous. If they were in it for the money, a client was anybody who had the fee.

Jane stayed down the street in her car until it was nearly light. When she saw movement behind the blinds just before six, she pulled away from the curb and drove around the corner. She didn't want to try for a first look at C. Langer at a moment when she was the only person on the street, and C. Langer could see as well as she could. She drove down to the beach to find a hotel where the dining room opened for breakfast early.

Jane spent two days learning about C. Langer's car. By a process of elimination she learned it was a red Mazda Miata. It struck Jane as an impossible choice. Sporty little cars attracted attention, even if they weren't expensive. Convertible tops were easy for a thief to slash open to get the radio, and a runner had to be careful to stay off police blotters. It was possible that C. Langer had a second car hidden somewhere and that this was a decoy, the one he or she wanted watchers to get used to seeing.

Jane was curious enough to try to find it. California law required drivers to carry proof of insurance, and C. Langer would be careful not to break any laws. Jane waited until after the street was dark and empty, then cut a slit in the convertible top that was just big enough to let her reach inside and open the door. She found the insurance card under the visor on the driver's side, wrote down the company and policy number, and went home.

The next day she called the company and gave the woman who answered the policy number. She said she was a loan officer and C. Langer had used the car as collateral on a loan. Was the insurance on it current and valid? Liability, collision, and so on? Payments made on time? Cost of policy? Were there other vehicles on the policy? There was also a new Ford Escort, and the woman gave her the license number.

It took Jane another day to find the Escort. There were few places in Santa Barbara that would do for a runner's car. It had to be accessible at any hour, it had to be close to where he or she lived, and it had to be unobtrusive. Jane found it in a carport behind an apartment building two blocks away.

It wasn't until she had been studying the house and the cars for three days that she saw C. Langer come out the front door, walk down the steps, and get into the Miata. C. Langer was a man in his early thirties. He wore a crisply pressed pair of khaki pants, Top-Sider shoes, and a short-sleeved polo shirt. He had the sort of sunglasses that Jane had always favored for her runners, with big photosensitive lenses that kept a bit of tint in dim light and became practically opaque in the sun. He looked lean and walked with more energy than he needed to expend, and his skin showed that he spent quite a bit of time in the sun. Even in the short walk to the car he was watchful. His head was high and his eyes were in motion, scanning the middle distance from left to right as though he had been taught to take in the sights one sector at a time to avoid missing anything. Jane stepped on the accelerator of her car so she would be beyond the corner before he could get around to looking at her.

She drove to the supermarket and bought a cookie sheet, then bought a pair of tin snips at a hardware store nearby, and went to a big drugstore on State Street for a box of thin, disposable latex gloves, a small flashlight, and a roll of adhesive tape. She cut a thin strip from the middle of the cookie sheet, wrapped one end of it with adhesive tape to make a handle, and she was ready.

Jane had predicted that the bathroom window and the kitchen windows would be the least troublesome, and she had been right. The bathroom window had no screen, so she could simply insert the thin strip of metal upward between the wooden frames of the two panes of glass. When it was in, she pushed forward to bend it slightly so it slipped behind the latch. She had made it long enough so she was able to use it as a lever to pry the latch around and unlock the window.

The architect had probably assured somebody that the window was too narrow for a man, but it was wide enough for Jane to slither halfway in. It wasn't until she reached her hips that she had to turn onto her side, put her right hand on the sink, and pull her legs in.

She closed the window behind her before she went out into the living room. She paused at the doorway. This wasn't the way runners' abodes usually looked. They almost always took furnished lodgings first, and kept them until they grew more confident. Even then, they tended to own things that they wouldn't mind walking away from.

C. Langer had an antique sideboard. He had a dining room table inlaid with squares of bird's-eye maple. He had a television set with a screen so big that it had gone beyond being obtrusive to just being a black wall. And C. Langer had a grand piano covered with framed photographs.

She moved closer. There was a picture of a man who looked as though he might be related to C. Langer standing on the deck of a sailboat. There was another of two children on a ski slope with a blond woman who looked like a model. The pictures were impressive. They looked old. She wondered whether Sid had made this man a few relatives. Of course, there were no pictures of C. Langer himself. A runner had to be able to walk away without leaving a fresh portrait of himself in the middle of the living room.

She moved into the kitchen and opened the cupboards. C. Langer's kitchen didn't look as though he did much cooking, so she began with the one beside the stove where the pots and pans were. It took her only a moment to find the pistol. She pulled it out of the pot gingerly because she could tell by the weight that it had a loaded magazine. She held it up. It was a Glock 19 nine millimeter. She put it back and looked in the refrigerator.

There was a milk carton that was too far back, and didn't slosh when she lifted it. Inside were a driver's license and credit cards in the name Frederick Henry Waldman, and underneath them were about fifty hundred-dollar bills in a plastic bag. The Waldman cards had no scratches from being swiped through magnetic readers, so they had to be a second set of forgeries he kept in case somebody saw through C. Langer. The milk carton was his escape kit.

Jane moved into the bedroom. Maybe the face-changers had taught him so well that Jane would not find what she was looking for. Maybe they had searched his belongings, cut the tags out of his clothes, removed anything that related to his old life, packed the boxes in Chicago themselves, and sent them on only when they were sure they were clean. But she had met few runners who had willingly taken that last step. Usually they tried to keep something—an old driver's license, a birth certificate, some piece of paper—that would let them go back if some miracle happened and home suddenly became a safe place.

Jane took the top drawer out of the nightstand, held it up, and looked to see if anything was taped under it. As she moved to put it back, she saw the second pistol in the bottom drawer. This one was a Walther P99. She slid the drawer in over it. This was a man who didn't waste money on cheap, unreliable firearms. She slid the drawer out and felt under it and behind it, but there was nothing taped there either.

Jane moved to the dresser and began removing the drawers, beginning at the top. It wasn't until she tried the bottom drawer that she found the wooden box. She opened it and looked at each item carefully. There were two watches—a Patek Philippe and a Cartier, but neither had anything engraved on it. There were a couple of tie tacks and some cuff links. Then she picked up the ring, almost unbelieving. It was a Yale class ring that said 1965 on it. C. Langer wasn't nearly old enough to have graduated in 1965. Was his father young enough to have? Just barely, if he had married young.

She tried to see it as a prop. Maybe he had bought it in a pawnshop to help with C. Langer's identity. But if he'd done that, he must have expected to alter the year somehow. She looked at the side and made out the initials B.R.V. He would have to do something about those, too. But there was something bigger than that wrong with the idea. If a runner wanted to hide and develop a safe identity, pretending to be a Yale alumnus was a rotten idea, and wearing a Yale ring was a worse idea. If a college was necessary, it should be something like the University of California, which had nine campuses, each as big as Yale, and must be so familiar to people around here that nobody would think about it. Apparently the face-changers hadn't bothered to teach this runner the first rule: don't answer any questions until somebody asks.

Jane looked around the room to be sure that she was leaving it undisturbed, then picked up the pistol in the nightstand and went to the living room to wait.

Just as she sat down she heard the Miata drive up and stop in front of the house. She heard the car door slam, and suddenly the sights she had seen began to come together into a suspicion. The Yale ring, the money he had spent on the furniture and the guns and the two cars, the photographs that looked a little bit like him were all wrong. Everything in this house was wrong. C. Langer wasn't an ordinary runner.

Jane stood up and moved silently into the bedroom, replaced the gun, slipped into the bathroom, and opened the window. She heard the key in the front-door lock as she was slithering out the narrow opening, then heard the door swing open. Jane lowered herself to the ground and slid the window closed, then crouched beneath it. She heard his footsteps approach. She heard him urinate, then flush the toilet. She knew he was directly above her, his face inches from the window as he washed his hands at the sink.

After what seemed like a long time, she heard his footsteps receding. Jane found a spot for her home-made latch opener behind a low bush near the window and left it there, then slipped along the back fence and across two yards to her car.

The next morning Jane waited until C. Langer had gotten into the Miata and driven off before she climbed in the bathroom window with her video camera. She turned it on as soon as the window was closed, then walked through the rooms, one by one. She made images of the furniture, recorded the serial numbers of the two guns, made close-ups of the photographs on the piano, the jewelry, the class ring, then laid out the Frederick Waldman identification cards and recorded close-up shots of those too. Before she left, she made sure that nothing was out of place. Then she closed and latched the bathroom window from the inside and left by the front door. When C. Langer came home, he would put his key into the dead bolt and turn it. Unless he was very astute, he would not be sure that the key moved too easily for the dead bolt to have been locked.

As soon as Jane was outside, she felt an almost uncontrollable impulse to escape from this place. She wanted to get into the car and drive as fast as she could, away from Santa Barbara. She promised herself that she would do it, but not yet. There was still one thing she didn't have on tape.

33

Jane placed the video camera on her car's dashboard in front of the steering wheel, zoomed in on C. Langer's doorway, and tossed a sweater over it so it wouldn't be visible from a distance. She came back to the car two hours later, when the tape would be used up, and drove off with it.

When she reviewed the tape in her hotel room, she had shots of C. Langer leaving the house, then an hour later coming back. But someone had taught him well. He always wore the dark glasses, always moved as though he were in a hurry. When he approached the door he already had the right key in his hand, and his body was close to the door and his head down when he opened it. When he left, he moved out of frame just as quickly. She was beginning to understand why police surveillance tapes were always so appallingly bad.

Jane recharged the battery in her hotel room and went out to buy more blank tapes at the big drugstore on State Street. It occurred to her that the people watching Carey at home must know how to get a clear picture of a man's face. But then she remembered that they were doing pretty much what she had—parked in front of the house and started the camera.

She had to get closer, and to do it at a time when the light was good. The next day, she studied his movements from a distance. There seemed to be no way to get close to him with a camera. If she followed him during his trips away from the house, it was hard to imagine a way to take a tape of him without being seen. When he had disappeared into the house for what Jane judged would be the last time, Jane went back to her car and drove up the street.

That evening she studied the tapes she had taken of C. Langer, running them over and over. But this time she was not looking at the male figure flashing across the camera's field of view. She looked at the shapes that did not move. She held her eyes on C. Langer's car, on the windows of the neighbors' houses, on the shrubbery in C. Langer's front yard.

As she watched, each object caused her to formulate a plan and dismiss it. The light fixture just above Langer's door was in the perfect position, but it wasn't quite big enough, and the glass globe was not transparent. No windows in the nearby houses were at the ideal angle and distance to afford the right view, even if she could have gotten inside. The shrubs that were thick enough to hide a video camera were too far from the door. The only plants near the door were the potted ones on the porch, and they were too sparse. She studied the pots. The biggest one, with a ficus in it, looked as though it might be plastic. She could enlarge the drainage hole in the bottom, bury the camera so the lens was pressed against the hole, and tip the plant so it looked as though the wind had blown it over. He would see it, squat or kneel close enough to the pot to tip the plant back up, and go inside. No, it was unlikely that he could see the hole and not see the lens.

She evolved a plan for C. Langer's car. She could create a minor problem in the engine that would stimulate him to open the hood. The camera could be attached to the engine compartment low and just in front of the firewall, disguised to look like one of the electronic boxes that belonged there. He would fix the problem—replace the radiator cap, or reattach the hose—then shut the hood, and drive off. She could open the hood and retrieve the camera the next time he parked the car. But Jane didn't know anything about C. Langer. He might be one of those men who knew every nut and bolt in a car and would see the camera instantly, or he might be the other kind, who wouldn't even open the hood. He'd call a mechanic to come and do it for him.

She watched the tapes again. The porch was where he was most visible, but there was nothing on it that she could use. It was a few minutes later when she realized that she had been staring at the solution all evening and failing to see it. She reminded herself that this was its most appealing quality, because C. Langer would look at it and not see it either.

Jane watched her tapes one more time to be sure. There was a small wooden square on the side of the porch that had to be an access hatch. Wooden porches felt solid and looked solid, but they were just platforms with boards laid over them and the sides enclosed. They were very dark inside. She prepared her video camera, then drove toward C. Langer's house. On the way, she stopped at a drugstore and bought a copy of *The New York Times*.

It was four o'clock in the morning when Jane emerged from under C. Langer's porch and replaced the hatch. Without stepping on the porch, she reached through the railing and placed the copy of the newspaper in exactly the right spot near the door, half on the doormat and half off. Then she went back to her hotel and went to sleep.

Jane waited until the next night to find out how her plan had worked. When she was sure the whole neighborhood was asleep, she drove back to C. Langer's house. She parked on the next street, slipped between Langer's house and the one beside it, crawled under the porch, and retrieved her camera.

When Jane returned to her hotel, she held her breath and played her tape on fast forward. There was a long pause, when the image was total darkness. It gradually lightened, until she could make out dim, blurred shapes of black letters between the sides of the hole she had widened in the porch floor. That was the newspaper. After thirty seconds, she stopped the tape and ran it at normal speed because she was afraid of missing something. Now she could hear the sounds the camera's microphone had picked up. Birds were singing in the trees near the house, cars started, and doors slammed.

At last, she heard a footstep. Then she heard a door closing. There were more footsteps. Suddenly, the screen was filled with glaring light, and then the automatic light meter adjusted: C. Langer had lifted the newspaper off the hole in the porch. Jane clenched her teeth. Langer was holding the paper between the camera and his face, reading the headlines. She could see his legs, his hands and chest, and then the newspaper. "Come on," she whispered. He turned a few pages, then folded the paper. He straightened, so all she could see was a clear image of the underside of his jaw, his nostrils, and his sunglasses.

He reached into his pocket, then produced a set of keys, but when he pulled them out, a couple of coins came out with them, clinked, and rolled. As he bent over to pick one of them up, she could see his face descend close to the camera. Jane stared at the screen and grinned.

But C. Langer frowned. He had noticed something that didn't look familiar. One of his hands came down and touched the crack Jane had widened between the porch floorboards. Then the hand came up and took off his sunglasses. He stared at the hole for three breaths. Then he gave a little sigh, stood up, and stepped out of frame. Jane heard him unlock his front door again, and heard the whispery sound of the newspaper being tossed inside, then landing with a flap. The door closed, the key turned. Then C. Langer reappeared long enough so that Jane could see him use the toe of his shoe to push the doormat an inch to cover the hole.

That night at 11:15 the guard at the front gate of Senior Rancho in Carlsbad recorded the entry of Julia Kieler to visit her father, Alan Weems. She had called him from Los Angeles, and when she pulled into the parking space assigned to his unit, he was standing at the door.

Jane walked immediately up to him and gave him a hug so she could place her body in front of his while she pulled him inside and locked the door. "I know this is probably as safe a place as any, but standing in lighted doorways is not a great habit for you."

"I know, I know," Dahlman muttered. "It's the first occasion when I've felt the impulse, and it'll probably be the last."

"How have you been?"

He scowled. "If you have something to tell me, then out with it. If you don't, we can go back to inquiring about each other's health."

"I have something I want you to look at." She held up the videocassette. "Do you have a VCR?"

"No," said Dahlman. "There's one in the rec room, but the old ladies are probably in there now watching some old movie that they can recite by heart."

"It's okay," said Jane. "It'll just take a few minutes to hook up the camera to the television set and play it back. You do have one of those?"

"Over here," said Dahlman. He pointed into the living room. "I don't use it much."

"No?" She plugged the line into the camera, then unplugged the lamp to plug in the camera's AC adapter.

"No. The first couple of weeks I watched all the news, waiting for them to talk about me. Once or twice, they did. After that, it was pretty much what you said would happen. I'm old news."

"You sound disappointed."

Dahlman shook his head. "I was working up to thanking you, so I guess I should just grit my teeth and say it. Thank you."

"You're welcome." The television set was crackling with snow and emitting an annoying buzz.

"Now what?"

Jane switched the channel. "Nothing. You just have to put it on an empty channel." The buzzing stopped, then started again. "I'm rewinding it."

He scowled. "I knew that."

"Now be quiet and come closer and look."

He stood where he was and watched. The picture flipped once, then settled to reveal the interior of C. Langer's house: the bathroom, the living room, then closer and closer to the piano. "Somebody's house?" said Dahlman. "Am I supposed to have been there or something?"

"Just watch." Jane kept her eyes on Dahlman's face.

The camera moved close to the first of the framed photographs on the piano. The sight of the woman and two children on the ski slope meant nothing. The picture of the man on the sailboat went by, and Dahlman's arm shot out at it. "Stop!" he said. "Can't you stop this thing?"

"We'll go back to it," said Jane. "Watch the rest."

The camera moved into the kitchen. She watched Dahlman out of the corner of her eye when the camera zoomed in on the false driver's license she had taken from the milk carton and laid on the counter. He straightened, then knelt on the rug to get closer. "How did you find him?" he murmured.

"So this is the one?"

Dahlman's head turned sharply and the little gray eyes glared at her. "Of course it's him. It's the man who called himself James Hardiston. I operated on him."

"Let me ask you this," Jane began.

"But—"

"Wait. Could the man you operated on have graduated from college in 1965?"

"1965?" Dahlman was distracted by the image on the screen. "That would make him—"

"Mid-fifties."

Dahlman squinted, then nodded. "Yes. He could easily be in his fifties. Go back to the beginning."

Jane stopped the tape, rewound it, and started it again.

"Get ready to stop it."

When the tape reached the figure of the man in the sailboat, Dahlman snapped, "Now."

Jane stopped the tape. The image quivered and lines of static rolled upward across the man's face like passing shadows.

"That's him too," said Dahlman. He was so excited that he stood and sidestepped back and forth. "You thought it was someone else, didn't you?"

Jane let the tape run again. "I thought it was supposed to be his father," said Jane. "I thought Sid Freeman cooked it up."

"What's that?" asked Dahlman as the image of the first pistol zoomed upward into focus.

"His gun. I wanted the serial number, and it's better than writing it down."

The second gun came on, and the tape reverted to snow and static. Dahlman looked disappointed, but Jane said, "Keep watching."

The camera was on the front of the house. The door opened and C. Langer walked out to his car. Dahlman frowned. "It's so hard to see from that picture."

Dahlman clenched his jaw and watched. Each time the man with the dark glasses would come in or go out, there seemed to be less of him to see. He looked at Jane in confusion. "I think that's the man, but he's moving so fast, and he turns away, and those glasses—"

"Keep your eyes on the screen."

There were a few seconds of darkness, then the printed letters of the newspaper, so close to the lens that they were difficult to make out. "What in the world is that?"

Jane had no time to answer. There was the flash of light, and then the man standing up holding the newspaper.

Dahlman waited impatiently until the moment when C. Langer bent over to pick up the coin and took off his sunglasses. "There!" Dahlman shouted. "That's him!"

Jane stopped the tape and pressed the rewind button. Dahlman grinned at her expectantly. "Where is he?"

"At the moment he's living in Santa Barbara. That may not be where he intends to end up, but it looked to me as though he was planning to stay put for a while. The house is pretty well chosen, and he's put a lot into making it right. I don't mean it's expensive, although it is. I mean everything is consistent. He's building an identity, a personality."

"Fine," he said impatiently. "So how do we do this—give the tape to the police?"

Jane looked at him apologetically. "I know you would like this to end. But I think that even if we could get the Santa Barbara police to hold this man and run his fingerprints—something I can't imagine them doing— it probably wouldn't solve your problem."

"It proves I told the truth. I said I performed surgery on a man claiming to be James Hardiston. Any physician could examine this man and verify the plastic surgery. They might not be able to accurately describe every procedure we used, but there would be no argument about the fact of surgery. And I think the fellow's fingerprints will prove he's some kind of criminal living under a false name."

"Yes," said Jane. "But what kind?"

"That's the job of the police—finding that out."

Jane sighed. "He's a runner. He spent a lot of money to get a new face and a solid identity and a lot of first-class treatment. Maybe his fingerprints will show that he's done terrible things. Will they show he killed Sarah Hoffman?"

"Of course they don't prove he did it personally. When she was killed he was still recovering from his last surgery."

"Then what good are they to us?"

Dahlman slumped into a chair by the wall and closed his eyes. "I see."

Jane stood and disconnected the cords from the television set and the wall and coiled them, then put the video camera back into her bag. She stood in silence for a few more seconds, then said gently, "We've come this far. Maybe we can make it the rest of the way."

Dahlman shook his head. "At the moment I can't conceive of how to do that."

"The first step is to find out who he is," she said. "Maybe after that we'll know the second step."

34

While Jane drove through the darkness up the coast toward Santa Barbara the optimism she had feigned for Dahlman faded. When she thought of Dahlman, her memory kept conjuring images of Carey, and she had to fight the urge to cry. He had labored at becoming a doctor, and then at being one, with a kind of intensity that was heartbreaking. The work had changed him, and changed the world he lived in. For any human being, seeing was not the eye receiving pictures of what was really there, but the brain reaching out to grasp what it needed. When Carey looked at a person he saw a biological entity, a marvelously intricate and interesting creature that was doing its best with what it had. He wanted to learn from the creature's experience and impressions, and he wanted to help it. If he could no longer do that, he would be lost.

Jane had trained herself over the years never to let her mind go down this path. Thinking about the consequences of failure was like thinking about falling from a high place: it would distract her, weaken her, and make her afraid. For weeks she had concentrated on what she had to do, and not what would happen if she made a mistake. But tonight her tired mind could not fight off the fear she felt for Carey.

If she failed, it was almost certain that Carey was going to be convicted of a felony. She was not positive that this meant the state would revoke his license to practice medicine. Almost certainly it did, but the wording of some law wasn't what mattered. It was hard to imagine a hospital that would grant surgical privileges to someone with a criminal record, or a company that would approve him for malpractice insurance. Surgery wasn't something he could do by himself at home. He would be like Dahlman, sitting in a room somewhere with nothing to do. Or it could be much worse than that. If the police found enough evidence for the wrong kind of charge, and Carey drew the wrong kind of judge, he would go to jail for a very long time.

Jane felt the tears beginning to come. She gritted her teeth and shook herself, then stared hard at the dark highway ahead. She wasn't going to keep those things from happening by crying. If she could prove that the man Carey had helped to escape was innocent, then Carey would be saved too.

As she wrestled her mind back to what she had to do, old methods and tricks began to occur to her. It was a few minutes later that she decided it was time to resurrect the Furnace Company. The Furnace Company was a genuine entity that had been incorporated in Illinois ten years ago. Its assets consisted of a post office box in a strip mall in Chicago and ten computer-printed receipts showing that it had paid its annual five-dollar fee for retaining its tenuous hold on existence. The only one of its officers who had ever breathed air was a woman named Mary Sullivan, and that wasn't the name she had breathed it under.

Jane arrived at her hotel in Santa Barbara in the early morning. She checked her watch and dialed an 800 number she had used a few dozen times over the years.

A man's voice answered, "Memory Publications, Manny."

Jane said, "Manny, it's Mary Sullivan at the Furnace Company."

"Well, hello," said Manny. "I haven't heard from you lately. Tell you the truth, I thought you'd gone under, like half the country."

"Gone under?"

"Yeah, Chapter Seven, Chapter Eleven, whatever. The business climate in this country is poisonous right now. You've got to be a big player, or you're squashed under the weight of mailing costs and government regulations. You know anybody that's making any money this year?"

"A few."

"Then you know a better class of people than I do."

"Maybe worse," said Jane.

Manny chuckled. "I just remembered why I missed you, honey. What can I get for you today?"

"This is a bit out of your usual line. Did you ever publish a directory of alumni for Yale University?"

Manny's voice turned sad. "No, honey. High school class reunion lists we do. Colleges, they don't need Memory Pubs. They've got better printing facilities, and they got people keeping track of their graduates to hound them for money."

"Too bad," said Jane. "I could have used it."

"What exactly do you need? Maybe I can find a different way there."

"Yale, classes in the 1960s. It's for a special direct-mail campaign. We want to sell nostalgia for New Haven in the sixties: sell them back their youth. When they're twenty-two they're inundated with souvenirs—class rings, yearbooks. But they're in their fifties now."

"Not bad," said Manny. "This is when they've got the most money. Have you tried the college?"

"No help there," said Jane. "They charge for the use of their name and logo. You ask, and they smell money. That's what I hate about nonprofit institutions. They feel no guilt."

"I hear you. What exactly will you offer?"

"What I'd really like to try is something with then-and-now portraits of each alumnus on it. You know, play straight for the ego."

"Sounds depressing. Where does the 'then' come from?"

"Yearbooks."

"That I might be able to get, but you'll have to find out for yourself what the copyright situation is."

"How can you get them?"

"That's proprietary information."

"Everything I've just told you is proprietary information."

"Don't worry about me," said Manny. "I'm just like your gynecologist. I see yours but only for your own good, and there's no reason to show you mine. I've got a supplier who buys up yearbooks for me."

"Old ones?"

"Sure," said Manny. "He picks them up at garage sales, estate sales, and from printers if there's an overrun. He pays just about nothing, and charges people like me like they were antiques. I only use the high school ones, but he gets thousands of them. He might have Yale. I'll call him now."

An hour later the 1965 Yale yearbook was in an express-mail pouch on its way to the Furnace Company's post office box, and Jane was on the way to catch a flight to Chicago. When she arrived four hours later, she checked into a hotel near O'Hare Airport and slept until it was time to pick up her mail at the strip mall.

When she returned to her hotel, she sat down on the bed, opened the express-mail envelope, and pulled out the book. She slowly opened it, then began to leaf through it.

It was full of black-and-white pictures of various groups and activities and buildings, things she sensed would have been resonant to somebody who had been in that place at that time. She was an intruder who couldn't know what the people in the pictures would feel if they looked at them. It occurred to her that she knew immeasurably more than these people between eighteen and twenty-two years old knew, because she knew what was going to happen in the next thirty-odd years. But then, all of these bright, cocky kids with smooth, unlined faces were in their fifties now, and they knew it too.

She reached the section where the rows of head shots were arranged alphabetically. She turned a handful of pages at once, first to the Ms, then to W, then back a few pages to the Vs. There were not many names that began with V. His picture was the first one her eyes settled on.

In those days he had been Brian Reeves Vaughn, from Weston, Massachusetts. He had worn his blond hair fairly short, considering the year. Then she scanned the pictures of other boys in the class, and discovered that her assumption had been wrong. A few had hair in curly halos around their heads, and a couple had straight, stringy hair to their shoulders, but only a couple. She had once heard somebody say that the sixties began in 1968, and she got the impression that she was holding evidence that it was true.

She turned back to the Vs and looked again at Brian Reeves Vaughn. He didn't look naive, exactly, just young. She tried to see the picture of the boy who stared back at her as happy. After all, three decades later the man he would become had walked away from his home, whatever family he had, even his name, but he had kept the ring that would remind him of those days at Yale. He didn't look happy. He looked a little bored, maybe just tolerating the photographer who was taking his picture.

She guessed that the assessment he must have arrived at that those days were the ones he wanted to remember had come in retrospect. That was normal, she supposed. For a runner, it was almost inevitable. No matter what a normal life had felt like at the time, it had certainly been better than whatever happened that could goad a person into trying to disappear, and it was also better than the experience of running.

She looked at Brian Vaughn more closely. He didn't seem to be the type to go misty-eyed about his days at Yale, when the whole world had seemed bright and limitless. He might be the type who felt sorry for himself and got secretly bitter. Secretly bitter, she repeated. That was what seemed wrong.

Keeping a class ring with his initials on it was stupid. She knew almost nothing about him, but she knew something about Yale. They didn't admit people who were stupid. This picture was taken in Brian Vaughn's senior year. If he had gotten that far, presumably he was as intelligent as he needed to be for most practical purposes.

She began to move backward through the rows of portraits. When she found the Hs, she understood. There, in the middle of the top row, was James Walter Hardiston. Vaughn had not invented him. He had gone to school with him. He had probably known him, picked up details about him and his family that had made the impersonation convincing. The class ring wasn't a sentimental souvenir. It was part of the disguise he had used to fool Sarah Hoffman and Richard Dahlman.

Jane picked up the telephone and started to call Dahlman in Carlsbad, then set it down again. What she had learned wasn't worth telling him. She knew what B.R.V.'s name had been, and she knew why he had been so good at impersonating a Hardiston. But she didn't know why he had wanted to.

The next morning she arrived at the big public library at ten, when the doors opened, and began to move backward in time. Christine Manon had seen the face-changers shipping C. Langer's belongings to Santa Barbara about two months ago, and that must have been shortly after the man impersonating James Hardiston had become C. Langer. When had he chosen to become James Hardiston? Richard Dahlman had said the series of surgical procedures he had performed on James Hardiston had taken about eight months. So the transformation to James Hardiston from Brian Vaughn must have taken place at least ten months ago, and possibly as long ago as a year. If Brian Vaughn had begun to worry about being recognized a year ago, then his problems must have begun before that.

Jane couldn't be sure how long it had taken Vaughn to get that worried, so she decided to begin with two-year-old stories and work forward to a year ago. She started by eliminating the possibility that he had been involved in something that had made national news. The *Reader's Guide to Periodical Literature* would tell her if he had been the subject of a magazine article. He had not.

She tested the theory that if an old Yale graduate was accused of a serious crime, or simply disappeared, it would be considered local news in New Haven. She slowly worked her way forward through a year of the *New Haven Register* and found no mention of Brian Vaughn.

Brian Vaughn's entry in the yearbook had said he was from Weston, Massachusetts, and that meant the big regional journals were the Boston papers. By the time she had scanned the local and domestic sections of a year's issues of the *Boston Globe* it was evening. She was too tired to look at anything that had print on it, so she ate dinner and lay on the bed in her hotel. Whatever trouble had come to Brian Vaughn, it had not been the sort that sold newspapers.

Jane sank into a fitful sleep, and when she saw the empty sky around her, she was afraid. She was standing high above a wide river on the top of the steel arch of a bridge. She had never gone to see the bridge in Washington that her father had been building when he died, so this one looked like the Peace Bridge over the Niagara River to Canada. She cautiously turned her eyes to the south, because she was afraid that if she moved she would fall. She saw the river widen to become the endless expanse of Lake Erie. She tried to look in the other direction, and felt herself tottering, so she crouched and clung to the steel arch. Below her she could see the wide, blue river moving away from her toward the north.

The wind was strong up here, and she could feel it tugging at her hair. With her head down, she could see the concrete blocks where the bridge supports were anchored. They were shaped like boats with their prows pointed upstream toward Lake Erie, and from here she could see a wake of eddies downstream as though it were the bridge that was moving. Each block was as big as a house when you were down there on the river, but now the white gulls that glided high above the eddies looking for fish were so far down they were just specks of white moving against the deep blue.

Then a long, black shadow passed over her and she had to look up. There he was, standing on a steel I-beam. There were thick, twisted cables on the ends, and an enormous crane was moving him across her field of vision toward the bridge. She recognized his blue jeans, the yellow hard hat, and the bright red flannel shirt.

"Daddy!" she called, even though she knew he couldn't hear her from so far away in this wind. He was so tiny and alone, surrounded by the blue sky with nothing but the blue water below him. He held one of the cables with his right hand, and raised his right arm to wave, but she knew he wasn't waving at her. He was giving some signal to the crane operator. She could barely hear her own voice as she said, "Please, please don't die."

But the cable that held the I-beam snapped, as it always did. The big piece of steel tilted, then slipped out of the loop on the other end and dropped. He was free of it now, and falling more slowly because his arms and legs were away from his body and moving, and the resistance seemed to hold him back a tiny bit, the sleeves of his red shirt fluttering and flapping.

She tried to close her eyes and cover her face, but it didn't change anything. She could still see him clearly, the red shirt getting tinier and tinier as he fell, turning slowly until his face stayed down and he had to watch the surface of the water rushing up at him. There was a little white splash, but the current moved so fast here that before it disappeared it was downstream.

She clung to the girder, closed her eyes, and sobbed in anguish. Then she heard the soft, kind voice. "You have to get up, Janie."

She looked along the arch, and she could see her mother standing on the narrow steel a few feet from her face. She was wearing a blue silk dress Jane remembered, which her husband had picked out to match her eyes. "I loved him," Jane said. "I love you both so much."

"We've lost him. He's not coming back." Her mother waited expectantly. Jane bent her knees, held her arms out from her sides like a tightrope walker, and stood. The wind seemed perverse now. It came in gusts, so she had to lean into it to stay upright, and then it would stop and she would almost fall.

Her mother's blue dress was flapping in the wind, but she turned around in a slow circle, looking off at the horizon.

"What am I doing up here?" asked Jane. "Was there something I could have done?"

Her mother looked at her, puzzled. "You mean so he wouldn't have gone up? Not ask for a new pair of shoes, or eat less food?"

"I don't know . . ."

"Everything that happens matters, but we don't know how." Her mother stared down the river toward the falls. "You can't break ground within a hundred miles of here without hitting bone." She looked at Jane with deep sadness. "Every single one of them loved somebody so much that when they closed their eyes at night they would think of something they forgot to do for them today, or something funny they wanted to tell them tomorrow."

"Don't."

"Men, women, children," she persisted. "In the Old Time when a baby died, the mother would bury him next to a trail. She thought maybe when some other woman came up the path to work the cornfields, his soul would go into her body so he would get another chance—not so she would have him for herself, but maybe some other woman would get him, who wouldn't make whatever mistake she had made."

Jane was frustrated, miserable. She wanted her mother to stop, but she was trying to tell her something. "That's it, isn't it—I made a mistake? What is it?"

Suddenly the shadow passed over her mother, then over Jane. She looked up. The crane was swinging the girder out over the water again. There was another man standing on it. She looked at her mother again.

She could see that her mother was anxious, almost afraid to answer her. "It's the brothers doing this. The world they beat out between them is a battlefield, and the fight doesn't stop. You don't get to fuss around for months, watching and poking around while your enemies are busy."

Jane watched the steel I-beam rise into the sky. The man waved his arm, but this time he was waving at her. She felt her heart stop. It was Carey. "No!" she screamed.

"If you want him, you have to go up there yourself."

She froze. "That's the price?"

Her mother spoke quietly. "That's always the price. That's how the brothers play. They won't stop until somebody loses everything."

She stared at her mother. "But I don't know enough yet. I know a name—Brian Vaughn. I don't know what he's running from, or who is hunting him."

"You know something just as good."

"What?"

"You know people who will hunt anybody." She stopped and watched Jane. "People who are hunting you."

Jane stood on the arch of the bridge as Carey rose higher and higher. The crane operator made some move that was a little faster than he had intended, and the girder began to swing away. It reached the end of its swing, then began to come back. It moved closer, closer, and Jane knew she would have just one chance. As it stopped, ready to swing away again forever, she jumped for it. She felt herself falling faster and faster, the wind tugging at her hair, the water rushing up at her, and then she woke, lying on the bed in the dark room.

35

When Alvin Jardine saw her he happened to have his head back to drink the last sweet, muddy residue of sugary coffee at the bottom of his cup. He took in a breath and nearly choked. She was coming off a flight from San Francisco and her eyes scanned the way their eyes always did, then snapped straight ahead. Jardine shut his briefcase and stood to turn away while she passed, then decided that the briefcase might be a problem. He pushed it into a rental locker, dropped the quarters into the slot, and took the key. He didn't need a Wanted poster or printed circular to remember that face. There was nothing in print on her anyway, and he knew he didn't want to get close to her encumbered by baggage. He quickly walked to the big open portal toward the concourse.

This was just another piece of evidence to prove that life presented prizes that were better than anything anybody could wish for. Here he was, waiting for any one of two dozen small-time bail jumpers and parole violators to step off a plane and into his custody, when in walks a trophy as rare as the last damned whooping crane. And here is Al Jardine, one of probably twenty bounty hunters in the whole world who would have known what he was looking at or had the slightest idea what to do with it.

He watched her from two hundred feet back as he followed her down the crowded concourse. She still had that long black hair, and the rest of her was exactly the way he remembered—legs that looked as though they went on and on. They reminded him of the tricky nature of the task ahead. She was not entirely defenseless. He remembered that very clearly from the one time when he had happened to see her work.

Jardine had been waiting at the Los Angeles County lockup on Vignes Street, watching the door that opened once each day to emit a few prisoners. A man named Hayward was due to be released any day, and Jardine had a fairly strong opinion that he had been jailed and served ninety days under a name that was not his own. It was Jardine's theory that Hayward had spent most of his life as Bobby McKay.

McKay was worth fifty thousand dollars to an armored-car company. He was also reputed to be big, violent, and uncomfortable without the weight of a pistol somewhere on his person. The best way in the world to take a man like that was at the jailhouse door. He couldn't be armed and had no chance to prepare. If he proved to be too much for Jardine, then the sight of Jardine getting pounded into the sidewalk would bring cops from inside.

The steel door opened and the gate was sliding out of the way. That day's excretion of rehabilitated citizenry was already streaming out into the sunshine. The sparse group of friends and relatives were pushing forward to meet them when Jardine became aware that a car had pulled up behind him. He turned and saw the tall, thin woman with black hair come around the car and open the passenger door. He saw a small, frail-looking woman with stringy blond hair separate from the rest and step toward the car, and he felt better, because that assured him the car wasn't there for Hayward.

There was a sound that set Jardine on edge. It wasn't loud—just the sound of feet moving fast on the concrete—but anything sudden or unexpected was out of place here.

Jardine had turned his head just in time to see a tall man in a suit arrive at the car and lean forward to lunge past the woman with long black hair to make a grab for the little blond woman in the seat. But the woman with the long black hair had heard him coming. Her elbow caught his face, and Jardine could still bring back the sound of it. He wasn't sure if it had been the crack of some facial bone breaking, or if the blow had just clapped the man's jaws together so the teeth clicked. But his head jerked sideways and his body reeled in approximately the direction she had sent his head. She spun counterclockwise. Jardine's eye had taken it as a quick pivot to begin a retreat around the front of the car to the driver's seat before the man could collect himself. It was more. As she turned, she was leaning her weight on the hood, swinging her right leg way too high. Her kick clotheslined the man at about eye level, dropped him onto his back, and followed through. The momentum helped her roll over the hood of the car and land on her feet on the driver's side. She was inside and accelerating away before Jardine fully appreciated what he had seen.

Jardine had instantly induced in himself an uncharacteristic concern for the welfare of the man in the suit. He had knelt and used his handkerchief to stanch the flow of blood from the man's nose, muttering quiet bits of optimistic nonsense about his condition. He had helped him to his feet and driven him to the hospital emergency room.

It was at least an hour before he had managed to get any answers to his sympathetic inquiries about what had brought this poor man to Vignes Street and what had led this woman to drop him on the pavement like a sack of garbage. When Jardine had heard that the man was a bounty hunter from New York, he had begun to feel rather festive about the whole episode. Jardine had no love of outsiders who came into his city to hunt his game.

The blond woman, it seemed, had been doing exactly what Jardine had suspected Bobby McKay of doing. She had gone to jail on a disorderly conduct charge and spent thirty days picking up gum wrappers along the freeway while the people who had been chasing her wore themselves out.

Like many hunters, Jardine had always been a convivial companion and an avid listener to his colleagues' stories of the chase. It was his main consolation in times when nothing seemed to work, and his best celebration of victory. But it also had a practical purpose, because the tales often carried information he could use. There had been times when he had heard things about a particular fugitive he had been chasing that had helped him make money, and other times he had heard things that had convinced him to turn his attention elsewhere. It was not a good idea to chase a fugitive who had once been convicted of something known to be the exclusive province of organized crime—large-scale gambling, or trafficking in stolen securities, for instance.

But along with the rest of the stories came rumors and tall tales. One of them he had heard several times was about a woman named Jane who made people disappear. He had not taken the Jane stories seriously, because they had always been about the one that got away. Some enormous payday had not come for some hunter, and here's why it wasn't his fault.

But on that day three years ago when the little blond woman had gotten away, he had begun to listen to the rumors, and to connect Jane with the names of fugitives who had not been captured. Maybe the stories weren't all true. Any time there was a ready-made excuse for failure, most people would take it. But he was sure that enough of them were true to make this Jane woman worth some effort. If someone managed to put her in a cage, he'd have the aliases and addresses of all the people she had ever hidden.

Jardine was having a difficult time believing his good fortune tonight as he followed her down the concourse toward the escalators. His mind worked frantically. He had just seen her come off an airplane. She could not possibly be armed. If she even owned a gun, it could only be disassembled and the parts scattered around in some big piece of luggage she had checked in. If the baggage claim was where she was headed, then he would simply have to move in close before she had a chance to claim the suitcase and get it out of here into a private place.

Jardine's gun was in his car, parked right across the street in the short-term lot, where he could get to it quickly. He would have no trouble with her if he kept the initiative and stayed a little bit ahead, so she wouldn't figure what she should have done until that "should have" had been firmly built in. She had almost certainly never seen Jardine before except on that one day three years ago, when she'd had other things on her mind.

As he watched her he could see that she was working. She wanted to give an overeager pursuer a chance to move in too early and show himself. She stopped to stare into a store window. Then she went into another and came out the farther doorway. Alvin Jardine was not a novice. He didn't want her in this crowded, brightly lit, heavily policed airport. He wanted to materialize in her path after she was alone out there in the dark.

He began to worry. She might be doing these things because she knew that someone else was following her that Jardine didn't know about. Jardine stopped in front of a display of guilty-husband presents in a window: perfume, jewelry, stuff with flowers and hearts on it. He tried to keep Jane in sight while he let the crowd behind him go past. He picked out two men who were possibilities, then let them get ahead and watched.

One went into the rest room, and the other walked so fast that he caught up with her and passed her. Jardine was elated. He didn't have to worry about having to fight over her. She passed the spot where the security people were herding passengers through the metal detectors, then stepped aside into the cafeteria. Jardine went past the doorway and loitered near the television sets where the schedules were posted so he could see which direction she would face when she sat down. She picked up a tray and got into the line of people sidestepping along in front of the food counter. About halfway through, she dropped something and squatted down to pick it up, and that gave her a chance to take a glance at the people behind her. Jardine had seen it coming, and looked away at the television screen.

He moved off while she paid for her food and went to sit in a booth at the wall so she could watch the doorway. Jardine waited on the other side of the wall, where he could see the doorway too. Watching her go through her precautions had made him feel eager. He had noticed before that sometimes people who were running seemed to have a vague premonition, to sense a change in the air that told them trouble was close, but not that the trouble was Jardine. Jane's extreme caution validated his belief that she was worth having, and he knew that each feint or detour she completed was helping her silence her own intuition and prove to herself that she was safe.

Jardine slapped his back pocket to feel the two sets of plastic wrist restraints. He liked them so well that he had given up carrying handcuffs even on the occasions when he didn't have to pass through a metal detector. They were quick and easy and gave a better fit, and getting out of them wasn't a question of picking a lock: they had to be cut. He had to remember that this time he wasn't going to be able to grab her and intone some meaningless words about warrants for her arrest. She would know that the words were meaningless as well as he did. He would be a fool if he didn't use the second set of restraints on her ankles.

He saw her leave the cafeteria and move toward the escalator. He waited until she was descending and hurried to the elevator, then walked across the first floor to be outside before she was. He watched the long line of glass doors until she was out. His luck seemed to be getting better and better. She had not stopped in the baggage claim. She didn't have a gun, and she wasn't going to have one. She stepped to the island to join the half dozen people waiting for the shuttle bus to take them to the distant long-term lots.

Jardine knew not only where she was, but where she was going. He hurried across the street to the short-term parking structure, ran up the stairs, and got into his car. He pulled out of the space and quickly made the first circuit of the parking structure to the ground floor, then stopped to look at the island. The shuttle bus pulled up to the stop and the people began to get in.

Jardine idled his car and watched to be sure she actually climbed aboard. Then he pulled forward out of the shelter of the parking structure and up to the kiosk to pay. In a few seconds he was on the long circular drive, following the shuttle bus. It stopped several times in front of other terminals to pick up passengers, but she never got off. When the bus finally passed the last stop and left the airport, Jardine could feel his lungs expanding in his chest. He drove far behind the bus, giving it plenty of space.

When the bus pulled into its special entrance at Lot C, Jardine drove on to the public entrance, took his ticket from the machine, and waited for the arm to lift to let him in. He drove slowly on a straight course down the middle aisle of the huge lot, watching the shuttle bus going back and forth in front of him, stopping every two hundred feet to let passengers off.

Slowly the bus emptied; people put suitcases into the trunks of cars and drove toward the exit. Jardine's luck seemed to be growing at every turn the bus made. She was going to be one of the last people out. That meant the others would be on their way home, and the empty bus would go back to its bus stop to wait for its next run to the airport. She would be virtually alone.

Finally the bus stopped and she got out. She walked along an aisle with few cars in it, staring around her as though she had remembered the row, but not the space where she had left hers. Jardine tugged the ends of the plastic restraints out of his pocket so he wouldn't have to dig around for them when the time came. She had found the car. She reached into her purse as she walked up to it. He could see she was going to have the keys ready when she got there. He sped up, turned abruptly, and stopped a yard away from her. He was out of the car and moving when she turned to him.

Her arm came up to her waist, and her white teeth glowed blue from the overhead light as she smiled.

"Hello," she said. She held a small black shape in her hand. He couldn't see much in this light except that the muzzle seemed to be lined up with his chest.

He tried letting some of the surprise and outrage he felt escape his lips. "What is this?"

She was not susceptible to doubt. "Be quiet and listen," she said. "I don't have any desire to kill you, so you won't need to do anything desperate."

"What do you want?"

"Just a ride."

"The key's still in the ignition. Get in and take it."

She moved around the back to the passenger side. He could see that she was giving him a few seconds to look around him. His inability to detect any other human beings in the vast parking lot was not comforting now. If he ran, he might get as far as the nearest parked car before she shot him, but he had nothing that would keep her from coming there after him, and reaching the first one wouldn't get him to the shelter of the next one. If he did as she said, he might be able to get his gun out from under the dashboard. She didn't seem to have any idea who he was.

Jardine climbed into his car and started the engine, glanced at her, and felt his jaw drop. He had given her too long alone in his car. The gun she was holding now was his. He said, "Look, I don't know you, but I'm sure you don't want to get in any worse trouble than—"

"Nice try, Alvin," she said. "I know you, and you know me. I knew you would be at the American Airlines terminal. I knew you would recognize me and follow. So here we are."

"Mind telling me how you got a gun in past airport security?"

"I didn't," she said. "Before I flew out this morning, I left it on the other side of the checkpoint." She looked at him in mock sympathy, then at his gun in her hand. "I guess you forgot to do the same."

He reached the parking lot exit, his mind churning, trying to catch up, while she read his mind aloud. "You're trying to convince yourself that you never heard of me killing anyone, so I probably won't shoot if you try to get help at the gate."

He looked at her out of the corner of his eye. "The thought had crossed my mind."

"You don't know me that well."

He handed his ticket and his money to the attendant at the gate and took his receipt, then drove out of the lot toward Century Boulevard. She let him get a few blocks, then said, "Take La Tijera." He turned onto the long, straight road. When they approached a small, dirty-looking motel she said, "Pull in over there."

He stopped the car in the motel lot where part of the low pink stucco building shielded it from the street. Jardine turned off the engine and tried to settle himself. He had felt intense shock when he had seen the gun, but in his experience, if the trigger didn't get pulled within the first few seconds, the danger went away. The story of how she had managed to walk out of an airport carrying a gun made him uneasy. She was a bit too wily for Jardine's taste. He reminded himself that these were just little potholes on the approach to his triumph. She had picked exactly the sort of place he would have, where the odd sound now and then wouldn't make anyone nervous because every ten seconds a jet plane came over so low you could see passengers' faces in the windows.

She said, "Room eleven." He got out and walked toward the door, listening for the sound of her feet behind him. He couldn't hear them, so he was not sure how far away she was—not sure enough. He stopped at the door and she reached around him and held out the key. She was close enough, but he could feel the barrel of the gun against his back. "You'll open the door, turn on the light, and step in where I can see you. Don't turn around."

He wanted nothing so much as to be indoors and out of sight with the door locked before he made his move, so he obeyed. In a few seconds, things would begin to go his way.

"Make yourself comfortable," she said. "Lie on the bed on your back."

He sat and swung his long legs up onto the bed. "This could be a night to remember."

She raised the pistol a little so it pointed at his chest and stood at the foot of the bed, where he couldn't get at her.

"Just a little joke," he muttered. "What do you want?"

"Take one of the wrist restraints out of your back pocket."

His eyes widened. How had she known? He had let them hang out because he had wanted them to be ready, and then forgotten. Fool. "You don't need those."

She said, "It's for your safety. If I know you can't reach me, I might not get startled and shoot you. Put it around the bed frame and your left wrist."

As he connected his wrist to the steel frame, he was already trying to work out the way to free himself. He could lift the frame off the slot in the headboard and slide the restraint to the end, but to do it, he had to get his weight off the bed. Maybe she would have to use the bathroom. "There. Satisfied?" He tried to sound patronizing.

She said, "I'm going to try to make this quick and simple. You know who I am, and I know who you are, so we won't waste any more time on that."

"What are we going to waste time on?"

"Tell me about Brian Reeves Vaughn."

He smiled. "If you tell me about Rhonda Eckerly." He studied her face for a reaction. "Or about Mary Perkins, or Coleman Fawcett, or Ronald Sitton."

She frowned and shook her head. "Silly me. I forgot to tell you how this works."

She took out of her purse a small silver picture frame and tossed it to him.

It was the photograph of his mother taken on her eightieth birthday. He was outraged. "You've been in my house."

"I found that on the mantel in your living room, and it looked as though it might have sentimental value. I figured you might want to keep it, so I brought it . . . just in case."

"Just in case of what?"

She looked at her watch. "It's now one-thirty. You can usually drive the speed limit at this time of night. If you do, you can make it from here to your house in twenty-eight minutes."

"So?"

"At two-thirty, the electric timer on the coffee maker in your kitchen will turn it on. The pot is filled with gasoline, and the heating element under it is covered with black powder. I'm betting it won't burn the whole house down before the fire department gets there."

"What if it does?"

"Then I will have wasted a lot of money on the heroin that's in your bedroom. But that's okay. There's some in the garage too."

She was bluffing. She had to be bluffing. But the picture of his mother staring him in the face reminded him: she had been there. He smirked. "You telling me you flew in with heroin, too?"

The way she shook her head gave him a sinking feeling. "No," she said. "I didn't know where to buy it in L.A., but Artie Macias did."

"Artie Macias?" It was a grave injustice. Maybe when he had taken Artie Macias in, he had been rougher with him than he'd needed to be. But Jardine wasn't the one who had jumped bail. And Gary the bondsman had offered to pay extra if an example got set for the rest of his customers.

"Yes," she said. "When I told him who it was for, he couldn't do enough. He said to make sure you knew who got it for you."

He stared at the ceiling. He had thought this was his lucky night. "So if I don't tell you what you want to know, you don't let me go in time to get there by two-thirty. My house burns down, and the firemen find a lot of heroin."

Her eyes were steady and unblinking. "Then you get to see what it's like to be a runner instead of a chaser."

He stared at the ceiling again, the muscles in his jaw working. He hated her. He wasn't sure whether he was going to kill her tonight, but he sincerely felt he should. He knew that was absolutely the wrong way to think. She knew things that could make him rich in a day. He would give maybe ten thousand dollars for the pleasure of breaking her skinny neck. Ten million was too much to waste on one night of pleasure. He had to keep her alive, so he would have another chance. In fact, he admitted to himself, he had to do what she said or he was in trouble.

"The time is going by," she reminded him.

He looked at her, beginning to feel the seconds now. He had to do this and get out of here. "I don't know where he is."

"I didn't ask," she said. "I want to know why he's running."

Jardine's brain began to work again. "He came to you, didn't he? He wants you to hide him."

Jane said, "If we both answer questions, it's going to take twice as long."

Jardine took that as a confirmation. Brian Vaughn had run out of ideas on his own, and somebody was about to cash in on him, so he had inquired about hiring professional help. It was actually funny. She wasn't sure he met her standards. "You don't even know who he is?"

"This is a lot of trouble to go to if I know," said Jane.

"Why did you pick me?"

"Because of the way you work. Most bounty hunters get hired to find somebody in particular. You're one of the few who just sits in one place and watches faces. In order to do that, you need to have a current list of which faces are worth money. You tell me why Brian Vaughn's is, and I'll let you go home and unplug your coffeepot."

Jardine stared at the ceiling again to focus his thoughts, but he found it took more strength than he had to overcome the awareness of each second ticking by. What if tonight was one of those nights when Cal-Trans decided to repave a section of the freeway between here and his house? "The reason you couldn't find any Wanted posters on Brian Vaughn is that he hasn't been charged yet."

"Charged with what?"

"Murder."

Jane nodded. It was what she had expected. "Where is he wanted?"

"Well," said Jardine, "he isn't, exactly, but he is. The police in Boston found a car with a deceased young lady in it. When they did the tests, they found that she had been freshly fucked."

"Raped?"

"Not sure," he said. "That's always the theory when they're dead, but she had all her clothes on right. No signs of a struggle, but her blood showed a fatal dose of a sedative. The car, it turned out, wasn't hers. It belonged to Brian Vaughn."

"Did they arrest him?"

"Here's where we get into things I heard that I can't swear to. He was rich—old money. He lived on an estate in some little town outside Boston. I heard the local police brought a detective or two from Boston out to the estate with their hats in their hands to inquire whether he might have something he'd like to get off his chest. It seems he wasn't at home. But while they were on the way from the station to the house, some caretaker called to report that the car was missing."

"Where was Vaughn?"

"Supposedly some servants said he was in Europe, some said they didn't know. Anyway, the stories didn't exactly match."

"Did he have a family?"

"Sure did. His parents were really old—living in Florida. They said he had mentioned some time before that he was going to Europe. Anyway, you get the idea. Nobody knew which country he was in or when he left, but everybody was sure it was at least a week before this girl shows up dead in his car. Nobody can get in touch with him. Only suddenly, he's got a lawyer."

"How did the lawyer explain that?"

"The usual. He's a family friend, he wonders if he can be of help to the police, and so on." He looked at her nervously. "What time is it?"

"One forty-three. Do you know the lawyer's name?"

"I never asked. It wouldn't mean anything to me."

"What happened next?"

"The police look closer. It seems Vaughn has a record."

"What kind?"

"On paper, it's spoiled-kid stuff. Driving fast and parking wherever, then not paying until the car gets impounded. But they also turn up a few people who hate Brian Vaughn, and one of them gives them the names of a couple of young ladies who were given large amounts of money years before. Sure enough, they're real. Both decline to say what the money was for. The money came from Vaughn's parents."

"Go on."

"The police are drooling. Now they want this guy bad. They don't have enough to charge him with anything, and there's no way they can go public and treat him like a fleeing suspect."

"The car wasn't enough?"

"They can't shake the alibi until they find out what it is. They figure if they give him a DNA test, he is almost certainly going to be the missing player in the sex scene. He is also going to have to prove how and when he went to Europe, how his stolen car got to Boston without being hot-wired, and numerous other things too time-consuming to mention when my fucking house is about to burn down." He sat up.

"You've got time," she said as she raised the pistol. "Why do you know all this?"

"Who hasn't been heard from?"

"The girl's family. Who was she?"

"She was from New York. Vaughn definitely knew her. But everybody thought she was in New York that night, and there's no proof Vaughn was around. Her family had a little money, and they hired a guy—a detective—to unravel all this stuff, and this is what he found out."

"Was any of this in the papers?"

"Sure. 'Amanda Barnes found dead in stolen car. Owner could not be reached for comment by press time.' "

"How did Vaughn manage that?"

"I don't know. Maybe the lawyer was working overtime. And maybe the police helped. They don't usually want it all over the news that a guy like this is their only suspect until they've got their hands on him. He had the money and the sort of history that would make them think he could stay in Europe forever. They asked Interpol to watch for him and let him know they wanted to talk. Big silence on the other end."

"You still haven't exactly said how you heard. Did you know the detective?"

"Not personally."

"Then how?"

"Word got around."

"How much is the girl's family offering?"

"A hundred grand. I added him to my list when I heard about it. I figured if he was in Europe, his smartest move wouldn't be to fly into Logan Airport or Kennedy. It would be to stay in Europe until somebody gets around to losing some physical evidence or they arrest somebody else for something similar. But if he got homesick, he'd fly in at L.A., where nobody's expecting him."

Jane nodded. "We only have about five minutes left. The police haven't charged him. If you saw him, you couldn't grab him and drag him to a station. You couldn't handcuff him and take him on a plane to Boston. Just what were you supposed to do for a hundred thousand?"

"Detain him."

"Detain him for whom?"

"For whoever is willing to pay me the hundred thousand." He fidgeted. "Now, can I go?"

"Which was it? Were you supposed to do it yourself, or tie him up and call somebody?"

His eyes shifted wildly. He looked at the door, he looked at her, then at the door again. "The hundred was for killing him. If I could keep him alive long enough for the girl's father to fly out here and blow his brains out, that was two hundred."

Jane sighed. She glanced at her watch and stood up. "All right," she said. "You've got thirty-three minutes to go save your house and your spotless reputation."

She held the gun on him as she walked close to the bed and used her pocketknife to slice the wrist restraint.

Jardine stood up. In the back of his mind was a reckless urge. He had insurance on the house, and his equity in it was less than forty thousand anyway. Having her in his hands would be like having millions. What was in the house, anyway? Cheap clothes, furniture that was ten years old and had stains on it from things that had gotten spilled, and . . . oh, yes. Heroin.

He took a step toward the door, then went back to the bed and picked up the picture of his mother, and his eyes met hers. "I won't forget this."

"You're welcome."

"I mean next time I see you I might just kill you."

Jane shook her head. "No," she said. "You wouldn't take the chance that I might be worth money."

Jardine stared at her and heard his breath hiss in and out through his teeth. He half-formed a plan to stop at a phone booth and call someone to break into his house while he waited for her outside. His friends and colleagues paraded through his mind, but each face had something hidden behind it—maybe greed, maybe the suspicion of unspoken malice. He turned, rushed out, and ran across the little parking lot toward his car. As he flung the door open he heard distant sirens. He muttered, "Don't let that be a ten-car pileup on the freeway." To whose ear he had spoken, or why he had taken three precious seconds to say it, he had no idea.

Jane waited until she had seen Jardine drive as far as the freeway entrance, then walked out of the building and down the street to her car. When she had started the engine and was almost to the same freeway entrance, she allowed herself to feel relief. For some reason, the part she felt most relieved about was a tiny detail. She was glad that he had chosen to move in when she had wanted him to—when she was walking up to a car she had never seen before in the middle of a deserted parking lot and pretending it was hers. Once he was standing in front of her, she had been too busy to feel afraid.

As she drove north toward Santa Barbara, her thoughts turned to Brian Vaughn. Jardine had insinuated that the family had been supplying him with money since he had disappeared. Certainly he had spent more than he could have carried with him. The face-changers had gone to extraordinary lengths to keep protecting him afterward. They would only do that if they thought the money was going to keep on coming and they couldn't get their hands on it all at once.

Other little details made Jardine's story seem right. If the police were playing Vaughn carefully, trying to lure him home, they might behave as Jardine had said. Vaughn had been in a very difficult position. The police had not charged him, but they would certainly keep quietly looking for him until they found him, so he couldn't go anyplace where people would recognize him. He also had to worry about how many people like Jardine might be looking for him. The only solution had been to stop calling himself Brian Vaughn, and stop looking like Brian Vaughn.

What had not struck Jane as right was the story Jardine had told her about the crime, but she had to take into account that it had probably been of little interest to Jardine. The dead girl had been found in Brian Vaughn's car. She tried to imagine how that could have happened.

One possibility was that Vaughn had picked her up in New York and taken her to his house in Weston. He had drugged and raped her, then realized that he had given her so much sedative that she had died. He had loaded her body into his car, intending to take her back to her apartment in New York. He had somehow been trapped—had mechanical trouble, run out of gas, gotten stuck in snow or mud—and had seen no alternative to abandoning the car. Maybe he had thought he was leaving temporarily, to walk to a gas station or something, but the police found the car before he could get back. But the story had to account not just for what had happened but for what Brian Vaughn had wanted to happen.

What would he have wanted? He certainly wouldn't have planned a crime that included dragging a dead—or even unconscious—woman from Weston, Massachusetts, to New York, then into an apartment building where people could hardly be expected not to see him. He would want the whole event to take place indoors at one address: but which address? He certainly would not want a woman he had raped to wake up in his house in Weston. He would want her to be in her own apartment in New York all evening, and wake up there not positive about the details of what had happened to her. Just waking up alone at home might make her feel that whatever had happened was over. After reflecting on what she remembered, and what she would have to face if she called the police, she might decide it was better if she didn't. But she hadn't been in New York, or even in Weston. She had been found in the place Vaughn was least likely to want her—in his car.

Jane tried another version. Vaughn and the woman had spent the evening together in Weston. After making love, maybe he fell asleep and she couldn't. She found sleeping pills in his medicine cabinet and accidentally overdosed because they weren't hers, or took her own and got a bad reaction because she had alcohol in her system. He woke up and found her unconscious, then put her into the car to rush her to the hospital in Boston. On the way he saw she was dead. He panicked. No, that didn't quite work. If someone was that sick, you didn't drive them to Boston. You called an ambulance.

What Jane had kept thinking all the time while she was listening to Jardine was that everything he had said was possible. But it was strangely neat. There was an odd perfection to the stories of all of the runners she had found on this trip. Vaughn was rich. He was used to having people provide expensive personal services for him. He seemed to have a history of offenses against women that might not be rape but were serious enough to require hush money. That was important too. He had bought his way out of serious trouble before. If a man like that got into this kind of trouble and happened to find his way to the face-changers, the face-changers would be lucky. What if they had picked him out and designed a particular kind of trouble just for him? It would look a lot like this.

36

The security technician had been introduced to Marshall only as Maggie, with no last name. "Maggie can piece the whole thing together for you," the shift commander had said. Marshall didn't feel comfortable calling the young woman by her first name, but he had waited until they were alone and said his name was John.

He had been in the Los Angeles International Airport security control center for over an hour, and he was still feeling admiration for their new surveillance system. It was a simple extension of what had been done in lots of public places, but it was a generation past the old systems, and the money they had spent was all visible on the screen. Maybe he was just prepared to admire anything that gave him hope. He said, "Can you take it from when she gets off the plane?"

"Sure," said Maggie.

Marshall watched the tired, bored passengers eagerly walking out of the boarding tunnel into the waiting area. Almost all of them seemed to be carrying full-sized suitcases and bags with things on hangers. He had noticed the change before, but he had not quite figured out when it had happened. One day people had simply decided they didn't trust the airlines to take care of their baggage, and the airlines had tacitly admitted their incompetence by letting them cram it all into the overhead compartments.

He watched the woman come out of the tunnel and take a quick look around to orient herself, just as the others did. Then she seemed to focus on something. "Can you freeze it for a second?"

The image stopped moving, the woman's head turned at an angle of ten or fifteen degrees. "Can you tell what she's looking at?"

"Not exactly. Here's the other camera." There was a refreshment area with twenty or thirty people sitting at tables, and behind it were the rest rooms and storage lockers. Between the woman and the lockers there were at least a hundred people. "I think it's the man at the third table, drinking coffee."

"Okay," he said.

The woman began to move again. She walked quickly across the vast room, down the concourse, into a shop, then into the cafeteria, then down the escalator toward the baggage area and into the street. As she moved out of the range of each camera, Maggie picked her up on the next one.

Marshall said, "Wait. Let's look in the cafeteria."

Maggie pointed to the next screen. "There." Jane walked in, got a tray, sidestepped along with the line of people sliding their trays along the shiny metal counter, taking plates of food and bottles and cans out of display cases. Jane took a pastry, then a cup of coffee, and put them on her tray. As she waited, she opened the purse hanging from her shoulder, and pushed things aside to reach for her wallet. Something fell out of her purse to the floor. She quickly bent her knees to duck down. Her right hand came up under the counter to steady herself while her left hand picked up the . . . he looked more closely . . . keys. The body pops up, the right hand stays where it is, which is now at belt level, then into her purse before it goes back to the counter. Why into the purse? The left hand was the one that should have gone into the purse, to get rid of the keys. But she had set the keys on the tray. Marshall couldn't be positive, but he had a very strong suspicion that something had been in that right hand.

Marshall watched the rest of the sequence of tapes patiently, this time looking at the people ahead of Jane, and behind her. If they had been using the airport as a drop, what could it be that they had left for her? Messages? Money? Maybe his mind was so bored with the sight of videotapes that it was inventing new images.

Jane gets on the shuttle bus. Jane gets off at Lot C. Jane is approached by a man. Jane gets into a car with him and drives off into the night. "Any luck on the man yet?"

"Oh, yes," she said. "That was easy, because you can see the license number on the Lot C footage. His name is Alvin Jardine. He's a private detective, officially."

"What do you mean, 'officially'?"

"That's what his license says, but the L.A.P.D. said he's basically a bounty hunter."

"Does he work the airport often?"

"I checked back for the last month, and he was here nearly every night. I don't have anything earlier than that."

"Is he here now?"

Maggie shook her head. "I already checked that too. I think he might have been the one she was looking at when she got off the plane, but I can't be sure. I couldn't be positive of the match, or even what her eyes were focused on—just the angle of her head. What about her? We were told you wanted her for questioning. Is she a suspect or a witness or what?"

Marshall stared at the screen. "I don't know," he said. "I know some of what she is, but I can't put a name on it yet."

The beep of his pager made them both jump. As he walked out into the airport to find a pay telephone where he could use his credit card, possibilities kept occurring to him. Maybe the bounty hunter had found Dahlman, and she had come to buy him off. Maybe she had some optimistic notion that Dahlman was innocent, and she was here to hire the worst possible person to find evidence to clear him. Novices often seemed to be drawn by some obscure law of nature to hire a fox to guard the henhouse.

He dialed the number on his pager and heard Grapelli's voice. "I hope I'm not interrupting anything, Marshall."

"I wanted to find a pay phone."

"Where are you?"

"L.A.X. They've been very cooperative. Mrs. McKinnon seems to have been here last night. She took a plane from Chicago to here, flew to San Francisco and back, met a man at a long-term parking lot, and drove off in the moonlight."

"It's not often you get to see such romance in this day of cynics and nihilists," said Grapelli. "Where does that leave us?"

"Chicago could mean she had gone to look for evidence or witnesses in the Dahlman case. Or it could mean she just happened to change planes there. San Francisco is a mystery, because she was there for no more than an hour or two. Since nobody has turned up a suspicious prescription for Dahlman's antibiotic yet, maybe she was making a black-market buy. L.A. could mean something."

"L.A. means just about as much as Chicago," said Grapelli. "Who's the guy?"

"He's a private detective–slash–bounty hunter. But since she wanted to meet with him, I have to assume he's on her side."

Grapelli's silence had a sour sound to it. Finally he said, "Do we know what the hell it is that her side wants to accomplish?"

"I have a theory," Marshall offered.

"Do you?"

"I think that she's got part of this situation figured out pretty clearly. Her husband definitely had something to do with Dahlman's escape, so he's in trouble. Her house has been under surveillance for long enough so she knows that nobody's going to write him off and go home. What's her way out? I'm not saying it's a safe way, or a smart way, just that it's a way, and there aren't any others."

"Divorce the stupid bastard and claim she knew nothing?"

"I mean for both of them," said Marshall. "Go out on her own and prove that Dahlman didn't do it."

"Give me a break," muttered Grapelli.

"Think about it," said Marshall. "If Dahlman stays out, does that help her and her husband? No. We'll watch them until the end of time. If Dahlman gets caught, does that end it? No. It's worse, because we'd have no reason to keep their home intact waiting for Dahlman to call or show up. They'd be subject to arrest. But what does get them off?"

"Very optimistic of her," said Grapelli. "Only, if Dahlman does come in, even if he's got absolute proof that somebody else killed that woman, the McKinnons are still guilty—aiding and abetting, obstruction of justice, and so on."

"She's blinded by love," said Marshall. "Otherwise she'd know that you're going to demand federal prosecution of a reputable surgeon and his beautiful wife who helped an innocent elderly doctor stay out long enough to solve our case for us."

"Well, probably not," admitted Grapelli. "But she can't know that."

"What else has she got to think about?"

"Very interesting theory, anyway," said Grapelli. "One of your better ones."

"Thank you," said Marshall. "It's nice to feel that I'm growing as a theorist, especially in these times when I'm unable to actually put anything into practice."

Grapelli's voice changed. It was lower and quieter, and the ironic edge was gone. "I'm afraid I wasn't calling to check up on you, John. I was calling to tell you what's going on here."

"About time," said Marshall. He could tell it was something he was not going to like, and he could tell Grapelli knew it and felt he still had to do it. Marshall determined to keep his feelings to himself.

"It's time to bring her home. Since she seems to have a flair for going where she pleases without being picked up, I only know one way to do it."

Marshall reminded himself that he was going to keep the disapproval out of his voice. "I have no way to prove this, but I think we're giving up on the strategy too early. But it's your call, and I respect that."   .

"Thanks, John," said Grapelli. "You want to come back to be there when she comes in?"

Marshall thought for a moment. "If you need me, I will. But I have a few leads I'd like to check here. This bounty hunter she met ought to be interviewed, and if he gives the right answers, I might be able to follow her in. Somebody should try to see where she stops on the way home."

"We'll call when she shows."

37

Carey sensed that something had changed. There was an odd, charged feel to the air. While he was in the shower, he kept imagining that he heard not sounds, but parts of sounds coming from somewhere in the old house—doors opening but not closing, single footfalls that were not repeated.

He turned the handle and heard nothing but the last of the water falling from the showerhead and making tiny pops as each drop shattered on the tile near his feet. He dressed quickly. He was sure now that he had picked up some alteration that was too subtle to be identified, and his own mind had supplied the explanation that it must be a sound.

Carey went from room to room, not sure whether he was doing this to verify that the police had not come into his house or because of his growing suspicion that his time had run out. That was it: he had given it a name. He was looking into each of the rooms in the house where he had grown up because he was afraid he might never see them again. He glanced at his watch. It was all right, he decided. If this was the day, then he had done it. If it wasn't, then let this serve as the last look. He would not need to look again.

He walked down the staircase to the small foyer and through the living room and the dining room to the big old kitchen to make his breakfast. As he was taking out the eggs and the frying pan he suddenly stopped. Somehow he had a feeling that this morning he should leave the kitchen spotlessly clean, with no dishes in the dishwasher and nothing out of place.

He went out the back door and locked it, then to the old carriage house in the back that his grandfather had been the first to call "the garage," and glanced at the yard. The two gigantic maple trees behind the house that shaded the windows of the master bedroom reminded him of the day he had shown Jane the revised deed. It now said Carey McKinnon and Jane McKinnon. She had chuckled at the idea, and he had asked her why. She had said, "Because I love you and because people are so funny."

"Funny? Why?"

She had left him standing in the back entry and run the sixty or seventy feet to the trunk of the taller maple tree. She had called, "Look at me." The trunk was nearly four feet wide at the base, and at this distance he could use her height as a measure and count upward ten times to the tallest branches. It had been big and old before his grandparents were born. He had walked out to stand ten feet from her.

She had bent back to look up at the huge, thick limbs, some of the lower ones wider around than her body, and his eyes had followed hers. "See?"

He had nodded. "So what's funny?"

She had raised an eyebrow. "Do you think it knows that I own it?"

Carey got into his black BMW. The car was perhaps his only idiotic purchase. It had cost too much, but he decided he was glad about that too. Even if this was the last time he drove it, and it had to be sold while he was in jail, it hardly mattered now. There was no sense in having a few more dollars for a retirement he and Jane would never reach, or for children who would never be born.

He pulled out of his driveway and watched the car behind him to see whether the policemen did anything differently. They stayed the usual two blocks behind him, drifting along near the curb because he was close to the median stripe. The other cars nearby weren't familiar and didn't seem to have policemen in them, but he knew that such impressions meant nothing.

He drove to the hospital by the usual route, introducing no changes. He certainly didn't want to behave erratically and precipitate some action they were only contemplating. If they were already committed, then he would gain no advantage by letting them know that he suspected.

He parked in his reserved space, then walked into the hospital with his head up and his eyes ahead. He went into his office in the surgical wing and sat down to review the files of the three patients he would be operating on today. He was glad they were fairly routine: Mr. Reardon's gall bladder, a hernia repair for Don Schwartz, and Mrs. Miller's partial colostomy.

Today might be his last day as a surgeon, and that made him concentrate harder on the X-rays he had in the viewer on the wall. He knew that no matter how the day ended, he was going to need to tell himself that this part of it had ended well.

He put the files back on his desk and stood up. It was time to scrub. As he closed the door behind him, he left inside all of the thoughts about his life and his personal worry. He thought about the specific movements his hands would need to perform to make Mrs. Miller's trouble go away.

Four hours later, when he was leaving the operating room for the last time, his mind seemed to awaken. It was saying, "What's next?" and the answer settled on him.

He showered and dressed in a state of passive receptivity. Nothing came to startle him. He carefully made his way out of the wing through the recovery room and then slipped into the first empty room he came to. He went to the window and looked out at his car in the parking lot.

The three vans that had been there the night he had operated on Richard Dahlman were back. The long booms on their roofs had been extended, and there were men and women in jeans inside doing something technical. He looked at the other vehicles in the lot. There were no regular police patrol cars, as there had been that night, but he could see two large, plain American cars with audio antennas above their rear windows and little emergency lights inside over the back seats. He walked to the bed and pressed the remote control for the television set high on the wall.

There was a cartoon mouse swinging a meat cleaver down toward a cat's head. The cat leaped into the air, spun around, and shot off like a bullet. Carey pressed the channel button and let the television set cycle through flashes of channels until he found a picture of the hospital. The *Channel Four Noon News* woman was saying, "—have said they would be making an official announcement concerning the mysterious disappearance of murder suspect Dr. Richard Dahlman in just a few minutes." Carey turned off the television set and left the room.

Jane had said it would begin without much warning, but that he would see it coming if he looked. "There will be people you haven't seen before," she had said. "They don't like to burn a surveillance specialist by having him scoop up the likes of you on television. There won't be guns in sight, because they know you're not dangerous. You have to see the signs, and then you have to move before they're ready."

Carey had thought about all of the ways and the times when this might happen, but somehow he had not imagined it would happen at the hospital. That was absurd, he realized. He spent ten or twelve hours a day in this building or in his office down the street. He had assumed that they would not want to arrest him in public, but why wouldn't they?

He spent a moment gathering his thoughts and then started off down the hallway. He slipped into the staircase to avoid the elevator, then went down two floors to the cafeteria. He saw Leo Bortoni and Sal Feinman sitting at a table together, but when Leo looked up and waved him over, he pretended not to see. He walked past the piles of cafeteria trays beside the hot table and stepped into the wake of a young man pushing a tall rack of dishes through the swinging doors into the kitchen.

He followed the rack through the food-preparation area. He had not been in the kitchen since he had taken a tour when he had accepted his appointment to the hospital staff. He had a vague memory that dishes were washed farther back somewhere, and that it was done by a big stainless steel machine with a conveyor belt that raised the water temperature above the level that any of the common microbes could survive. He heard lots of rattling dishes and water running on both sides, but he didn't dare look.

"Carey!"

He turned and saw Lana McLiesh wearing her white lab coat and a hairnet over her blond hair, carrying the clipboard she always seemed to have. "Hi," he said. "I was looking for you."

She pulled him aside and handed him a paper cap from her pocket. "Put this on. You're not supposed to be back here, you know."

"Sorry," he said. "I was on my way out, when it occurred to me that I didn't order for my morning surgeries."

She squinted at her clipboard and flipped a couple of pages. "Miller, Reardon, Schwartz, right?"

"Oh, that's right," he said. "I think I signed it yesterday. Joy must have put the order in. How have you been?"

"Terrific," she said. "My cooking agrees with me. How about you?"

"Same here." He looked around him, pretending to be disoriented. He pointed. "I can get out that way, can't I?"

She looked a little uncertain. "You can, but that's the way the garbage goes out. You might want to—"

"No, it's fine," he said. He leaned closer. "There seem to be a lot of reporters around today, and I'm not really in the mood to answer questions about Richard Dahlman."

She winked. "Gotcha. Just watch your step. The floor back there is perpetually wet."

He stepped out onto the loading dock in the back of the hospital and resisted the temptation to jump to the driveway below. From here he could see his office building, so he turned to look. In the parking lot behind the building he could see the roof of a police car with the bar of emergency lights across the front. He supposed that if he had needed confirmation, that would have been it. He walked down the steps.

Jane had made a foolproof plan for him, but he had no idea how he could get from the place where he now was to the place where the first steps of the plan began, at Jake Reinert's house.

He heard his pager go *bee-beep, bee-beep, bee-beep.* He reached to his belt and held it up to confirm his suspicion that it was the central desk trying to locate him for the police. But the number on the display was the emergency-room number. He heard a siren in the distance. It was an ambulance, and a moment later it pulled into the driveway and up to the emergency room.

Carey turned off his beeper and began to walk quickly toward the street. He would duck into a restaurant a few blocks from here, call Jake Reinert, and ask Jake to pick him up. Even if they really needed an extra surgeon in the emergency room, he had seen Leo in the cafeteria, and Leo was a capable surgeon.

Carey was almost to the street when he heard the second siren. He slowed his pace a little and listened. The siren cut off, but he heard the engine roar as it went up the drive. They never did that unless it was urgent and somebody had only a few minutes left. They usually slowed down at the entrance to the driveway. He stopped. He could hear other sirens now: two more, or was it three? Something terrible must have happened.

He held himself as though he were balancing on a thin wire. His mind filled with Jane's image. He had been so close to her, but now he could feel her slipping away. With her went all hope, all possibilities. He had been foolish to imagine that he could go off with her. He had been like a big, clumsy plow horse trying to jump the fence so he could run with the deer.

Carey pivoted on his heel and ran up the lawn of the hospital. He reached the driveway just as Leo Bortoni came out on the loading dock, craning his neck to look for him.

"Carey!" he yelled, and beckoned.

Carey climbed the steps three at a time, and hurried through the kitchen beside him. "What is it?"

"Don't know much yet. Some kind of explosion at a factory. Lots of third-degrees, probably, and a lot of flying metal."

As Carey hurried across the polished floor of the cafeteria, he could see that Pankowski, the hospital administrator, was in the hallway saying something to two uniformed policemen. He turned his head as Carey and Bortoni reached the doorway. The two policemen brushed past Pankowski.

One of them came close to Carey's shoulder, but did not touch him. "Dr. McKinnon?"

"Yes?"

"As soon as you're out of surgery, we'd like to talk to you."

"Oh?" said Carey. He glanced at the officer's face. It was the face of a decent man, who was willing to gamble that his job didn't require stopping a surgeon from saving somebody's life. He was asking for a promise; if Carey didn't make it, he would have to follow the order he had been given to arrest him now. Carey hesitated, then made the promise. "I won't be going anywhere."

The next night, Jane stepped to the newsstand on State Street, opened the *Los Angeles Times* and looked at the headlines, then moved her eyes down the page. Dahlman was not mentioned in the news anymore. She put the paper back in the pile and went to the set of cubbyholes by the wall where the out-of-state papers were sold. The newsstand didn't carry the *Buffalo News*, but she saw the *Chicago Tribune*. She picked one up, opened it, and saw the article at the bottom of the front page. DOCTOR SUS-PECTED IN DAHLMAN ESCAPE. She calmly folded the paper, walked to the little counter under the green awning, and handed it to the man with the unlit cigar in his mouth. She gave him a dollar and turned to walk up the street to her car. The newspaper in her hand was an object that felt both fragile and dangerous, like a firebomb or a poisonous snake.

She sat behind the steering wheel and opened it again, feeling her heartbeat at the sides of her head. Her eyes swooped to the article, clutching phrases because she was too impatient to follow sentences: "taken into custody," "questioned by the F.B.I.," "could be charged." She read that twice. If he could be charged, then he had not been charged. That gave her the momentum to relinquish the first page and move to the second. Charged with what? "Accessory to murder." Her mind protested: Not a chance . . . not yet, anyway. But she saw it was just the culmination of a list. "Aiding and abetting an escaping felon, obstruction of justice, making false statements in a police report."

Jane closed the newspaper, tossed it to the floor in front of the passenger seat, and started the engine. There was no more time for waiting and watching and looking into the past, trying to gather a pile of evidence that Richard Dahlman was innocent. She was going to have to take a chance on Brian Vaughn.

38

Charles Langer went out to breakfast, as he often did. When he had still been Brian Vaughn he would not have dared show his face in a spot like the Santa Barbara Biltmore. Now Brian Vaughn's face didn't exist, and there was no disadvantage to showing Charles Langer's. Since he had been in Santa Barbara he had seen four people who had known him when he was Brian Vaughn, and two of them had been at the Biltmore.

The first time, he had been eating lunch at an outdoor table on the patio. He had been staring past the tall cedar tree on the broad front lawn, beyond the shoreward rolling of blue, sluggish Pacific swells, at a squadron of tiny white sails just poised on the horizon so their hulls were invisible and their forward progress was almost impossible to detect. A shadow had unexpectedly fallen across the white linen in front of him, he had looked up, and standing over him was David Rollins.

Langer had become flustered. He had been warned that moments like this might happen someday, but someday had always seemed far away. But Rollins had not said "Brian!" or even "Don't I know you?" He had said, "Excuse me, but is anyone using these chairs?"

Charles Langer had not dared use his voice. He had smiled and shaken his head. Rollins had taken two of the extra chairs to his table, said, "Thanks," sat on one of the chairs, and picked up his menu. The other chair had been for Rona Pellham, apparently Mrs. Rollins now. Langer was sure that she would not fail to recognize him. As soon as she looked in his direction, he was going to have to say something false about not being who she thought he was, and bail out of Santa Barbara. But Rona had not appeared to even glance at him. It was a miracle. He had known her very well—actually made a serious attempt to Do the Deed with her once, with enough acquiescence so that he could knowledgeably judge the terrible things that time and gravity had done to the poor woman since then.

Nobody had recognized Brian Vaughn looking at them from behind Charles Langer's face, and the chance meeting had been wonderful for Charles Langer. He was liberated, giddy with power and license. He reminded himself of Claude Rains in *The Invisible Man*, capering around and practically tweaking people's noses with absolute impunity.

He had stuck to all of the precautions they had taught him during the long period since he had needed to leave Massachusetts. But after seeing Rollins, these safeguards had come to seem like the old civil defense drills of his childhood, when he had dutifully crouched under his desk to escape bombs that never fell. He was now convinced that the only necessary precaution had been taken for all time. He was a brand-new man with nothing much to worry him.

Langer finished his breakfast and walked on the beach for an hour. He liked walking away from Santa Barbara, below the big homes above the cliffs, toward the Montecito side. If he walked in the morning like this, he could often go for long stretches without seeing another human being.

He came back up the beach just ahead of the incoming tide, got into his Miata, and drove toward his house. He would spend a little time cleaning the place and then go to the library before he went off for his golf game. That way he would have something fresh to read this evening.

Many of the things he liked least about being the Invisible Man had gradually been mitigated. At first he had found it frustrating to live in a place where he could have golfed on almost any day of the year, except that he wasn't able to join a club or even scare up a foursome. Now he simply went to the public course and told the starter he would fill in on any threesome who showed up. Most days it meant he would not have to wait as long as he would have with three partners. When Langer wanted to swim, he would pay for a day's admission to the Coral Casino across the street from the Biltmore and share the best pool in town with a sparse gathering of ephemeral strangers who sat in cabanas, ordered a few drinks, and then moved on.

His search for something to fill the time after sunset had not been as satisfactory, but it was not painful. He now kept his days busy and active, lingered late over dinner at a pleasant restaurant, then spent the latter part of the evening reading the books he had borrowed from the public library.

Langer had spent only a few months in this place, and already the social prospects were showing small signs of improvement. Several times at the golf course he had run into men he had played with before, and when they had seen him alone as usual, they hadn't waited for the starter to form the foursome but had invited him themselves. There were also two young female librarians who made it a practice to smile and joke with him when he came in, and he had actually had a real conversation with the prettier of the two a week ago. At first he had been a little wistful and regretful when she had seemed to like him, but then he had remembered that he wasn't fifty-five anymore. To her he looked about her own age. Maybe next time he would find out more about her so he could concoct exactly the right invitation to make her go out with him.

As he drove up his street, he studied all of the cars parked at the curb, glanced at the windows of the houses nearby, and then stopped without taking the keys out of the ignition and looked again. The precautions they had taught him were all habits now, and each time he performed them he actually felt better. After all this time he would have noticed anything that was out of place.

He got out of his Miata, walked up the sidewalk, unlocked his door, and slipped inside, then stepped directly to the corner window to ascertain that his arrival had not triggered any movement outside.

He counted to ten, then stepped back, turned, and gasped. He felt the hair on his scalp bristle. A woman was sitting motionless on the couch, and at first his mind didn't know what to do with her: ghost-burglar-accuser? Was his eye assembling shadows into a human shape?

"I'm sorry to startle you," she said.

"What are you doing here?" he asked, then realized he had said it wrong. He sounded scared and ridiculous. He had not missed the soft, melodious sound of her voice, and there was a little catch in it that was mildly erotic and appealing. He couldn't see her very well because his glasses hadn't adjusted to the dim light on that side of the room. The outline of her was long, lean, and feminine like a cat. There was nothing to be afraid of.

"To tell you the truth," she said, "I had just sat down to rest. They called me in the middle of the night, so I had to take a red-eye flight to get here."

"Why?"

"Oh," she said. "Sorry again." She stood up and took a couple of steps where the light from the window reached her. He appraised the long black hair and the grace of her movements. "It seems that Santa Barbara is about to get too hot for you. I'm here to help you get out before the temperature takes its upturn." She walked into the bedroom, where he had no choice but to follow. "I've already packed almost everything, and given the place a quick scrub for prints. Don't touch any smooth surfaces in the house without wiping them off afterwards."

He saw his suitcase on the bed and walked toward it. He looked at it for a moment, then opened it and stared down at his clothes, his shoes. He could see she had even found the milk carton in the refrigerator, because the money and his next identity were tucked into the pocket.

"Come on," she coaxed from the doorway. "Don't worry about what I've got. Worry about what I might have missed."

He turned and stared at her. "Who's coming?"

She was ready for the question. "There's a man named Jardine in Los Angeles. He's a bounty hunter who's been asking a lot of questions about Brian Vaughn for months. Apparently last night he started asking questions about Charles Langer."

"What does that mean?"

She held her hands palms upward, then let them fall. "It means he probably asked the wrong person. But the fact that they called me in means that the problem isn't solved."

Brian Vaughn sat on the bed. "Do you know a lot about me?"

She sighed in frustration. "I know enough so I'll be mixing my own drinks on this trip, thank you. Beyond that, I don't care. I just came to get you out of here."

His voice carried quiet conviction. "I'm innocent. I didn't give her the overdose, or drive her anywhere in my car. When I left her, she was in her apartment in New York."

"Fine," said Jane. She was on her guard. Something was happening.

"It matters."

Jane looked at him apologetically. "I didn't mean to upset you," she said. "But I'm sure you must know that my helping you isn't contingent on my judgment of whether you did it or not. If you could prove that, what would you need us for? We're in a business. You pay, we take care of you. Now, my best professional advice is to get up, get into the car, and let me take you someplace safe."

"Where?"

Jane had hoped this would not come up until he was in the car. "I'm supposed to get you back to Chicago. From there they'll start you over again in a new place. Do you care?"

"Not really," he said. "I guess it was idle curiosity. I'm not going."

Jane's muscles tightened. Chicago was where Christine had seen his boxes. He had spent months there getting his face changed, so she had guessed he would consider it home base. It was also the only place where she could turn him over to policemen who would know where he fit in the Dahlman case, but she was sure that was not what had made him refuse. It was something else. "I'm not particular. If you have another place in mind where you'll be safe for now, I'll drive you there and explain it later. But let's get going before we have to fight our way out."

"You go," he said. "Thank you for coming to my rescue, but I'm going to stay here. Since I've been here I've met several people who once knew me well, and they don't now. I'll probably be fine."

"What if you're wrong?"

He shrugged. "Then I'll be dead, I suppose."

She leaned against the wall and folded her arms. "Suddenly, after all this effort, that doesn't matter to you?"

His face flashed an expression that began as a smile and ended as a frown. "I made a bad deal. I've done what I could to live with it, and begun making a comfortable life here. I'm through being ordered from place to place, and told how to look and act."

"If you want to disappear, that's how it's done." She shrugged. "You must have known that when you decided to run."

He looked at her again, his face less troubled. "When I told you I was innocent, I wasn't sure why I was saying it. I thought it might be a simple reflex, trying to defend myself from what you had said. But it was for me. You see, time moved too quickly for me. One night I was in New York, having just left a young lady at her apartment and gone to my hotel. The next morning my lawyer was on the phone telling me that I was about to be arrested. After that all I had time to think about was playing my part in this elaborate hoax. But since I got here, I've had time."

"Time for what?"

"Until then I didn't have time to question what I was being told. The simple statement that Amanda had been murdered—I never examined it. Amanda might very well have come back to the hotel, borrowed my car herself, and accidentally taken an overdose. Maybe it was suicide. Any number of things might have happened. I accepted the assumption that it was murder, and the assumption that being innocent would be irrelevant. But once I had made the first move to run, it was too late. I could only go forward. For a long time I told myself I had done the only prudent thing. Now that I've had time to think, I believe it was a mistake. I was too trusting of expert opinions."

Jane shook her head. "You picked a very bad time to start doing your own thinking."

"I know," he said. "I'm just telling you this as one human being to another, so you'll accept it and go on to something else. I'm no longer a client." He nodded with finality. "You can tell them that. I'm finished. I'm not paying another dime."

Jane looked at him thoughtfully. He seemed to be exactly what she had hoped he would be: a victim, who had run out of fear, not guilt. Maybe she had arrived at the right time, after he had already begun to understand the way the business worked. He had been the one to bring up money. Could she get him to understand what he had to do to get out of this mess? Christine Manon had been easy to nudge in the right direction, because she had seen enough to be scared. Vaughn didn't seem to be scared: he seemed defiant. She had to try. She shrugged and said, "You were too trusting. You're right."

He looked puzzled. That wasn't what he had expected her to say. She had to be careful now, and take him through the logical steps. She asked, "How much have you paid to stay hidden this long?"

He gave a mirthless little snort. "A fortune. I suppose we must be up over a million by now, wouldn't you say? If I went to Chicago with you, that alone would cost me another hundred thousand or more, and that much to get settled the next time. It never seems to end."

"No," Jane agreed. "And it won't. Do you think that they'll let you simply say, 'Thanks, but I'm as safe as I want to be'?"

"They won't?"

"They killed people to get you where you are."

He gaped, frowned, then said, "They did? Who?"

She let the amazement she felt show on her face. "Where have you been?"

"Here," he said. "Right here. Why did they kill anyone?"

"There's quite a list," said Jane, "each person for a different reason. But unless you know better, the first one was Amanda."

"How could that be for me?"

"I didn't mean it was for your convenience or safety. It was for you—in order to get control of you, to take over your life. After that they killed other people—four of them at the surgical clinic because they knew your new face and could connect it with the old one. That was to protect you, because you were theirs. They need to keep you unencumbered and willing to keep paying until your money is gone."

His face went through a series of fleeting expressions: skepticism, anger, fear. "You're saying that if I don't go to Chicago with you, they'll kill me too, aren't you?"

She was silent.

He pressed her. "But suppose I did go? At some point they'll get every cent I have, every cent I can get. What happens then?"

"I don't know," said Jane. "I met a woman client who ran out, and one of them implied to her that she could work off future fees as a prostitute. Maybe it was just a mean thing men say to scare women. Maybe it wasn't. I would guess that they would weigh the likelihood that you could keep bringing in money against the likelihood that you would be caught and talk to the police."

His eyes narrowed as though he were in pain. "It's amazing, when I look back on it. I thought about the way she died, and of course it had occurred to me that it was an intentional setup. But I thought it had to be someone who hated her—after all, I wasn't the one who was killed. It could be some enemy of hers I knew nothing about. Then I thought it could be someone who hated me, or wanted her and was jealous. But it wasn't. It was someone who wanted money and knew that if I were made desperate and miserable enough, I could pay and pay." He stood up. "I'm through."

Jane said, "Sitting tight and refusing to budge isn't likely to be your best strategy."

"I understood your threat," he said. "You didn't help me because I was in trouble. You caused the trouble so I would pay you to keep solving it. And now I have no choice but to keep paying."

Jane took a deep breath and let it out. Now was the time. "That's the idea, but I think you have a choice."

"I do," he agreed. "You can tell them that I'm going to make sure that if anything happens, the police know everything I know."

"I wouldn't advise waiting until something happens."

"Whose side are you on?"

Jane said, "I have my own side. And I'm going to make you an offer. If you want me to, I will risk my life to save yours. I can't make anything that has already happened go away. I can keep you alive long enough so you can tell your story to cops who will know what you're talking about, and who might think it answers questions that are on their minds. I can also produce two people who suddenly developed problems just as un-likely as yours and were both offered solutions. That's the best offer you're ever going to get, and it won't come again."

"If that's what you wanted to do, why haven't you already done it?"

"Because I didn't have the one piece of evidence that turns a couple of suspects' wild claims into one story that makes perfect sense." When she looked at him, her gaze was so intense that he wanted to turn away. "I didn't have you."

Jane watched him walk past her into the living room. He stood and looked down at the piano, then walked to the pile of books on the an-tique table near the door. His eyes rose to the gold-rimmed mirror on the wall above them. He said, "This is probably the part that I hate them for most."

"What is?"

"My face."

"I got the impression that it was an improvement."

He kept his eyes on the reflection before him. "It is. I look twenty-five years younger than I looked before. My imperfections are gone. But I look like a different person."

"Isn't that what you wanted?"

He sighed. "It sounded like a wonderful idea. I didn't really under-stand what it meant. People say that by the age of forty you wear the face you've earned. The scars and wrinkles and marks are supposed to be the punishment, and maybe the warning to other people. But the alterna-tive isn't exactly a fresh start. It's being fifty-five, looking in the mirror, and seeing a young face that has nothing in it you recognize. You have to study that face, and try to be what he seems to be. If you don't change, conform to the mask's contours, then you'll be discovered. It was a brilliant thing for them to do to me. I can't walk into a police station and tell my story, because my own face proves I'm a liar. Because I let them do this, they're safe." He turned to look at her and smiled, and the smile was winning, confident, and utterly false. In a few seconds, he let the muscles go slack. "I can't do what you ask."

Jane urged him. "I think you have very little choice."

He shook his head. "I can't tell the police I'm an innocent victim, a person who was duped. I'm a man who escaped from the authorities before they started looking, and then changed my face. How could they believe me?"

"They won't if you're alone—if the only story they hear is yours. But I have other stories, other victims."

"Who?"

"One is Richard Dahlman."

"Dahlman . . . the surgeon?"

"After he finished your surgery, all of the people who worked with him and saw your face were killed. Then they did to Dahlman exactly what they did to you. They made him scared, then offered him a way out that made him look guilty."

"A man like him? It's . . ."

"Unbelievable? Alone, neither of you gets anywhere. But together, you're pretty convincing. His story that the reason his friends all died off was that they helped him perform plastic surgery on a mysterious fugitive looks a bit better if the fugitive shows up. Your story of getting framed for a murder and talked into running looks a bit better if you know they did the same to him."

"I would be taking an incredible risk."

"It's a chance. If you wait until he's gone, you've got nothing. A man who volunteers to tell the police a story sounds better than one who tells it after they catch him." She paused. "And if you're killed, your side of the story never gets told."

He sat down on the edge of the couch and stared into the fireplace. Jane sensed that it was time to let him alone to think, so she moved back into the bedroom and waited. After a long time, she heard movement in the other room, and he appeared in the doorway.

"Before I walk into any police station, I'm going to need something better than a similarity to other people who make more convincing victims," he said. "I'm going to need proof."

"What sort of proof?"

He took a deep breath, and she could hear a shivering in it, as though he were afraid even to say it. "Tape recordings. I can get them to come here. If I say the right things, maybe I can get them to admit out loud that I didn't know anything about any murders—Amanda or the people at the clinic."

Jane frowned, then paced. "I'll be honest with you. I don't like the idea."

"I can do it."

"They have no reason to trust a person they've harmed. If they hear a wrong tone in your voice, a question they don't think you ought to be asking, you're going to die—not later, after they've had time to mull it over—right then, right there."

He said, "I know that. If they killed other people, then I'm no different. You want me to take a risk. All right, I will. But it has to be this one."

"It's much bigger."

"If I can get through five minutes of the right kind of conversation, I win everything. They go to jail, I go free, and I can be myself again. Five minutes of acting. Not five years of telling the same story over and over to hostile cops and judges and juries, and every minute of it being just as vulnerable as I am now. No, more vulnerable, because everyone in the country will have seen this new face." He gave her a pleading look. "If I turn myself in now, I'll never get another chance."

Jane stared past his clear, honest thirty-year-old face and into his eyes. "I hate the idea," she said.

"I'm not asking your advice," he said. "I'm going to do this, regardless of what you think."

Jane held her gaze on his eyes. He was perfectly serious. He was going to try to clear himself, and there was very little she could do to stop him. She couldn't hope to drag him all the way to Chicago at gunpoint, and even if she could, he wasn't going to be of much use to Dahlman unless he told his story. "If you have to do it, I'll try to show you how to do it right."

39

Marshall walked into the American Airlines waiting area carrying a manila envelope under his arm. Jardine was sitting exactly where the camera had shown him, in front of the row of lockers and between the two rest rooms, at a table where he could watch the gates.

Marshall approached the table, his leather identification folder already open in his hand. He stopped beside Jardine and held it in front of his face. "Hello, Mr. Jardine. John Marshall, F.B.I."

Jardine's eyes squinted at the ID, then looked up at Marshall. His eyes were guarded, not quite daring to be hostile, but the brain behind them was already aware that this was not likely to be good news.

Marshall said, "I'd like to talk with you for a few minutes."

Jardine made his eyes flick from side to side, already convinced that the arrival of the tall man in the dark suit had frightened off some valuable quarry. "This is kind of an awkward place," he said. "Can we go somewhere away from the gates?"

"If you'd like," said Marshall. He stepped back and waited while Jardine closed his briefcase and stood up. Marshall stepped off toward the concourse and let Jardine follow.

Marshall entered the cafeteria, sat down at a table, then gave Jardine an inquiring look. Jardine nodded and sat down. He had used the short walk to regain his composure. He leaned back in his seat comfortably, as though he were about to light a cigar and pass the brandy. "What can I do for you?" asked Jardine. He looked into Marshall's eyes and saw something that dispelled his confidence. His wariness returned. He straightened and sat in his chair with the palms of his hands on the table.

Marshall opened the manila envelope. "You're probably anxious to get back to what you were doing, so I'll try to make this quick." He turned the impenetrable light brown eyes on Jardine. "And I know you'll help me."

Marshall set three enlarged photographs on the table and spun them around, one after the other, so they faced Jardine. The pictures were grainy, so Jardine knew they must have been transferred from a videotape. But they were unarguably pictures of him with Jane in Lot C.

In the first, the two were standing beside his car talking. In the second the doors were open. She was seated and he was getting into the car. In the third, Jardine was driving out the gate with her in the passenger seat. Jardine looked up at Marshall.

"Who is she?" asked Marshall.

Jardine feigned a smile while he looked at Marshall and considered his answer. This man wasn't about to screw around listening to him say he didn't know. He knew that Jardine knew, and he was sitting here with his palms sweating, just waiting to catch Jardine in a lie. "I don't know a whole lot about her. The name she gave me is Jane."

Marshall's gaze seemed to lose some of its chill. He looked interested. "What was your business with her?"

Jardine felt cheated. It was just like the damned taxes. You owned something as long as the government felt like ignoring the fact that you had it, but you were just taking care of it for them. If they wanted it, they just came to you like this and took it. She was worth money to him. She might be the difference between retiring in a big house with a pool table in the basement and freezing to death in some alley in a cardboard box. He resisted. "Is there a reward for information leading to her apprehension and conviction?"

Marshall shook his head. "Sorry."

"Is there a bench warrant for her? Bail bondsman involved?"

"No," said Marshall. "She's just somebody we'd like to talk to. She might have information about a fugitive we're looking for."

"Who is it?"

Jardine detected that Marshall's patience had been exhausted. The look in his eyes returned. "This is a friendly inquiry. We would like to know why you were meeting with her the other night in Lot C."

Jardine felt alarm seeping into his veins to speed up his heart and slow his mind. The F.B.I. knew she was a criminal and had pictures to prove he had been with her alone. He stared down at the three photographs. They made it look as though he had met her at the airport and taken her somewhere. That was aiding the escape of a felon. It occurred to him that the appearance was exactly what had happened.

But she had been holding a gun on him. Why couldn't you see it in the pictures? He remembered she had been shielding it with her body when he had approached. Then she had backed up to keep it on him and her body was turned to the side. He had assumed at the time that she just didn't want a shuttle bus driver to notice, or a passenger starting his car to turn on his headlights and see it. But she had known exactly where the cameras were mounted, and had kept her back to them.

He searched for a way out. The F.B.I. could have his license pulled in a second, but that wasn't what worried him most. This guy could probably get him held in county jail on suspicion for a couple of days while he dreamed up a charge. Jardine thought about the prospect of being placed in the general population behind the walls on Vignes Street. The population always included a few who knew him professionally. He would never get out alive.

It was a gross injustice. Any kind of cop who got sent up would be put in solitary on a special block where the other prisoners couldn't get at him. Jardine was just as much a part of the justice system as any of them, but he wouldn't get special treatment.

He had to survive. "Here's the way it was," he said. "I don't really know her at all. She came off a plane. She looked a little bit like a woman who was wanted in Illinois. If I remember right, it was mail fraud and forgery, but I could be wrong. Anyway, she had that look. It was a slow night, and so I decided to tail her until I could make sure."

"How?"

"First on foot, then in my car."

"No," said Marshall. "How were you going to make sure? If you couldn't tell by looking at her in a lighted airport, what new information were you going to get?"

"I carry a collection of posters and circulars." Jardine swung his briefcase onto the table and opened it for Marshall. Clipped to the lid were rows of photographs reproduced on a copying machine. On some pictures, subtleties of skin tone and shading had been left out by the copier, and on others, shadows and textured details like hair had become dark blurs, but Marshall recognized a few of the faces. Richard Dahlman was one. "I thought I'd get really close—maybe talk to her, and see."

Marshall closed the briefcase. "So what happened?"

"I was wrong. I got to the C lot, pulled up, got out, and she looked straight at me. I had come too close to get out of it without saying something. She looked startled, so I was afraid she was going to scream or mace me or something. I said I mistook her for somebody, and was about to move on. Then she said she couldn't find her keys. Would I give her a ride?"

"A ride to where?"

"To her motel."

Marshall's face was expressionless. "Did that strike you as odd?" The eyes never seemed to blink. "The next shuttle bus would have come along in five minutes and taken her to the airport. She could have stepped out of it and walked ten feet to a cab."

Jardine felt hot and panicky. He had let himself get overconfident again, while he had described a procedure he had used many times. Spotting fugitives was a chancy business, so he had spent many evenings trying to get a second, closer look. He had gone too far. No woman with more brains than a ham sandwich who saw a stranger pull up in that parking lot at night would ask him for a ride. It had never happened, could never happen.

He had to get out of this hole. The F.B.I. knew who she was, but he couldn't let them know he did. "I was just getting to that," he said. "I thought, 'This isn't right.' " He glanced at the eyes to see how he was doing, and he judged that he wasn't out yet. "I thought maybe I ought to get out of there. Maybe she was one of those decoys that get you someplace dark and then a big guy with a tire iron cracks your skull and goes through your pockets."

"But you didn't leave."

Jardine shrugged. "It occurred to me that there were other possibilities. I thought it could be that she was another kind of decoy."

"What kind?"

"She didn't seem surprised enough, or in the right way. Maybe she knew who I was, or at least what I had been doing at the airport, and came through first to get my attention and lead me away before somebody else came through."

Marshall's face showed Jardine nothing, but he knew that Marshall had to be considering it. The only reason the F.B.I. would be interested in Jane was that they knew what she did for a living, and that was what she did. Marshall asked, "Did you figure it out?"

He shook his head. "I still haven't. I took her to the motel, drove off, and waited around outside for half the night for somebody to come to meet her. Just before dawn, I had to rethink the whole thing. It was going to be daylight, and you can't sit in a car she's ridden in and expect her not to remember it. If she was just trying to distract me, I might as well admit she had succeeded. If she just wanted me out of the airport or out of the parking lot, she had done it. There was nothing I could do to change it. If she was just a regular woman who thought I had the face of a gentleman—" He grinned comically. "Well, now how could anyone argue with her?"

"That's it?" asked Marshall. "You gave up?"

Jardine looked at him, puzzled. Maybe he should have told the truth. That woman deserved to have the F.B.I. hunting her for what she had done to him. But he still had to hope that some night he would get another chance to trap her and turn her into money. As it always did, the thought of money gripped his consciousness and left no room in it for rancor. "I was curious, but I'm afraid that I've got to be in business for money. I couldn't for the life of me imagine a way to make any out of her."

Marshall set a business card on the table and waited while Jardine looked at it, picked it up, and put it into his pocket. "Call me if you see her again." Then he stood up and walked away.

Jardine picked up his briefcase and tried to decide whether or not he should feel safe. It was possible that they had watched the rest of the evening's tapes and found something that made what he had said impossible. But the business card was his assurance. He could hardly see her and call Marshall if he was in jail. He stood up and walked out of the cafeteria. There were no other agents waiting for him, so he supposed he had done well enough. If he had guessed wrong, he had probably done no worse than put himself out of business. It was a lousy business anyway.

40

J ane finished testing the three voice-actuated tape recorders she had hidden in Brian Vaughn's house. The first one had gone into the heating duct in the living room. The second was hung on the wall above the door of the bedroom closet, so a person would have to step inside and turn around to see it. The third was in the drawer under the oven behind a couple of pans, with the microphone cord running up the back of the range to the inside of the control panel. A video camera was too risky for this meeting. If the face-changers said something useful, the words would be enough. If they saw a lens, Brian Vaughn was through.

She turned to him. "If you have any doubts about doing this—"

He interrupted: "I'm sure. I'm going to do it."

She sighed. "All right. Here's how it works. You just need to turn on the recorders as soon as you've made the call, and then forget them. They're voice-actuated, and you don't need to be anywhere in particular when you have the conversation. One of the microphones will pick up what's said anywhere in the house. If you don't feel right at any point, don't pursue it. Bail out of the conversation."

"You mean give up?"

"Absolutely," she said. "This isn't all we've got, so don't take risks to get more. The police do this kind of thing all the time, and sometimes it takes them a dozen tries to get anything useful."

"You think I'm going to fail, don't you?"

Jane shrugged. "I'd rather you didn't take the chance, but I can see why you would want to. All I can do is show you how it's done and let you make your decision."

"I'll remember."

"Don't turn it into a confrontation, because that's the way to get hurt. You're just not feeling as safe as you thought you would in this little town, and you want them to move you again. You're afraid that if somebody is curious about you, they'll know your new face."

"What do you think they'll say to that?"

"It doesn't matter very much. If they agree to the premise, then we've got about all we can hope for. But I think they'll quote you a price, and they'll want to know who's making you nervous."

"If you're right about them, won't I be putting somebody in terrible danger?"

"Yep," she said. "You will. That's why it's me."

He frowned. "That doesn't sound smart."

She walked across the kitchen toward the side door. "I'm the only candidate they'll take seriously. One of them has seen me already, and they know I'm looking for them. If you tell them something they already know, then whatever else you say will seem more likely."

Jane opened the kitchen door a half inch and looked out at the cars parked along the street, then stepped to the window and scanned the neighborhood. "When they leave, wait ten minutes and then call me at the number I gave you. I'll be waiting to get you and those tapes out of here."

She took a last look at Brian Vaughn, and touched his arm. "Remember, if you decide it's not such a good idea after all, I agree with you in advance. I'll take you out, and I'll make sure Dr. Dahlman shows up to tell what he knows."

Vaughn took a deep, shuddering breath. It looked to Jane as though in the brief time it took to fill his lungs, he was assessing his whole life. He let out the air in a scared puff. "No," he said. "That wouldn't be enough. I have to try."

"All right," said Jane. "Just call and I'll come." She slipped out the back door, across the yard, and out the garden gate.

Brian Vaughn stared at the gate for a full minute, then went to the living room and sat down on the couch with the telephone at his elbow. He stared at it, collecting his thoughts, then put them into words and repeated them silently. He picked up the telephone, then put it back down and considered what he was going to do. Finally, with the air of a man stepping to the edge of a cliff, he rapidly dialed the telephone and waited for the ring.

A half hour later, Jane sat in her room at the hotel trying not to look at the telephone. When it rang, it startled her. As it rang the second time, she realized that she had been hoping that this call would not come.

"Yes?" she said. She listened carefully to be sure there was no click of a second extension. She had given him the number so he could dial directly, and she would not hear the sound of the hotel operator hanging up.

"It's me," said Brian Vaughn. "They can't be here until tomorrow night at eleven."

"All right," she said. "Call me when it's over."

She hung up the phone and began to prepare. She had already rented a second room, at the hotel next door to this big, sprawling place. She had asked for a room on the southwest corner, so she could watch the parking lot of this hotel.

She went out through a side door, quickly stepped across the lawn to the sidewalk, then walked down Cabrillo Boulevard as though she were taking an evening stroll along the ocean. After ten minutes, she came back to the second hotel and entered her room. She sat for a long time watching the parking lot next door, until she had assured herself that nobody was searching for her car. After that she went to sleep, and began to dream.

Once again Jane walked out onto Cabrillo Boulevard. This time she turned south, and stepped along the narrow path beside the green pond in the park they called a bird sanctuary. It was different from the way it had looked to her while she was awake. The glassy surface of the pond was empty and undisturbed, as though the ducks and coots and shore-birds had suffered some kind of sudden kill-off. She left the path and turned up, away from the ocean.

Jane kept walking but had no sense of the pressure of the ground on the soles of her feet. The unchanging, bright sunshine lit every object she saw so that the surface shone, outlined against the shadows, but she felt no warmth from it.

She knew the streets of the city because she had been here a few times, but she felt none of the comfort that familiarity usually brought her in cities she visited. The scenery was beautiful, like the pictures in magazines meant to lure people from cold northern places for midwinter vacations, but it seemed flat and impervious as a photograph. There was no place to enter the picture and hide. The tall eucalyptus and palm trees grew fifty feet of trunk before they leafed out at the top, so they were like bare pillars down here where she walked. All the doors of the buildings were bolted and the gates were locked.

Jane knew where her steps were taking her. She heard herself say, "I don't want to go there," but as soon as she had said it, she was walking up the slight incline onto Ocean View Avenue. She walked directly to the apartment building at the end on the left. The last time she had been here, she had thought about what a good spot it had seemed to place a man like Harry—the street wasn't one that any casual visitor would be likely to notice, because it didn't connect with any of the long, straight ones that crossed the town. By the time she had come here for the first visit all that was to be seen of Harry was a big, dark bloodstain on the cheap yellow shag carpet in the living room.

In the logic of her dream, she felt relieved that old blood never really came out of carpets. The landlords would have replaced the carpet years ago, before they could rent the apartment to some unsuspecting tenant who'd arrived in town after the talk of the murder had subsided. The group memory about unpleasant events wasn't very good in places like Santa Barbara anyway. The bad things happened to strangers— transients and tourists. The victims were assumed to have brought both the causes and the perpetrators with them into the quiet town, and when they were dead the trouble went with them.

Jane knew it wasn't enough to walk past the building and say to herself, "This is the place where John Felker brought a knife across the throat of Harry Kemple and watched him bleed to death on the floor," like some tour guide. She was not an outsider.

She felt her hand on the cold iron railing and listened as her feet touched each of the short slabs of roughened concrete that formed the steps. She remembered the way footsteps made the railing vibrate and hum a little.

She reached the door at the top and touched the handle. When it turned she released it, but it was too late. The door was open six inches and she knew she was supposed to go in. She stepped inside and closed the door.

She looked down at the place on the floor where Harry had died, but she could not see anything different about it, so she lost her certainty that it was the right place, and tried to line it up with the window she had looked through that night.

She watched Harry step into the space on the floor where the bright afternoon sunlight beamed in through the window and illuminated the tiny specks of dust floating in the air. He didn't deflect them from their courses at all. He said, "I hate it here." Then he added apologetically, "But I'm a troubled spirit."

"The unquiet dead," she said. "That's you, Harry."

He made his familiar gesture of tugging at his collar, and she could see the seam that the undertaker had sewn to close his neck. That was the reason. She realized that the wound was bleeding again, little droplets seeping out where the needle had not closed the skin, as though being here made the blood flow. Jane stared down at the carpet, to look away from it.

Harry touched the toe of his worn, scuffed shoe on the carpet. "This is where I died. Did you know that?"

"Of course I knew that," she said impatiently, but seeing him staring down at it like this caused tears to blur her vision.

"I mean right here, where I'm standing now. They only replaced this little square—about five by five—and combed the shag over the seams so it would look the same." He raised his eyes and stared at her intently. "It's happening again, Janie."

She was held by his eyes. "How can it be?"

"Nothing lasts, but nothing really changes. The replacement is what it replaces. The brothers still stalk each other, and then they fight to the death. Over and over."

Jane waited, trying to understand.

Harry said, "They're so good at it that for a long time they've been able to read each other's minds. The Right-Handed Twin, the Creator, was born exactly as strong as the Left-Handed, the Destroyer. They both know it, but each one has a secret vulnerability, so he can't help thinking about it. Hanegoategeh, the Destroyer, thinks the truth, but Hawenneyu, the good one, thinks a lie." He paused. "Ever wonder why it isn't the other way around?"

"Because it never was a game," she said. "It's a war."

He nodded. "Anybody who doesn't live by his wits, doesn't live. Death is always a surprise." He held her in his melancholy gaze for a moment, and she could tell he was letting her think about what had happened here. The way you cut a throat was by using the right hand to bring the blade edge across from behind. First you had to get him to turn his back by making him believe you were a friend.

She said, "It's all going wrong, isn't it? I missed something else."

He said, "You know everything they know. And they know everything you know. You both know that, too."

Jane awoke suddenly, shocked to be in the light. Her head jerked to the side to search for something familiar, because she couldn't remember where she was. Her eyes settled on the clock radio beside the bed, and she read the digits: 5:55. She supposed the dream had been cut short by a sound. She heard a hotel maid moving her cart up the hallway.

She sat up and closed her eyes, trying to recapture the bits of the dream before they were dispersed by the sensory impressions that had come with consciousness. She was frustrated, because she kept catching herself thinking about Brian Vaughn. Then she realized that he wasn't a distraction. Their secret vulnerability was Brian Vaughn. And now he was her vulnerability too. But then, why had they picked him? Because he was weak.

41

Jane carefully constructed her package. The videotape of Brian Vaughn and his apartment and his false identification she surrounded with crumpled newspaper before she put it into the box. The box was addressed to Alan Weems at Senior Rancho in Carlsbad, and she used the return address she had given the Rancho people for his daughter, Julia Kieler, so he would know it wasn't a bomb.

She looked over her letter again. It began, "This is the tape of Brian Vaughn, the man you operated on. His address as of this date is 80183 Padre Street in Santa Barbara, and he calls himself Charles Langer. The other person I found who had been fooled by the people who killed Sarah Hoffman is Janet McAffee. She is living as Christine Manon at 9595 Timon Street in Cleveland, Ohio. If you hear of my death, or are caught, give both of them up to the police."

The rest of the letter was more difficult. It was an attempt to put down everything she had learned about the face-changers in a logical, comprehensible way. As she read it over, it seemed to her that what she had described was a collection of three separate stories that had collided and begun to overlap very early. The face-changers seemed to have gone into business with Brian Vaughn, but hiding him had forced them to manipulate, and finally frame, Richard Dahlman. The face-changers had already taken on Christine Manon when Dahlman unexpectedly escaped from custody. They had to devote most of their time to searching for

Dahlman, so they needed to put Christine in storage. They had made her wait in an apartment in Chicago while the boxes they had planned to ship to Brian Vaughn were still in the closet there. They had planned to move her to the apartment on Troost Avenue in Los Angeles, which was empty and new because they had undoubtedly just bought it with Brian Vaughn's money. Everything had affected everything else in small, incidental ways. She could only hope that each part would help to corroborate the others.

When Jane was satisfied that she had included every detail that she knew, she folded the letter, addressed it to Dahlman, and placed it inside the box with the tape. She had decided that the information belonged to him. If all of this misery ever resulted in a trial, then the name of the trial was most likely to be *The People v. Richard Dahlman.*

She drove to the municipal parking lot, walked to the big post office on Santa Barbara Street, and waited at the counter to send the package by express mail. Then she walked to State Street to do her shopping. At the first stop she bought a battery-operated household intercom, and at the second, a new battery and a fresh tape for her video camera. She walked a little farther and bought a cellular telephone as a present for C. Langer of 80183 Padre Street and had the number activated immediately. The last purchase she made was at a store she had visited before. It was a small, sensitive tape recorder exactly like the ones she had hidden in Brian Vaughn's house.

Jane spent the rest of the afternoon testing the equipment she had bought and looking out her window at the parking lot of the big hotel next door. Finally she could see that another whole row of cars had been gobbled up by the shadow of the long, low building, and the rear windows of the farthest row were glowing orange in the sunset. It was nearly time. She dressed and looked at the clock. It was Brian Vaughn's dinner hour.

She put her purchases into her shoulder bag, went out, and drove to Brian Vaughn's house, then slipped in through the bathroom window. She was not surprised that he had gone out. It would be maddening to him to sit in this house alone, wondering whether each movement he made was being picked up on the tape recorders. One of them was under his oven, so he would be afraid to do any cooking.

Jane sat down on the couch and dialed the number of the house in Amherst where she had lived with Carey. The telephone rang four times before the answering machine took over. She had been gone so long that she had forgotten what the recorded answer was. Her own voice startled her. "I'm sorry. We're not able to come to the phone right now. If you'd like to leave a message, begin when you hear the tone."

Jane gave a little sigh. She had hoped to hear Carey's voice. But there was the beep.

She said, "Hi. Some nasal-sounding woman just told me we can't come to the phone. I knew I couldn't, but I was hoping for a chance to talk to you. I've stopped off in Wisconsin, but don't try to join me, be-cause I'll be gone as soon as this powwow's over. I know that when you listen to this, you're going to be feeling very alone. Remember I love you, and take care of yourself." She hung up, then went to check the three tape recorders.

All three were still where she had left them, still had tapes and batter-ies and functioned when she turned them on. She left them turned off, then turned the fourth one on and carefully placed it behind a row of books high in the bookcase without disturbing the dust.

She plugged the intercom into the outlet beneath the headboard of Brian Vaughn's bed, pressed TALK, then turned on the receiver. There was a squeak of feedback that was rapidly growing into a shriek, so she turned it off again. Then she took the receiver with her, and quietly slipped out the bathroom window and through the garden gate to the next street. When she was in her car she looked at her watch. It was eight o'clock. Brian Vaughn had told her that the face-changers would be at his door in three hours.

Marshall was back in the cafeteria on the concourse at the Los Angeles airport. This time he was carrying a tray of food to a table. He automat-ically picked the one where he had talked with Alvin Jardine, but only because he had spent some time there and found it acceptable. He had come here to pursue a worry, and he didn't want to be distracted.

Jardine had been lying, which was what he would do if he were con-spiring with Mrs. McKinnon. But Marshall was not comfortable with the theory that a woman like Mrs. McKinnon would know how to look for a man like Alvin Jardine and get help from him. It didn't feel right. It also didn't feel right that Jardine would pass up the chance to drag in a fugi-tive of the stature of Richard Dahlman.

Jardine had not seen Richard Dahlman. What he had seen was a pretty woman with long black hair coming through the airport. Yet he had instantly decided to follow her all the way to the distant long-term parking lot. Marshall had watched the airport security tapes again. The woman had definitely been walking toward a white Buick in the parking lot. She had reached into her purse, presumably for a set of keys. Then Jardine had come along, and she had gone off with him. What nagged at Marshall now was that the Buick had not yet disappeared from the parking lot.

The car raised a great many questions. He had put a pair of agents in the lot more than thirty-six hours ago to watch it for her return. She had not come back, and the car was still there. He had been operating on the assumption that Alvin Jardine was some kind of ally of Mrs. McKinnon's. It seemed clear from the tapes that she had thought so too. But that didn't mean she had been right. It was just possible that Mrs. McKinnon had miscalculated, and Alvin Jardine had killed her.

Marshall had not yet reassured himself on that point, but in the past few minutes things had grown more complicated. Marshall had just come along the counter with his tray, intentionally dropped a fork, and bent down to pick it up in exactly the same way that Mrs. McKinnon had. He had found that he was not nearly as flexible as Mrs. McKinnon, but he had managed to put his right hand in the same place. The underside of the stainless-steel counter was plywood. There was a sticky residue of adhesive on the plywood in two rectangular strips about five inches apart. It was just as though something about that size had been stuck there with duct tape, and yanked off.

It had occurred to Marshall early in his inquiry that there was no obvious explanation as to why Mrs. McKinnon would have keys to a Buick registered to Gormby Boat Sales in Marina Del Rey, California. She had stopped to talk to no one from the time she had gotten off the plane until she had met Jardine. It was just possible that the F.B.I. should be more interested in how a set of keys to a clean, respectable car nobody was looking for got taped under a counter in an airport than in what had become of Richard Dahlman. For a decade there had been rumors that there were professional services that helped fugitives disappear.

The attractiveness of the idea was hard for a law enforcement officer to resist. Sometimes a person who should have been easy to catch seemed to vanish. But every time one of those fugitives surfaced, it seemed to Marshall that the fugitive had spent the time in plain view, hardly hiding at all. One had run a popular restaurant in Seattle; another had moved to a resort town in upstate New York and told people he was a film producer.

Just as Marshall set his tray down and prepared to lose himself in cogitation, his pager began to beep. He looked at the tray with grim resignation. He had come here as a way to check the counter, but he had gotten used to the idea that he was going to get to eat the food.

As he walked out of the cafeteria onto the concourse, he looked at the number on the pager: Grapelli. It must be time for him to fly back to Buffalo. It would be interesting to ask Mrs. McKinnon exactly why the keys to the Buick had been taped under the counter, and what she had talked about with Jardine.

He dialed the number and Grapelli said, "Hate to interrupt your dinner."

Marshall said, "I take it she turned up?"

"Yeah."

"All right. I guess you can't keep me from eating on the plane."

"Be my guest. But all they give you on those short flights is a bag of peanuts. She's not in Buffalo."

"Where are they holding her?"

"There is no 'they,' " said Grapelli. "And nobody is holding her. That's what I wanted to talk to you about. She called home. The phone tap recorded it and we traced it to a house in Santa Barbara. 80183 Padre Street."

"Can I hear it?"

"Stand by."

Marshall listened to the sound of Jane's voice. He felt a little sorry for her, and a little ashamed to hear the words she had meant for her husband. But then he heard what he had been listening for. If she had said she was in Santa Barbara, he would have called it a feint of some kind to draw attention away from somewhere else.

"Okay," said Marshall. "Good enough for me."

"I'll call ahead to get the Santa Barbara police to meet you at the airport."

"You mind if we wait on that?" asked Marshall.

"Why?" Grapelli paused. "Are you afraid they'll bust in on them before you get there?"

"They'll do what they're supposed to do," said Marshall. "They'll put a big circle of plain-wrap cars around the neighborhood so nobody can get out and nobody can get in. Including me."

"That doesn't strike me as a drawback."

"I want to take a look at the place before we do anything irrevocable. If Dahlman's there with her, then I'll call them in myself."

"So what are you worried about?"

"Once the neighborhood is surrounded, we're committed. We have whoever is inside it, and that's all we have. If Dahlman's with her, then the game's over, and we're still champions. But what if Dahlman isn't there? She's been traveling all over the place without him, so it's not a sure thing."

"Okay, so what if Dahlman isn't there? She must know where he is."

"Right. If we follow her, she'll lead us to him eventually. If she's in a cell, she's not leading anybody anywhere. She'll be just one more suspect who isn't answering any questions."

"You think she'll hold out?"

"After what she's done already, she doesn't strike me as a person who panics under pressure," said Marshall. "And the woman she used as a decoy started talking lawyers the second the door of her hotel room popped. These are not unsophisticated people. What her lawyer will tell her is to keep quiet."

Grapelli sighed. At last he said, "All right. Let's try this the easy way. Go take a look. The minute you've seen the place, you call me. But unless what you've seen is a good reason not to, what I'm going to tell you is to get a search warrant on the way to the police station, where you will pick up a few guys to kick down the door for you. Understood?"

"Understood."

42

Jane packed all of her gear and her suitcase into her car, checked out of her two hotels, and then drove off. If Brian Vaughn got through the meeting, he would try to call her, and he would probably feel a moment of panic when she didn't answer. But it would be only a moment, because within a few seconds she would be able to stand beside him and tell him there was nothing to worry about.

Jane glanced at her watch. She had timed this correctly. The sky was dark, but it was still two hours before the face-changers were supposed to arrive. She would have all the time she needed to get herself set and make sure she got a videotape of them walking under the street lamp and up to Vaughn's door.

She parked her car two streets away, moved into the little back yard through the garden gate, then stole along the back of the driveway to hide behind the garbage cans. She looked into the eyepiece of the video camera to be sure that she could see enough of the street to pick them up. Then she set it down, turned on her intercom, and listened.

A voice that wasn't Brian Vaughn's said, "If it's what you want, I guess we could arrange it."

They were here already. Jane's heart began to beat faster. She had come early, to see the house and hear what was going on inside before anyone could have expected her. They had come earlier. Since she had done it, she should have known that they would too. They knew what she knew.

The man said, "But we went to a hell of a lot of trouble to get you set up here. You put in months getting the locals used to you, so you're part of the landscape. That's a lot to throw away." There was a brief pause. "And it's expensive."

"How expensive?" That was Brian Vaughn's voice.

"Top-of-my-head figures? Let's see," said the man. "Suppose, just for example, it was Port Townsend, Washington, like you say. A pleasant little town, and a nice little house like this. That's maybe three hundred. We can't sell this one right away, so there's no help there."

"Why not?"

"We just bought it. If you're not safe here with a new face, we can't use it for somebody else, can we?"

"But I paid for it." Jane began to feel tense. His tone was too argumentative.

"We'll unload it in a year or two and you'll get the money. Minus expenses and commissions. So figure three hundred for a new house and furnishings up there, you sign over this one, and another hundred on top, it's going to cost you half a million to get moved."

"What's the extra hundred for?" Vaughn sounded angry. What was he doing? He was arguing over money he was never going to give them.

"Shipping and handling."

There was a sharp laugh. A third voice. It must be a two-man team. Jane held her breath and listened. Just because there were two didn't mean there weren't more.

"What's that?"

"That's our time and trouble."

There was a pause, and then Vaughn said, "All right." Jane rose to a crouch. He had used the wrong tone. It wasn't grudging and resentful enough. He couldn't take the man through all that by arguing, and then simply agree.

The man seemed to have sensed it too. He said, "That okay with you?"

Vaughn said, "Sure."

"You want to leave tonight or tomorrow?" That was the big question. The man was giving Vaughn a chance to salvage this, to save himself.

He gave the wrong answer. "I guess tomorrow. That would give me time to pack and make sure things look normal here."

The man said, "Sounds good. You got any coffee?"

"I'll go make some."

She heard him walking off. Then she heard the man who had been quiet say, "What's the best way?"

"We could cut his throat in the bathtub, so it won't be such a big deal to clean it up."

"I think we've got to get him out of here now, and do it on the way. We could drive him north of here, and pull off at one of those turnoffs for the beaches up there. Or maybe some campground."

Jane set down the intercom and started moving toward the house. If she could get there before Vaughn finished making the coffee and left the kitchen, there was still a chance. She slipped around the corner of the house, up to the kitchen door, and tried to peer inside. The blinds were closed, and she could see only a narrow slice of empty tile floor through a crack at the corner.

She flung open the kitchen door, but she couldn't see him. Where was he? She looked at the coffee maker on the counter. It wasn't turned on yet, didn't look as though he had even filled it. The voices were quiet now. Something must have happened in the brief time it had taken her to reach the house. They hadn't even let him get started. But if they hadn't killed him yet, she had to try. As she moved quietly toward the living room doorway, her breaths were shallow and quick, fighting the sick regret she knew she would not have time to feel.

She would have to read the pattern of sights in the room instantly while she was in motion—the positions of the men, where their hands were, what it would take to propel Vaughn out the door with her—and act before they'd had time to think. She stepped out of cover into the doorway, her eyes flicking about her wildly.

Brian Vaughn was alone, sitting on the couch, aiming a pistol at Jane. The three tape recorders he had watched her hide were lined up on the coffee table. From one of the them, the conversation resumed.

Vaughn's voice said, "The coffee will be ready in a few minutes."

"Thanks," said the other man's voice. "You know, Brian, we've been talking. We'd like to get you out of here tonight."

Vaughn's forehead was damp with a faint, sticky sweat. His skin seemed to have lost the suntan glow and bleached out to a pale gray. He looked terrified. His own voice came out of the recorder: "I'm a little bit worried about leaving without wiping this place for fingerprints and so on . . ." The sound seemed to distract him, irritate him, as though he was having trouble concentrating. He punched the button and the tape recorder stopped. He raised his head to yell, "She's here!"

Jane hissed urgently, "You've still got a chance."

He shook his head frantically, denying it as though he was trying to keep his ears from even hearing it.

"They were outside waiting for me to arrive, weren't they?"

He seemed angry at her. "Of course they were." Jane could see that he had lost his nerve hours ago, maybe blurted out the whole story the minute the face-changers had arrived. He hated her for not saving him, and for having tried. He hated her for his own collapse, and the longer he felt the danger that she had brought him, the more certain he seemed to be that she had caused it.

She stepped closer, whispering now. "You can still save us both."

In reply, he jerked the gun up to point at her face, his arm muscles so tight that it looked as though he wanted to jab her with it. Jane saw a faint smirk playing about his lips, as though he were trying it on, testing the way it felt. She sensed that he was determined to show the face-changers how loyal he was: he was going to be sure he was the one to kill her. He was utterly lost.

Jane had one final chance, and she would have to use Brian Vaughn's eyes to know when it came. She could hear footsteps coming up the walk toward the front door behind her. She heard a shoe on the bottom step, then one on the top. She tensed her muscles and watched Brian Vaughn's eyes.

At the instant the door behind Jane opened, Brian Vaughn's eyes flicked toward it. Jane leapt and spun to throw her shoulder into Vaughn's chest as she wrapped her arm over Vaughn's so it was clamped in her armpit, and used both of her hands to squeeze his fingers. The gun discharged into the wall beside the door. The man who had been coming in dived to the floor as Jane bucked to jerk her head into Vaughn's face. In the second when she felt him loosen his grip on the gun, she wrenched it out of his hand and dashed out the doorway the man had left open.

She veered to the right without having to choose, because it was harder for a right-handed shooter to follow a target moving in that direction. She dashed across the neighbor's flower bed and reached the first tree before the man on the floor could make his way back to the open door. He fired his first shot into the ground behind her feet, then overcompensated and fired again four feet ahead of her, and by then she was beyond the corner of the next house.

Jane ran up the next driveway toward the back of the house. She could hear heavy feet pounding the sidewalk along Brian Vaughn's street, then moving more cautiously up the driveway behind her. She could see this house had a six-foot board fence like the one behind Vaughn's. She had no time to look for a gate. She ran hard, took two long steps, sprang upward to grasp the top of the fence, and used her momentum to roll over it. She came down hard in the middle of another flower bed. She fought the urge to rise to her feet instantly. Instead she crawled ten feet on her belly along the bottom of the fence.

When the men fired through the board fence, they pierced it several times at the place where they had seen her go over it. She stood and dashed straight for the space between this house and the next. She couldn't run for her car. They were so close behind her that she could not hope to get it unlocked, climb in, and start it before they shot her. Instead she cut across the front lawn of the house, across the sidewalk and the street, then along the opposite row of houses to put the bodies of parked cars between her and her pursuers.

Jane ran for the corner of the fifth house, where she remembered there was an alley that separated the residential stretch of street from the beginning of a small business district. The alley was a logical place to park a car, so she had walked the route she was taking now in daylight and in the dark. It had turned out to be wrong: the far end opened on a municipal parking lot. It had been blocked by a row of steel posts set in concrete so only pedestrians could get into the parking lot that way. But she had kept it in mind because it had looked so right. She decided that tonight she would take it at a sprint, going as fast as she could run over the rough, potholed pavement where they would have to tread with caution. If some of them were following her in a car, this would be the place to strip away that advantage.

Jane glanced over her shoulder at the block of houses behind her, trying to detect moving figures, then turned to enter the mouth of the alley.

The sight of the man made her gasp. "Hold it!" he called. "F.B.I."

Jane veered away from him and dashed up the sidewalk along the first storefront. She had timed everything wrong. The face-changers had arrived hours early, and so had the F.B.I.

Now she could hear the footsteps of the F.B.I. agent on the pavement behind her. She knew she had to run faster, to make her legs pump harder and stretch for distance at each pace. She had done this to herself. She had intentionally put herself in the way of a group of men who were coldly, pragmatically violent. Next she had intentionally attracted the attention of a government agency whose whole purpose was meeting people like that with overwhelming force. But then she had failed to get out from between them.

The only way she had to get out of it now was to bet everything on her speed, to keep herself from thinking about how it felt to run blind into the darkness, what would happen if she twisted an ankle or didn't see an obstacle. She had to throw herself into the space ahead of her and hope that nothing had been left there that wasn't imprinted on the map she carried in her memory.

She turned up the next alley, looking for a place to hide. She ran a few paces, then saw the steps. A three-story brick building ahead and to her left had steel rungs built into the side so maintenance people could climb to the roof. She had no time to stop and judge exactly how much of a lead she had on the F.B.I. man, or to figure out the positions or numbers of agents with him. She had to move before she could think, or the lead would be used up. She came to the building at full speed, jumped high so her foot landed on the third rung, and began to scramble up. She knew she had to get out of view before the F.B.I. agent reached the alley entrance, so she raised her face to the night sky and climbed.

She could hear his feet on the sidewalk beyond the alley now, and they seemed to be hitting much more rapidly than she had expected. She tried to climb faster. Her foot slipped, her body dropped, but her terror had made her hands clutch the rung above her so tightly that when her arms extended, she stopped. She hung for a second, found her footing, and began to climb again. She was more timid now, cold and breathless. Maybe all she would have to do was get above his normal eye level, and he would pass.

She heard one foot hit hard, then stop. His voice was below her, off to the left. He called up to her, "Stop, or I'll have to shoot."

Jane had been half-expecting the words, as she had heard them in her imagination for years. The sound was not as she had expected. The words were softer, less angry and brutal than they had been in her mind. He wasn't shouting them out so some witness would testify later that he had killed her legally. The words were for her, to remind her what they both knew he was supposed to do.

Jane gritted her teeth, gazed up at the sky, and thought, "I did this." Her legs pumped and her arms stretched above her, following her eyes up into the sky. As she climbed, she listened for the loud noise and relaxed her muscles to receive the pain. She was aware that there had never been the night when the average F.B.I. agent could not drop her in one shot.

She had not climbed more than thirty feet of the way up, and he was maybe another thirty feet from the foot of the ladder.

Why was he hesitating? Was he deciding whether he had meant it? No, he must be aiming. Jane climbed faster, and the shot came. It was so loud that she cringed, trying to protect her ears with her shoulders. Then there was an aftersound that hung in the air as though the report had jarred the molecules and changed them somehow. She scrambled higher.

That had been the warning shot. The next one was going to shatter her spine. Her right hand reached up for the next rung and slapped down on a flat, abrasive surface. Her hand had touched the roof.

Her fingers spread to get a firm hold on the level, featureless spot. She forced herself to relinquish the left hand's grip on the last metal rung to press both palms downward, pull herself up onto her belly, and slither onto the flat, tarry surface.

She lay there for a moment, panting, as she finally allowed herself to feel the terror. She assured herself she was up, out of sight, and he had not shot her. She heard a metallic ring, and her next breath caught in her throat. It was the sound of his shoe touching the lowest rung of the ladder.

She raised herself to her feet and spun her body to look around her frantically. She had assumed there would be something up here—a door, a vent, anything she could pry open to slip down into the building. But she was on a flat, open rectangle of black tar. On all sides she could see the roofs of other buildings, at varying distances. She looked back the way she had come. She couldn't go back down the ladder, because he was on his way up from the alley. On the opposite side was the street. She whirled her head from side to side. The closest building was the next one along the alley.

Jane walked, less quickly than she wanted to, toward the edge of the black rectangle where she was trapped and looked toward the other roof. It seemed to be about eight or nine feet away. Jane gnashed her teeth, scared, frustrated, and angry at herself. She was more afraid than she had been when she had thought it would be a bullet. She tried to be rational. There were people who could take a running start and jump twenty-seven feet. This was one-third as far. She was uninjured and in good physical condition. She was a terrific runner.

But as she was marshaling the arguments, trying to convince herself, she knew that the arguments worked only if she could goad herself into running straight for the gap between the roofs at full speed. If she judged the paces wrong and stutter-stepped, or lost her nerve at the edge and hesitated, she would fall to the pavement below.

Jane cautiously approached the edge of the roof in a crouch, unable to stand up straight for fear she would get dizzy and topple over. She judged the distance again. It wasn't that far. It was no more than she could have done with ease on the ground.

Jane heard the sound of the man's feet on the metal rungs on the side of the building. She could hear his breathing now. He was a little winded, but there was no tremor or shallowness in his breaths. He wasn't afraid.

She turned away from the edge and paced back toward the other end of the roof. One, two, three, four . . . she had to try. Seven. She could not stand here and get cornered and arrested by the F.B.I. while the face-changers drove off somewhere. Ten, eleven, twelve.

Jane took three deep breaths. In a moment he would be up here. She leaned into her first step, to force her left foot to come down and catch her weight. The second was slightly easier, and the third was like a reflex, the fourth unconscious. She ran faster, harder now. Dig, dig, dig. Four steps left—here it comes, one more—and leap! She pushed off with her right foot, then took another half step in the air, her arms flailing for balance. As soon as she was airborne, she knew that she had made it easily. She came down five or six feet past the edge, hit gravel, slipped, and tried to break her fall with the palms of her hands.

She slid on the rough, loose stones. Her hands stung, her thigh was scraped, but she was alive. She felt her lungs expand, taking in too much air, refusing to exhale until she stopped them. She huffed out a breath, then another. She had made it.

She got to her knees, then hurried to the edge beside the alley to look down and find the ladder. She lay on her belly to peer over at it. There was no ladder. She had made a horrible mistake. The fact that the last one had a ladder didn't mean this one did. Reluctantly, with growing trepidation, she looked back at the last building. The man was climbing onto the roof.

All Jane could see was his silhouette, but she could read his thoughts. He looked quickly around the roof, then at the building where Jane lay. He stepped closer, as though to judge the distance between the two buildings. He saw her. He was thinking, "If she can jump it, so can I." He backed away from the edge, but he didn't seem to be looking at the chasm between the buildings. He was looking at her.

Jane stood and turned away from him to look at the building beyond hers. It was the same kind of jump that she had just made. She walked toward it, then changed her mind. She had no time to count the steps. She sensed the place where she should begin, fixed her eyes on the gap between the buildings, and leaned forward. Her left foot came down, and then the right, and she was in a full run. When she reached the place where she had to spring upward, her foot landed on gravel. She dug in and felt for friction. Her trajectory seemed too flat, too low. Behind her, she heard bits of gravel rolling off the edge. As she flew, she thought, "I'm dead," but then it didn't seem so certain. She brought her knees to her chest, hit the next roof, and slid forward on her back. After a second, she heard a handful of gravel hit the ground far below.

Jane was shaken, and this time the impact had scraped the skin on her back. She glanced behind her and saw the F.B.I. man take the leap to the second building. For an instant her mind interpreted the silhouette as having wings, but she realized that it was just his sport coat flaring outward in the wind as he jumped. He was only one building away again.

Jane turned and walked only close enough to the fourth building to see it clearly, then backed up and ran for it. This time her steps were sure, and she landed on her feet and took a few steps to stop herself. Then she looked at the fifth building.

This one was different. The little row of businesses was ending, and the next building was just a big house with a sloped roof. She looked back at the F.B.I. agent just as he made his second jump. He was tall and strong, and whatever he was afraid of, this wasn't it. He landed hard and trotted forward a dozen feet to stop his momentum, but he was already looking ahead.

Jane felt despair. A terrible moment was coming. She could see it clearly, and there was no way that she could think of to avoid it. The big F.B.I. agent was alone. She didn't know why he was alone, and there was no time to wonder. He just was. She could see from the way he carried himself—standing upright and then running ahead to leap each gap between buildings—that he was positive that the woman he was chasing was unarmed. The thought made her reach to the pocket of her jacket and touch the pistol she had taken from Brian Vaughn.

She stared at the agent's shape in the darkness. He was what she had told Dahlman to worry about. He was not some evil, greedy psychotic who wanted to turn people into money. He was one of the good guys— the best of the good guys, because he spent all of his time protecting the weak from the strong. She had challenged him to come after her, and he had to do it, but he didn't have to do it this way. He could have shot her while she was climbing up here, but he had decided that it was better to risk his life jumping from rooftop to rooftop above the sleeping city, where the street lamps were far below and threw no light.

She watched him moving forward to look at the next stretch of empty space he would have to cross. He would be so easy. She could sit down on this flat surface where she now stood. She could take Vaughn's Walther P99 in both hands, steady them on her right knee. If she squeezed off the first round just as he went up, she could probably put two or three more into his chest before his limp body slammed into the side of the building.

Jane took a deep breath and held it for a second, then pushed the air out of her lungs and turned away from him. He was going to be on this roof with her soon. If she let that happen, it was over. She stared at the next building. There was no choice as to how she must do it. The peak of the roof was higher than this flat one, and jumping up there was physically impossible. She would have to leap for the place where the slope matched her level, and hope that after she hit, she would be able to stop herself be-fore she slid the rest of the way down and dropped off at the eaves.

Jane leaned into her first step and ran hard. She threw herself into the air, then landed with her left leg bent, so both feet and then her left hand hit the shingles. As soon as she felt the impact, she turned a little so her momentum would make her flop onto her belly.

Jane completed the turn, and stopped. She felt herself begin to slip. She clawed at the shingles with her fingertips, but her face was four inches from the roof and she could see it moving upward past her eyes. She felt the rough, grainy texture moving under her fingertips and nails, then felt her fingers slip down to the next shingle. She grasped at one with her right hand, jammed her thumb under it and pinched it, then did the same with her left. Her arms extended, trying to slow her down as her sweatshirt rolled upward under her belly and she felt the scratchy shingles on her bare skin. Then she stopped. The buckle of her belt had caught on the shingles. She lay there, straining to hold herself and afraid to move.

She heard the man's running footsteps, then heard the heavy impact as he landed on the roof of the building she had just left, then four more steps as he stopped himself.

Jane spread her legs apart and felt for a footing on the shingles, keeping her knees and the insides of her toes touching the roof. When she sensed resistance, she pushed herself upward a little with her feet and reached for the next shingle, then the next. A few inches at a time, she pulled herself up the roof toward the peak like a mountain climber.

The F.B.I. man was at the edge of the next roof now, looking at her. He called, "This looks like a good place to quit."

She pushed his voice out of her mind and reached up to pinch the next shingle between her thumb and forefinger, feeling the strain all the way to her wrist. She used her feet to push her body up to it.

He tried again. "Whatever happened back there, the penalty for it isn't as bad as the penalty for falling." His shoes made crunching sounds on the other roof three times, as though he were sidestepping to get a better look at her. "I can get the fire department to bring you down with a ladder."

She longed for it. They would drive a truck up and extend the ladder. Some big, strong guy would climb it to the peak and anchor a rope up there, then lower a harness that would fit under her arms like a mother's hug, then slowly ease her to the ladder. She looked up, and she could see that she was making progress. Her thumbs and fingers were numb, but the peak looked closer. She put her face close to the shingles and kept climbing.

Then she reached up, and felt the slightly rounded shingles running along the spine of the roof. She put both hands over the apex and pulled, and she could look down the other side to the street in front of the building. She swung one knee over the peak and began to crawl unsteadily away from the F.B.I. man toward the far end of the roof. When she reached the chimney she leaned her back against it, then slid her shoulder blades up it to rise to her feet shakily and look for a way down.

The loud, harsh sound of the shots made her squat down quickly. Why now? Why kill her now? But the shots had not been that close. They were coming from somewhere below. The face-changers had not run back to their car and driven out of town. They were here.

Then she heard a different set of shots—one, two, three, four in rapid succession. That had to be the F.B.I. man returning fire. There was an irregular volley of shots from below, then silence. They weren't shooting at her. They were shooting at him.

The pause lasted a long time. Maybe after all of that noise they had decided they had to leave. She slowly raised her body against the chimney, then craned her neck to search for the F.B.I. agent. She picked out a shape that must be his on the next roof, crouched and looking away from her along the row of rooftops they both had crossed.

She kept her eyes turned in that direction. She knew she should be spending this time searching for a way down, but she couldn't. She saw movement. The F.B.I. agent fired twice, then ducked down. Muzzle flashes erupted far down the line. Jane pulled out Vaughn's pistol and waited. She thought she saw the shadow of a man appear on the farthest roof and tried to aim, but lost it in the shape of another building. Then another bobbed up from the ladder. She tried to lead them as they crouched and ran, but it was too late. They flopped down on their bellies so she couldn't see them.

The F.B.I. man fired two times at their prone figures. Then there was a click as though he had removed the magazine from his pistol. The two men heard it too, or sensed it. They popped up and fired eight or ten times while he slid his next magazine into place.

One of the two men made a run and jumped to the second roof. Just as he came down, the F.B.I. man fired once. But the other man had been waiting for it, and he fired wildly in the F.B.I. man's direction to keep his head down. He used the pause to make his run and jump to join his companion on the second roof.

When the F.B.I. agent rose to fire at him, he got off only one shot before the man's companion fired a rapid salvo to make him drop down again.

Jane watched anxiously as the two men used the same strategy to reach the third roof. Each time the F.B.I. agent tried to raise his head to aim at the one who was vulnerable, the other one would lay down a barrage of fire that forced him to go down again. Jane had led them both into a terrible place. Jane was already trapped on a roof with a steep slope, and she could not hold a view of the two men long enough to fire. All she could tell in the darkness was that they were moving closer and closer, and the F.B.I. agent had gone as far as he could without being trapped beside her.

He had fired probably ten times and then he had needed to reload. Why wasn't he carrying a government-issue Beretta 92 with a police-only fifteen-round magazine? He had been walking around town alone, in a jacket and tie. He had been looking for a doctor's wife, not conducting a raid on Brian Vaughn's house, or getting into a firefight. He was probably using something smaller that he could carry without attracting attention, with a single-stack ten-round magazine like the ones they sold in every gun store. It was very unlikely that he was carrying more than one extra magazine.

Jane saw him beginning to crawl toward the edge of the roof closest to the two face-changers, and her heart skipped, then beat harder. It was much worse than she had guessed. He had not been reloading his pistol. He had been checking the magazine to see if he had another shot left: ten in the magazine, one in the chamber. He was out. As she watched him, she found that she could feel his thoughts again, and she felt despair. He was moving to the spot where he believed the first man would leap to his roof, so he could jump the man, disable him, and take his gun. It was a desperate, hopeless plan.

Jane watched as the first man began his run. They must have sensed what had happened too. They knew he was out of ammunition, just as she did. The man ran harder. He was going to jump.

Jane stood up and screamed, "Hey! Over here!" The man hesitated, slipped, and barely stopped himself from toppling over the edge. His friend dashed to his side and grabbed his arm to steady him, and they both ducked down.

The F.B.I. man turned, sprang to his feet, and ran across the fourth roof toward the last gap. He launched himself into the air, landed on his side, and rolled to his belly, as Jane had. He slid a few feet downward, then stopped just as the two men realized what he had done and fired.

He had landed high enough on the sloped roof so that they couldn't achieve the proper angle. Their shots cracked over his head into the sky.

From the peak of the roof, Jane called down, "Stay on your belly and come up at an angle, toward the chimney. It's higher than their roof, so they can't quite see you."

"I'll try," said the agent. He didn't sound very optimistic.

"Don't pretend to be nervous," said Jane. "You're Superman."

She could hear the agent give a little huff of air that might have been a chuckle. "What's to stop them from doing the same thing?"

She said, "I'm leaving a little present for you on the upper side of the chimney. That should help." Then she moved along the crest of the house, away from him.

When she reached the edge, she lay on her belly, grasped the shingles again, and let herself slide, hand below hand, down the slope of the roof.

At the very end, she turned and looked down to be sure that she had seen clearly from above. A thin black cable stretched from the telephone pole across the alley to the corner of the house.

She reached down and tugged on the wire. It was looped once around a metal hook screwed into the clapboard, then stapled once to the wooden trim, and finally it disappeared into a hole drilled into the house. It seemed to be a cable-television hookup. Her eyes followed the wire across the alley to the telephone pole, but she could not tell how it was connected on the other end. As she grasped the wire and slowly eased her weight off the roof, she tried to convince herself that it would hold her. She reached out farther on the wire with her right hand, and her body swung and bounced a little. The swing helped bring her left hand up to the wire for the next grasp. She began to move out over the alley, swinging from hand to hand.

She heard a sound behind her, then felt the cable jerk and begin to sag. The loop had tightened, and the metal hook was threatening to pop out of the clapboard. She moved her hands faster, trying to keep her body from swinging.

Jane dropped four or five feet as extra cable began paying out of the drill-hole in the house. She heard a loud crash, and something like broken glass from inside the house, and then a thud against the wall. Jane knew what it was. The coaxial cable had been screwed into the back of a television set, and her weight had pulled the television set off whatever it had been sitting on. The set was caught against the wall, and the only thing that could be holding the cable to it was that little metal connection.

Jane began moving toward the telephone pole again. In her imagination she could see the television set jammed against the wall, and she remembered that the backs of all the television sets she had ever seen were just brittle plastic. Maybe the metal connection would come right out, but with its base, it would be too big to go through the hole.

She was dangling over a spot just past the center of the alley when the cable gave way. She fell straight down a few feet, but then the connection at the pole caught and her fall became a swing. She loosened her grip on the thin cable to go lower, but the telephone pole seemed to be coming toward her at an incredible speed. She held her feet up in front of her to cushion the impact, but then she twisted in the air. Her shoulder glanced off the pole and she lost her grip. She hit the ground hard, rolled, and lay on the gravel, dazed.

Jane had to get up and move. Her shoulder and side hurt, and there was a dull pain in her left ankle. She tested her weight on it and found she could walk. She took a few steps, then a few more, heading toward the end of the alley.

She stared up at the rooftops, but could not see any of the three men. She began to trot, and she could tell that she would be able to run after all. She stopped, turned, and cupped her hands around her mouth. "Hey!" she shouted. "Doesn't anybody want to say good night to a lady?" She pivoted and began to run.

She passed between two of the posts at the end of the alley and into the municipal parking lot, then dodged to the left to run along the only line of cars left there this late at night.

She reached the end and prepared to turn right to head for the cross street that would take her under the freeway, and then saw the pay tele- phone on the corner. She told herself it was too soon to stop. She should get far enough ahead to be sure they wouldn't convert a glimpse into a clear shot. How could she possibly be more exposed to their view than she would be standing under a street lamp at the first intersection? She took a step toward the telephone. There were plenty of telephones far- ther away. She had seen lots of them along the beach.

Jane paused and listened. There were still no sirens. She was sure that people all over town must have heard the shots. But there was nothing in this neighborhood except closed shops, so apparently nobody had been around to tell the police exactly where the shots had come from. Their only way of finding out was to get into cars, patrol the streets, and listen.

Jane ran to the telephone, lifted the receiver, and dialed 911. She heard a female voice say "emergency" something, but Jane said, "There's an of- ficer under fire on a roof by the parking lot at Chapala and Castillo. I re- peat, officer under fire." She left the telephone hanging to be sure they could trace the call if they needed to, but she didn't run toward the free- way underpass to reach the beach, as she had planned. Instead, she turned away from the ocean and ran along the sidewalk. She ran in the open, under the glowing street lamps because that was the way to move at top speed. She did not know this street, but she could tell the direction it was leading her, and she knew that she would not miss the corner where she wanted to turn. It was the street where Brian Vaughn lived.

43

Marshall crouched in the darkness on the steep roof, with his back to the chimney. He felt behind him with his right hand, and his fingers closed on a familiar shape. He clutched the grips and raised the weapon close to his face. He could make out the word "Walther" and the model number P99 stamped into the receiver. It made a nice, timely gift, he thought. Without it his death would be about a minute away. Maybe it was, anyway.

Marshall moved around to the far side of the chimney and stared down at the building he had just left. He saw the first man make the leap back to the building beyond it. After a couple of seconds, his partner joined him. They were trying to make it back to the one with the ladder. She had done it. They were going after her.

He stuck the pistol into his coat pocket and began to crawl along the peak of the roof. He said to himself that he was too old to be this stupid, or maybe too stupid to have grown this old. He had come into Santa Barbara alone because he had wanted to get the woman's cooperation. He had gotten her cooperation, all right. And that was only after he had emptied his sidearm punching holes in shadows from fifty yards. Now he was going to do something else that was even more stupid.

He had nearly reached the edge of the roof. He raised his head a little to verify what he had remembered about the height of the building. He rose unsteadily to his feet, straddling the peak of the roof. He took two steps forward, then the third right on the bent shingles at the crest, then the fourth, fifth, and launched himself into the air.

He had guessed that the peak was high enough above the flat top of the building beside it to make up for the fact that he couldn't get a running start on a sloped roof. As he began his fall, he was not certain that he had been right. But after a second his optimism returned. He braced himself for the landing, tried to break his fall, but felt the impact from his ankles, up his spine, to his shoulders. He rolled, pulled the pistol out of his belt, and brought it up.

One of the two men was lying on the next roof with his arm extended toward Marshall. But Marshall was in the same position, the gift pistol's single-dot sight already settling on the man's head. Marshall squeezed the trigger and the man jerked once, then lay still.

Marshall ran forward and jumped to the roof where the man lay. He saw the second man run across the next roof, then leap to the one with the ladder. Marshall heard the sound of running feet in the alley below . . . police? He heard a voice shout, "This way."

He ran to the edge of the building and looked down into the alley. There was a third man waving at the man on the roof. He had stayed on the ground, and must have been working his way along the row of buildings, waiting for a shot at Marshall or the woman. But now he was a hundred yards ahead of the other man, and he was going after her. Marshall knew that the man who had been retreating toward the ladder would reach it in a few seconds, and the shot at him was the more likely of the two, but this one was close enough behind the woman to have a chance of catching her.

Marshall turned his body away from the man on the roof to bring his right arm beyond the edge below his feet, and straighten it. As he looked down into the alley, the gift pistol in his hand was already part of his field of vision. He brought the single white dot between the two dots of the rear sight, let it settle on the top of the running man's head, and squeezed the trigger.

The man's left leg was striding forward, but when the foot hit the ground there was no life in it, and it didn't hold his weight. From above, it looked to Marshall as though he were suddenly ducking to run downward into the ground.

Marshall pivoted and dashed for the gap between the buildings. He landed on the next roof still running, then leapt to the last one. When he reached the ladder, the alley seemed to explode into glaring white light. He involuntarily flinched and turned his head to shield his eyes. Across the roof he could see that the fronts of the buildings along the far side of the street were lit up by the colored warning lights of police cars, flashing, then sweeping across the facades, then flashing again. Doors slammed, hard rubber shoes pattered up the alley below him.

Marshall stood above the ladder and raised his hands high, so the men below could see him clearly. He shouted loudly, so they would hear. "F.B.I. Special Agent John Marshall," he called. That seemed to satisfy the policemen below him, for the moment. None of them seemed inclined to shoot.

A couple of them looked away from him at the three policemen who were bent over the man he had shot from above. "That's not all of them," Marshall called down.

"How many? What description?"

He hesitated for a half second, then pointed away from the direction the woman had run. "One male. Armed. He took off that way on foot."

Jane made her way back along the quiet, empty streets, listening. There were distant sirens, but the sky a few blocks south of her was already bright with the lights of police cars blinking garish colors into the foggy night air. She supposed the sirens were the reinforcements.

Jane moved along the street behind Brian Vaughn's house, winded, sore, and dazed. She knew that the only sensible thing to do was to get into her car and try to make it out of Santa Barbara now, but she had been drawn here. She could not let all that had happened come to nothing. She had to salvage one piece of evidence that something had occurred tonight besides three unidentified shooters trying to kill an F.B.I. agent.

Jane cautiously stole up the driveway and into the back yard of the house behind Brian Vaughn's. She moved to the fence and pulled herself over it. The lights in the house were still on, and the kitchen door was ajar, as though everyone had dashed outside to escape a fire that had unaccountably gone out.

She saw the video camera lying where she had dropped it behind the garbage cans when she had run to the house. She picked it up and looked at the little window. The tape was still in it. The intercom was a foot or two away, so she picked it up, too.

Over the soft hissing of the intercom came the sound of footsteps. She listened. Somebody was still in the house. She took a step closer to the back door, and her head came forward to bring her body into a crouch.

She heard the steps moving quickly now, almost a run. Then she heard the front door slam. She dropped the camera and the intercom at her feet and sprinted along the side of the house on the driveway.

Just as she reached the corner of the house, a man crossed the sidewalk, stepped to the curb, and reached for the door handle of Brian Vaughn's little red Miata. His fingers closed on it, the door swung open, and the dome light came on.

Jane saw the face and drew in a breath: she knew it. It was not the face of the man she had seen in Vaughn's doorway, or of either of the men she had seen when she was with Richard Dahlman. It would not even have surprised her if the man she had electrocuted in L.A. had merely been stunned and lived to drive up here for the pleasure of seeing her die. This was the face of a genuine ghost.

The man got into the car, started the engine, then suddenly turned his head in Jane's direction. She stepped back into the shelter of the house, but it was too late. The ghost had seen her too.

She hurried back up the driveway, staying in the shadows close to the clapboards of the house, where he would have a hard time getting a clear shot at her. But in a moment she heard the car accelerate up the street and away.

Marshall stood outside in the midday sunshine while the forensics team completed the search of the house where Charles Langer had died. He had watched them from the doorway for a long time, moving slowly and methodically outward from the body, and by now they would be close to the perimeter. He had seen this process too many times. Hours and hours ago, while he had stood in the alley answering questions, he had watched them searching the ground and the roofs, marking each spot where a brass casing had been ejected from a gun, drawing diagrams and taking pictures, and he'd had time to evaluate their competence. They didn't need his advice on how to handle this house.

He heard an engine, and watched without interest as another unmarked police car pulled up and two men in sport coats got out. The older one with thinning blond hair walked up the sidewalk and stopped in front of him. "Are you Special Agent Marshall?"

"Yes," he said.

The man gave him a look that was friendly, but not quite a smile. "I'm Lieutenant Harris. I've been assigned to help out."

Marshall nodded. In a town the size of Santa Barbara it was hard to imagine a case that would distract them much from this one. Every detective they had would be engaged for at least a few days.

"I've got a couple of things in the car you might want to take a look at."

Marshall walked with him to the curb. There would be lots of conversations like this in the next day or two. They would want him to resolve inconsistencies in what their eyes were telling them, and he would try, and fail. He accepted the plain manila envelope the lieutenant handed him, and looked inside. There were several enlarged photographs. The first two were pictures of the two men he had shot in the alley, but now they were lying in a morgue. There were two small x's marked on each picture in a random pattern over each man's torso.

"What's that?" asked Marshall. "The marks."

Lieutenant Harris looked at him mysteriously and pulled the two photographs away to reveal the next two. The two bodies had been photographed with their shirts off.

Marshall looked at the lieutenant. "Bulletproof vests?" he asked. "They were wearing bulletproof vests?"

"That's right," said Harris. "And not some cut-rate piece of trash that won't stop a bean-shooter, either. This is regular police-issue body armor." His friendly expression tightened into a conspiratorial smile. "The x's are your hits. Two each. They must have hurt like hell— staggered them—but I'll bet you wondered why they didn't fall down. Kind of disconcerting."

"Yeah," said Marshall. "I was disconcerted out of my wits."

The detective chuckled, but his face was more sympathetic than amused. The pictures reminded him of his own vulnerability. "That's why you went for the head shots, isn't it?"

Marshall shook his head. "I took what I could see." He put the photographs back into the envelope, but he noticed there were others. "What are the rest of them?"

Harris nodded toward the house. "Those are him." He frowned. "Now, there's another mystery."

"What do you mean?"

"His driver's license says his name was Charles Langer. But it seems his prints don't match the ones the D.M.V. has on file."

Marshall said, "So it's a false ID."

"Not the kind we usually see. His face matches the picture they have of Charles Langer. It's not often you see somebody who lets the state take his picture but goes to a lot of trouble to give them the wrong prints." Harris shrugged. "I'm not even sure how he did it." He looked at the house as though he could see through the wall. "And he's had some surgery."

"Plastic surgery?"

Harris nodded.

"How do you know?"

Harris smiled again. "I confess I didn't see it right off. I've been a cop in this part of the world for a long time, so I ought to be able to see it. But the coroner picked it up. There are a couple of spots with faint scar tissue, but you wouldn't notice even if the hair hadn't covered it. Then he did an X-ray that proved it. There's evidence of bone sculpting. The clincher is that when they do a face-lift, they put a couple of tiny titanium pins right up here above the temple to stretch the skin on. They take them out afterward, but it leaves a mark."

"Lieutenant?" The voice came from the front steps behind Marshall. One of the officers searching the house was holding something in a plastic evidence bag. Marshall followed Harris to the steps.

The officer said, "We found another tape recorder stuck behind some books in the bookcase. This one had tape in it, and it was still turned on."

44

Jane stepped off the plane in Rochester, Minnesota, and paused for a moment in front of a shop that sold newspapers, then walked on toward the car-rental counters. It was too soon for anything about what had happened in Santa Barbara to have reached print, and if there were any articles about Carey or Richard Dahlman or Janet McAffee she should not read them. She could do nothing now but what she was doing, and any distraction would weaken her.

She rented a Toyota Camry and drove up Route 52 toward Minneapolis. It seemed to her that a lifetime had passed since she had driven to Minneapolis with Richard Dahlman, and nearly that long since she had come back to watch Sid Freeman's house.

As she drove on the dark highway, she could not help composing versions of what she was going to say. "I don't know why you didn't kill me while I was in your house. Maybe you're so crazy that you forgot."

Sid would protest. "Janie," he would say. "It wasn't me. I didn't have anything to do with these people except what I told you that night to your face."

Jane would say, "I saw Quinn."

He would be silent, trying to work out all of the implications in an instant but not able to, and she would hear him breathing through his mouth. Maybe he would say, "You're going to kill me, aren't you?" She would answer, "I don't do that kind of work. Kill yourself."

The last words she would say were, "Better get packed, Sid. The police will be here in five minutes." She amended it: "three minutes." That would be enough time for him to get frantic, but not enough time for him to scrape up twenty years' accretion of incriminating evidence and make it into a fast car. She would wait until she could actually see the black-and-whites speeding along the lake road.

She thought through the conversation in so many variations that she almost failed to notice when she was getting too close to the lake road. She turned off at the next corner, circled the lake on the hillside high above Sid Freeman's house, then parked her car on the street two blocks from the house where she had rented her room.

It was after midnight when Jane walked along the top of the hill above Sid Freeman's house, among the tall old trees. She held the cellular telephone in her hand, but carried nothing else. She could have driven to the bank in Chicago, opened the safe-deposit box, and taken out the Beretta Cougar nine-millimeter pistol she stored there with a few spare identities. Maybe she would be making that trip sometime soon, and maybe in a few minutes she would wish she had done it tonight. If she did, the feeling of regret would probably last only a second or two before darkness came. She knew that tonight it was not a good idea for her to have in her hand the means of killing Sid Freeman. He had gotten very adept at taking away people's whole lives and changing them into something that they did not want to be. His final act on earth was not going to be taking away Jane Whitefield.

Jane was afraid of the people who lived in that fortified house. She was in awe not of Sid Freeman but of his craziness. The strange, uncivilized teenagers he had brought in were one manifestation of it; his extreme premeditation was another. She could picture him sitting in that dim library, working all of it out as though the world outside were some enormous chessboard. As she walked along, a lot of sights and sounds that had struck her as little surprises came back to her.

Sid had said he had been watching television and reading newspapers and magazines and had not run across some runner who had come to his house. In the old days, Sid had never paid the slightest attention to published news. He had gotten all of the information that interested him from the people who came up the path to his house—and from Quinn. That was what had made it seem true: Quinn was dead.

She had bought without question the statement that Quinn was dead. It had seemed inevitable, even overdue. Selling commodities and services to criminals was a risky activity. Sid had stayed in that house in Minneapolis with lookouts and armed guards, while Quinn, and sometimes Christie, had traveled the country foraging for things that could be had only from people who didn't care about laws, and delivering them to people who used them to commit crimes. All transactions had been in cash. When Jane had heard they were both dead, she had been only mildly surprised.

Of course they would be dead—if not now, then next week, or next year. The only part of the announcement that had even held her attention was that she had trouble imagining Sid without them. When she had tried to bargain with him, she had been surprised that the one who left the bigger void was not Christie. Christie had always floated in the background like some weird wraith, the only constant in Sid's fortress, where everything was always in motion and even Sid couldn't hold onto one identity for long. But now it seemed to Jane that Christie must just have been a young woman who had gotten some kind of titillation out of the excitement that surrounded Sid's repulsive person.

It was Quinn that Jane had kept missing. She had kept thinking of him while Sid was talking, catching herself glancing suddenly into the shadows and expecting to see him. It occurred to her that he probably had been in the house that night. She had somehow sensed it—maybe smelled some subtle personal scent that human beings gave off, or heard him in another room whispering to Sid's kids, just below the level of conscious hearing.

That made her wonder why Sid had not told Quinn to kill her. That was the way it would have been done. Quinn was the permanent second in command, the junior partner. He had always made her tense and careful, not because he wouldn't do as Sid asked, but because she had never seen him experience a moment of reluctance. It had been as though his craziness had been worse than Sid's, and Sid's deliberation and physical torpor had held it back from its natural excesses.

Jane still wasn't sure why Sid had not killed her. He had sent the two teams of men all over the country looking for Dahlman. She sensed that she had missed something, so she tried to remember events in order. After that night, the men had not come close to Dahlman. Maybe they had stopped looking. As soon as Sid had seen that Dahlman was in Jane's hands, he had quit. Was that what he had wanted? Yes. He had, maybe on the spot, decided he liked the idea of having Dahlman disappear. It was much better than having him dead. If Dahlman was killed, then the police could not escape the conclusion that someone must have done away with him, and wonder who. If Dahlman just vanished, then the only killer was Dahlman.

Jane reached the vantage point that she had been looking for, and stared down at Sid Freeman's house. The high, dark brown building looked different, and at first she wasn't sure why. She moved her eyes along the row of upper windows. There were no lights, no shades. Usually it was possible for her to pick out the room where the lookout with the spotting scope was stationed, because it would be the only room on the floor with no lights. She looked at the ground-floor windows. There was the usual dim glow of inadequate, old-fashioned ceiling fixtures. Sid had never been good about changing bulbs.

She moved closer to get a better look, her heart beating a little faster. She studied the front of the house. The steel-mesh security door was slightly ajar. It wasn't squared with the jamb, so the lock was not engaged. She had known it was possible that Quinn would simply have driven to the nearest telephone to tell Sid it was time to stop being Sid and get out. During her flight she had put that notion aside, because it was a thought that could lead to no possible change in her actions. She had to come here.

She could not leave him alone and let him use her name to fool helpless runners into giving him whatever money and freedom they had left. And she couldn't go back to being Mrs. McKinnon knowing that some night she might wake up next to Carey and hear the sound of Quinn cocking the hammer.

Jane had to see. She kept to the land above the house and behind it. She approached it from the corner so she would not be directly in front of any window. She walked with such care and silence that she could not hear her own footsteps, and she stayed in the deepest shadows with her back to a stand of trees up the hill. She kept moving until her hand touched the cold, damp brick apron along the side of the house.

She barely breathed as she slowly edged along the stonework that was taller than she was. It had been designed so that if Sid was standing, no bullet from outside would pierce the siding and take off his head. Jane felt no indecision about where she should go. Sid was nocturnal, and the room he used for his work was the library to the left of the foyer. If he had not left, that was where he would be.

She stepped close to the window. Had it always had bars on it? She had never seen them before, because the shutters were kept closed. Why were they open now?

She moved her left eye close to the corner of the window and looked in, then pulled back quickly, her back pressed against the cold stones. She studied the image she had brought away with her. The body on the floor seemed to be genuine. It was not some other big man in late middle age who had been turned into a corpse so Sid could be presumed dead. This seemed to be Sid. The open blinds and the unlocked door made sense. If the little monsters had turned on him, they wouldn't bother to lock up. Jane began to step toward the front of the house. She would have to go inside and get a look at his face in the light. She heard a faint sound: the window latch.

Jane dived away from the side of the house just as the arm jabbed out between the bars and fired a pistol down into the ground directly below the window. The arm swung upward like a pendulum, firing a shot every yard or two along the stone siding, as rapidly as the finger could pull the trigger. The sound of the pistol with its suppressor was like the strike of a snake, so the ring of the brass ejected against the stone was almost as loud.

At the end of the swing, in the instant when the arm reached horizontal, Jane leapt. She pinned the forearm to the wall with her left shoulder and hammered the fingers with her right fist.

The yelp was Quinn's. He yanked his arm back and dropped the pistol so he could get his hand back through the bars quickly. Jane picked up the gun, ducked behind the trunk of a tree, and waited.

"Jane?" She could hear his position as though she could see him. He was under the window, where no bullet could reach him through all that stone. He wanted to hear where she was.

She decided that she would need to keep up with where he was, too. She had to make him talk. "What, Quinn?"

"It occurred to me that we have a problem."

"Do we?"

"If I moved away from this wall—say, toward the door—you would shoot me through the window, wouldn't you?"

"It's possible," she admitted. "I don't like you."

"But you're behind the tree. If you move away from it, I'm going to be able to pop up and shoot you before you could get to the next one."

"Assuming you have another gun where you can reach it." She ventured a glance around the tree at the window. He was letting her see the end of the barrel over the windowsill. She aimed the pistol at it and waited. Just a tiny bit of his hand would be enough. The barrel disappeared.

"Janie? You here to see Sid?"

"I just saw Sid," she answered.

"Oh," said Quinn. "Hey, do you smell fat burning? Sid must be in hell already." He laughed. "Courtesy of you."

"How did I manage that?" she asked.

"Sid died for your sins. I couldn't let you tell him that all this time the one sending him runners was me."

"You mean he didn't know? He really thought you were dead?" Of course, she thought. She had not caught Sid lying, because Sid had not been lying. He had been fooled, too.

Quinn laughed. "How else was I going to leave Sid and take a lot of Sid's money with me?"

"What about the lovely and talented Christie?"

"She's really dead. Nothing to do with me. Got killed in New York, I heard."

Jane was silent for a long time. Had his voice come from a different spot? She listened for fainter sounds that might be movement.

Quinn broke her concentration. "You know, there's one good way to get out of this, Janie." He was still under the window.

"Maybe more than one."

"I said one *good* way. I can do everything Sid ever did, and you seem to be back in the trade. We could get pretty rich if we'd help each other."

"Great offer, Quinn. But your last partner seems reluctant to give you a reference."

"You know what really killed him?"

"Besides you?"

"He didn't get out enough," said Quinn. "He lost touch. He knew zero. He sat here all alone, waiting for everybody to come to him, and without me—"

"All alone?" said Jane. Was it possible he didn't know?

"Yeah, all alone," Quinn repeated. "He sat here on his fat ass. He didn't even change the locks after I got killed. So ten minutes ago, I walked right in and—"

Jane said, "Quinn, listen to me. Get out of that house. Get out now."

Quinn laughed again. "I head for the door, you pop me through the window? Sure."

"No, you don't understand. Sid wasn't alone. He must have sent them out on some errand. I swear I won't go near the window. Just get out now. They'll kill us both." She took three steps from the tree.

The barrel of Quinn's gun appeared above the windowsill, and Jane dived back toward the tree. She heard the gun spit four or five times, and a stone near the base of the tree jumped upward into the weeds.

She lay behind the tree listening. She had not heard a car pull up on the street, but now she heard doors slamming and running feet. She was not sure whether Quinn's sudden silence meant he was listening too or he was just moving to another window to get a better shot at her. Then she heard the roar of the Ingram MAC 10 tearing his body to pieces.

Jane lay still as a young girl appeared at the window. Jane could tell this was the one she had seen hiding at the top of the stairs on the night she had come here with Dahlman. The girl pressed her thin, feral face against the metal bars and her sharp eyes stared out into the dark.

Then Jane heard the voice of the boy she had seen that night. "What—you think somebody went out through the bars?"

The girl bristled. "Maybe I need some air. Do you mind?"

"He's dead, and the other old guy is dead. You want to be dead too?"

The girl sighed in heavy annoyance. "Go pack the car. I'll look around for money."

Jane heard the boy's shoes on the floor, hurrying out of the room into the foyer. The girl stayed where she was for a moment, then moved toward the door after him. She looked down at the body. "Bye, Sid." Her voice sounded like the voice of a little child. Then Jane heard her move out into the foyer after the boy.

Jane stood, wiped the gun off, and left it on the ground. She whispered, "Bye, Sid," picked up the cellular telephone she had brought, and moved off into the darkness toward her car. As she drove, she made three telephone calls. The first was to an apartment in Cleveland, the second to a retirement home in Carlsbad, and the third was to the Minneapolis Police Department.

As soon as she had made the last call, she stopped the car at a parking lot beside a picnic area overlooking the Mississippi. There was only one street lamp near the entrance to the lot. She drove to the far end of the pavement and turned off her lights. She left the car running, got out, walked across the lawn to the edge, and hurled the telephone into the slow, dark water.

Jane turned and walked back to the car. She sat down in the seat, pulled the safety belt across her chest, and fastened it. She put the car into gear and began to make a wide turn toward the entrance.

"Jay-nee . . ." It was a soft, female voice, like a song just above a whisper. It made the hair on the back of Jane's neck stand.

Jane's foot hit the brake and the car jerked to a stop. She whirled in her seat to look behind her, and what she saw made her breath catch in her throat.

The woman's face was illuminated in the glow of the single street lamp. It looked supernaturally pale under the long, black hair, but the red lips were set in the same amused, knowing smile that Jane remembered. "Jay-nee," came the voice again. Then came the horrible, mocking laugh. Jane could see the big, square-looking .45 pistol held just above the woman's lap with the muzzle aimed at the center of Jane's backrest. They both knew the car seat wouldn't stop the bullet.

The voice rose to a normal volume. "Say something."

Jane said, "Everybody around here seems to come back from the dead. First Quinn, now you."

The woman looked irritated. "Not exactly. I'm not Christie anymore. Quinn and I figured you must be dead, so I died too, only the death I came back from was yours."

Jane said, "You're supposed to be me? That's why you grew your hair long and dyed it. You're Jane?"

Christie shrugged. "I was the only one who had the qualifications. I got rich at it. Did you?" She seemed to enjoy the thought for a moment, then said, "You surprised me tonight, though."

"By staying alive."

Christie nodded. "I knew you were coming. I sent Quinn in to do Sid, so you could be Little Red Riding Hood, and Quinn could be the wolf. I spent the evening driving around, waiting for a rental car like this to appear in the neighborhood."

"Why?"

"If the one who came out of the house was Quinn, great. If Sid came out, still okay: I could make him believe anything—that I was Quinn's prisoner or something. But if the one who came back was you. . . . What could I do?"

"Christie," said Jane. "You don't have to—"

"I'm not," Christie interrupted. "I'm sick of the whole business. Without Quinn or Sid, it's too much trouble. I wanted to let you know. Drive

back to the dark part of the lot and park. When you get there, I'll get out
and you drive off. I'll be watching until you're out of sight, so don't do
anything strange. Don't even look back."

Jane turned the car and drove in the direction of the river. Christie was
lying. There was no reason in the world for Christie to do anything now
except pull the trigger. Jane pressed her foot down on the gas pedal a little harder. The car was moving faster now, slowly gaining speed. She had
not turned the headlights on when Christie had appeared, and she didn't
turn them on now, in the hope that Christie would not notice just how
fast the car was moving.

The voice came again. "Slow down."

Jane said nothing. Christie was more alert than she had expected.
There was no hope of hiding the speed now, so Jane accelcrated rapidly.
The faster she was going, the fewer options Christie would have. It was
already too late to shoot and jump.

"Stop the car or I'll blow your head off."

The car left the pavement and bumped onto the uneven surface of the
lawn without losing speed. Jane watched the rearview mirror and saw
the arm come up carrying the gun, then swing hard at her head.

Jane ducked to avoid the impact, but the gun caught the back of her
head in a glancing blow that knocked her forward and made her see a
red afterimage. Then she realized that the car had already reached the
end of the grass. It shot outward, and it felt for a moment as though they
were suspended in the air, and then the car began to fall. Jane's seat belt
seemed to tighten and drag her down out of the sky.

For a second she was aware that Christie was rising behind her in
the back seat, both hands pressed against the ceiling to keep it away
from her. Jane straightened her spine and sat up in her seat, looked out
the windshield, and tried to see the surface of the river below. It was all
darkness. She waited a second, then another, and then came the
shock.

The car seemed to stab downward into the water at an angle. There
was a bang as the airbag exploded out of the hub of the steering column
and flattened Jane against her seat and, at the same time, a heavy thump
as Christie was thrown forward behind her. Almost immediately, Jane
heard a rushing noise in the dark, like a waterfall, and then the sensation of cold water on her feet.

It took Jane a second or two to determine that she could move. She fought the airbag to free her right arm, unbuckled her belt, and slipped sideways to the passenger side. She fell against the dashboard. The car was sinking front-first, the heavy engine weighing it down.

The water began to rush in faster. Her legs were in water up to the hip. Then she could hear more water, and she could feel that it was coming in through the weakened seal around the windshield. Jane listened, but she couldn't hear Christie, so she tried to stare between the front seats toward the floor of the back seat.

At that moment, Christie moved. She pushed off against the back of the driver's seat and brought the pistol around. There was a deafening report, and the airbag beside Jane deflated. Then Christie climbed higher onto the back seat, and Jane ducked lower.

Jane let the torrent of water coming through the open side window pour over her. She held herself against it with all the strength in her legs, and groped for the door handle. When she found it, she grasped it and stayed down. The water was up to her chest now, then her neck, and she held only her face above it. She knew that no human being could open a car door against the rush of water. She would have to hold on to the door handle and wait until the door was completely submerged.

The seconds went by, while Jane listened for another shot. Then she could hear nothing, because the water was up over her ears. She lifted her face above it to take a breath of air, pushed down on the door handle, put her shoulder against the door, and used her legs to press against it. The door opened. Jane slipped out and swam. She counted her strokes: one, two, three; her head broke out of the dark water, and she gasped in a breath.

Jane swam on the surface to the little margin of pebbles and mud on shore, pulled herself onto it, then looked back. The front of the car was completely underwater now. The only parts visible were the rear window, the trunk, and a bit of the roof, but it was sinking. Suddenly there was a shot, and a hole appeared in the rear window.

"No!" Jane shouted. "Get out the way I did! Swim down to the door!"

But there was no way Christie could hear her. There was a series of five muffled shots, and Jane saw bits of glass sparkling in the muzzle flashes as they exploded upward out of the rear window. Christie had created a ragged row of punctures, but she had not created an exit for herself. The car sank more rapidly, and the water reached the rear window. Christie's shoe kicked against it once, making it balloon outward an inch or two;

then the leg was pulled back to kick again when the rear window collapsed inward and Christie disappeared. The water poured in, and the car sank from sight.

Jane jumped to her feet and ran a few yards downstream, where the lazy current had carried the car, then sloshed back into the water until it was up to her thighs, and ducked into it. She dived downward, trying to reach the car. But the water was black, and she could not find it. She tried over and over, but her hands touched nothing except soft mud and stringy weeds. There was nothing that felt like metal. After what could have been ten minutes or a half hour, Jane crawled back onto the shore and lay there, panting.

Before she had fully regained her breath, she forced herself to stand. She took one last look at the slow, untroubled surface of the river. Then she turned away and began to walk.

45

Early one morning in late August, a young woman with long black hair parked her rented car in a small lot around the bend from the Glen Iris Inn at Letchworth State Park in Livingston County, New York, and walked along the park road to one of the narrow paths leading down into the gorge of the Genesee River. She descended the steep steps cut into the cliff in a zigzag that sometimes took her within a foot or two of the top leaves of a tall tree, then came back again beside the trunk and then passed once more near the place where the roots had dug in among the rocks. The land had been made a park in the 1860s, so the woods were thick and old. She emerged from the shadows of the trees, walked the last hundred feet on flat weedy ground, then stepped out on a smooth stone ledge above the water.

She looked around her and listened. The river was shallow here, and it made a whispery sound as it rushed over the rounded pebbles and flat shelves. She could hear the birds above the wooded path she had just left, but there was no sound of a human being yet. In an hour or two, hikers and picnickers would be crowding the trails, making the last, sweet week before Labor Day loud with their usual desperate enthusiasm. But now it was just a Seneca woman standing alone by the Genesee River, and this could have been any morning since the last Ice Age.

The Genesee River was the place where the Stone-Throwers, one of the tribes of Jo-ge-oh, lived. They were said to be no taller than the length of a person's foot, so they were called Little People, but they were very strong. On the few occasions when they had allowed themselves to be seen, they had done it to intervene and save a person in extreme danger. They would take him out of the world for a time, to hide him from his enemies until the danger was over.

The Seneca woman took the purse off her shoulder, set it on the rock ledge at her feet, and pulled out a pouch of pipe tobacco she had bought at the Rochester airport. She took a pinch and tossed it into the air, then watched the wind carry it down onto the rocks below her.

"It's me, little guys," she said. "Jane Whitefield." She waited for a few seconds, listening to the water whispering over the stones, then poured more tobacco to the rocks below her.

"I brought you the usual presents." The Little People liked tobacco, and their only source of supply was the Senecas, who had not lived along this part of the Genesee since the Buffalo Creek treaty of 1826. She emptied the rest of the brown shreds of tobacco from the pouch and reached into her purse again.

This time she had a plastic bag containing the clippings of her fingernails. The Little People particularly valued the fingernail clippings of human beings, which they used to fool foxes and raccoons into believing that big people were nearby. She sprinkled the little moon-shaped clippings onto the rocks to make a wide zone of safety for the Little People.

"Thank you," she said. "Thank you for keeping my husband safe." She stood looking at the river for a few minutes, then said aloud, "I'm going home to be with him now."

Jane drove the length of the park road, then turned onto the Genesee Expressway at Mount Morris and headed north to change to the New York State Thruway west of Rochester. As she drove, she could see signs that the summer had reached its fullest perfection and was about to end. The leaves on the maple trees had all matured, opened flat, and grown as big as a man's hand.

In the Old Time, the people's lives had followed a cycle announced by signs in the world. Each spring, when the white oak leaves were the size of a red squirrel's foot, the women would go out to the fields to plant the corn, beans, and squash. When the leaves on the deciduous trees had opened a little farther, and the foliage was thick enough to hide a human shape in the forest, warriors would slip away, sometimes in parties of three or four and sometimes alone. They would travel in silence just off the trails, until they had reached the countries of enemies. They would stay for most of the summer watching, listening, and studying until they had found the enemy's weaknesses and vulnerabilities.

When the nights were just beginning to turn cool and the days shorter, and the corn in the enemies' fields was beginning to ripen, the scouts would begin the journey back to the land between the Niagara River and Sodus Bay. They would travel quickly through the forests, often from as far west as the Mississippi River and, more rarely, from beyond it to the eastern slopes of the high mountain range they called the Rim of the World, where the Left-Handed Twin was reputed to wait for the souls of the dead.

They returned to take part in the Green Corn ceremony that was held when the ears on the stalks standing in the women's fields had ripened enough to be edible. Green Corn marked the end of the female half of the year, when the country of the Senecas was warm and fruitful, and the corn, beans, and squash they called the Three Sisters grew to feed the people. The festival began on the day when the people knew that for this year, at least, they would not starve. Their lives had been preserved.

A few weeks later the crops would be harvested and the male half of the year would begin. In the dark, cold half of the year, the celebrations were given by the men. There were hints that the men's ceremonies came from a time when the land between the Niagara and the Hudson had been much colder and barer, and the people had lived by following the migrations of herds of large animals. Every year, as soon as the harvest was completed, the men went off to hunt deer and bear or to attack the enemies that the scouts had observed during the summer. But Green Corn was a time when all of the people came together.

When Jane reached the edge of Amherst, she stopped along the road, tilted the rearview mirror so she could see her face, brushed her hair, and put on her makeup. Then she readjusted the mirror and drove on.

She turned into the driveway of the big old stone house, glanced in the rearview mirror, and watched the woman in shorts and a T-shirt strolling along the other side of the street stop, open her purse, and fiddle with something inside it, her lips moving. She was apparently muttering to herself about something she was looking for, but Jane smiled in the mirror at her and said, "It's me, all right. Tell them I said 'Hi.' "

Jane got out of the car and walked toward the front of the house. The door swung open, and Carey stepped onto the porch.

Jane said, "How was the rest of the movie?"

He shrugged. "A cynical attempt to pander to the romantic, sensitive female audience. You would have been putty in my hands."

"Didn't understand it, huh?"

"I put some estrogen in the popcorn after you left, but it didn't help." He rubbed his chin. "Didn't have to shave for twenty-eight days, though."

She put her arms around him and held her cheek against his in a long, hard embrace. "It seems to have worn off."

"Yeah," he admitted. "I got tired of the popcorn." He suddenly bent to scoop her off her feet, carried her inside the house, and pushed the door shut with his foot.

Jane said, "Nice of you to give me a lift, but I can only stay a minute."

He withdrew his right hand so her feet swung to the floor. "These nightmares are beginning to get a perverse, teasing quality to them."

"I came to get your opinion of a place I rented. Would you be willing to take a look at it?"

"I was going to do a crossword puzzle, but I could work on it in the car . . ."

"Well, then, come along. It's kind of nice." She took his hand and tugged him toward the door. "I promise you'll like it. It's got four hundred rooms, and a bed in every one."

He brightened. "A hospital! You finally got me a hospital."

She wrapped her arms around him again and kissed him. She broke it off and looked at him happily. "No," she said. "I didn't." Then she swung the door open and pushed him out toward the car.

Dr. and Mrs. McKinnon did not return to the house in Amherst that night. At eight the next morning they were seen driving from a hotel in Buffalo eastward to the Tonawanda Indian Reservation. At nine-thirty the mobile surveillance team was ordered to break off contact, and the team at the house in Amherst was told to dismantle their observation post and stand down.

John Marshall arrived in Tonawanda in the afternoon. He parked in a small blacktop square near a long, single-story building with a door and a chimney at each end and a row of windows along the side. There were two smaller buildings nearby, where he could smell food cooking and now and then hear women's voices and the clatter of utensils.

He entered the long, low building he had been told to call the longhouse in time to hear several speeches in a language so alien to him that he was occasionally incapable of discerning even the mood. He guessed correctly that the first one was a prayer.

The prayer was spoken by a man who'd held an office in unbroken succession since Deganawida and Hiawatha convinced five warring nations to form the Iroquois confederacy at least five hundred years ago. The prayer was much older than that, and it contained a skeleton of the Seneca cosmology. In it the people thanked the Right-Handed Twin, Hawenneyu the Creator, for making all parts of the universe and, at the same time, thanked each of the parts themselves. The prayer began with the lowest earthbound beings, the warriors and women, then moved upward to the water, the herbs and grasses, the bushes and saplings, then the trees, the corn, beans, and squash, the game animals, the birds. Then the people thanked the Thunderers, the winds, the sun, moon, and stars, and finally Hawenneyu. There was nothing in the prayer but thanks, because the Senecas did not believe in asking for anything. They only expressed gratitude for what had been created and preserved.

After that there was a recitation of an abridged version of the Gaiiwio, the "good word" that the prophet Handsome Lake had received in his visions two hundred years ago, during the worst moments of Seneca history, when the world had seemed to them to have changed terribly but really had not changed at all. One of Handsome Lake's visions had told him to preserve the ancient cycle of feasts.

Marshall listened as an elderly man with a stentorian voice addressed the people on what appeared to be another matter of profound seriousness, upon which the audience burst into laughter, stood up, and went about preparing to serve food. Marshall drifted through the crowds and began his search.

Once Marshall thought he saw the one he was looking for, but as he stepped toward her, a hand touched his arm. He turned and found Violet Peterson with her face close to his. She said quietly, "If you're here to arrest somebody, you picked a rotten time."

"I didn't—"

"Would you go to a church on Easter and haul somebody out in front of his family?"

He said, "I'm not here to do anything like that. I was just hoping that they would be here. If you see them, will you let me know?"

She said suspiciously, "If I see them, I'll let them know."

Marshall saw huge cauldrons brought in from the kitchen building, and matrons ladling food into bowls for eating in the dining hall next door and into covered containers for taking to people who were not here.

Twice he thought he saw her, but each time it was another young woman with long black hair. He didn't find the one he had come to look for until early evening, after the dancing had begun. He saw her only because she was standing along the wall close to her husband. The drums throbbed, the singers wailed, and the turtle shells made a noise like ghosts whispering in Marshall's ear as he approached.

She seemed to feel his presence rather than hear it. She turned to face him and stared into his eyes for a moment, then lowered her head and took a step. Her husband started to follow, but she shook her head.

She led Marshall out of the western door of the long, low building, down the wooden steps, and into the night. She turned again to look up at him.

He said, "I heard you were going to be here."

"I didn't say it. I left a note in my house for my husband."

He was silent for a moment. Then he said, "My name is John Marshall."

She nodded. "My husband told me. He remembers you from the hospital."

Marshall said, "I was the one in Santa Barbara."

She said, "I've never been to Santa Barbara."

"I didn't think so," he said. He looked in the direction of the longhouse, where the sounds of singing and dancing had grown louder. "What are you folks celebrating?"

Jane seemed to ponder for a moment, as though she were compressing a great many complex matters, then answered, "Being alive."

Marshall smiled. "Me too." He started again, looking at her intently. "I know you must have heard Richard Dahlman turned out to be innocent. All the evidence—a witness, tape recordings, videotapes even—all turned up miraculously. The charges were dropped."

"I think I read something about it in the newspapers."

He looked down at his feet. "There was a woman I met not long ago who reminded me of you. She gave me a present." He reached into his pocket and handed her a small black box that looked like a transistor radio. "This is something I thought you might like."

"What is it?"

"It's kind of a safety device. It detects even the very faintest resistance on any electrical line. If, for instance, there were some very small appliance that was draining voltage on your house—say, a transmitter of some kind—you could pick it up and find it." He shrugged. "Silly gadget, but it could prevent the wires from heating up some time."

"Thank you," she said.

He began to back away from her. "Don't mention it."

She stared into his eyes. "I never will." Then she added, "Unless I happen to meet that woman."

"What woman?" He turned and walked toward the longhouse parking lot, then got into a car. She watched the car moving up the road until the two taillights diminished into a single, glowing spot of orange-red light no bigger than a firefly. She listened to the pounding of the drums and the shuffling of many feet on the wood floor inside.

This was the first night of Green Corn. This morning babies born since Midwinter had been given names, and adults who were taking on new names had announced them. Tomorrow there would be the chanting of personal thanks for good fortune and accomplishments, the appearance of the Society of Faces to cure the sick, and more food and dancing. And on the final day, there would be the casting of the peach pits, one side white and the other burnt black. The pits would be thrown down and read, over and over, until the black side or the white side triumphed, in imitation of the eternal battle between the Creator and his identical twin brother, the Destroyer.

THOMAS PERRY was born in Tonawanda, N.Y., in 1947. He received a B.A. from Cornell University in 1969 and a Ph.D. in English literature from the University of Rochester in 1974. He has been a laborer, maintenance man, commercial fisherman, weapons mechanic, university administrator and teacher, and television writer and producer. His other novels include *The Butcher's Boy* (awarded an Edgar from the Mystery Writers of America), *Metzger's Dog, Big Fish, Island, Sleeping Dogs, Vanishing Act, Dance for the Dead,* and *Shadow Woman.* He lives in southern California with his wife and two daughters.

ABOUT THE TYPE

This book was set in Photina, a typeface designed by José Mendoza in 1971. It is a very elegant design with high legibility, and its close character fit has made it a popular choice for use in quality magazines and art gallery publications.